GW01398566

THE ESQUADRON

Legacy of Wrath Book 2

CHARLIE FREELANDER

TABLE OF CONTENTS

PROLOGUE

Elsewhere, a while ago...

PERI SAT FOR A LONG MOMENT, TOO DRAINED TO FEEL much of anything. Velimir had not left a body behind. At the moment of death, he had vanished in a blink of golden dust. *His madness—the same madness that lurks within me—consumed it?* The lurking madness was far more than hidden feelings or thoughts—it was a physical, visceral thing. Ever since Ewynne and she had been on the road after leaving Eilean de Taigh-Sholais behind, it had become more distinct and tangible. Whispers. Shapes. No discernible words...yet. But something beckoned to her. A dark vortex pulled her.

Peri glanced at Ewynne gathering her scattered spell components. She lightly ran her finger over Velimir's greatsword. *We avenged you, Connor...well, sort of. "We" is generous. Some weird-ass warp thing happened here, and Ewynne accidentally summoned a demon.* Ewynne's simple goblin-summoning spell had probably reacted in an unexpected

1

manner to the latent Dimitrian energies seeping from the abandoned temple and its surroundings. Velimir had accused her of wanting to *steal* the demon from him and proceeded to command it. *Surprise, surprise. It promptly killed him.* Peri smirked. It was almost funny—but she didn't much feel like laughing.

Connor's killer was dead, and she and Ewynne were alive. So why was she so miserable? At first, she had only wanted Velimir dead. For taking Connor from her. For revenge. But gradually, she had come to understand the magnitude of Velimir's madness and pain—that there might have been something worthy of Tomoe's devotion inside of him, at least once. *I wish I wasn't so alone with this. I wish I could have saved him to the extent I have been saved.* Peri sighed in resignation. *He would have understood like no-one else could. I know you were trying to protect me, Connor...but you shouldn't have kept me in the dark.*

Ewynne sat down next to her. "Tomoe was right. He was too far gone. I know you didn't want to believe it, sis, but it was always a long shot. I know I should be glad that he's dead, and I am. We live! But you are still sad."

Peri sighed and hugged her sister, not able to explain to the genuinely kind and good Ewynne what was going on inside of her. *She doesn't know that she is one of Dimitri's "weak" spawn...I can sense them now. That is why Connor must have adopted her, too.* Her ability to sense the other Dimitrian siblings, and other things, had changed since Connor's death. It was as if that abrupt shattering of her world had put something in motion. As far as Ewynne was concerned, Velimir had broken the perfect idyll of their existence, and that was the beginning of a nightmare. But Peri felt that the nightmare had always lurked below the surface. She was the one who, even as an infant, had brought it to the island, not Velimir. His actions had just plunged Peri's world into the final chaos it had always been heading to.

I can't lose myself. I can sense that Dimitri wants us of the strong blood—to hunt his weak progeny. Velimir called me "a mongrel like him" and took the answers with him wherever he went. She sighed and finished strapping Velimir's sword to her backpack. It was way too big for her to wield, and anyway, she preferred a regular longsword. But she wasn't about to leave the sword behind. *It is all that I have left of my brother—of the one who is like me.*

Ewynne watched Peri pull a bundle from her backpack, then unwrap it to reveal a simple, unadorned wooden box. She brought it close to her face and closed her eyes, inhaling deeply. Ewynne caught a whiff of cedar.

"What do you intend to do with it?" Ewynne asked. The box was a gift from Connor for Peri's seventh birthday.

"It will serve as an urn. We will bury Tomoe. I...I know she helped to kill Connor...but I can't help feeling for her. She knew what love meant, and she was a brave warrior. A warrior deserves a fucking grave. She has lost everything else."

Ewynne didn't fully understand what it was about Tomoe that had touched Peri's heart so deeply, but she didn't want to question Peri's right to feel what she felt. That was how it always had been between them, and Peri had been more and more brooding and withdrawn as of late. "I felt sorry for Tomoe," Ewynne said. "I mean, she might have been a great person if not for...How can anyone love Velimir?"

Peri shrugged. "I, for one, am grateful that love is not

reserved only for those who deserve it." *Gods know I have needed it.* She beckoned Ewynne to follow, and the girls walked closer to the edge of the ancient dead sea. "Here. Close to the waterline. There's no tide here."

The sisters made a pyre, gathering gray driftwood that had dried at the edges of the shallow puddles. They set Tomoe's remains ablaze with a spell and stood quietly, watching the flames die down and the ashes cool. Once the ash was cool enough to touch, Peri gathered it and the bits of bone into her box, hissing when her fingers grazed an ember. With the murky bottom of the ancient half-dried sea as their witness, the girls dug a small hole in the moist and sticky ground with a wedge-like bit of a broken gravestone. They placed Tomoe's weapons in the ground with the urn. Peri patted the small hill with her hands. *Not even a headstone. Just a little mound in the mud.*

"Rest in peace, warrior," Peri whispered. She tossed her hair to the side and flung the backpack over her shoulder. "Come on, Wyn. Let's leave this place and never return."

———— • ● • ————

THE FIRST SENSATION WAS A CHILL THAT CREPT INTO Kiril's bones. The air was humid and thick, leaden gray. There was no sun or moon—just heavy, soggy clouds hanging low. Mist twisted and swirled everywhere. There were deformed half-dead pine trees, some covered with frost, others slowly dripping water. Kiril lifted his numb fingers to touch his face. It felt solid but cold—so very cold. He exhaled frosty vapor.

He took a few tentative steps towards the bank of a black river of slowly flowing slush. There were slimy rocks here and there at the banks of the river, some rust red with dried blood under the half-solid ice. There was a handful of withered dark red berries growing in the ground. He picked a few and tried a simple scrying spell for illusions or magical charge. Nothing. He frowned and mouthed the syllables again. Nothing. The warm hum of latent magic he was so used to summoning *wasn't there*. Just unresponsive emptiness. A knot of dread tightened in his throat.

Kiril sank to a slimy, cold rock, taking in his new situation. A bird was close by—a gray pigeon. The bird cocked its head and watched him intently for a few seconds. Kiril laughed humorlessly and spoke to it. "This is death, then? Cold and gray and emptiness? And my magic is gone."

"Countless lands of the dead sprawl across the ether that makes the multiverse, mage," the bird responded. "You have ended up in one land of the Nether, drawn here by the way you lived your life. You hardened your heart in bitterness. You scorned love and compassion and hope. Here it is reality. Here in Manala, everything is as bleak and hopeless and loveless as you claimed to be, to justify yourself."

"And speaking birds too, of course," Kiril replied, running a hand through his hair. It looked like a regular, unremarkable pigeon. But here it was, speaking to him, regarding him with its inquisitive beady eyes. "But, bird, I…discovered that love is real, after all. Yet at that point it was too late for regrets."

"Indeed. But you still have a chance, Kiril Belaja. There is someone who loves you, who wants to save you. The Lady of the Valley of the Lilies, a favoured devotee of Lord Milostra, has sent me here as a messenger," said the bird and pecked at a red berry.

"The Lady of…Jelena. You mean her. She revered Milostra. Jelena has sent you?"

"She has been in the service of Lord Milostra ever since she crossed over. The Forbearing God recruited her upon arrival. She resides in Milostra's corner of the Elysian Fields of the Yonder—the Valley of the Lilies. But all that happiness, all her meaningful work in the Forbearing God's service, can give her no solace, because she has been following your misguided life and waiting for you to cross over."

Kiril could not tell if the bird—if it really was a bird—disapproved. He motioned for it to continue.

"She doesn't have the power to come to the Nether. The denizens of Yonder are not welcome here, but gray pigeons can go unnoticed where white doves would attract attention, even though a pigeon and a dove are one and the same. I was able to slip by hostile creatures, to look for your soul. To instruct you."

The white dove was Milostra's holy symbol. His clerics carried an amulet depicting one over their sand brown modest robes. Whatever this pigeon—or dove—was, it was no ordinary bird. *Brilliant deduction there, Kiril. Was it the fact that it is speaking to you that gave it away?* Perhaps it was a magical animal made of subtle matter, like a mage's familiar. They, too, were able to manifest a flesh form when it suited them. "It seems that I still have a body," Kiril remarked.

The bird cocked its head. "For now. Gross matter builds anew around a soul, in most circumstances. But here in Manala, souls fade away. They become apathetic wraiths and forget who they are. As their will, desire, and memories fade, so does their flesh. Then they listlessly wander here forever. That will be your fate, Kiril Belaja, unless you heed my message."

Did Jelena know everything? Kiril fervently hoped she didn't. Would she still love him enough to send a messenger to this bleak land of the Nether he had ended up in? "I'm listening," he said.

"Every moment you spend in Manala increases the danger that you will become one of the roaming wraiths—or something worse. Malevolent beings with green bile for blood prey on the lost souls, and without magic, you are helpless. But if you manage to avoid succumbing to the inertia of this place and evade the predators for long enough, you stand a chance to reunite with the Lady of the Lilies. It is a bold plan, born of desperation. But a chance is a chance."

Something white floated in the slush of the river. It was a dead infant, milky eyes staring at Kiril and the bird. Kiril startled and again instinctively reached for a divination, only to feel the mute throb of nothing. *Damn...*

"That thing is not dangerous," the bird said. "A desperate mother drowned an unwanted child somewhere. Innocents don't end up in this place, so its soul is somewhere far away. What floats in the river is a visible reminder of the mother's guilt and shame. The desperation and self-loathing that makes the fabric of this place—that gives it shape and form. Remember that. Though there are predators, the most dangerous thing in this place is your own mind. Your despair."

"You said...there is a chance that I could be reunited with Jelena?" The idea of facing her after all he had done terrified Kiril. All the same, the spark of hope warmed his numb limbs.

"As I said, countless lands of the dead sprawl across the infinity of the multiverse," said the pigeon. "There is a people of fierce warriors in another world—Northmen, they are called. And it so happens that a great mystical ash tree is the axis of their universe. It has a root in the Nether, and at that root there is a spring from where all the rivers of the Nether flow. This one"—it nodded at the sluggishly flowing slush— "is no exception. Thus, if you follow this river, you will find your way to the root of that tree. The tree is called Yggdrasil."

Kiril glanced at the river, flowing from the foggy grayness of the horizon he was barely able to see through the mist. He nodded for the bird to continue.

"The All-Father of that universe—Odin by name, though he goes by many others—performed a sacrifice at the tree and gained great power and wisdom. The tree might be powerful enough to give you your magic back, so that you are strong enough to find your way to Lady Jelena. She will try to make her way to the part of the Yonder where Yggdrasil has another root—Asgard, the home of the gods of the Northmen, and their revered fallen. Deal with the ladies who guard the tree. Do what you must so that they allow you to make a sacrifice. Keep your head down, your mind focused. Don't attract attention. Follow the river. Find Yggdrasil."

For a moment, the bird turned luminous white, then it reverted to its gray form and disappeared in a blink. "Wait! Where—" Kiril called after it, but it was gone. He had so many questions. But the warning and the straight-forward instructions would have to suffice. In all likelihood, Jelena was not familiar with the magnitude of his sins and the grand purpose behind them. But...perhaps she would understand and forgive. He had failed already, after all. What did it matter now? He had a chance to reunite with Jelena.

But what of Velimir? Cornered and raving mad, it was

likely that the boy had met an unfortunate end—an end that Kiril bore a great deal of responsibility for coming to pass. Perhaps, if he got his powers back, he would be able to help Velimir somehow.

One foot after another. Follow the river. Evade predators. Find Yggdrasil.

PART ONE
VELIMIR

"I'd strike the sun if it insulted me."
—Herman Melville, Moby Dick

1
THE ABYSS, JUST ANOTHER SHIFTING PLANE

VELIMIR ENTERED THE PORTAL, BRACING HIMSELF FOR whatever intolerable pain would be unleashed on him upon arrival. Nothing. He opened his eyes and looked around. He was in the kitchen of Rosinin's old Oligorsk home. Cautiously, he took a few steps and touched the table, Jelena's shiny kettles and pots on the shelves, the stove. Everything seemed to be real.

The door opened, and Radek arrived, smiling cruelly as he did when he was still confident of his supreme ability to control both Jelena and Velimir. He had a nine-tailed barbed whip in his hand. Wherever did the bastard come from?

"Velimir! What a pleasure," he sneered. "So, you wanted me dead all along, and that bitch of yours did the honors. She will have hers, too...but first I will continue what was interrupted in our mortal life. Disciplining you, dear son. Take your clothes off, for you are in for some whipping."

"You've *got* to be kidding me," said Velimir, knowing he could snap the man in half without breaking a sweat. He stepped forward to do just that, when he was suddenly transformed into the body of a seven-year-old child. Radek, now towering above him, grabbed his arm and lifted him upwards.

Velimir was helpless in the man's grip, and no divine power was coming to help. He could feel Dimitri's mirth as the celestial feasted on Velimir's horror.

"I don't think so," murmured Radek. He ripped Velimir's shirt effortlessly, yanked his trousers down, and tossed the boy face-down on the table, then started to whip him relentlessly. Velimir tried to yell, his voice the high-pitched tone of a child, but he started to choke on his tears. This was worse than any pain before, the barbs ripping and gouging, the nine tails twirling around his limbs and flaying flaps of his skin, the blood flowing liberally on the table in little streams.

Had he truly had a body and been alive, he would have lost his consciousness. But the agony continued and continued, his eyes open, blood coming from his mouth, his eyes bulging. He was limp, subdued, waiting for death that would not come, wondering how long it would take before his skin completely fell off.

"This is what I ought to have done when I had the chance. I always was a man with too gentle a heart," muttered Radek. He disappeared and appeared in front of Velimir's eyes, this time dragging Tomoe with her. Tomoe was bound and gagged, struggling in her ropes.

"She *is* a nice piece of ass. I have to give you that much,"

Radek continued. "Too bad she has a nasty habit of murdering respectable citizens. Well, now she is going to pay for that, and you get to watch."

Velimir, unable to move or do anything but look on in repulsion, horror, denial, saw him ripping Tomoe's clothes, leering at her, taking his time, exploring every crevice of her body, thoroughly having his way with Velimir's lover, breaking the spirit of the proud warrior reduced to his pleasure slave. At first, the woman tried to struggle, grunt and fight, but then she lay still and offered no resistance. After the man was done, calmly regarding his possessions, Tomoe stared ahead, breathing, but her spirit was dead. *This can't happen, this can't! It isn't right!* Velimir's mind screamed, but there was nothing he could do about it. His mind began to fall apart.

Dimitri wasn't talking to Velimir anymore, nor sending him visions, but he still felt the fallen celestial alternating between all-consuming rage and cruel amusement. All those soothing visions had been but lies. Despair started to sneak in. Velimir's eyelids drooped. But Radek poked his head, grinning again.

"You think that's all I have in store for you, son? Oh no... watch..."

Jelena entered the kitchen—beautiful, whole, humming and starting to make tea. She looked right through the two slumped heaps and her husband, apparently not able to see them.

NO! Mother, run! But Velimir's voice didn't work, and he couldn't move.

Radek quietly moved behind her, then spoke in a soft voice layered with malice. "Jelena...Jelena dear..."

She turned around and gasped, and Radek brandished the garrote.

"Velimir will save me. He won't let this happen," said Jelena, taking a step back.

"Velimir?" laughed Radek. "He can't even save himself. Why, he's watching right now and not able to do a damn thing about it." He placed the garrote around Jelena's neck. She tried to push her hand in between in vain.

"Velimir! Please!"

Radek started to squeeze, and the garrote cut into her neck, her eyes bulging.

"Velimir…please save me…son…" she pleaded in despair.

Velimir tried, with all his might, to get up—but his strength was gone, his despair gripping him as painfully as the garrote gripping Jelena's neck.

Suddenly, it hit him. What could his poor mother ever have done to end up in this place of torment? Surely, it wasn't really her! And if it wasn't her, then all of it was a lie!

"I call your bluff, demon!" he yelled, and was magnificently pleased to find that his voice was the deep bellow of a large man again. "You are playing with my mind, trying to make me despair!"

At the words, Jelena and Tomoe dissolved, as did the environment, replaced by a nondescript barren wasteland with large craters everywhere. Radek dissolved, too, and in his place stood a vaguely humanoid shape, reddish, yellow-eyed, molten and full of rage and malice. It still wielded the nine-tailed whip and roared in intense displeasure. Velimir knew this would be an excellent time to scram, so he ran as fast as he could while the creature tried to recover from its frustration. As he jumped over the first bottomless-looking crater, he felt a tug of magic and was portaled somewhere… dark.

Dark and damp…a cave. Quiet, pitch-dark. Cold stone against his cheek. At least at the moment, nothing threatened to consume him, so he collected himself and settled down. The creature had been able to read his fears and memories sunken in the deep, dark fjord of the things he didn't want to think about. He shuddered. But he had beaten it for now. This also proved he was correct. Giving in—despair—was what would make him stay here forever. To become one with this depraved and hopeless place. He would never let that happen.

Knowing the nature of his divine father now, he prayed to the only beautiful thing he had faith left in.

"Mother, give me strength. Mother, thank you, it wasn't true."

2
WALLILA GATE

THE YOUNG MAN TOOK CARE TO LOOK EXACTLY LIKE ANY other citizen milling about at Wallila Gate's busy central square. Fortunately, there was an abundance of peddlers with their wares, street performers, and folk from faraway lands from all over Valkama. People strolled leisurely, finding plenty of interest around them. He, too, pretended to slow down to take a look at this or that, focusing his eyes on something novel, without appearing to be tracking the Morishiman courier escorted by two young women.

The escorts formed an odd pair. The one was unsmiling, a sword at her waist, donning a leather jerkin—obviously a warrior. She was on the short side, her body strong and stocky, her hair a glossy reddish-brown veil reaching her waist. *Peri of Eilean de Taigh-Sholais.* His mark. The other girl was taller, but slender. Her face was round and friendly, her hair reaching her shoulders dyed emerald green.

Ewynne, Peri's sister and sidekick. One of Dimitri's weakling spawn, collected by the late brother Connor to protect. A mage of some skill, taught by her stepfather.

"We have now arrived at our destination," said the Morishiman courier, patting her satchel and smiling courteously at Peri and Ewynne. The woman was disheveled after the long and hot journey. She adjusted her traditional hairstyle. "I am delighted that our journey was without an incident, though I have no doubt that you would have kept us safe had it been otherwise. Genjiro-san will deliver you the payment in the tavern, as agreed. I bid you goodbye," she said and disappeared into the office of a company trading in Zmaj-Vostokan imports.

"You can always tell the ones who haven't been here to the West for very long," said Ewynne. "They speak so formally. Nice and steady income in protecting the couriers and escorting caravans. I know the other jobs make us more money, but I like these ones. Most of the time, the bandits and muggers don't bother us. I'm glad—I don't like to hurt people."

Peri shrugged. "If they attack what they think are defenseless travelers, they have it coming." She frowned for a moment. *Most likely she welcomes the opportunity to slaughter—she is one of Dimitri's true progeny*, thought the young man tracking the girls and pretending to be delighted with the show a juggler was putting on next to the girls. *But she may be hesitant to say so to her weakling sister she seems content to keep around for now.*

Then Peri grinned and perked up. "We make a good team," she told Ewynne. "I think there are basically two approaches to protection. The other one I would call the 'in your face' approach. I'm not a large woman, but I do give that 'fuck off' vibe. My training and slight paranoia from being on the road and dodging Velimir's bounty hunters shows."

"It...is more than that. Always was. You know that." Ewynne didn't smile back or otherwise respond to Peri's deliberate cheerfulness.

"I guess. I'm changing. Physically. Stronger and faster, my senses sharper. More vicious." Peri looked grim for a moment, then grinned again. "I swear to you, I have not been bitten by a werewolf. Don't get me wrong. Part of me enjoys this. That people don't even think about jerking me around. But I know it can rub people the wrong way. I guess...in our job, the wrong way is the right way."

The young man turned his face to observe the desert-born juggler performing for a group of giggling children, but made sure to keep the girls in his peripheral vision.

"Okay, sis, so you are the 'in your face' approach. But you were saying that there is another approach." Ewynne leaned forward eagerly.

"The other approach I would call the 'what the fuck' approach. When someone has something bad on their mind and they don't expect any resistance, then see something that confuses them. Something 'what the fuck.' Something that makes them miss a beat. And that beat is enough for you to finish them. You with your friendly face and green hair are the good kind of 'what the fuck.'"

The observer acknowledged to himself that Peri made a good point. While there was a distinct aura of menace around her, the last thing one would associate with Ewynne was danger. Smart of the girls to use that to their advantage in teamwork. But then, Dimitri's true offspring were nothing if not resourceful. Perhaps Peri's strong blood ignited Ewynne's weak spark so that the little mage was not completely useless. *Either way, she won't live for long. Perhaps Peri will slaughter her herself when the time is right—or the Esquadron will have them both before that happens.*

"That...actually makes me more dangerous than you, doesn't it?" said Ewynne, a spark of enthusiasm in her voice. "Sure, you can scowl and make a show of your weapons—but I have to actually kill them if it comes to that!"

"There you see," Peri said. "Let's go to Bucc's now. I could definitely use a drink."

———•●•———

THE YOUNG MAN SLIPPED IN THE CROWD AND MADE HIS way through the shadowy alleyways to the remote, white-washed building. He sighed in relief as he stepped into its cool interior, wiping his perspiring forehead. The dour-looking tall, blonde woman and the young man with sallow skin, shiny dark hair, and bright, black eyes waited for him. "Mistress Rajsa. Master Darien. The leads were correct. I have tracked her to Wallila Gate. I observed them both with my own eyes," he said.

"Excellent!" exclaimed the man called Darien brightly and flashed his perfect white teeth. "Do sit down. She is still traveling with her sister?"

The young man accepted the offered refreshments—olives, hard salty cheese, and bread with chilled wine and a pitcher of cool water—and nodded. "Ever since they left Lughani Vos, they have been selling protection services to travelers and couriers. They journeyed the coast eastwards, selling their sword on the way. An odd job here and there clearing out bandits and monsters—your normal sellsword stuff. But now they have settled in Wallila Gate, for the time being at least. They lodge in the Buccaneer's Respite at the port. It is the hub of local sellswords. Prospective employers leave messages at the bar, or just approach the sellswords when they are drinking."

The blonde woman called Rajsa nodded curtly. "Yes, yes. There is a place like that in any big port town."

"The girls work for the local Morishimans, particularly one trader that lodges in the same inn. But not only for them. The local business—legal and otherwise—is quite cutthroat, so business is lucrative for swords-for-hire. The girls, too, sell their services to shady characters. Spying, breaking and entering, even enforcing—I get the impression that they are borderline assassins at this point. Lately, they have been working for a guy named Tejero. A local slumlord," the young man explained to the duo.

Rajsa kept fingering a small leather pouch hanging on her neck as an amulet. It was the holy emblem of clerics of Stribog—after the pouch where the grandfather of winds kept them contained according to legend. Darien leaned forward, eager like a coiled spring.

"They have been trying to lie low ever since leaving Lughani Vos," Darien said, "and for a long while, they have been successful. Well done! The Esquadron will reward you well. It is essential that we get Peri, and to keep it neat, we'd better get her unsuspecting."

———————•●•———————

WALLILA GATE, THE BUSTLING TRADING HUB AND CAPITAL of Yalifa, was nestled between the sea and the mountains that shimmered blue in the distance. The ancient city had seen nations rise and fall, tribes and peoples come and go. It had always, however, been a center of trade and seafaring. Peri and Ewynne passed the Cathedral of the Three: Cijeli, Milostra, and Juris. The clerics of Cijeli the All-Father wore richly embroidered golden robes and observed the folk passing by under the arches, welcoming worshippers to the halls of the imposing building. Though the church of the Three was prominent in Yalifa, there were temples and shrines of all imaginable faiths from all over Valkama.

"I know you miss the island, Wyn," said Peri. "But I don't. I love it here."

"I know." Much to Ewynne's sorrow, Peri had wanted to leave long before…the horrible happened.

"It is…small. People know you. Look at you. Judge you. I would go to the Inn Island, talk with sailors and pilgrims, fuck one if I felt like it…I was so *hungry* to see everything, to *live!* And now I can." She had said it all before—but she hoped, perhaps in vain, that this time Ewynne would understand, *truly* understand. They were just passing a shrine dedicated to a feline luck goddess from faraway Feng Guo— another example of how the whole wide world was now Peri's to conquer…and Ewynne's, if she only would open her heart to adventure.

"Do you…miss Connor at all?" There was a slight reservation in Ewynne's voice. It was almost as if the death of their stepfather had set Peri free, while Ewynne was still heartbroken.

Peri stopped in her tracks and turned to face her. "Of course, I do! He was…what kept me from going insane. He was my father." She turned abruptly and started to briskly walk towards the port, Ewynne hurrying after her.

"Forgive me, Peri," she said. "It is just...you are so happy here. It is like...you have moved on. I haven't. I still mourn. I miss the island. I like to adventure, a bit, but then I want to go back home."

"There is no home for me," said Peri, her mouth still a tight line. "Nor will there be. I don't want one. I hope the bastards one day will welcome you back, but now..." her voice trailed off. Of course, the small-minded bastards blamed Connor's adopted charges for bringing murder and chaos to the island. Peri herself had it coming—she had attracted Velimir's madness to hers—but Ewynne? The kindest and warmest soul there was? *That's people for you.* Peri glanced at her sister and smiled, though the smile didn't reach her eyes. But she did so in order to demonstrate to Ewynne that she was not angry at her.

"...the dreams are worse now, aren't they? I can sometimes hear you moaning in your sleep," Ewynne said.

Not just dreams, sis. Peri nodded. "It's okay. Let's not dwell on crap that can't be helped."

———————— •●• ————————

"FAIR WINDS AND FOLLOWING SEAS, GENJIRO," SAID PERI as the man approached her at the table in the Buccaneer's Respite Inn. "The goods arrived intact. No major trouble on the way."

"...fair winds and following seas," answered Genjiro, arching his eyebrow, smiling just a little. A silky wisp of black hair was plastered on his forehead. There was a scar crossing the eyebrow. "Curious phrasing, my friend."

"It is a phrase that Eoghain's devout use...and I was

raised on his holy island," said Peri. "But I am far from pious, just...old habits die hard."

"No doubt. But this confuses me. They say Stribog is the godfather of winds, and many offer to him, fear him. He even has a mighty merchant house named after him. But Eoghain...is he not a wind god, too?" Genjiro sat down with his glass of ale.

"Eoghain is the kind god of travelers and favourable winds. Stribog wants to dominate the winds and their destinations. Eoghain wants to follow the winds to the unknown. Or so Connor and the monks taught me." Peri shrugged. "I don't know. Winds are winds. What about you? Any wind gods back home in Zmaj-Vostok?"

"We...don't have gods like your people do. We have thousands and thousands of *kami*—every thing, no matter how big or small, has a *kami*. I'm sure there are wind *kami* everywhere, but they have no names or fathers or followers." Genjiro spoke excellent common, but he had a distinct accent.

"This is what I like about Wallila Gate. People from all over Valkama, everybody with tales to tell, nobody standing out from the motley crowd," Peri said. "They don't look at you sideways, because everyone and no-one is odd here."

"Coin is the common tongue here. Abundant freedom, yes...but no-one looks after the defenseless either."

"I guess," Peri said, wondering if Genjiro found that regrettable. *Like Ewynne.* "We can handle ourselves. Ewynne, my mage sister, is starting to accept that we sometimes have to hurt people."

"Ah, she of the green hair. I suppose hurting evil people does not bother you—you are a battlemaiden."

"Evil…I don't know. Some of them are greedy, others desperate. I have a job to do, and that job is to stop them. I'm no battlemaiden, anyway." Peri found it easy to talk to Genjiro, and for the first time after leaving Eilean de Taigh-Sholais behind, she felt the urge to tell more about herself to a relative stranger. "I studied fighting at a garrison, but I was not a soldier or training to be one. Just wanted to learn to… handle myself. To kill, even. Turns out I have something of a talent for it. And Ewynne learned magic from our father."

"Well, it seems you both have made good use of what you learned. You came highly recommended, and my compatriots are not easy to impress. Which reminds me. I owe you the agreed payment for services well rendered, again. You are starting to build a name for yourselves."

"I hope not," said Peri, frowning. "I came here because…I want to blend in with the scenery. Be a sword for hire like any other."

"My, my, the intrigue thickens! Does Peri the battlemaiden have dark secrets in her past?" Genjiro regarded her from behind half-closed eyelids, looking slightly amused.

Peri rolled her eyes. "Does that smooth talk actually work for you, Genjiro?"

"Sometimes," he replied, never taking his eyes off Peri, lips still curved in the enigmatic smile.

"You are determined to annoy me by calling me a battlemaiden, aren't you?" Peri sighed, but then grinned. "I fight hard and dirty if I must, but I try to slip by unnoticed. Mislead and confuse. I recon, spy, observe patiently. Make a plan. If I have to kill something, I prefer to ambush it."

"That is the way of those who walk the path of shadows," said Genjiro, dropping his smile.

There was an awkward silence. Genjiro peeled the agreed upon notes from a roll for Peri, who nodded, leaned back, and closed her eyes.

"...fair winds and following seas. Correct?" said Genjiro.

Peri, without opening her eyes, gave him a thumbs-up, and he went his way.

3
THE ABYSS

THE DAY PASSED INTO WEEKS. THE WEEKS INTO MONTHS. Velimir had been portal-jumping for a while now. Though he had always taken pride in his imagination, he had learned more about different interesting ways of suffering than he'd expected to be possible or would have liked to get first-hand experience of. That never failed to amuse Dimitri, whom Velimir tried to ignore. It was not as if he could do anything about the vengeful bastard tormenting him. Velimir's eyes had sunken a little, hollow in his wraithlike form, but he had not lost his grim resolve. He would find a way out of here.

As he traveled, he managed to gather information from those he came across. A bored succubus, a lost warrior, a portal-hopping wanderer from a world far beyond Valkama, hoping to visit all the portals of the multiverse…Velimir had a plan. He would have to reach the river Styx, the only known way out of the Abyss. He would do whatever he had to do to pay the ferryman and travel to the evergrey hopelessness of Manala. Somewhere within its soggy gloom, the legend stated, grew a root of a tree growing through an entire faraway world of fierce warriors. By following the root to their corner of the Yonder, one would come across a rainbow bridge that led back to the world of the living.

Finding his way out of the Abyss and to that tree became Velimir's single-minded focus. He'd make his way back to the world of the living. He would figure out how to get a corporeal form and his life back. He would find a way to power and glory again. He would stab from hell's heart at anyone standing in his way!

Occasionally, he felt as if Tomoe's sad face watched him through the haze of the chaotic memories of his fall. Judging. Pleading. He embraced his anger and determination with renewed fervour whenever that happened. Tomoe had chosen to be a lesser being and done her level best to drag him down with her. It was her fault that he was dead now—but he was determined to live again.

The problem at hand, though, was that he had no idea how to get to the Styx. It would have been easy to despair, as the ever-shifting layers were infinite, and he was jumping the portals without the faintest idea where they would lead. But he was confident he would eventually meet someone or something that could lead him to the Styx. It would perhaps have been safer to stay somewhere where the torment was bearable instead of taking chances. But it was not in his nature to lay low. Only by moving on, clinging to his plan, would he prevent the nagging enemy—despair—from taking residence and making him one of the surrendered beings of this depraved place.

Again, Velimir was reminded of his childhood in the streets. He remembered the old beggars who didn't care about anything but food and shelter, and how his spirit yearned for more than that. He would keep his spirit yearning.

No sooner than coming through the latest portal, he was grabbed by two stern-looking beings, different from the beings normally encountered in the Abyss—like an unnaturally radiant elf and human, so very robust and healthy: blonde and beautiful, perfect teeth, surrounded with faint light. In their eyes was something familiar. Velimir was reminded of the priestesses who had tried to sacrifice him to Dimitri.

"We will have you know, sinner, that we do not normally dwell here. We are custosi from Panoptica, and we are on a special mission," said the elven-looking one in a cultivated, and a tad snobbish, voice.

"Oh." Velimir saw that the creature was dying to elaborate, so he didn't ask anything.

"That means we are the high-ranking spirits whose ultimate reward of righteous life and continued service of Lord Bentham is on the plane of Panoptica!" said the female human-looking one.

"Nice for you," said Velimir. The custosi hauled him into a chair. There were rows and rows of chairs, with damned souls of the Abyss seated on most of them.

"We, the custosi of Panoptica, have a sad duty to make you, the evil souls condemned to the Abyss, watch what you would have received had you lived your life in the right fashion as we and our charges did. You are sealed in with us, and the magical enchantment makes you unable to avert your eyes or close them. Look at the place where the righteous dwell! Look at their reward! Lament your fate, for this is now forever denied you!" intoned the other custosi. They were dressed in full battle gear, white and shining.

A large, shimmering portal appeared, apparently a visual connection to the plane of happiness. *No doubt they have a similar one there so that the happy souls get to watch us writhing in pain*, Velimir thought. In the vision, there was an elaborate garden where every bush and plant was neatly clipped in symmetrical perfection. The folks strolling the spotless and perfectly straight lanes were exceptionally healthy. They wore symmetric smiles with perfect white teeth. They were tall and robust. Everybody was polite, groomed, and well-dressed.

"Panoptica is the land of ultimate good. Laws are made for the good of everyone. Natural harmony is maintained religiously," explained the male elf, blind to the irony. "The evil are attacked on sight without mercy, the non-committed are escorted to the borders. Those with good intentions but misguided beliefs are referred to correctional facilities."

The focus of the vision shifted to wildlife, but it, too, seemed to arrange itself symmetrically for the viewer's benefit. The landscape, plants and animals seemed to strive to be perfect specimens.

"The truly righteous are protected, able to enjoy all the happiness this perfection can offer—"

Velimir snapped. It was insufferable that these patronizing zealots could imagine that he, Velimir, would long for such an infantile, impotent life under their yoke! Dead and defeated or not, he still was a man of will and dignity, on his way to rediscovering power. He bolted upwards and started to bellow, his hollow eyes blazing as they had when he was alive.

"Even given a choice, I'd *choose* this eternal torment over that mindless life of a well-fed farm animal! Yes, the pain is incredible. Yes, every new layer of suffering is worse than the previous. But at least it is *my* pain, *mine* to wander, *mine* to endure! What doesn't kill me can only make me stronger, and as I'm already dead, I can only grow in power! I swore at the bitter ashes of my mother's grave that I'd crawl and scratch my way back to the land of the living, and, by the fallen celestial that is my father, so I will!"

The custosi gasped, drawing their shining swords.

"Erm. If I may be so bold and take this…disruption with me." An observer stepped out of the shadows. He looked like a demon, complete with the horns and hooves, but there was a faint blue glow surrounding him, something that Velimir had not seen before.

The custosi nodded stiffly, and the demon made a nonchalant motion. He teleported away with Velimir, and both found themselves standing on another dusty plain.

"Why, you have some spirit," chuckled the demon. "I am Azul, here on recruiting duty, and I was wondering if you'd be interested in some Abyssal warfare."

4
WALLILA GATE

"It will take two seconds for me to cast a *crn-prasak*. I don't know how to do spell triggers yet," said Ewynne, her green hair pulled up and covered by a dark hood. "I didn't prepare a flaming arrow—it takes so long to cast, and we are expecting several targets." Instead of the high-impact lance of elemental fire, she had prepared several *crn-prasaks* and a one target hold spell that would immobilize the target for a few seconds. "Mass hold would be awesome, but if I had prepared that, I couldn't cast any other spells." Mages gained more capacity with the combination of experience and careful study of subtle energy. One day she would be able to immobilize all the targets and rain elemental damage of her choice on them, but that day was not today.

Peri nodded. They were planning their ambush in the office of a warehouse their employer expected to be burgled.

"Plenty of time for them to react. I don't like this. On the other hand, if we drop one in the doorway, it will hinder them...but then we can't see what the rest are doing. Can you...hold the spell, ready to release, like a finger on the trigger of a crossbow?"

"I can, for a while, though better not make it too long," Ewynne said.

"So...we will be waiting at the rafters," Peri said. "Elevated position. They will start searching the place as soon as they enter. I imagine they'll start with the desk."

"I planted an obvious trap in the first drawer," Ewynne said. "They'll think they cracked it and feel relieved, anxious to get the loot."

"And then I'll drop the net by the door." Peri pointed at the contraption she had devised. "When the net drops, you prepare the *crn-prasak*. When the drawer clicks open, I drop the one who opened it, and you drop the one that seems most dangerous."

Ewynne nodded. "Even if the *crn-prasak* doesn't kill them, it will certainly knock them back."

"They shouldn't be expecting any resistance, but even if they do, we have them like fish in a barrel. Let's just hope they don't have mages or clerics," Peri said. Divinations could mess up the best of ambushes, and spellcasters had all kinds of nasty tricks to deal with shooters at an elevated position.

"And then, we just...kill them all...in a pile," Ewynne said wanly.

"Wyn, they are bad dudes. Slavers—or sent by them, anyway," Peri said. Peri decided to appeal to Ewynne's sense of reality. "You know that the city guard is completely corrupt, and most judges, too. They'd be back in the street before sundown. We are just doing what the city guard should be doing." The rationalization sounded hollow in her ears even as she uttered it. *Fuck it, I just want to kill something in goodish conscience.* She hoped Ewynne bought it, anyway.

"Yeah, but it's not like Tejero is doing this to stop slavers! He may not be a slaver, but he extorts poor people who live in his houses with nowhere else to go…maybe sells shinedust across the border. He just wants to stop the slavers from getting the upper hand," Ewynne answered, while climbing up to the rafters and settling for a balanced spot lying across the beam.

Peri sighed, loading her crossbow. "It is what it is, Wyn. Perhaps we will have a chance to off Tejero at some point. But then what? Another rises in his place? Could be worse than him. Very likely, it is not a particularly benevolent person interested in helping the poor tenants, or he wouldn't have hired us to off Tejero. It's frustrating to think about. You'd have to change this entire nation, perhaps the entire world. There is a certain simplicity to this I find appealing. This town is full of scumbags competing with each other, and they pay us to eliminate the competition's scumbags. So—we eliminate scumbags. Isn't that heroic or something?"

"I can't deny that the spying and scouting and making all the plans and ambushes and stuff is fun," Ewynne said. "I just…Maybe we should use our skills for something better. For helping people."

Peri shrugged. "Maybe. I don't know. They'd just want to be helped more and more and more, and it still won't make a dent in how things are. Maybe we could take some job that takes us out of town. An adventure! But for now, let's focus."

The girls waited silently at the rafters. After a while,

they could hear the warehouse door creak open and hesitant steps in the hallway. The burglars treaded lightly. The group of three entered the office. The narrow face of an elven woman glanced at the rafters, but she didn't see the dark-clad girls, who kept still.

"Look," she said after studying the desk for a while. "What a pathetic trap! You'd think Tejero would have secured this a bit better—"

Her remark seemed to alarm a companion—a human man—who looked around. "Exactly," he said. "What if Tejero has gotten wind of us?" He started to wiggle his fingers.

Ewynne felt fluttering dread in the pit of her stomach. *A divination?* It would reveal their presence immediately. She glanced at Peri, who, face tight with anticipation, nodded and released the string of her trap. Ewynne started to cast the *crn-prasak*, quietly mouthing the syllables. Peri trained her crossbow at the elf, waiting for the agreed upon signal.

There was a brief flash, and their silhouettes started to glitter. The mage released his finger and hurled a flaming lance through the air. *Oh shit, he had a spell trigger prepared!* It didn't hit Peri squarely, but it made an impact, and Peri screamed, dropping her crossbow. Ewynne gasped, and her spell was released, missing the mage by an inch. The *crn-prasak* flew through the air like a glowing black missile and ricocheted from the floor, knocking back a stunned third burglar. Ewynne focused her gaze on her fingertip. *Calm center in the middle of chaos. Focus. Act.* She started to prepare the hold spell, *budimiran*, pointing her index fingers at the mage, who had drawn his arm back. A lightning bolt started to form and hover above his palm.

Peri, still screaming, leaped from the rafters at the mage.

She pulled her sword while leaping—a trick she had rehearsed—and aimed to use the momentum from her leap for a devastating strike into the mage's gut. But the sword bounced uselessly off him. *Shit! Svetilje sphere!*

Peri started to shimmer and vacillate between her familiar form and something taller, smooth and perfect, radiant. She growled in frustration and turned to face the elf, who had recovered from her surprise, and the third burglar, who looked terrified. The elf drew a dagger and slashed at Peri, but she dodged and thrust her blade in the elf's abdomen. Ewynne trained her fingers on the third burglar, realizing that the *Svetilje sphere* would dissipate her hold spell.

Now Peri stepped on the corpse and pulled her blade out. She flickered and vacillated between three different forms— the one of pure light, her own, and that of a demon, like the one they had released in the old Dimitri temple but smaller. Her eyes shifted between that menacing pool of molten lava with pinpoints of hatred, then serene, commanding and golden, then her own grayish-green. Ewynne's hold spell encased the terrified burglar, while the agitated mage released a second spell trigger—a *crn-prasak.* It knocked Peri back, making a sickening sound. Peri screamed in pain and dropped the blade. Then her fingers transformed into black gnarled talons! She laughed, but the voice was not her own. She thrust the talons in the mage's belly, gripped, and started to pull the innards out. The mage made a chortling noise and his eyes went glassy.

Peri was nowhere near done. She ripped and grunted, splattering herself with gore. She sank her teeth into the mage's forearm, yanking and ripping it off the body. Then she slowly turned to face the remaining burglar, who was pale, shaking, and had peed his pants. The hold spell had worn off, but he made no attempt to move. Peri shifted back to her own form and started to grin. The burglar closed his eyes and moaned.

Ewynne leaped off the rafters and grabbed her arm. "Peri! Peri! Stop! Stop! Don't kill him! Please!"

Peri grunted in annoyance but hesitated, facing Ewynne. She shook her head and took a few breaths, regarding her surroundings as if seeing them for the first time. "What… the fuck…just happened here?"

Ewynne jerked her head, nodding at the burglar. Peri crouched next to him. "Go," she said. "Tell the scumbags who sent you not to mess with Tejero." She sank to her knees as the burglar hurried away, whimpering.

"Peri…" Ewynne said, measuring her words carefully, "you…transformed into something. Two things."

Peri glanced at the gory mess that had been the mage, then studied the entrails covering her hands in wonder. "You have said that I sometimes look different when I…well, kill."

"Not like this. Before it has been a momentary flicker—a trick of light. But now…"

"Motherfucker burned me! It pissed me off."

"Yeah, so I gathered. Ripping his guts out with your hands and biting his arm off were kind of a dead giveaway."

Peri suddenly looked like she was about to cry. "Ewynne. That is not your line. It is me who says things like that. Not you. Don't turn into me. What am I even saying? I am some kind of monster now."

"I know this is a lot to take in. I will explain to you what happened, but let's get out of here first. Okay?" Ewynne offered her hand to Peri, who allowed herself to be led out. It had always been the other way around. Ewynne had always relied on Peri to protect her, especially now that Connor was gone. *But she is lost. And I kill people. I see a thing like that and it is just...something that happens to me. Like something within the parameters of normal. Velimir did this to us. Connor would have protected us from whatever god-awful thing this is.*

But Connor was gone. Ewynne would have to deal with this on her own.

5
THE ABYSS

This was the best time yet that Velimir had so far in the Abyss. He had just been in a battle, on one of the countless abyssal planes. Aside from the fact that the ground was molten, burning his shadowy feet, wielding steel again, to fight, made him feel alive. At times, he glanced at his side for an affirming nod to orchestrate his combat moves with…Oh, he was alone. Tomoe was no longer fighting by his side. *Nor would she be worthy of being my sister in arms, the traitor.* But no matter how true that was, a pang of pain always surfaced when he realized that she did not have his flank—that she would never have his flank again. *Insufferable!* Not even death had rid him of such pathetic impulses. *I refuse! I will not acknowledge that the traitor ever meant anything to me.*

His wraithlike, translucent form allowed him the ability to grasp items and manipulate them, but unfortunately also the full sensory experience of excruciating pain. It didn't require food for nourishment, but he did feel the need to fall into the deep, pitch-dark nothingness of sleep. At times, the nothingness was a relief, but it unnerved him—what if he were not to wake from it? What if there was an even more final death, a true annihilation? What if his desire and will sputtered out and his spark died? *NEVER! Hostile landscapes? Tortures of mind and body? So be it.* He'd endure all that and more, as long as his desire kept him yearning for power and glory!

The demons they had fought didn't look much different from the demons Velimir fought for. Why they hated each other so much seemed to be a profound difference in basic philosophy. The demons opposing Azul's troops wanted to rule with an iron fist. They were strategic and organized, and masters of twisting the meaning of bargains struck with mortals foolish enough to deal with demons. Their mission was to conquer and settle all the Netherworld, and they were reaching to the Abyss from Ratas, their looming fortress city state somewhere in the Nether.

Azul had explained this to him, contemptuously. The demon saw their own way of doing things—the random, vigorous, spontaneous rage—as more virile and adaptable. The display of true power. And so, the free-roaming demons fought the would-be conquerors, hoping to wipe out the other ones and rule all the underworld. To Velimir it seemed pointless, as there always would be uses for both approaches, but he kept his mouth shut. It was to his advantage that the demon considered him an ally rather than a plaything. Yet that could change if he presumed too much. Demons were nothing if not fickle and malicious, with the cruelest sense of humor.

Azul knew what Velimir was—had been—when he was alive. The demon had equipped his form with a suite of armor and a sword, standard issue but well-crafted. Velimir felt such a gratitude that he almost wept and thanked the demon, only his instincts preventing him from doing this. There were lesser demons and undead among their troops. Even a few newly dead mortals had joined the group—no small feat. These ones had bodies of flesh not unlike the ones they'd had on the face of Valkama. Velimir's Dimitrian essence must have burned away whatever it was that made a normal mortal capable of obtaining a body in death.

The recent battles had just been disposing of a small force of demons from Ratas trying to sneak into the Abyss, but Velimir noticed that fighting seemed to give more substance to his form. It made him somewhat more alive, or at least corporeal. This gave him pleasure and hope, both of which he treasured in his heart and didn't flaunt so that they wouldn't be crushed. Dimitri naturally was displeased, and tormented his soul with renewed vigor.

"Well, well, child of Dimitri," said Azul, in good spirits. "That's it for those Ratas wretches. It seems your legendary battle prowess was not just divine power channeled through magical armor and sword. Indeed, your fury and skill almost make you worthy of being a proper demon."

Velimir knew this was meant as a compliment, but still he caught himself before flinching. There was a certain *enslaving* quality in the particular brand of ambition and cruelty that demons represented. A quality they were blind to themselves. Velimir wanted no part of it. "I was a warrior a long time before that armor was forged," he answered.

Azul did not bother responding to the remark. "Now, I want you to take part in a bigger campaign—something more demanding than this one. We are to join forces with other commanders, and then launch an attack under a demon prince called Sozmoth."

"Where would the rallying point be?" asked Velimir nonchalantly. He certainly hadn't shared his plan of escape and living again, as the demon would never allow him to leave. And he knew better than to trust the creatures of the Abyss or to make pacts with them.

"The commanding center of Parola, close to the Dragsvik craters. In fact, I believe we are about to be summoned there this minute," answered the demon.

And so they were, along with numerous other troops. They stood on a dusty plain, a too hot sun above their heads. Nearby was a series of white-hot craters filled with molten iron.

"There are the craters," Azul said. "An important source of iron, so we have a stationary force here. The Ratas strike forces attack Dragsvik plains every so often as they try to cut our access to the iron." The demon pointed to an iron stronghold serving as the command center.

Velimir looked around. The troops were in a state of apprehension, wandering about the yard, waiting for something to happen. Farther away, Velimir could see outlines of other strongholds along with something dark and snake-like. *This is it.*

"Is that…a river in the distance?" he asked, in a carefully crafted tone designed to convey an impression of small-talk, not particular interest.

"Indeed it is. The great Styx in its festering glory," said

Azul. "They come by the river at times, trying to cut out our access to the iron."

"Oh. All right," said Velimir in a bored voice, but his mind was racing. Who knew where the war would take him? Perhaps he would be slain for real and truly be obliterated, the desire and will that was his essence snuffed out. *Never!* He must act now and reach the Styx. And he'd better succeed, or Azul would be very displeased. Deserters were not looked upon kindly, even by commanders of mundane wars on the face of Valkama. How would a demon prince react to such a betrayal? *Mother, protect me. Mother, give me strength.*

"I'd like to take a look at the stronghold," he said casually. The troops wandered around, some of them setting camps, others trying to amuse themselves by what meager means they had available. The lesser demons pouted, as they had been forbidden to amuse themselves with their non-demon squad-mates.

"Come along, then," said Azul. "The commanders will have a conference and plan the attack. You can put the guard duty together, as you have previous experience as a military commander."

Yes, and I was more of a commander than you are, demon. Instead of saying so, Velimir nodded and walked to the upper levels of the stronghold with Azul.

The demon disappeared behind the barred doors to the conference with the other commanders. Velimir climbed atop the building, his confident stride reminding him of his mortal days. He had briefly considered the option of trying to improve his situation by advancing rank in the senseless demon wars, but decided against it. However skilled he was, he still was here at Azul's sufferance, and he didn't much like his deferential position. The demons were the ones who ruled here, plain and simple, and he was either useful or amusing, nothing more. Perhaps it was possible to turn into a demon once your memories faded and your personality started to dissolve into the horrors of this place. Velimir didn't want that either. *No.* He would be Velimir, now and always. He'd get out of here and, once again, hold sway of his own soul.

He gazed at the hopeless dusty landscape and spotted the dark festering river in the distance. There…there was his way out. But judging from his vantage point, it was a rather long trek. He would be missed too soon. Also, he had yet to figure out how to persuade the ferryman to take him to Manala. After a few moments of quick thinking, a look of grim resolve formed on his half-corporeal face, and he had a plan. He approached the door behind which the conference of the demon commanders was held and knocked.

As soon as the door was opened, the assembled demons glared at Velimir. They had a high-ranking succubus matron with them—a snake-like being with a torso of a beautiful woman, if you didn't count the unmistakable cruelty in her features.

"What is that…thing doing here?" asked the succubus matron, her voice chilling Velimir. It was like the seductive voice of an expensive courtesan, but with a metallic, dead ring to it, as if she was talking inside a huge metal barrel.

"Forgive my intrusion," said Velimir, gritting his teeth at the humility he knew was wise to convey. "I wouldn't have dreamed of entering, but I spotted a suspicious force moving in the vicinity of the river in the distance."

The succubus arched her perfectly manicured eyebrows

and glanced at Azul. "This would be the one of yours, Azul?"

"Yes. One of Dimitri's progeny, though his divinity is gone. He has been very competent so far," said Azul.

"Well, let him deal with the threat, then. Must be another strike force or just scouts, but we can't be distracted now," said the succubus and extended a polished and garishly painted fingernail to move a miniature denoting a fortification. "His squad can join the stationary force once they have disposed of the nuisance."

"Very well," said Azul. "Son of Dimitri, I want you to take the...entities you feel you need from our troops to form a squad and go investigate. Kill them on sight and return. With luck, you'll be here before the campaign begins, but we can't count on it."

Velimir nodded curtly and walked away.

Excellent. Now they wouldn't miss him for some time, and he had a legitimate reason to move about the river. And when the commanders started to wonder where Velimir was and realized that the only proof they had of the threat was his own testimony, he'd be far away. Already he was strengthened by his stay in the Abyss. His spirit was tired, but the shock had worn out, and it helped to keep himself focused. He wasn't sure whether his mother was able to hear his prayers, but the mere idea of her gave Velimir strength and helped keep him from despairing.

"Hear me out," he addressed the troops he had been traveling with. "A suspicious force has been spotted near the river Styx, and I have been assigned to lead a scouting mission. Any volunteers?"

A young female human raised her hand, a recently dead mortal. She must have been a warrior of remarkable skill in life, or the demons would have been more interested in tormenting than enlisting her. "I would be glad to join," she said. Velimir nodded and motioned to her. Another dead mortal followed suit, a dwarf with rough features. Naturally, they wanted a chance to stand out from the masses.

"Hmm…An interesting prospect, child of Dimitri," lisped a pale, raven-haired woman.

Splendid. A vampire.

"I would join you, for I bet you are interesting company. My name is Myra, and I can take my pets with us. They are quite resilient and never complain." She gestured towards a group of zombies staring mindlessly ahead.

The things gave Velimir the creeps, but he supposed they were better than lesser demons as they had no minds of their own. Even the stupidest and weakest demons resented him already for the attention Azul gave him. If they were directly under his command, they would be all too glad to squeal on him if they suspected something was amiss.

"Very well, lady. I believe we are enough," Velimir said. "Any more would render a scouting team ineffective."

Velimir would have to figure out what to do about his companions, but he was sure he'd come up with something. *Kiril could always be counted on to have an idea.* He felt a twinge of guilt for stabbing Kiril, but shoved the emotion away. *He shouldn't have betrayed me.*

The group started its trek, and Velimir silently prayed to his mother to bestow a blessing upon his daring gamble.

6
WALLILA GATE

PERI KICKED THE SWEAT-SOAKED SHEET OFF HER LEGS and squinted at the vague shapes of the furniture in the darkness of the room. The Buccaneer's Respite was a watering hole for folks from all walks of life and a hub of trade for the local sellswords. Prospective employers would seek mercenaries from the inn and leave messages at its notice board. But the inn also served as a lodging house. Peri's and Ewynne's room looked over the docks and the silhouettes of the ships. Peri could see the closest one, the Soaring Falcon, swaying gently in the breeze. She heard the creaking of the ropes as they strained, and smelled the tar.

Again, Peri couldn't get any sleep. Again, she was restless while Ewynne snored peacefully at the other side of the room.

SHE SLEEPS SO PEACEFULLY. ALWAYS DID, THE SIMPLE SOUL. NEVER TOSSING AROUND, RESTLESS

AND AGITATED, WANTING TO FALL ASLEEP SO BADLY BUT HER MIND RACING. AND THEN WHEN YOU FINALLY DRIFTED ASLEEP, SHE'D POKE YOU AND CHIRRUP IN YOUR EARS AND CHEERFULLY WANT YOU TO 'WAKE UP ALREADY' EASY FOR HER, ISN'T IT, WHEN SLEEP NEVER ELUDES HER.

Shut up. Dimitri had started to speak to Peri. The bastard seemed to know all her secrets, feelings she had never revealed to anyone. Yet Dimitri's attention wasn't entirely unwelcome. Dimitri showed compassion to her. Dimitri understood her like no-one ever had. Nobody had ever cared that she had trouble sleeping at night. People were supposed to jump off the bed early in the morning, like the cheerful Ewynne effortlessly did. People who lingered in bed and were grumpy in the morning were lazy. Weak. *Here, I can sleep as late as I want. Ewynne lets me sleep, tiptoes out of the room. It's not her fault that she's a good sleeper.*

THE WORLD IS OUT THERE. IN ITS ABSURD GLORY. YOU ABHOR BEING TRAPPED, MY DAUGHTER, AS IS ONLY FITTING FOR SOMEONE WITH A SOARING DIVINE SPIRIT. YOU HAD ALREADY DECIDED TO LEAVE WITH THE SHIP BOUND TO WULANI AND BEYOND—BUT SHE DIDN'T WANT TO LEAVE. MADE YOU FEEL GUILTY WITH HER PASSIVE-AGGRESSIVE POUTING. SHE 'NEEDED YOU' SO YOU COULDN'T LEAVE EITHER.

As if in a trance, Peri rose from her bed and grabbed her dagger from under the pillow. She took a few steps towards Ewynne. It was dark, but she sensed rather than saw Ewynne's veins pulsing in her neck.

YOU CAN FEEL THE LATENT POWER OF MY

BLOOD IN HER, CAN'T YOU? THE WEAK PROGENY. THEY ARE PREY FOR YOUR KIND. THEY STRENGTHEN YOU. AND YOU, MY DAUGHTER, ARE SO FAVOURED BY ME—YOUR THIRST FOR FREEDOM IS A MARK OF A DIVINE MIND.

Peri nodded. It did seem to make sense. Her blood was very hot in her veins, and she felt divine. Like she understood so many things that all these insignificant people she had been surrounded with her whole life didn't understand. It was only natural that she longed for more than them.

IF YOU EMBRACE YOUR DIVINITY, YOU WILL NEVER GROW FEEBLE, OLD, ILL. YOU WILL NEVER BE TRAPPED BY THE MUNDANE HUMDRUM. NOBODY WILL WEIGH YOU DOWN. YOU CAN FLY TO SPHERES BEYOND IMAGINATION, SEE WONDERS FORBIDDEN TO MORTALS. YOU WANT TO. YOU KNOW YOU DO. SHE IS A DEAD WEIGHT. DRAGGING YOU DOWN. LIKE AGE. LIKE TIME. NOBODY UNDERSTANDS HOW FREE YOU YEARN TO BE.

"...yes," Peri whispered. It was as if an external force was leading her hand—and the dagger—towards Ewynne's throat. Suddenly, she gasped and jerked, throwing the dagger to a faraway corner. She stumbled back a few steps, blinking back shocked tears.

Ewynne startled and squinted, frowning in the dark.

"I...had a nightmare," Peri whispered. "Just sleep, okay?" She hurried out of the room, grabbing her sword as she went.

———————— •●• ————————

IT WAS LATE AT NIGHT, BUT GENJIRO SPOTTED PERI sitting at the pier. The girl was holding a bottle of wine, and she poured some of it in the water, whispering something as she did.

"Fair winds and following seas, battlemaiden Peri," he said as he approached and sat next to her. "What are you doing? Why pour precious wine away?"

"Fair winds and following seas, indeed," she replied, looking vaguely embarrassed. "Precious is definitely debatable. It is the cheapest not horrible stuff they sell at the Bucc's." She paused to take a long swig from the bottle and offered it to Genjiro. "But anyway...I told you I was raised to revere Eoghain. And that I'm not terribly pious. Yet...he is the god of travelers and the unknown. Right up my alley. I hadn't even properly realized that before I started to live on the road." Peri waved the bottle in her hand in a wide arc so that some of the red liquid spilled on the weathered planks. "That was a sacrifice for him. I could have walked all the way to the lighthouse," she said, pointing at the lighthouse in the distance which shed its light on the waves. "All lighthouses are shrines to Eoghain. But I'm a lazy bastard, so I couldn't be arsed. Instead, I offered some of my wine to him. 'If you have no other means of worship available, you can always offer a gift for the Voyager to the waves or the winds.' Waves it is."

"But why would you sacrifice to your god in the middle of the night?" Genjiro asked. He could tell that Peri was upset, even though she was trying to grin drunkenly. She also had her sword with her.

"Because...I'm really fucked up! And I want him to help me get a grip!" She hesitated for a moment, then continued. "Gods, it's been so long since I've talked with...well, anyone. Except Ewynne. Let me tell you about my life on the island, before we came here. It was a perfect idyll. A beautiful holy place. A kind stepfather. An armsmaster to teach me. A sister. A lively island to have fun at, just a short boat trip away."

"But you were not happy," Genjiro ventured. Water lapped under the pier and a seagull mewed in the distance. All the drunken noise of the port-side taverns had died hours ago—it was the dead of the night.

"Correct. I was, as a child. Often, I would watch the horizon and the ships disappearing in it. I felt such a longing to be on board, to see what is beyond there. It didn't bother me at first so much—it was like a sweet longing." Peri shifted her weight clumsily then crossed her legs.

Genjiro nodded for her to continue.

"Then I grew up, and it started to burn me. It bothered me how the island was so small, how everyone knew everyone, and they all cared so much about the small things happening there, things that didn't matter in the large world," Peri said. "I would fuck pilgrims and other travelers." She paused for a moment, staring Genjiro in the eye, as if to gauge his reaction. When the man's expression didn't reveal anything, she went on. "Hearing their tales made me hungry to see the world. But they often were older than me, and patronized me, telling me how I should be grateful to have such a wonderful home. And it was, I'm sure. But they didn't understand. No-one did." She paused. "Not even Ewynne."

"But she adventures with you, doesn't she? I can tell you are good friends as well as sisters."

"We are! The best. But she is with me because she can't go back home. She would want to. Anyway, what I was getting at…I once met a pirate. He didn't advertise, seeing as it is kind of illegal to be one—but he told me. And I decided that

I'd leave with him, with the ship. All I could think of was how we'd sail to Wulani, and I'd see the Grand Bazaar, the desert, the mirages, the djinni, the cities of sand…and then we'd sail on, and I'd see even more fantastic lands! I told Ewynne, expecting her to be happy for me. But she started to pout. She wanted to stay at the island, and she guilt-tripped me into staying, too. "She needs me," Peri mimicked. "She loves me, do I not love her? And what about Connor—our stepfather? His heart would break!" Peri's voice was scornful. "So…I stayed. But I suppose I have always harbored resentment."

"I…can see it from the point of view of both of you," Genjiro said. "Family is important. A sister's love…but I have seen wondrous lands, experienced absurd situations, seen so many things I couldn't have imagined growing up in Morishima. Life is such a marvelous thing. How could I be content to stay forever in one place familiar to me, when there is an unknown place to see beyond the horizon?"

Peri smiled and grabbed his hand, holding it to her heart, great intensity in her eyes. "I knew you would get it! We are the same," she said. "I do love Ewynne, but…there is…something inside of me. Something…bad." Whatever that bad thing was inside of Peri, she liked it. Relished it. It was part of her. And it was growing.

7
SOMEWHERE IN THE NETHER

Kiril wore penitent's rags. His shoes soaked through with the slush he was trudging in. Gone were his finest black silks—low-key elegant, light, and comfortable. Where had the rags even come from? As far as he remembered, he had worn them ever since he had died and "gross matter had built anew his soul" as Jelena's messenger had put it. *A fitting attire.* What a mess they had made of things. Kiril visualized himself explaining to Jelena what he had been up to since she died. *Oh, you know, we tried to start a war in order to make Velimir a new god of wrath. And yes, we did manage to kill quite a few people in the process.* It sounded like a gibberish plan of a madman. Kiril wasn't sure it wasn't exactly that.

How long had he been following the river? It was impossible to tell, because the suffocating grayness was so impenetrable. Every moment held the dim grayness just short of darkness. It might have been something like nine days. But who knew how time passed in the land of the dead? *Or if it passed at all.* Maybe the river was, in fact, a circle and he'd be forever looking for Yggdrasil in vain. Maybe Yggdrasil didn't even exist. Maybe it was all a cruel joke.

Nevertheless, he knew that he'd better keep walking and thinking about the tree that would give him back his magic— if he was able to convince its guardians. When he stopped to rest, doubt crept in. And with doubt came anguish—the anguish of what kind of man he had been. *A glorious child was given to me to guard and foster—and I drove him to madness.* The fog became thicker the more the anguish gripped him. His flesh looked a tad whiter, more transparent. When that happened, he thought of Jelena. She was his anchor, as she had been for that short, sweet while in life. *I denounced your values, my love. Now I will heed you.* If there was still a small chance that he'd be able to make things right, perhaps even see Jelena and Velimir again, he'd fight for that chance. One step at a time.

Gray shades moved about. Judging by their looks, they had once been mortals, but now they were transparent, their eyes hollow in their gray faces, apathy set in their features. He knew from previous encounters with others like them that, if asked questions, they'd shrug and say that they didn't know—or care, for that matter. The most nondescript and shadowlike ones didn't remember their names. They didn't know anything about the landscape, or if they once had, they had forgotten. *That will be me, if I think too much.* Kiril had always been in the habit of thinking a lot. It was his means of solving problems and dealing with challenges, as well as his pastime and pleasure. But here, it was the enemy. With so little reference point at the outside, the mind weaved a tangled web that snared him if he indulged in it.

Kiril kept ignoring the shades as they shuffled by. Then one of them sidled away from the group, little by little, as if trying to sneak away. That was curious. The shades didn't care—about anything. Perhaps it was a newcomer, still trying to figure the place out. In spite of himself, Kiril felt a spark of longing—for another human being who still remembered how it was to desire things. The shade, its face downcast, approached him. It didn't shuffle quite as listlessly as the other shades. Neither did Kiril. He hadn't succumbed yet. How much he suddenly longed to talk to someone—anyone—who loved something, desired something, *cared* about something!

Its face was obscured with limp, graying hair and a hood. It slowly pulled the hood off and looked him in the eye. An elderly woman—confused and unsettled, her eyes searching for answers, her mouth twitching nervously. She hesitantly extended a slightly trembling hand. The joints looked swollen with arthritis.

"Greetings. You are a recent arrival at Manala, too?" Kiril asked.

"Manala…?" Her croaky voice shook.

Right. Kiril hadn't known that there was a land called Manala either. He had been welcomed by a messenger, as he was loved even in death by someone whose love he very much didn't deserve. Probably this poor woman had been dumped here unceremoniously by whatever circumstances had led to her death. Perhaps she didn't realize yet that she was dead. Perhaps she had lost her wits long ago in life and withered away. *The unpleasant fate of too many people who are 'blessed' with a long life.*

"We are all dead here. But there is death, and there is—" Kiril hesitated. The essence of this place—its very physical fabric—was loss of hope and desire. Jelena's messenger had delivered him the antidote—hope—but did he want to share it with this poor addled thing and then be saddled with her? A stranger, a person who meant nothing to him? Who perhaps had already turned into a listless shade, even in what passed for life for those forgotten to die by their kin. He had enough trouble as it was! Yet...Jelena would never have turned away from a stranger in need. *So be it.* "Lady, let me help. Let me explain to you what I have learned about this place."

Kiril supported the old woman's arm, and she watched him with her confused watery eyes. Her lip twitched—no doubt an involuntary tic that came with age. "Would you? Would you be so kind?" she asked, a spark of hope rising in her eyes, her gaze now more focused. She took a step forward but slipped, collapsing onto Kiril, who took hold of her, steadying her frail form in his embrace.

"You are so kind. So kind...I didn't expect..." she whispered, hugging Kiril and pressing her face against his chest. Kiril responded by patting her back, faintly reminded of his great grandmother who had died before his fifth birthday.

"I didn't expect to find...such a firm, fleshy man in Manala," the woman murmured. Her voice didn't sound quite as croaky anymore. Her grip around Kiril's back tightened.

Kiril tried to pull back, and she squeezed. Kiril tried to push her away, but her grip was like pincers. She looked up, her face inches from Kiril's. What had he been thinking? How had he imagined her eyes to be watery and confused?

They were sickly green with pinpoints for pupils, sharply focused on Kiril. The woman cackled and exhaled foul vapor.

A bile hag! Kiril rarely had ventured to locales with monsters, but any mage of his caliber knew how to deal with them. Elemental fire. Well prepared spell triggers that would activate in case anything managed to get in melee range. Spheres that absorbed magic as well as natural elements such as acid. A capable team would include a cleric to deal with negative energy, curses, or undead. But now he was helpless, like a rag doll in the jaws of a boisterous puppy. Kiril wiggled helplessly, straining to get away, panic causing bile to rise in his throat, not certain whether the sour, suffocating liquid came from his own throat or if the hag emitted it.

The hag sank her teeth into Kiril's elbow. The bite burned and chilled at the same time, and he went limp, like he always had as a boy when the bullies pushed him around and beat him. *Before magic made me strong.* There was the curious, indifferent peace that came with giving up, with watching your own pathetic form from the outside, watching yourself be the plaything of stupid, gleeful, and cruel children. All was lost now. *What next? The mercy of oblivion? Or something worse?*

The pain in Kiril's shoulder was not so bad anymore. He heard cartilage cracking, could no longer feel his fingers. He felt as if he were drowning in gray slush, his vision dimming. For a moment, it was as if Jelena's eyes watched him. And young Velimir's—the piercing, questioning golden eyes. The eyes of promise—the promise he had turned into a weapon to avenge his pain on the world. Regret washed over him. The awaiting oblivion was a good thing.

"You will make an excellent servant, once I suck all the

yummy flesh from your bones, dear," said the hag. "You taste of latent magic. A skeletal mage at my command…yes, that will be so nice."

No! Please, let me be a shade instead! Kiril tried to scream, but he was paralyzed. Then someone materialized from the fog. A shape of a tall, lean man, face obscured by a wide-brimmed hat, wearing a traveler's cloak.

The stranger nudged the hag with his staff, gently but firmly. "Now, now, *amma*," he said in a voice Kiril had to strain to hear, "is that any way to treat this poor man? Go now, find another plaything." The stranger frowned at the hag from behind bushy eyebrows—and Kiril noticed that he had but one eye. Once again, the bile hag's body felt frail and trembling against Kiril's chest. The old woman averted her watery eyes, her mouth twitching. *Was* it a bile hag? Had it *ever* been a bile hag? Kiril wasn't sure anymore.

"Forgive the lady, *vinr*," said the stranger in his low, gravelly voice. "She is just lonely. Can get feisty if she gets company. She is quite sweet when you know her, I'm sure." He regarded Kiril with a frown and unsmiling countenance, yet there was a hint of mirth in his manner.

"Uh, thank you for the timely rescue," Kiril managed.

"*Rescue?* I see you have a flair for melodrama, *vinr*. A lonely old lady talks your ear off, and you speak of *rescue*. But no matter! I like dramatic souls. The best skalds who have tasted the mead of poetry are like that."

Despite more pressing emotions to tend to, Kiril bristled at being characterized as "a dramatic soul." Then he assessed the man. The stranger carried a staff. *Check.* He wore a wide-brimmed hat and a cloak. *Check.* Though far from feeble, he sported a long, white beard and bushy eyebrows. *That seals it. A mage, even if he doesn't go for the gaudy robes.* Kiril had always ridiculed mages who loved looking the part—in Vari Domoi, that would have been most of them—but now he didn't feel in a position to do so. "Dare I assume that you are a fellow magician?" Kiril asked his rescuer.

"A *fellow* magician, *vinr?*" asked the stranger, arching his bushy eyebrow. "You seemed very distressed, yet I didn't see you using magic to rid yourself of the pesky old lady. A violent spell would have been just rude, I agree, but there are subtler ones. As I'm sure you, as a magician, would know."

Kiril flinched, then sagged. It was true. And it hurt. He was a mage no more than a hobbling cripple was a runner. "I...used to be a mage. No more, true. I guess the fact hasn't properly registered yet."

The one-eyed mage smiled briefly. "I have been known to dabble with magic now and then during my travels, yes. But it has been a long time. I am just a weary wanderer— Grimnir, by name."

A wanderer? Perhaps the stranger could help Kiril once again. "During your wanderings, have you ever heard of a tree called Yggdrasil? A magical tree that is the axis of another world. I...have heard that it might be able to give me my magic back."

Grimnir cocked his head and regarded Kiril. "Why, I have passed by Yggdrasil once or twice."

"You have?" The surge of hope frightened Kiril. But the tree must exist—this person had seen it! *Unless this is all a dream—a figment of my imagination.* Kiril shoved the spiraling feeling of doubt and madness aside and focused. "Please, tell me how to find the tree. I have been following this river, but everything looks the same, day after day."

Grimnir leaned on his staff, pondering. "The tree is powerful. It was there before the world itself was created, before the giants and the humans. It has always existed. But it might want something in return. It...generally does."

Kiril was still shaken by the helplessness he had felt in the bile hag's grip. *Or was it just an old woman, and I imagined it all? Who can tell in this—quite literally—godforsaken place?* Kiril had always avoided thinking about his childhood, as it wasn't very pleasant. An intelligent boy, mostly ignored by his parents, ridiculed by his teacher, shunned by his peers. He still remembered the watery, stupid, and mean eyes of the stockier boys who tormented him, pushed and slapped him around, ripped his books. His first motivation in his dedication to the Art was to show the bullies. To rain lightning and fire on them, drain water from their bodies, watch them writhe in pain. But when he gained that kind of power, his anger had waned, and his motivation now was to perfect the craft and bow to nothing but pure intellect, the application of the Art. Stripped of his mastery of the complex humming web of energies at his command, he had been taken back to that helpless, desperate anger. And just like then, Kiril very much wanted magic to make him strong again.

"Please, take me to the tree if you can. I am willing to do a service to it. I want...I *need* the magic back. I was beginning to lose hope. I've been following this river forever. No sign of the tree."

"No sign?" Grimnir frowned, then smiled. "Look, *vinr.* The tree is right in front of you." He waved his hand, and it seemed as if the mist dispersed. Indeed, some thirty feet away stood the root of an enormous ash, its bark gnarly and dying in some places, new growths sprouting from it in others. It reached somewhere beyond the heavy-hanging leaden grey impenetrable clouds, while the leaves of the lowest branches almost brushed Kiril's face. He rubbed his eyes, shook his head. Had it really been there all the time? No matter. Here it was.

"If you want to deal with Yggdrasil, you must talk with the Norns," Grimnir said. "I've a mind to take you to them. It is dangerous out here. If you walk the wrong way, you may end up on the Final Shore, where a very unpleasant serpent sucks on the corpses of the wicked. We wouldn't want that, would we, *vinr*? Asgard is a long way from here, but I know the right root to follow."

A raven descended from the mists to rest on Grimnir's shoulder. Kiril was reminded of his own stuffed raven and absurdly felt a flash of dread, as if the bird could somehow know that he had possessed a stuffed corpse of its kin and used it for decoration and rituals. He swallowed uneasily and said, "I'm very pleased to hear that. Lead the way, Grimnir."

As the men started ahead amidst the chaotic twisted maze of the enormous ash's roots, Kiril spotted another raven that followed them from a distance. Perhaps it knew also. Perhaps it was all his imagination.

8
THE STYX

"Velimir, I can see you were a handsome man in your life. You would have made a gorgeous vampire," lisped the vampiress, giving Velimir a sensual look.

"Thank you," answered Velimir, feeling a serious need to flinch. Myra looked glamorous and beautiful in the alabaster dramatic way vampires did, but that only served to remind him of his current less-than-perfectly-alive state. "Alas, blood doesn't truly flow in my veins anymore...though I still feel as if it does, and as though my wraithlike form is reshaping."

"Such a waste," sighed Myra. "My gift wouldn't make you a vampire now. Had I preyed upon you in your life, we could have been lovers...shared a most glorious undeath in my mansion in Kalmisto when we were not on a hunt."

"Kalmisto?" Despite his distaste for undeath in any form, the more he knew about this wretched place, the better.

"Yes, Kalmisto. The dimension of the Abyss where the undead rule. All of it is frozen, the ice sparkling under the pale moon. Sepulchers, crypts, mausoleums. Ghosts glide across the cemeteries, zombies and ghouls roam around. We vampires are the patricians of Gorod Smerti, a necropolis overlooking a frozen ocean," she said, smiling dreamily. "My home is the tallest mausoleum overlooking all the houses of the dead...and on the highest cliff we leave our slain prey. The winds steal their memories away, it is said, and as they descend to the city in their new undead forms, they remember nothing of their former lives."

"Is that what happened to you?" asked Velimir.

The vampiress nodded. She didn't seem sad about it. She continued her tale, reminiscing of lost glory even as she traversed the dusty plains. "If you travel long enough on the frozen ocean, it merges with the Otherworld, and you find a place where it isn't so cold anymore. There is a spiral cliff emerging from the waves, and on the top, in the center of the spiral, there is a little crypt where candles are always alight, safe from the wind. On the way, there are memorabilia for those who have died at sea...sunken warships, drowned sailors and fishermen...someone always carries flowers and lanterns there. I've heard that from all the oceans, people can enter that place, but they may never find their way back to their own world again."

Velimir had never thought there could be anything beautiful in the Abyss, yet perhaps he was wrong. Still, undeath put him more on edge than the demons did, so he'd take the vampire's word for it and refrain from seeking Kalmisto out.

He pondered how to gauge the goals of his companions. He'd either have to get rid of them somehow or take them with him in order to escape on the Styx.

"Your home sounds like a beautiful place...I suppose. Why are you battling here?" he asked.

"Suffice it to say, politics. It would not be to my advantage to stay in Gorod Smerti now." Myra sighed. "And...what else is there to do? Those damnable demons have power over me, just like they have over you, I imagine. What *are* you anyway? You are not like the other dead mortals, as you don't have a flesh body...but then you are not undead either, nor a demon or other native monster."

"I am a child of Dimitri," said Velimir. It was the truth, even though the divinity was gone.

"A half-celestial, then. There are others of your kind, but from you I get the impression of exceptional willpower and strength."

Velimir merely nodded. In all the bitterness of his defeat, he knew, all the same, that it was true.

"What do you hope to gain, Myra?" he asked. The vampire seemed to like him well enough, but her kind was not to be trusted. Still, perhaps she could be more of an advantage than a hindrance.

"What do I hope to gain?" She laughed bitterly. "To roam around and feed on things that bleed. Perhaps, some day, find a way out of the Abyss to happier hunting grounds, as they say." She flashed her fangs.

Good. A possible ally, and a powerful one at that if she didn't turn against him. What of the two dead mortals? The dwarf and the human woman marched behind the group of zombies, deep in conversation. Velimir had heard snippets of their conversation and concluded that both were avaricious fools hoping to rob some demon lord's treasure. He had to give them points for having guts, though, but there was such a thing as excess greed. Myra and he could kill them easily, even though they were skilled warriors. On the other hand, they could be useful. Perhaps Velimir could persuade them to follow. Then it struck him that none of his group knew his exact orders. He smiled to himself.

As the group started to approach the river, a foul stench of rotting fish guts, former parts of human anatomy, and diseased flotsam polluted the air. The human and the dwarf gagged. Velimir nearly followed suit but resisted the urge. The water of the river bubbled with grease and putrid remains festering. Velimir ordered the troop to a halt.

"There is no sign of the troop I spotted. Our orders are simple. Seek and destroy. So, we have no choice but to follow the river to the other planes in order to prevent them from reporting. We must split. The two of you will part ways from us," he spoke to the dead mortals, "and the zombies will be given orders to obey you. You seek a force of Ratas demons. Kill them if they don't overpower you significantly. If they do, you will follow them unnoticed, and we will catch up with you. We will travel in the opposite direction and find you later. Questions?"

"How do ye know they have traveled the river?" asked the dwarf, doubt in his eyes.

"I don't. But if they have not, they are still in the Abyss and can't report back," said Velimir. "The river is the only way out of here."

"How will you find us?" asked the woman.

"You should know that vampires are powerful spell casters. Myra can cast a divination once we are back. Can't you, Myra?" asked Velimir pointedly, hoping she either could or would play along.

"Certainly," said the vampiress and flashed the dead mortals an unnerving smile.

The mortals nodded, apparently a little scared of the prospect of searching a nether realm by themselves with a bunch of zombies.

"I assure you that you will be greatly rewarded if the mission succeeds," said Velimir. "Lord Azul mentioned weapons created in an unholy forge by a high-ranking demon forgelord."

That did it. Their greed wouldn't let them pass up such an opportunity.

The ferryman they encountered first was a dead mortal with eyes of a hunted animal. Velimir guessed the man had got his job after sucking up to his torturers for long enough. At first, the ferryman was reluctant to take the troop with him, as he had no orders from a demon. Velimir supposed they could try to find another one, but this one was scared. So Velimir decided to go on gambling and manipulate the ferryman.

"I'm traveling with Commander Azul's authority," he said in an unwavering voice, frowning in the calculated annoyed manner of a man who really had better things to do. "I suppose I could trek back to the commanding center and let the force we are tracking gain advantage. You would risk his most severe displeasure, but I suppose he would be just and merciful…after all, you are only doing your job." Velimir smiled wolfishly.

The ferryman flinched. "Oh. I will ferry you, certainly. Come aboard."

The party settled in the rickety barge, and the man

started to paddle in the festering sludge. The dead mortals probably were veterans of war, and it was an automated habit for them to make themselves comfortable and rest whenever they could. So, the woman and the dwarf were soon sleeping, curled close to the huddled zombies.

Myra and Velimir sat silent for a while, watching the eddies in the dark, polluted water and the grayness ahead. When he looked up, Myra was gazing at Velimir in the eyes.

"There isn't any devil troop, Velimir, is there." Her voice was quiet. It didn't sound like a question.

Velimir shook his head. If the vampire guessed as much already, there was not much point to lying. Besides, his instincts suggested that she wouldn't turn against him.

"You want out of here, too," she said.

Velimir nodded and quietly told her about the mystical tree growing somewhere in the Nether.

"You may travel with me, Myra, if you wish. You can find a place where you can be happy and free to hunt as you please. The dead mortals are only after their magic toys. Once they realize no-one is coming, we will be far gone."

Myra was quiet for a while, then faced Velimir with a single tear rolling on her cheek. "I...thank you, Velimir," she said and kissed his cheek. Her lips were like ice, but Velimir felt oddly moved.

He felt a sense of pleasure at having nothing to lose. He had thrown the die. Already they had gone a long way. He would get out of the Abyss. Then, in that moment when he felt better than he had ever felt since his death, a powerful grip of magical force pulled him away. He hurled helplessly through time and space.

9
THE BUCCANEER'S RESPITE INN

WHAT THE FUCK WAS I THINKING? I TOLD GENJI THAT Wyn is also a child of Dimitri when Wyn herself doesn't even know! Truth was, keeping that knowledge from Ewynne had taken a toll. Peri meant to tell her one day. *Soon.* But then she would have to answer the obvious question: how did Peri know that? *'See, Dimitri is talking inside of my head and urging me to murder you. Don't take it personally. He wants me to murder all his other children, too.'*

But it had felt natural to tell him. Peri and Genjiro had started spending more time in each other's company. After Ewynne went to bed, they'd grab a bottle of cheap wine and sit at the pier, listening to the lapping waves and watching the stars, talking about everything under the sun. After telling Genjiro about her dark heritage, it was easy to tell him other things, too. About Velimir. About murderous urges. About how she regretted the death of her brother more than she should. Genjiro didn't judge her. In return, he regaled Peri with tales of the underworld of Morishima's capital, Shorioka, and his journey through the Shimmering Sands, the splendour of Feng Guo, the fierce, wind-swept Steppes with their feuding horse lords.

Fuck, I had no right to tell him before I tell Wyn. But it just...slipped. Peri stretched and yawned in a semi-drunken stupor. She pressed her face to the pillow and fell back asleep.

———————————— • ● • ————————————

THE INNKEEP OF THE BUCCANEER'S RESPITE INN YAWNED and started to tidy up the bar, glancing at his last customer nodding off in front of him.

"Time to go home to your wife, Eliot," he said. "It's late. You can finish your drink in peace, but I'm closing up."

Eliot was a kind, timid man who liked to nurse his drinks while reading and sitting in his thoughts. The man smiled and emptied his glass, standing up as to go.

At that moment, the inn door creaked open. A grim-looking man dressed in a black cape and wearing black high boots entered with a crossbow, shooting a bolt into Eliot. Eliot made a strange startled sound and collapsed, dead before hitting the floor. The innkeep stared at the shooter, his blood cold in his veins, his innards turning to water.

The cloaked stranger stepped towards the innkeep, followed by five other strangers—all dressed in matte black and armed. A dwarf in chain mail, a brutal-looking spiked hammer in his hand. An elf holding a bow, wearing leather.

69

A human woman wearing mage robes. And two huge war-riors who seemed to be twins. They all had cruel eyes that missed nothing, and they sneered at the innkeep, who swal-lowed uneasily, opting to stay quiet and pray for survival.

"Two young women: a warrior and a mage with ridic-ulous green hair. They live here. Which room?" asked the leader in a thin, chilling voice. "I don't have to tell you what will happen if you lie to me or try to warn them."

Forgive me, Milostra, but I'm just an innkeep. I don't want to die. Receive their souls if not a miracle saves them, thought the innkeep. "It is number five," he whispered.

Without wasting a second look on him, they ascended the stairs. Though armed, they moved stealthily, not making a sound.

———————————— • • • ————————————

Ewynne heard a slight...*hissing?*...sound. Like someone moving, dragging his feet just a little too much. She squinted, her eyes adjusting to the near darkness. She glanced at Peri, who seemed to be sleeping soundly. She had stumbled in just a few hours ago, having been drinking at the pier with Genjiro again. Ewynne felt a vague sense of dread. Now she was sure. A lone floorboard creaked the slightest bit. Her heart jolted in her chest when she heard the door handle move ever so slightly. She silently but quickly rose, dreadfully aware that she had depleted al-most all her spells. She grabbed the loaded crossbow from the nightstand. Her heart nearly pounded its way out of her chest. *Peri, wake up. Please, WAKE UP!* But she dared not make a sound.

The door slid open. A figure wearing a black cloak,

followed by four more, nodded at Peri's shape in the bed. Two massive intruders started to approach her while a third one raised a bow. Two others focused their attention on Ewynne's side of the room. Without hesitating, Ewynne launched a bolt at the intruder holding a bow and started to scream. The bolt hit the assailant in the elbow, and they dropped their bow. But the intruder just grunted and grabbed at their elbow, snarling. "Ares! To me!"

There was a short moment of chaos as Ewynne frantically tried to start an incantation, even as the calmer part of her mind realized it was futile with them mere feet from the edge of her bed. She could hear Peri screaming, then snarling something, as she was dragged out of her bed by the two massive intruders and held in place. Ewynne glanced at Peri, who made muffled and infuriated sounds, struggling in the grip of the two.

The person who had entered first muttered a syllable, and the dim green light of a floating orb flooded the room. The man had a smug and triumphant expression on his face. "Well done, crew," he said in a thin, chilly voice. He was not tall and had a light frame, but he looked quick and nimble, and his eyes were dark and mean. His hair was shiny and black, his complexion sallow, his teeth disturbingly white. The elf Ewynne had injured was panting, gripping her bleeding wound.

"My pleasure, Darien," answered a dwarf gruffly. He was built like a barrel and his grip of Ewynne felt like iron pincers. She bit her lip in order not to whimper. "Good that the wench was drunk. Got her with little trouble."

"Little trouble! I was wounded by that little bitch's bolt, Ares!" exclaimed the elf sharply.

71

"And I put a stopgap spell in it immediately, so shut yer mouth," the dwarf grunted.

"Silence!" snapped the man called Darien. "Don't bicker in front of our prey. Unbecoming."

"So Peri ye wanted alive. But what about this one? She is one of Dimitri's too," said the dwarf.

Darien seemed to consider it for a moment. "...Nah. She's just a weak spawn. Kill her however you wish. Peri is all we need."

The elf snarled, "Oh trust me, I will! And in what a manner—"

At that moment, it was as if someone sounded a foghorn in the room. The scream split the air. The frames of the door and the furniture started to shake, the earth to rumble. A blinding light emanated from Peri, who grew. Everyone dropped their weapons and held their bleeding ears in agony as they fell to their knees.

Peri seemed to hover in the midair, but...she wasn't Peri anymore. She was larger than a normal man, and so luminous and blinding. Her face was smooth, perfect, and commanding. Her eyes shone golden, her hair blazed, she shimmered. She continued to scream and raised her arms, an expression of heavenly fury on her face.

Darien sprang up, his eyes darting around, glowing momentarily red. He seemed to disappear in the shadows. Peri, still hovering in midair, convulsed a few times and started to roar. The piercing scream transformed into a beastly roar, and Peri turned into a demon again. This time, the form was larger, and a multitude of what looked like nails sprouted forth from her head. Her mouth became a deformed maw too full of teeth. She exhaled acid that burned Ewynne's eyes as she squeezed her ears shut. Peri's fingers were again gnarled talons. She lunged on top of the fallen twins and started to slash, pierce, and grunt. The roar covered the anguished screams of her victims as she shredded them to a bloody pulp. She leapt in a flash toward the remaining victims, shredding them, too, in mere seconds. Then she convulsed a few times and fell flat, unconscious and pale, now looking like herself again, still covered with blood, entrails, and brain matter. To her relief Ewynne could see that Peri was still breathing.

10
THE ABYSS, DIMITRI'S FORMER REALM

HELLO, SON OF MINE. NICE TRY, BUT IN VAIN. WELCOME TO MY FORMER REALM.

This was the first time Dimitri had spoken to Velimir since his arrival in the Abyss. His chuckling mirth confirmed Velimir's enraged suspicion. He had been snatched from some place deep in the bowels of the Abyss, and his hard-won plan of escape was ruined. He tried hard to suppress his smouldering rage, so as to not give Dimitri the pleasure of reveling in his frustration, but he had little doubt that the bastard felt it anyway.

Velimir's surroundings shimmered, shifting and taking shape as he tried to take the situation in. Before the deity's imprisonment, Dimitri had ruled a part of the Abyss. *Somewhere here?* After Dimitri's defeat, Cijeli's troops had warded and sealed his sanctuary, the place of his final stand—but perhaps some residue of his essence remained.

Velimir also felt another presence beside Dimitri. *Peri?* He felt the same terrifying intimate vulnerability he had felt that fatal day of his fall, when Peri had confronted him at the old temple. It was as if Peri could see right to his core, as if she somehow could see that shameful failed pathetic child he had been when he had picked up the baby and tried to drag it to safety with him. As if part of the sniveling worm Velimir had been remained with his sister even when she was rescued as an infant, leaving Velimir behind to die. Nothing had ever made him feel as naked as Peri's presence.

Thus far, Velimir had avoided thinking about his sister, focusing his willpower on escaping and drawing strength from the idea of his mother. But now, all the nagging bitterness returned. It was only fitting that she was behind this. Was it not enough to ruin his plans and send him to the pits of hell? Now she had to drag him here and spoil everything he had worked so hard to achieve? Velimir growled in rage.

She still held the Dimitrian essence inside of her—the essence that was lost to Velimir forever. He recognized its intoxicating hum and *yearned* to have it burn in his veins. But Peri wasn't dead—she was here because of something else. Perhaps she sought to gather all the essence, to be the last remaining sibling and take this place over? She would then wield the power Velimir had died seeking. It was still there to take. The prophecy still held true.

Twisted, gnarled shapes, stony faces in anguish. Sulphureous pools, fiery ponds, and dry sand plains. Deep, dark pits, ominous archways. Nothing Velimir hadn't seen before. And then the shifting ceased, and he stood in a vast hellish cave.

SHE HAS BEEN DRAWN HERE BY A CLASH BE-
TWEEN HER AND ANOTHER CHILD OF MINE. IT DE-
STABILISED HER. SHE STUMBLES ABOUT, POWER-
FUL BUT LACKING DISCIPLINE, AS IS THE WONT OF
MY CHILDREN. HER MIND RESONATES WITH THIS
PLACE, IT SHIFTS ACCORDING TO HER WHIMS. YOU
SEEM TO HAVE A BIG PART IN HER SOUL, ENOUGH
THAT SHE SUMMONED YOU HERE.

Velimir heard faint humming and strained his hearing.
The humming grew louder. Moans, screams, and thuds like
he had heard in his dreams in life.

DO WHAT YOU WANT WITH HER, SON...USELESS
AS YOU ARE, YOU HAVE ONLY GROWN IN POWER.
WHETHER SHE IS SLAIN OR NOT MAKES NO DIFFER-
ENCE TO ME...FINALLY ONE OF THE CHILDREN WILL
REMAIN, AND IT IS MOST AMUSING TO WATCH.

Velimir felt a tug of the despair he had fought so hard.
He wanted to cry, scream, pound the walls in vain—but then
he noticed that his body felt more real and solid than it had
felt before. And not only that. He was wearing his old armor,
wielding his sword. This was, of course, Peri's influence. That
was how she remembered him. She had never seen his true
face—only the golden eyes gleaming from behind the visor.

What if they fought again and Velimir defeated her?
Would she die and become another wraith lost in the infinity of despair? Wouldn't that be true justice? Not that
Velimir had anything to gain by it. On the other hand, perhaps it would be interesting if it was this sibling who was the
one to ascend. One who, as a fellow "mongrel," seemed to
have a special link to his soul—special enough that she had

summoned him here, special enough that he could feel her presence? The beast lurked beneath the intoxicating rage. The part of Peri that was not her at all, but Dimitri's latent avatar. Which would be better? See Peri destroyed and enjoy the revenge? Or see her succeed and satisfy his curiosity?

The girl entered, her form shifting and shimmering. She was panting and disheveled, covered with gore.

"So, we meet again," said Velimir, his face a tense mask, still unsure what he hoped would happen.

"Velimir. I'm not *that* surprised to see you here," answered Peri.

"You shouldn't be. My divine essence joined that of our father after you murdered me, as will happen to all children of Dimitri—save the last one."

"*Murdered?* You were the one who tried to command the damn demon! But...does this mean that I'm dead, too? An eternity here? Joy."

"Fool!" Velimir's patience started to wear thin. It was infuriating that Peri still had the chance, still could take what he could not anymore. She stumbled blindly about, everything carried to her lap. "You are not truly dead, not yet. Why do you think you are here? Do you think *I* get to form this place with my will? No such deal for one who has lost his divinity...dear Peri," he snarled.

Peri frowned. "Why have you come here, then?"

"Gods, what a dullard! To think that *you* killed me! The indignity of it!" growled Velimir. "I am here, fool, because the essence of our father still present in your blood is shaping this place as you go. You have summoned me here because your mind now holds sway here. What is it that you want of me? Speak quickly!"

"I didn't ask for this, Velimir, and I'm not enjoying my-self," said Peri. "None of this is intentional—I have not called you here. I was attacked...and after that, I remember noth-ing. That's why I thought I was dead."

"As you would be, if there were any justice!" Velimir snapped. "Such power in the hands of an inane cretin!"

"What makes you think you can judge me?" asked Peri, the first hint of irritation in her voice.

Velimir had finally managed to make her angry. Her eyes momentarily grew red, but her shape started to flicker be-tween her own and that of a smooth, luminous being. *Like how Dimitri looked sometimes.*

"If there was any true justice, I would rule this place now! You and your damned blind luck!" Velimir said, his eyes narrowing.

"Great, I've always wanted a scalding place with a smell of sulfur and dry sand everywhere!" Peri snapped.

"That's all you can think of, is it? True power shoved within reach of one totally devoid of vision! You...you pa-thetic...this is beyond exasperating!" It was so *infuriating*, her standing there, not appreciating what she had, not even caring! Suddenly, Velimir knew what would make her lose control. "I relished splitting your precious Connor with my blade! I should only have done the same to you, then!"

"You dare speak of Connor?" Peri was pale now, her eyes dark with anger.

"Oh yes, *finally* you feel something! Summon the wrath we were born of. Show respect to your heritage for once." Gleeful, Velimir was enjoying himself, as Peri was shaking with anger. Her form was shifting, her eyes burning with murder. Could it be? "Oh yes, summon the power in your blood. Because if you cannot, then you are not worthy of your destiny. It should have been me! Fight me and prove your worth!"

And then Peri was not Peri anymore, but a thing flickering between a luminous celestial and a taloned demon with molten lava eyes full of hate. It emitted earth-splitting screams. It slashed with the vicious talons. It towered above Velimir, attacking him in blind fury, nothing but madness in its eyes, and with supernatural strength and speed.

YES! The Edge! The prophecy holds! A wave of euphoria, an echo of the intoxicating invincibility of the lost taint of his blood, warmed Velimir. He had made this happen.

"Yes! Finally! A worthy opponent, like only a 'mongrel' can be!" he bellowed. Then he parried and thrust.

He had never fought anything this powerful, but he did well. He was an even better warrior dead than he had been in life, for the horrors of the Abyss and the fights with the demons had honed his skills and given him strength. He felt alive, almost like when he truly was, as he laughed, jumped, dodged, and struck.

They fought for minutes, hours, but the beast wouldn't be quelled. Then it managed to rip Velimir's sword from his grip and grab him, throwing him across the cave. Velimir was slammed against the wall and tried to stand up, panting. Then the claws of the beast ended the battle, and there was darkness.

Hurts. Hurts so much. Velimir felt as if all his bones were broken. And his form, so much shadier than it had been... *beaten.* Dimitri ripping his soul again. *Empty. No-one here.* Velimir sat up, grimacing in pain, and buried his head in his hands.

11
THE BUCCANEER'S RESPITE INN

The door was kicked open, and Ewynne raised her hands, determined to try to defend herself with the remaining *crn-prasak*.

"*Plavosvetljo!*" It was a deep male voice, uttered by one of the two dark-skinned men that had just entered. From his raised palm spread a cone of clear and pure blue light that illuminated the room. "Halt, girl! We are here to help!"

Ewynne shivered, slowly lowering her hands. The pair observed the carnage and the corners of the room in the blue light, their weapons drawn. "No-one here anymore," said the other man. He was younger than his companion, his skin even darker. His eyes were gray and stood out on his face.

He sheathed his mace and slung his shield behind his

shoulder, then stepped in front of Ewynne and bent to one knee. "My lady," he said, "Jussuf al-Rasid at your service. Fear no longer. We are paladins of Juris."

"Indeed," said the older man in his deep, cultured voice. "I am Razeem al-Farouq. We were tracking your assailants, but it appears we were late. Lady Ewynne, you are safe now. Please tell us what has happened here."

The paladins didn't seem intent on killing her, so Ewynne relaxed a little and sat on her bed. "They tried to ambush us. They wanted Peri...my sister...alive, but they were going to kill me." The paladins listened intently, their faces grave. "She...transformed into a beast and...well, you can see what she did to them. And now she just lies there and won't wake up."

The younger man, Jussuf, kneeled to examine Peri. "She seems unharmed, but she is...not here."

"Let Kauno try to help her." It was yet another voice. Everyone turned to face the newcomer. She was a tall woman with a long face and watery blue eyes. Her long hair was tied in a chaotic mess of loose braidlets and was the color of straw. She wore a dull brown garb, and a small bird was perched at her shoulder. A sparrow. There were all kinds of strings and knots hanging from her belt, as well as a few small pouches.

"Hello, Kauno," Razeem said, looking relieved. "Good that you are here. See to her as you wish. We will talk with Lady Ewynne." He sat next to Ewynne on the bed. Kauno knelt next to Peri, her veil of hair obscuring them both from the rest of the company. "Kauno is...a friend. She is from Balatsky Taiga and knows about that kind of healing."

"What kind of healing?" asked Ewynne.

"Healing of a soul," said Jussuf. "Sometimes, when things go awry, a soul may drift away from the physical body. It has a body of its own, normally animating the flesh body and tethered to it with a silver thread. My healing, a gift from Juris, is no good in such circumstances. Kauno...is touched by the spirits."

"Tell us about the beast, Lady Ewynne," said Razeem. "To save some time and equivocation, we know of Peri's heritage. And yours. That is why we are here."

"It...wait a minute. *Mine?* What do you mean?" said Ewynne. She recalled in a flash that the assailants had referred to her as "Dimitri's too." She had a sinking feeling, as if plummeting down an abysmal chasm.

The paladins shared a long look. "You are...not aware that you, too, are of Dimitri's blood?" Razeem frowned. "But... please, my lady, tell us about the beast first. It is urgent."

Ewynne leaned back, banging her head on the headboard. She exhaled slowly, then decided to focus on the matter at hand. "Peri has turned into it once before. It flickers. At one moment, it looks like...a celestial, I guess. It looks golden and smooth and perfect. And furious. And terrifying. And the other moment, it is just like the demon we...a demon. You know. Eyes of fire. Talons for fingers. Rips everything to pieces." She gestured at the carnage on the floor.

"The Edge. As we feared," Razeem said. "By Juris, this has happened before? This is not good."

"Yeah...a few months ago, Peri flipped when we faced a mage who burned her with a flame arrow. She slaughtered him like this. But...this time was something else. The screaming. How it shattered everything. My ears still hurt. And the demon was bigger. Looked different. And she was so fast!"

"Yes...it is progressive," said Jussuf. "The group you were fighting then...were they as powerful as the one that attacked you?"

"Oh no. We have never fought a group this powerful. The mage was an unpleasant surprise, but the other two were just little thugs."

"And praise Juris for that," said Razeem, and scratched his gray stub of beard. "Lady Ewynne, what you are describing is called the Edge." The two sat down next to Ewynne and watched as Kauno tended to Peri.

— • ● • —

THE VORTEX OF BLOOD-RED PAIN AND ECSTASY STILL throbbed in her heart, but it started to ebb. She remembered vaguely that she had a name. *P...peri?* There were things that had mattered a great deal to this Peri, but she didn't remember the things. There had been people this Peri had been attached to, but she didn't remember the people. *No no no!* She wanted more of the ecstatic rage, even if it hurt. But she was also wearing thin, the humming in her ears drowning the intense tugging of this Peri and her memories. She wavered between confusion and dread, as she couldn't get hold of the rage.

Blue eyes. Eyes that looked at her, the beast, and didn't falter, didn't judge. Kind eyes, like the eyes of someone this Peri once knew. The person with the eyes sang at her. A calming song, a lullaby. She slowed down, settled down. All would be well.

— • ● • —

PERI BLINKED TWICE. A WOMAN CROUCHED OVER HER and watched her with watery blue eyes. "You...," Peri said and gingerly raised her torso, leaning on her elbow. "You were there...and Velimir. I don't remember...Am I dead?"

"No, honey," answered the woman. "Kauno came to retrieve your soul. Back to Wallila Gate, to your sister." She held Peri's hand. The grip was just right: not squeezing, not limp. The hand was dry and warm.

"I was in...hell. I think. And Velimir was there. How—"

"Do you remember the attack?" Kauno asked.

"I...Ewynne! Is she—?" Peri looked around frantically, but Kauno patted her hand. Her smile made Peri feel like cooling herself in the waves of the sea by the cliffs of Eilean de Taigh-Sholais as a child.

"Ewynne is fine, honey," Kauno said. "Kauno and two paladins of Juris—they'll introduce themselves in a minute; Kauno is sure—we came here to help. We were late. You had already killed them all and been whisked to Dimitri's realm—but Kauno was able to follow you."

"Velimir was so angry. He goaded me...and then a feeling of rage and joy...and then just..."

"Kauno found you there, wandering in the ether. Waited for your rage to die down. Took you back when you were ready."

"I remember your eyes," Peri said. "They watched me, so calm. And you asked me to follow and...now we are here."

"Kauno has seen many lost and angry spirits before. Not another of your power—but Kauno knows the hurt at the heart of it. Kauno knows how to invite them back."

"So, Kauno," Peri grimaced and sat up, "Pleased to make your acquaintance. Sorry about the corpses."

Two men approached her. The younger man was very dark-skinned, but his eyes were gray. He was lean and broad-shouldered. *Very handsome.* He offered his hand to Peri. "My lady," he said, and helped Peri to her feet. "Jussuf al-Rasid, at your service."

"And I am Razeem al-Farouq," said the older man in a deep, cultured voice. "We are indeed, as Kauno said, paladins of Juris. We were tracking Darien, who seems to have escaped the carnage. He is a rogue and stealth specialist of no small skill. The progeny of Dimitri's acolytes are powerful, each in their own way."

"Um, about that 'my lady' stuff. Trust me. I'm not. But... you were tracking that bastard who ambushed us. Why?"

"Perhaps we could go downstairs and have a proper conversation in the inn. There is no doubt a crowd, and the city guard wanting answers. The assailants murdered a patron in order to convince the innkeep to cooperate. And the noise and the earthquake you created...," Razeem said. "I will talk to them. A senior paladin with authentication will put their mind at ease, for now."

The group descended the stairs. Peri and Ewynne lagged behind the others, Peri looking at her sister quizzically.

"I'm glad that you are okay, Peri, but I'm not happy," Ewynne said in a voice simmering with anger.

"I can tell. What is it? I didn't mean to do any of that, I'm sure you can—" Peri started.

"Not that. I know that you can sense the 'weak' Dimitrian spawn. You have told me so. Velimir could too."

"Oh." Peri's heart tightened. "I only wanted to—"

"—protect me? Huh? You have known all the time! And said nothing! You have been complaining about Connor, how he didn't tell you more! And you did the same to me! Are you even capable of seeing the irony?"

Peri tried to think of something to say when she became aware of the innkeep staring at her. Kauno was talking with the man, but he only saw Peri. His face was white and his eyes wide, as if he was observing a dangerous animal that would attack any moment—an animal he would put down if he could, and feel completely justified. Peri realized that she was still covered with blood and entrails. There was a corpse slumped in front of the bar, a crossbow bolt buried in its back.

Genjiro descended the stairs and ran to Peri, embracing her before she could say a word. "You are alive! It sounded like demons or monsters, so I stayed in my room until it was quiet. What on Valkama has happened here? Is this about—"

"Yeah. Big time. But we'll need to talk with these...paladins. You can join us, I suppose," Peri said. Genjiro hadn't looked at her with fear and loathing. Just relief. Peri's throat choked with emotion.

The group was huddled around a table in the faraway corner of the inn. In her peripheral vision, Peri could see guardsmen carrying the killed patron away and the pale innkeep numbly starting to clean the place up.

"This is our friend Genjiro. He knows about Dimitri, so he can stay," Peri said. Ewynne glanced sharply at her, and Peri grimaced. *She didn't know* that *either. Didn't want to tell her that I've told Genjiro...*

"I spoke with the city guard and attempted to soothe the crowd," said Razeem.

"Did it work?" Ewynne asked.

"To a point. The innkeep testified that they killed a

patron in cold blood, so I managed to convince them you acted in self-defense. But people are terrified. The innkeep promised—reluctantly—that we can spend the night, but he wants us all gone at our earliest convenience." Razeem didn't quite seem to know how to continue.

"This is the part where you tell us why you were tracking that Darien and what you know about what is going on," Peri said, regarding the paladins neutrally. She glanced at Kauno, almost as if looking for safety from the woman.

"War is brewing in Wulani," Razeem said. The paladin had a Wulanian scimitar at his waist, though he wore a Western style chest plate. "There are others like you—progeny of Dimitri's chosen acolytes—and these strong ones, like Darien and his group, seek to murder all the remaining ones. It is the duty of the Order of the Eye to deal with this—but we are ill-equipped to do so. Very little is known about the ancient prophecies. To this day, they were thought to be just legends or allegories."

"Okay, but Peri turned into that...thing," Ewynne said, drawing circles on the worn-out table with her index finger. "You know something about that, at least."

Razeem nodded. "It is called the Edge. It is an avatar of doom, portending the rise of a new Lord of Wrath." The paladin paused for a moment, as if contemplating the gravity of his words. "This is conjecture, but we believe it will wear what remains of the host's—Peri's—own soul thin. It has happened twice now. She could turn into it once more, maybe twice—but after that, whatever remains of her would be gone. She would become something else—perhaps a vessel for Dimitri's ascension, perhaps a beast at his command. But of Peri herself, there would be nothing left."

87

"How do you know?" Peri asked, frowning.

"Because that is how transcendental energy behaves," the younger paladin Jussuf said.

Peri nodded grimly. She didn't doubt it. She remembered very little of her battle with Velimir. The second time she had transformed into this Edge had been more extreme than the first.

"This coalition of strong Dimitrian spawn—the progeny of his chosen acolytes—is seeking your death. It seems that Darien went through a lot of trouble to get to you, personally," said Razeem. "You have been lying low here—but your heroics in Lughani Vos, slaying the Dimitrian madman Velimir Rosinin, drew attention. A powerful demon was released during those events"—Ewynne winced at this, while Peri just continued to stare at him neutrally—"and our best exorcists have been working hard to track it in order to banish it to the Nether."

A conflicted emotion crossed Jussuf's face. "My lady... Peri—there is more. There are many in the Church of the Three who want you dead, too. They say that if you are of the same progeny, you are dangerous and need to be put down. We were to be tasked with that deed, but Razeem refused."

They all turned to the older paladin.

"I could never be part of such panicked travesty," said Razeem, indignation coloring his deep, cultured voice. "Dangerous heritage or not, you are a young woman of free will and a soul flowing from the grace of the All-Father. The faithful of Juris, and we paladins in particular, are the vigilant guardians and protectors of all such creatures. Not executioners of convenience! Other paladins have been willing to go after others like you. But I quit the Order and pledged to seek you out and assist you when you struggle with your nature, and to fight the enemies coming after you."

"Razeem gave up much by refusing to take part in your execution. He left a respected and comfortable position for a life on the road," Jussuf said.

"And you, my faithful second hand, followed," Razeem said.

"Uh...thank you. I guess," Peri said. "So...if not for your refusal, not only these other Dimitrian spawn, but the church of Juris, would be after my ass, intent to kill me?"

"That's about the size of it," Razeem said. "I apologize for my brethren. So...we pledge ourselves to your service until such time that the Dimitrian turmoil is resolved one way or the other."

Peri regarded them all for a long moment. Ewynne, still grumpy. Genjiro, puzzled. Kauno, serene and friendly. And the two holy warriors, seemingly righteous and true. Paladins were the quintessential righteous knights in a shining armour. They followed a strict code of honor, modeled after their patron god Juris the Ever-Vigilant. They dedicated themselves to righteous causes and pledged themselves to worthy individuals. Sometimes they also rescued virtuous damsels in distress. And now they were about to pledge themselves to *her*? On both counts, they were sure to be sorely disappointed. The corners of her mouth started to twitch. She started to giggle, as if melting into a puddle. Her shoulders were shaking, and she almost sobbed. "Paladins. Paladins pledging themselves to my service. Sure. Why not."

12
DIMITRI'S SANCTUARY

VELIMIR SAT EMPTY, DRAINED, AND BROODING FOR A long time. He stared ahead, aching all over. His body was very shady now, the hard work of reshaping it with the strength of his spirit undone. *Why did I have to get so enraged? I made her turn into the Edge. I wanted her to finally feel something...but it was so powerful. If Kiril were here, he would lecture me now...I grant you it is not fair, he would say, but whoever promised anything was fair?*

In spite of himself, Velimir was a bit curious about what had happened to Peri. She was no longer here. As angry as Velimir had been, he almost hoped that Peri had survived. Perhaps he would get to see what came of all this business with Dimitri's progeny. After all, he was in Dimitri's former home realm, and the time of the prophecy was at hand. According to the legend, the Edge was a formidable avatar of Dimitri, one demonstrating his dual nature. An avatar that would manifest in the times when Dimitri's ascension was nigh. And now it had. The Edge would manifest and loosen the wards of Dimitri's sanctuary. Velimir had always assumed that it would be he who would manifest as the avatar after his ascension, assuming control of the sanctuary and Dimitri's former realm. But however Peri was going about the business, control didn't seem to enter it. It appeared as if she had no idea what she was doing—and why would she, if she had no knowledge of the prophecies?

Velimir took a few tentative steps. Naturally it hurt. How long would it take to gain back what he had lost because of his temper? Was he stuck here, or would it be possible to try to escape the Abyss again? Velimir had a sinking feeling—even if he did get out, the commanders of the demon war forces were no doubt extremely displeased with him, and right now he was very weak and tired. Perhaps the torments inflicted upon him would break his spirit and make him dissolve into a mindless little demon.

ENJOY YOUR ETERNITY, SON...THERE IS NO WAY OUT.

Damn you, you bastard! Don't you have anything better to do than gloat over my misfortunes?

FRANKLY, NO. THERE IS LITTLE TO DO IF YOU HAPPEN TO BE IMPRISONED IN AN ABYSSAL PRISON.

Velimir sank downwards, leaning on the rocky wall. He buried his face in his hands, then clutched his knees. He teetered at the edge of a true soul-snuffing despair.

* Velimir...don't despair...Velimir...your destiny isn't over yet...you are still loved...*

He sensed rather than heard his mother's voice. It was very quiet, and perhaps it was just a figment of his imagination. Still, it made a small surge of power flow into his veins.

"M...mother? Can you talk to me?" he whispered.

There was no answer. But he was sure he had heard it and held his head high, resolve on his face.

He stood up and limped a bit when he noticed an area still shifting and forming in the distance. Something that looked like a vortex, or a portal. Was Peri's mind still at work here? He knew the girl was gone; he was able to sense her if she was nearby. But her blood could still hold sway here, if she had survived. Could it be the sanctuary? Her loosening its wards, as the legend stated? Could Peri, unstable as she was, be forming that concentration of divine potential with her mind?

Velimir fought his way over the rough terrain, grimacing and hissing in pain, and saw the shimmering turmoil shaping the landscape. He felt the force emanating from it, and a faint displeasure from Dimitri, who had been enjoying his suffering. His mind was racing again. So, the bastard didn't like the shifting vortex. Perhaps Peri, wittingly or—more likely—without a clue what she was doing, was attempting to stabilize it for herself?

DON'T GO THERE, SON. YOU WILL DIE LIKE A FLY IF YOU ENTER. THE GIRL HATES YOU, AND HER HOSTILITY WILL SNUFF YOUR SOUL.

Is that so, Father? I wonder why the sudden eagerness to give me good advice.

Velimir continued, too exhausted to walk, so crawling on the hot ground, grabbing the stones that burned his palms.

I CAN GIVE YOU SOME ESSENCE BACK...

I just bet you will.

Velimir's ears were buzzing. He had to get in before he lost consciousness.

Finally! His fingers bleeding, his nails chipped, his palms blistered, he dragged himself into the shimmering area. Just before passing out, he felt a relief he had forgotten was possible—Dimitri couldn't torment his soul anymore. He couldn't feel the dead celestial, and his soul was left alone. Grateful, he fell asleep, and again there was just darkness.

———————————•●•———————————

Velimir woke up still aching all over, but that felt insignificant compared to the relief of having his soul free of Dimitri's attention. He looked around. The decorations were not much of an improvement, but perhaps Peri would pay more attention to that if she indeed was the one who was chosen to be the new Lady of Wrath. This was naturally better than being at Dimitri's mercy, but Velimir still was stuck here. It could get boring at some point. But Peri would be here eventually. Without seeking to do so, she had drifted to Dimitri's former realm and summoned him there. The time of the prophecy was upon her, and all Valkama, for that matter. Velimir felt the familiar resentment at how easily the girl got everything he had fought to gain and failed.

But there was another side to that. She was stumbling about with no clue where she had to go and what to do. Perhaps...perhaps Velimir could offer to help her. And surely she knew by now that there were no such things as free lunches. If he told her what he knew about the prophecies... if she willingly took him with her...perhaps, in this place where much of Dimitri's old power was there for the taking, she was even powerful enough to give him a spark of life. Velimir started to smile.

"Er...hello."

Velimir whirled around, eyes wide. An imp. It had an annoying, squeaky voice. The imp's skin was leathery gray, a few strings of dry hair covering its skull. Its beady, alert eyes regarded Velimir, the expression not unfriendly but very inquisitive. Velimir felt an instinctive urge to smash it, but perhaps that would be a bit hasty. It might have some information.

"And what, or who, are you?" Velimir asked.

"I'se the master's faithful companion! I'se Casimir! You'se got lost and wandered here, maybe? The master's blood gone from you?"

Velimir nodded wearily. The imp seemed brightened by being correct in its deduction.

"I'se been waiting for the Master! But the Master's been gone for a very long time!" it said. "Maybe can's be faithful companion to the redhead—she has strong blood of the Master."

"Don't I know it," answered Velimir gloomily. Undeniably, the "redhead" had manifested as the very avatar of Dimitri, while he, Velimir, was reduced to this.

"You'se still nice, though," said the imp, and patted Velimir's arm.

Velimir grumbled at Casimir's idea of a compliment. "I suppose I should thank you. Is Peri going to be your master, then?" asked Velimir. He was reminded of the company Peri kept and scoffed. "Why not the other one, while we are at it?"

"Peri has red hair! Not green hair, but red!" The imp seemed all worked up. "But the green-hair also has the blood of the great one. But me'se not can be faithful companion to the green-hair, because the green-hair not feels like the Master, but Peri feels like the Master so maybe can's—" he babbled on.

"Calm yourself, imp!" Velimir snapped. "Slow down. Are you confirming that…you used to serve Dimitri, but now you are considering serving Peri instead because she 'feels like' Dimitri?"

"Oh yes, oh yes," Casimir said, an eager gleam in his eyes. "The green-hair also has the blood, but she's *sooo* sad and she not at all wants to have the blood. She all teddy bears and sugar and smiles and gentleness, Ewynne. Not at all murder, gore, blood, hate—"

"I get the picture," Velimir interrupted. So now diabolical creatures, even as ridiculous as this one, were considering serving Peri and anticipating her ascension. And a silly green-haired slip of a girl had more divine blood than he, Velimir, did—sacred seed spilled to mundane ground or not. What kind of justice was that? The usual kind, he guessed. *Non-existent.*

"Do you know who I am?" he asked Casimir, out of curiosity.

The imp tilted his head.

"You'se…Velimir! Very very very much blood of the great one, but then all boom! Killed and no more blood of the great one!" The imp smiled with a kind and rueful expression on his face. "You'se all sad, me knows."

"Your delusional comments aside, do you have a grip on what is going on?" asked Velimir, stretching his shadowy legs out and leaning back on a large lava rock.

"Me's the faithful companion! Me wait and wait and wait

but the Master just not comes back...." the imp looked positively sad now, sniffing a little.

"Here I am, stuck with an insane imp with the most irritating voice there possibly could be," said Velimir.

"Me's voice irritating?" Casimir asked, his eyes huge with uncomplicated, childish hurt.

"It could be...in some circumstances...perceived as... such," said Velimir, deep down cursing himself for not being able to be more blunt. What did he owe to the stupid imp? And it really *was* irritating.

"Me's can's not help the voice," said Casimir.

"Do not trouble yourself over it. Nobody's perfect," answered Velimir gruffly, in spite of his better judgement. How had this creature ended up being Dimitri's "faithful companion?" But here the creature was, in Dimitri's sanctuary, the place of his last stand. And apparently, it had been waiting for the celestial to return ever since. Silly as the thing was, it had actually known Dimitri before his defeat.

"So! You'se my new best friend!" Casimir lit up. "We's celebrate my birthday soon! Me's 1347 years old now."

"Congratulations. An...impressive age," said Velimir.

"You'se just a human! Just a few, few years! You'se could maybe travels and be friends with Peri and the green-hair, yes? Peri is all mad at poor Velimir, but Casimir give her cake, too, and then she'll like Velimir!"

"No doubt she will," Velimir answered dryly.

"Me's make you pancakes, yes?" asked Casimir shyly. "You'se all sad your great one blood went BOOOOM! Yes?"

"Pancakes." Velimir felt a sudden, fierce headache.

"Oh yes, oh yes! Me'se makes many kind of jellies, oh yes! Me'se a good cook! Me'se make good pancakes...you'se not like…me's pancakes…?" The imp looked so sad and hurt, like an accidentally kicked puppy.

"You'll notice that I have a wraithlike form at the moment. Therefore, I don't exactly need to eat," said Velimir.

Casimir just kept staring at him relentlessly.

"Oh, all right. Conjure pancakes, and I will…consume them." He tried to tell himself he was just obliging the imp because it could give him some valuable information. After all, that was the only rational reason he had not already killed the irritating thing. It surely couldn't be that he wanted company or felt sympathy for the annoying creature. Surely not.

13
THE BUCCANEER'S RESPITE INN

FOR ONCE, PERI WAS SLEEPING LIKE A LOG. TURNING into the Edge had drained all the strength from her. Ewynne, still angry that Peri had kept her in the dark—and told Genjiro about Dimitri!—didn't get much sleep. Ewynne yawned and stretched, then poked Peri.

"Half an hour before we meet the others downstairs," she said.

Peri mumbled something and burrowed deeper under the pillow.

"Seriously. You need to start waking up," Ewynne persisted.

"Mmm. Okay. Look, my eyes are open. I'll be there." Peri exaggeratedly widened her eyes.

Satisfied, Ewynne dressed in her traveling tunic and

descended the stairs. Jussuf waited for her at the foot of the stairs, hesitant, as if he had something to say. Razeem was already seated at the table, accompanied by a rather dapper-looking man. The man wore a scarlet doublet, embroidered pants, and shiny boots. He nodded thanks to Razeem, who was pouring tea or coffee for him, and pushed a few stray strands of blonde hair in his feathered cap. Looking closer, Ewynne could tell that the man wasn't as young as his exuberant habitus and colorful clothes had led her to think. His face was long, his eyes blue and a bit watery.

Ewynne squinted. She glanced at Jussuf. "Is that—" she asked.

"Kauno sometimes dresses like a man, sometimes like a woman. Sometimes you can't tell," Jussuf said. "And today he is, well, a he."

"Huh. To each their own, I guess."

"I…was taught that people like him are an abomination," Jussuf said, lowering his striking gray eyes for a moment. "And I believed it. Who was I to question my parents, my entire upbringing? But Razeem told me that I was wrong. That being different is not evil. And…Kauno is kind, and wise, and brave. He is a wandering mystic…a shaman, a sorcerer, whatever the forest-born call them…but like a paladin, he helps those in need without expecting compensation. He goes where whim and the spirits take him. I was a foolish git to look down on him."

"At least you learned the error in your ways," Ewynne said. Judging from what Jussuf said, it seemed like Razeem was a kind, wise man. *Like Connor.* Jussuf pulled a chair out for Ewynne and the two sat at the breakfast table.

Kauno still had the sparrow perched on his shoulder.

"Kauno's deepest apologies for neglecting to introduce Varpu," he said, cupping the bird in his hand and extending it for everybody to see. The bird tilted its head and watched the party with unblinking eyes.

"Is Varpu he or she?" Ewynne asked. "I hate it when people call animals 'it.'"

"Varpu does not lay eggs, so you may call Varpu him," Kauno said, smiling kindly. Seeing Ewynne's confused frown he continued. "Spirits have no sex. They wear a suit of flesh and identity for a while, then move on to pick another. The entire creation is a delightful divine game, the Dreamer playing hide and seek with itself. Kauno likes to play this game in this life already. One day, of course, every spirit will wake up and realize that it has been the Dreamer itself all the time."

"Got it," Ewynne said, though she wasn't sure that she did.

"Reality is way less fixed than people typically think, that is for sure," said Razeem. "Not many return to tell their tale from the planes of the Yonder and the Nether, but what we know indicates that reality shifts and sprawls there in ways not known to mortals of the Hereworld."

Peri arrived, only raising her eyebrow at Kauno's new habitus. The chair squeaked as she heavily sat down. "So. Good morning, everyone."

"Say hi to Kauno's friend," Ewynne said, her anger at Peri starting to dissipate. "He is called Varpu."

Varpu chirped and glanced at Peri.

"Hello there," Peri said. Little surprised her anymore. "Now the innkeep can't have us gone soon enough," she continued, "so we need to move on. We had some contracts here in town..."

"I don't think you understand how terrified people are,

Peri," said Razeem. "For all they know, a demon from the pits of hell rattled the inn on its foundation, caused the earth to tremble, and shredded five people to pieces. The guards who saw the carnage have no doubt described the scene, and the rumors take on a life of their own."

Peri nodded. "But where do we go then? Somewhere people don't know us? We could take on contracts for swords for hire, I guess. Paladins do that, right? If the cause is just?"

"It is frowned upon," Jussuf said, "but as you say, not forbidden if the cause is just."

"The prophecy will find you, Peri," Kauno said, smiling ruefully. "Kauno is no scholar, but he can feel the times upon us. The spirit world is charged, the spirits agitated. Something grand is happening. And it is coming your way."

The innkeep kept glancing at the group, pointedly polishing already gleaming glasses. Genjiro smiled at the man, but the innkeep's frown just deepened.

"I want nothing to do with the motherfucking prophecy," Peri said. "I had a good life—growing in skill and power, free to go as I please. I wasn't done with Wallila Gate, but I was going to move on at some point, anyway. I just want to follow the road to the unknown." Peri laughed. "I really am more of an Eoghainite than I ever thought I was! Who would have known—I was always bored shitless in the services and snarking at the monks and even Connor when they tried to teach me."

Razeem cleared his throat. "The prophecy states that Dimitri's wrathful blood drives his offspring to slaughter each other all over the shores of the Starlit Sea, vying for the prize of being the last remaining one and ascending as the new lord of wrath." Razeem glanced at the innkeep who gazed at the group, offering the man a reassuring, yet authoritative smile. He turned his attention back to Peri. "Apart from that, we know very little. There is a free-for-all war between Dimitri's offspring in Wulani, but this coalition who tried to capture you is organized and determined. They found you once, Peri, and your notoriety will only grow after this incident."

Peri let out a long breath. "Unfortunately, the mother-fucking prophecy seems to want everything to do with me. And I definitely can't keep turning into that thing. I fully believe that it is as dangerous as you say."

"Not only that, the other Dimitrian spawn will seek you out. Why they want you alive, I don't know. It is frustrating to know so little—but tolerating frustration is part of a life of service," said Razeem. He sucked his lips in, then continued. "I do have an idea, if it can be called that. By Juris, all my life, I have been a servant of...well, Juris. I joined the Order of the Eye at a young age. It had been my childhood dream."

The paladin paused and Peri nodded for him to continue.

"I have served my Lord to the best of my ability. But it has always meant operating within a framework of relative simplicity. The church and the Order are part of the powers that be—the establishment, if you will. The evils they fight are known and clear-cut. I am, and have been, an uncomplicated, practical man."

"Such is the way of the samurai of my homeland," said Genjiro, watching the paladin intently. "They know who they are. Who their enemies are. They have a respected public position for all to see. But sometimes that is not enough. Sometimes it is not simple. Sometimes things are not what they seem. And then you need to venture to the unknown.

To seek power and answers from where shadows are tall. Is this what you are getting at?"

Razeem raised his eyebrow. "That, indeed, is my predicament. I could not have foreseen a merchant from a land as far away as Morishima to be the one to see that so clearly. I suppose people are people everywhere."

Genjiro nodded. "That is…a role that I have played in the past. Been the one who seeks answers where there are readily none. From places where nothing is simple, where nothing is as it seems."

"My proposition is pretty much a shot in the dark—but if you are predisposed for adventure, Peri, perhaps it will please you," said Razeem. "Are you familiar with the tales of Siri?"

"Am I ever!" Peri said, her eyes sparkling. "The forgotten city in the desert? Carved in stone? Used to be the capital of a great civilization?"

"That is the one," Razeem said.

"The city has known many names," Kauno said. "Siri, it was called in its heyday, and that is the name the Wulani call it when it is whispered. Yalifans named it Veranis. When the horselord conqueror Ulagan held Siri, he called it Tenger."

"I was going to go look for it!" Peri said. "When I was planning to leave Eilean de Taigh-Sholais with a…a crew."

"You do know it is most likely haunted? Inhabited by demons and djinn and who knows what horrors? It has long been in ruin," Jussuf said. He frowned, then smiled cynically, his eyes a tad colder than before when regarding Peri. "Or is it the treasure? Is that why you would venture there?"

"They said something about treasure." Peri shrugged. "I didn't really care about that. I just read in the monastery's library that they had starwatchers who could read the skies with their open-air laboratories. Collect water from the rain to create a garden with floating islands—in the middle of the desert! They worshipped bird gods and knew magic that is now lost. I wanted to see it all."

"Siri's exact location is not known," Razeem said. "This crew you were planning to travel there with was not the first to seek Siri's lost treasure. Most return empty-handed, having found no sign of the city, and some not at all."

"Those who did not return may even have found it," Jussuf said. "The desert is full of roaming monsters, and even in ancient times, the Wulani would have protected mausoleums or hoards with potent magic."

Razeem rewarded his fellow paladin with an affirming nod. "In ancient history, Cijeli's faithful had dealings with the people of Siri," the older paladin continued. "The best healers and ritualists would consult with Siri. They had to walk a 'Sjenka's shadow path,' whatever that is, every time they visited Siri, so that they could not return uninvited. If there's anything, anything at all, left of the old knowledge in the ruins...needless to say, Sjenka and her adherents don't welcome the servants of Juris."

"Sjenka, the Lady of Shadow," said Genjiro. "I frequently hear her mentioned."

"Yeah, no doubt," Peri snorted. "Seeing as you hang out here and at the docks all the time, doing business with—" she glanced at the paladins "—never mind. Criminals usually worship her. All kinds of sneaky types, really."

"Connor said that Sjenka has a more benevolent side to her," Ewynne said. "Artists, entertainers and storytellers, everyone who creates illusions to delight and entertain, worship her, too. Wandering troubadours sure do, like the ones who passed by last month, remember?"

"Let that be a relief for us, then," said Razeem dryly. "This is the best I can do. Chase a most likely djinn-infested ghost city in the middle of the desert and dabble with the goddess of stealth, lies and subterfuge, on the off chance that some knowledge of how to rid yourself of the Edge remains. My apologies, Peri."

Peri waved her hand. "Are you fucking kidding me?" She laughed. "We travel to the unknown for some absurd reason, not knowing what's going to happen and what will become of us. I was kinda getting bored with Wallila Gate already. I couldn't *ask* for a better life than that! Perhaps things will improve after all! I already have three new friends traveling with me."

"I would want to come with you," Genjiro said. "I...am no warrior or skilled fighter. But I know about finding things out. I traversed the Shimmering Sands and made my way to Yalifa from Wulani. I believe I can be of use."

"But why would you want to?" Jussuf asked, frowning. "You have a...business here, and we are heading into danger."

"I am sure there is profit to be made," Genjiro answered. "And I respond to the call of adventure. I think, being at Peri's side, things never get boring."

Peri flashed him a smile. The group shared glances and shrugs. "It is decided, then. To Siri and the shadow path of Sjenka—and whatever else fun we run into on our way to Wulani! Cheers to that!"

PART TWO
PERI

"The great Gaels of Ireland are the men that God made mad,
For all their wars are merry, and all their songs are sad."
  —G.K. Chesterton, The Ballad of the White Horse

14
THE COAST OF THE STARLIT SEA, SOMEWHERE BETWEEN YALIFA AND WULANI

For a month now, Peri and her companions had journeyed towards Wulani and the ancient desert city of legend, Siri. The road followed the coast of the Starlit Sea, in the shelter of the shimmering mountains, snaking through olive groves and orange orchards. The evening was cooling, and the waves lapped at the shore, next to a modest inn between Yalifa and Wulani. The paladins had gone to bed early, as was their wont, while Kauno and Ewynne had set out to collect herbs and enjoy a walk. Peri and Genjiro were gambling and drinking.

The silence was thick as the rolling dice slowed down, then came to a halt. Peri erupted into a triumphant cheer, standing up and slamming her tankard to the table. Genjiro cocked his head and raised his tankard, too. The men sitting opposite to them frowned and muttered, then produced the agreed upon coin and went their way.

Genjiro leaned back. "Lady Koun favoured us tonight."

"Another *kami* of yours?" Peri asked.

"Yes...she is the fickle *kami* of fortune. When the night falls, Peri, and all the decent folk of stature sleep, the floating world of *ukiyo* is alive. You know that I...associated with yakuza." For the past weeks, Genjiro had regaled her with tales of the Morishiman underworld and the crime families with their colorful tattoos, entertainments, and games of fortune.

"As it happens, yakuza is 'in your face,' as you put it. They are covered in tattoos depicting dragons, manticores, lions and the like. They are wild in public. But there is much secrecy going on in Shorioka's night, too." Genjiro was fiddling with the coins they had just won. "Secret societies of powerful people—*maho-tsukai* or magicians, as you call them— advisors of the clans, wealthy merchants. Yakuza shelters their meetings."

"So, what do they do in those meetings? Share secret handshakes? Sing secret society anthems?" Peri gulped down some more ale.

"You jest, but trust me, there is a lot of ritual secrecy involved. Morishima is...not like here. Your public standing, your 'face,' is *everything*. Being in the wrong place at the wrong time can be deadly." Genjiro did not return Peri's smile. "And the societies...they are secret for a reason. They may be plotting the downfall of a clan. Worship evil kami. Practice *noroi*...evil magic that deals with the dead

109

and curses."

"Necromancy." Peri knew that so far Ewynne had not dabbled with it, but every mage needed to know the basics if she wanted to get far.

"Once Aiko—that *bakuto* I had an...understanding with, if you remember...and I had to smuggle a Watanabe courier back to the court at dawn. The man had drunk himself comatose in a secret society meeting. He was terrified and nauseous, and for sure he would have been in great danger had he been seen or not made it back in time...but in truth, it was hilarious." Genjiro's face relaxed as he smiled at the memory. "We had to loan a raft from a fish peddler and bribe a *wako* fleet that was watching an opening to a tunnel that goes under the *shiro*—the castle—up at the cliff. We paddled the shivering and vomiting courtier to the half-forgotten pier that only smugglers use."

"And *wako* are pirates, right?" Peri asked. Genjiro's hand brushed hers as he gave her an affirmative nod. "By the time we make it to Wulani, I'll speak Morishiman. You'll have to teach me more swear words, though."

"It will be a while yet," said Genjiro.

Peri pushed a handful of coins around on the table. "I wish there was something to buy with this coin we won."

"We just bought beer," said Genjiro.

Peri frowned. "Dude! I mean something fancy. Something we absolutely don't need and shouldn't waste money on." The party had traveled on foot towards Wulani for a month now, and while the trade routes were busy, there was little entertainment available at the inns along the road. Peri didn't even know what she would want to buy. But she wanted to celebrate extravagantly, to spend gold like there was no tomorrow, because it was so good to feel triumphant, wild, magnificent, and alive. "In the next city, let's buy a huge dinner in the best restaurant we can find. Hire a band of troubadours to play for us."

"All we won was pocket change," Genjiro said. "But it is true that we could afford to celebrate a little. For me, having a bath and soft linen to sleep in would be a celebration in its own right." The party had sold its sword along the way. There were always monsters around, couriers and merchants to protect, common folk in need of help. They had also been attacked by bounty hunters and Dimitri's unaffiliated offspring, but the party had made short work of them.

"And Kauno could make a small fortune with her knots if she wanted," Peri said. "That's how she makes money when she needs to." It was believed that warlocks from Balatsky Taiga could command the winds. So Kauno—and many others from the region—sold strings with wind knots in them. One for a mild breeze, two for a gale, three for a storm. If it didn't work, nobody had come back to complain.

"You need new boots, too, remember?" Genjiro said. "Buy really good ones before we blow the rest celebrating, okay?"

"Yes, Dad," Peri said, rolling her eyes. As she stood up in order to go to the privy behind the inn, she spotted a few beggars in the shadows. One of them sat in a rickety small cart. Peri stepped closer and Genjiro followed her. In the flickering lantern light, they could see that the beggar had no legs. He was a middle-aged man with large eyes and a hardened face. Peri stepped closer and opened her mouth to speak, then hesitated. The man frowned at her. Peri saw two items in the cart with the man. Looking closer, she realized they were two lumps of iron with handles in them.

Her eyes welled. She fumbled through her pockets, emptying all the coins and notes in her hands and shoving them into the hands of the beggar. "Take it…take it all," she whispered and rushed away, towards the shore, without another look at the man.

Genjiro shrugged and flashed a hurried smile at the beggar, then followed Peri to the shore. The last remnants of sunlight glowed orange on the horizon, and the choppy little waves lapped back and forth. Peri waded in the water. She had rolled her pants up to her knees, having left her worn boots on the shore. She didn't look at Genjiro, but instead ever so slightly turned her head away when he tried to establish eye contact. She waded deeper and watched the sun completely disappear behind the horizon.

The moon and stars illuminated the little bay and the aptly named Starlit Sea. Peri slowly turned to face Genjiro, wearing an expression he'd never seen on her face before— one of utter terror. Her eyes glittered in the moonlight. She looked him in the eye, with that startled expression of an ambushed guardsman who recognizes the danger too late. Genjiro had never killed anyone. He stayed back in the inn or the camp when the others went to fulfil contracts that required violence. Peri, he had gathered from Razeem's and Jussuf's muffled conversations, killed with gleeful savage precision. But right now, she looked like she was the prey.

"Genjiro," she said in a voice that sounded as if it was coming from far away, muffled. "How does he even wipe his own *arse?* If his friends can't be bothered, he has to drag himself around with those pathetic lumps." She waded back to the shore, to Genjiro, who wordlessly waited. She grabbed

Genjiro's hands with great intensity and pressed them to her heart. "If...if I ever..." She struggled for words with a trembling lip and welling eyes. "If I would ever become dependent on anyone's goodwill—unable to feed or bathe myself—you must promise me..." She bit her lip, staring at him, squeezing his hands.

"Promise you what?" Genjiro quietly asked.

"That you'll end me. End me! Or I'll...just promise."

Genjiro's expression was unreadable. "I promise."

Peri's face melted into an expression of profound gentleness. She was twenty-one, Genjiro knew, but now she looked even much younger. She planted a light kiss on Genjiro's cheek, like a being brushed with a feather, then pulled her boots back on, shielding her face with that mane of glossy reddish-brown hair.

As they walked back to the inn, Genjiro described Morishiman sailboats to Peri. Her bright-eyed interest seemed exaggerated, as if she wanted to erase the emotion that had overtaken her earlier. As they approached the inn, they heard raucous laughter and singing and could make out the refrain as the group finished the song.

"—and greet my brothers at the Fiddler's Green!"

The revelers fell silent for a moment, then someone spoke in a somber tone. "For the fallen."

"For the fallen," replied the rest.

As Peri and Genjiro approached, they realized it was the group of beggars gathered around the legless man in the rickety cart. One of the man's companions patted him on the back and said, "Sure you'll be fine, Pulaski?"

"I'm sure," answered the man. "The night is warm and I have my blanket. I'll just finish here and watch the stars by myself."

"Perros Callejeros! Brothers forever!" said another companion and bumped the beggar's shoulder with his fist.

"Perros forever," answered the man and bumped his friend's shin.

Peri gave Genjiro's sleeve a little tug and tried to steer clear of the man, keeping to the other side of the yard. But the man glanced at the two of them and shouted, "Girl! This booze was bought with your money! Come and finish the bottle with me."

Peri glanced at Genjiro, then at the man. "Okay," she said in a small voice.

"Goodnight," said Genjiro quietly and left for his room in the inn.

Peri approached warily.

"It ain't contagious," the man said with a half-smile.

Peri smiled feebly. "Sorry."

The man grunted and waved her apology away. "You're not the first one. Name's Pulaski. Janis Pulaski. Been a long while since we've had anything this good to drink. Old Port from Cadenas!"

"I'm Peri. And yeah, it's good stuff." Peri accepted the offered bottle, took a smaller sip than she wanted to, and handed it back.

"You ever serve, girl? You have that step."

Peri laughed. "Gods no. All those rules and early mornings don't mix with me. But I was trained to fight at a garrison, by the armsmaster as a favour to my dad."

The man nodded. "He taught you to step lively, I reckon. But you have seen combat. Can tell from the way you carry yourself, size everything up for danger."

"Yeah. Sword for hire, on my way to Wulani."

"So was I, once. Near twenty years ago. Before I joined the Perros. Officially, that's the *Twenty-Third Spearhead Cavalry Regiment of the King His Majesty.* The only cavalry regiment that accepts foreigners and commoners in its ranks. Hence, Perros Callejeros. Dogs of the street. Mongrels."

"In Lughani Vos, the cavalry was all noblemen, far as I know," Peri said. As a child, she had assumed it had something to do with the shining brass buttons and colorful uniforms she'd seen in parades on the mainland, but probably it had more to do with the fact that a trained warhorse was a big investment. *And you have to know all the posh drinking songs, not the kind commoners sing.*

"That's how it works in Yalifa, too. But the Perros, we are an exception. We would be the first to charge, straight into the enemy infantry, to drive them in disarray at the start of the battle." The man straightened his shoulders and narrowed his eyes, leaning slightly forward. Peri could almost see the young hot-headed cavalryman eager for a daring charge shine through the man's weathered and aged features. *"Despierta la rabia!"* He paused, then smiled ruefully. "That was our battle cry. 'Wake the fury.' A bit of a pun, too, as 'rabia' means both fury and the mad dog disease. And we were, well, the mad dogs. I spoke barely a word of Yalifan when I joined. Didn't even know the words of the damn battle cry. 'Perros' I understood. You pick a word here and there from the lands you travel as a mercenary, as you would know. I'm from Leshenkaya, yet I woke the fury in the name of king Jorge the First, in the name of Yalifa."

"Sounds badass. So, you were like the best of the best." Peri could see the appeal of it—being one of the crazy and daring who'd do the first charge, who even other soldiers looked up to, who had their own badass unit name and a battle cry. She wondered how the man could bear being a pitiable legless beggar after such a glorious youth. She didn't dare to ask.

The man snorted. "So we thought. That cavalry is only for them nobles, but they made an exception for us, because we were so brave and dashing and clever, commoners or not, foreigners or not. Turns out, the truth is that we were expendable. Did I know that I was risking my life for a country I barely knew, a king I've never even seen? Of course! It made the cry echoing in the valley and the clatter of the hooves even sweeter. No such rush!"

"Yeah! There's no feeling of being alive like facing death and laughing at it," said Peri. She inched closer to her drinking companion. She found it easier to look at the man now.

"What better way to go than hearing the steel singing, riding the wave of battle, leading the spearhead? A death like that, among your brothers, that didn't scare me. But that ain't how my life as a cavalryman ended. It was when my Ventoso stumbled into the enemy pike wall during a charge, and I was crushed under him..." The man stopped talking and his eyes welled up.

Peri's hand twitched. She didn't know how to comfort the man for the loss of what he had been. She wanted to pat his back, give him something, *anything*, to make up for it.

Then the man blew his nose and continued. "It's stupid, but give me something to drink, and I'll bawl about my horse. After all these years. Ventoso. The way he shrieked when he was impaled by the pikes..."

Peri bit her lip. *He's crying about his horse. Not about his*

116

legs. "I…get it," she said. "My sister loves animals. I just… never wanted to get close to one. Their lives are too short."

"You can say that again. But Ventoso was still a young buck. We were all so young…like you. Fiery, like you. But once I could no longer *despertar la rabia*, I found out why the cavalry regiment on the most dangerous jobs takes commoners and foreigners. We were not important. Expendable, and so proud and grateful for the chance to kill and die. When I could no longer kill for King Jorge, I was nothing to them, nothing to Yalifa. Just another dirty *perro*." Pulaski leaned back in his cart, forlornly staring at the last remnants of the Cadenan port.

"That…really sucks." Peri again fidgeted with her hands. She felt an almost irrepressible urge to pat the man's back or hold his hand, but doing so felt too familiar and intrusive. *Gods know people treat him like a lackwit or piece of furniture all the time. I can still treat him like a grown man I don't know well.*

"Bah, look at me all pitying myself. Many people have it worse."

"They do?" Peri blurted out, then slapped a hand over her mouth, eyes wide and cheeks flushed with embarrassment.

Pulaski smiled ruefully at her. "Do I wish I still had my legs? For sure. But I still have so much to live for. Some of my brothers who made it through the wars are still around. The innkeep lets me sleep indoors if it gets too cold. Beautiful sunsets."

Peri nodded but wasn't convinced. The mere idea of being trapped like the beggar suffocated her.

IT WOULD BE A MERCY, YOU KNOW. ALLOW HIM TO REUNITE WITH HIS BELOVED HORSE. WITH ANY

LUCK, HE'D REGAIN HIS LEGS IN THE HEREAFTER…

Dimitri. Shut up. However much Dimitri made sense, she had no right to decide for the man. *If he asked me though…*

Pulaski looked her in the eye. "You don't agree."

Peri tried to think of a tactful thing to say but came up empty.

"No offence taken. I would have thought the same at your age, when I rode with the Perros. But all is fleeting, girl. If nothing else, age will diminish you. Happens to us all."

Peri felt silent mirth from Dimitri. Her heart was too big in her chest and there was a lump in her throat. She hugged the beggar's shoulders—hugged hard—to make up for all the ways life was horrible. *Janis. Janis Pulaski. He has a name.* Maybe it was intrusive. Disrespectful. But he hugged her back, his arms still strong and sinewy as they must have been in his glory days.

"Goodnight and…I don't know…Eoghain keep you?" she said.

"He does. He sent you my way, didn't he? Goodnight, girl."

And a lot of good that *did to you. A bit of expensive booze, and then I go on my merry way.* Peri slipped into the quiet inn and made her way upstairs.

15
THE COAST OF THE STARLIT SEA, FARTHER TOWARDS WULANI

Days later, Peri smiled drowsily and gulped down some wine. Another evening, another nondescript inn, another pebbly shore. This one had a nice grove tucked next to a forgotten, leaky boat. *A fisherman died, or moved away, left his boat to rot?* Peri picked up a shell and followed the grooves with her finger. She wondered how long ago the shell had been formed, where it had come from, what ancient events it had witnessed. She was leaning on the boat as she heard movement near the edge of the grove. Genjiro, coming to meet her by the boat as agreed. Tonight, she would finally work up the courage and do *something*. Never before had she felt hesitation to kiss a guy and see where it

went from there. But this time, she didn't want to be rejected. If her feelings of longing for him were not returned, she
didn't want to know. But Genji *had* to like her. It was in the
spark of his eyes, the knowing smiles, the way he sought
her company just as she sought his. *Didn't he?*

As he approached, Genjiro's expression was unreadable,
but there was a great intensity in his eyes. Peri tilted her
head and smiled up at him, tossing her mane of hair behind
her shoulder. Their eyes met, and for a moment, there was
nothing but this connection that had been there for a time,
that Peri hoped would be acknowledged tonight. Then it
was abruptly broken.

Genjiro's face pinched up in pain, and he looked away.
"There she is," he quietly said.

Peri frowned and squinted when two shapes materialized from the shadows. Darien, the man with dark, piercing
eyes who had tried to abduct her before, and a tall, blonde
woman with a dour and humorless expression on her face.
The woman tensed her fingers, as if holding an invisible
globe in her hands.

Peri glanced again at Genjiro, looking for a benign explanation, anything. *No, no, no...*She knew Darien and the
stranger watched her every move, but she made to jump up
and draw her sword anyway...to no avail. She was unable
to lift a finger, let alone spring up. It wasn't the short-lived
dread of being encased in stone of a hold spell. It was an
overwhelming sense of lethargy. Her muscles didn't want to
move. They had simply quit and walked off. She felt a wave
of nausea roll over her.

"Genjiro..." she moaned.

Darien smiled thinly. "Your obligation is fulfilled,

Hanamori Genjiro. Go. Rejoice! You are free."

Genjiro kept watching his boots, arms protectively wrapped around his torso, face still pinched. "What...what will you do with her?" he whispered.

"None of your business, worm!" snapped the blonde woman. "Go, while you can, and be glad that we gave you a chance."

Genjiro turned around and slowly walked away, shoulders hunched, face downcast.

"Don't think about trying to call the Edge this time, girl," Darien said. "Rajsa here possesses clerical powers. She, and a concoction little Genjiro slipped in your drink earlier tonight, have seen to it that you'll stay docile."

Peri felt as if Genjiro had plunged a physical knife in her back instead of a proverbial one. *How very fucking great,* she thought. *I was so sure that we had...something. And trusted him completely.* It hurt so much that she concentrated on the sharp, acid edge of dread, the way it electrified the intense stares between the two intruders and herself. At any rate, she could not afford to dwell on her shock if she meant to survive. *Focus.* She strained to speak, fighting a wave of nausea. *Clerical...so she must have a patron god.* "You lunatics want a new god to arise. Why would an old one help?"

"How little you understand," the blonde woman named Rajsa said. Her voice was cold and crisp, precise. "But then, what can you expect from a mongrel? I serve Lord Stribog, true. But wrath, murder and destruction are not part of his domain."

"Oh yeah? Seems like his fucking Citadel caused a fuck ton of murder and destruction from what I could see," Peri replied.

"Means to an end, mongrel," said Rajsa. "Stribog is about exploitation and dominance. Dimitri and his offspring are creatures of all-consuming passion. A passion that, I'll grant you, possesses immense unadulterated power. So, a new god of wrath arising would make a great ally for Stribog. One of us was raised to become a priestess of Stribog for this very purpose."

Peri wanted to struggle against her invisible bonds but lacked the strength. *I'm a helpless prisoner to these megalomaniacal nutjobs,* Peri thought. *Though I'm not dead yet. Not sure if that's a good thing or a bad thing.*

"And you were the lucky one. My deepest congratulations. Why do you keep calling me a mongrel? You two have a pedigree or something?" Maybe if Peri kept them talking, she'd figure out a way to escape.

"She doesn't know, does she?" Rajsa said, exasperated. "She doesn't know how it began, how it all has been planned. The manifestation of the Edge on her is a sacrilege!"

"Don't underestimate her for her undeniable cluelessness," said Darien. "Brother Connor consciously chose to raise her as an ordinary child, as he no doubt saw Dimitri's essence as a destructive force. He believed exposing her to the knowledge of her heritage would make her more vulnerable to all the...temptations that come with it."

"You don't understand, Darien!" said Rajsa hotly. "You are intrigued by her, but she is filth. She, and her brother whom she eliminated earlier." The woman turned to face Peri, a cold gleam of intense purpose in her eyes. "Neither of you were supposed to live. You were sheltered by your stepfather. He simply clung to life out of sheer tenacity. But no matter! The improved plan is already in motion, and...

Enough. You don't deserve a villain's exposition."

A black, viscous, oozing stream emanated from Rajsa's hands. It encased Peri, as if she were drowning in murky water, and soon Peri knew no more.

16
ASGARD

Kiril watched Grimnir's back, the man's gray hair tied in a loose ponytail snaking from under his wide-brimmed hat. One raven perched on Grimnir's shoulder while the other scanned the skies high above. For a while, the two men had traveled side by side, but some time ago the seemingly endless maze of entangled roots had become too narrow. Other things had changed, too. At first, the mist had gradually become thinner, the chill receding from Kiril's toes and fingertips. The roots that had been covered with black, slimy, oily sap were now lighter brown in color and healthier, a light green sheen on them. The travelers could occasionally see the pale and distant sun beyond the thinning clouds. The massive trunk of the ash tree loomed in the distance, but no matter how long the men journeyed, they didn't get any closer.

Grimnir had told Kiril not to worry. He knew the way,

and indeed Kiril had already concluded that time and matter didn't behave in the Nether like they did in the mundane world. Now, however, the gap between the entangled roots widened, and eventually the rightmost one disappeared entirely below the ground. Grimnir slowed down and glanced at Kiril, who took a few long strides and resumed his pace at the side of his companion. Before they had been forced to walk in a line, Grimnir had been quite talkative. But what had the man been talking *about*? Kiril frowned. He couldn't quite remember, even though he remembered having been entertained.

"At long last!" said Grimnir. "We are in Asgard." The man tossed his head back and closed his eyes, a smile spreading on his face as he breathed a lungful of fresh air that smelled of soft fresh grass. "Not before long we'll be at the Yggdrasil, and then you'll meet the Norns. Say, Kiril, are there *jöttnar*—giants—in this Valkama of yours?"

"There were some at the mountains in Leshenkaya. I never personally encountered any."

"And what are they rumored to be like?"

"Violent. Cruel. Not too bright. Though that is the perspective of those who are at odds with the giants, so I would take that in account before making any firm judgements."

"Indeed that is what they are like as a race—creatures of chaos and destruction. But there is an oddity about that. It is as if fate rolls dice whenever one is born. Every so often, especially bright and beautiful individuals are born. There are men of great wisdom, maidens of great beauty—greater than that of humans."

Kiril licked his dry and cracked lips, and Grimnir noticed, passing him a waterskin. The weather was not cold anymore. The giant trunk of the ash tree loomed closer now, and Kiril could just barely see an outline of a building.

"There is the longhouse of the Norns," Grimnir said. "Reason I brought this up is that the Norns are actually giantesses. Three sisters, brought up in Jötunnheim before they settled in Asgard to tend to the tree and keep score of the lives of mankind. And like all those winners in this cosmic birth lottery of jötunnkind, they are not actually gigantic at all. They are both wise and beautiful."

Near the longhouse, a spring was nestled in the embrace of a thick, curved root of the tree, sheltered by the leaves of the low-reaching branches. Water lilies floated in the dark but clear water, and a woman drew water in a pail from the spring. She had long, blonde hair and a simple woven ribbon around her head. Her clothes were plain and fit for physical labour, but finely woven of good material.

"Verdandi, dear Verdandi! What a pleasure to see you again!" yelled Grimnir from afar.

The woman paid him no heed as she collected some light gray clay from the ground with a small shovel and started to mix it with the water in the pail, smiling to herself as she did. Only when they approached did she turn to them.

"Why, you wandering ruffian! You smell of Nilfheim, I do declare! And you have brought a stray, again." She rolled her eyes and kept stirring the clay into the water, then walked to the crooked, thick root and started to sprinkle the water over it. The tree almost seemed to groan in relief as the water nourished its bark. Its apex reached somewhere high up in the sky, beyond where the eye could see.

"I did, didn't I?" said Grimnir and clapped his hand over Kiril's shoulder. As the men walked closer, Kiril noticed two swans gliding between the water lilies. The bottom of the spring was fine white sand, and several bubbling hearts could be seen at the bottom. Yet closer to the middle, the bottom was obscured by fine strands of foam and white mist.

"I suppose the laws of hospitality compel me to invite you to dinner," Verdandi said. "Urd will be extraordinarily delighted to see you and your stray, I'm sure." All the time, she kept smiling. "Oh, but my manners! Well met, stranger. Do you have a name?"

"It is Kiril, most gracious." Kiril spotted something faintly glittering through the obscured middle of the spring. Even cut off from the source of magic, he instantly recognized that this place brimmed with it and Verdandi was a creature of great power.

As the men followed Verdandi to the direction of the longhouse, she and Grimnir chattered in a language Kiril didn't understand. He had already gotten used to Grimnir's theatrical manner, but now it seemed that Verdandi, too, was putting on an act. There was something eager and attentive about the way she carried herself, despite her professed exasperation at a vagabond turning on her doorstep. Was this whole act for his benefit? Kiril didn't understand, but there was little to do but to roll with it.

There was a rough-hewn wooden table outdoors in front of the longhouse. Another woman emerged from inside of the building. She was a bit older than Verdandi, more matronly and more soft. Her cheeks and eyes were round, and she had collected her wheat blonde hair in a bun on the top of her head. Her eyes lit up as she saw Grimnir, but she rolled her eyes in the same mock-exasperated manner Verdandi had.

"Right in time for dinner!" Verdandi exclaimed, switching to common tongue for a moment. "Do sit down, Kiril. This is but a simple stew, as we didn't expect company, but I hope it will please."

The stew was, indeed, simple but delicious. The carrots, potatoes and turnips were thoroughly flavoured with the broth, salt, and butter, and Urd served sliced cucumbers in vinegar, sugar, and dill as a side dish.

Grimnir, who in general ate very little, scratched the neck of one of the wolves that kept following him. The other one was curled at his feet, staring at the two women with its narrowed yellow eyes. The beasts ignored Kiril, as if they regarded him beneath their notice. Grimnir fed little morsels of meat to the wolves and sipped wine. Kiril wasn't sure how his body and mind would react to alcohol after going through death and...*reassemblage, if not rebirth?* But he didn't want to take chances. He stuck to water.

As the meal progressed, Kiril noticed that as his companions forgot about his presence, they had dropped their theatrical, good-natured performance and were instead frowning and talking in a worried tone. At one point, he noticed a dust cloud where the road disappeared into the valley. After a while, he could hear a distant sound of hooves.

"Skuld," Verdandi said. "Our youngest. She rides with the Valkyries, reviving the brave and deserving of fallen warriors and inviting them to feast in the so sadly absent All-Father Odin's halls."

"I do hope the All-Father appreciates us who keep everything in order when wanderlust takes over him and he goes on his journeys," said Urd, hand on her heart, wearing a sad and wistful expression.

"I am sure he keeps everyone fondly in his heart, wherever he goes," said Grimnir.

It was then that a great white horse galloped to the longhouse, rearing on its hindlegs, ridden by a laughing young girl with a sand brown long plait whipping behind her back, wearing a helmet and greaves, a spear strapped at her back.

"Any luck, Skuld?" asked Verdandi as the young girl greeted the company, dismounted, and started to tend to her horse.

Skuld bit her lip and shook her head. "I kept an eye on the fields as we patrolled, but no sign of the priestess. She must be slippery or else know some kind of elven magic not known to us."

"It is an embarrassment," Urd said, frowning.

"Ah, but perhaps it is a good thing that I brought a petitioner here then, hmm?" said Grimnir. "The elf was originally from his world."

The women turned to look at Kiril with a new interest.

"You did say that you would be willing to do a service to the Yggdrasil—and the world it guards—in return for an opportunity to get your magic back?" Grimnir said.

"I did," Kiril said. *What kind of service, though?* He was scrawny and gaunt and had no magic.

As if reading his mind, Skuld said, "*This* petitioner? How could this little dead man find a crafty and dangerous elven priestess?"

"He used to be a mage," Grimnir said, "and is quite clever. Perhaps he, with his fresh eyes and an outsider's perspective, can spot something that our own agents missed. Either way, you are busy with your duties. If he fails, then his bones will bleach under the midsummer sun at Asgard's fields. And you ladies will be none the worse off."

The Norns glanced at each other and shared shrugs and nods. "Very well," said Verdandi. "Listen then, Kiril of Valkama. There is a trespasser here in Asgard. She has escaped from a sanatorium in the Nether. I understand that it is some forward-thinking thing—something about how sickness causes people to sin and err, and so they are taken to a place of healing."

"But some of them are dangerous, so they are locked up," said Urd, ladling stew in a bowl for Skuld, who sat down and eagerly dug in. "This priestess had left behind the elven land of the dead, Silva Lunari. She wandered the planes and was caught breaking the planar laws by the custosi—the spirits from a plane of Panoptica. They are trying to settle and organize the chaos of the Nether, and they run this sanatorium."

"What planar laws did the priestess break?" asked Kiril. Not that it mattered. He had little desire to become involved with planar turf wars any more than he had to—but he couldn't help being curious.

"She was trying to go back to the land of the living. Looking for a necromancer to bargain with, and almost succeeded. So, they put her in the sanatorium. But now she has escaped and, apparently, is trying to use our rainbow bridge for the same purpose. I don't know what her plan is or if she even has one, but she seems to believe that she can somehow use the bridge to return to this Valkama of yours. She killed a number of custodians during her escape."

Grimnir was feeding little crumbs of bread to his ravens from the palm of his hand. "The custodians asked for us to return the prisoner to them. The ladies don't interfere with the Nether, as they have their hands full tending to the universe of the Northmen. But they do have an understanding with the people of Panoptica."

Verdandi was nodding. "They are dedicated to order, and we are dedicated to the order of our own world."

"So it is, shall I say, a bit of a planar embarrassment if we can't tend to our own backyard and return the fugitive in a short order," Grimnir continued. He fell silent for a moment, then he spoke louder, and his one eye seemed to almost glow red. There was nothing left of his ever-present good humor. "More importantly, this…outsider—this nobody who left her own Silva Lunari behind—thinks she can just come unannounced, like a thief in the dead of night, to use our greatest wonder, a holy passage, for her own purposes! Why, the honor—" he paused and smirked, almost deflated. The smile returned to the corner of his eyes. "I'm sure the All-Father would be most upset if he knew."

"I'm sure," said Urd.

"I'm sure," echoed the other Norns.

"So, Kiril, we'll give you good boots and clothes, rations and…maybe a crossbow?" Skuld said. "Find this elf and bring her to us. Her name is Vallara Silverbond. That is all I know."

Kiril nodded slowly. It did sound dreadful, but they expected him to try to be useful. He wanted the magic back so badly that he could almost taste it. And if—*if!*—he got the magic back, he might even live an afterlife worth living. Reunite with Jelena. Put things right. He had to succeed.

17
REMOTE
MARSHLANDS

PERI WOKE UP WITH A SPLITTING HEADACHE AND GRImaced. Raw red filtered behind her retinas. There was a much too bright light wherever she was that there was no escaping. She cautiously pried one swollen eyelid open. Everything was just...white. Bright, shiny white. There was a bar attached to the ceiling that emitted glaring, unnatural, too bright light. No windows. No furniture save for the gurney Peri found herself manacled to. She attempted to pull her wrist away from the handcuff but immediately hissed in pain as an acidic liquid burned her skin.

"The acid will nip in the bud the trigger that initiates the Edge," rang a voice from somewhere. There was no-one in the room. *Just white...* "Stress hormones, the body's natural alarm and emergency systems...we need to collect it, instead of letting it spring the transcendental energy into action. Minimal sensory input is required. The mind will create content on its own if there is none available in the surroundings…and that will serve our harvesting purposes."

Seems like someone is way too proud of whatever diabolical shit they've come up with that they can't resist a little villain's exposition after all, said a small, calmer part of Peri's mind. The larger part that held more sway of her was close to all-consuming panic. A needle was strapped to her vein with a hose connected to it, which disappeared into a hole in the wall.

Peri heard something like a valve opening, a hollow clang followed by a humming sound. The hose changed color. Something purple flowed through it, slowly, from behind the wall. Into her vein. *No no no!* She tried to back off, to buck, only to be cut by the sharp acid in the manacles. She felt a compulsive need to rock herself, to escape her own skin, to get *away away AWAY*, to recoil from the trap that was her own skin and flesh and blood. She could not discern an external reason for the panic, but her body had decided that it was there, and her mind could hold no sway. *I have to get away!* Her fingers and toes twitched uncontrollably, her blood felt too hot in her veins, her sinews bulged. *LET ME DIE LET ME DIE LET ME AWAY!* she screamed in the white emptiness…

The magnificent joy and rage struggled to fly free in the skies. But Peri was just writhing in the shell of her body, trying to rock herself, her throat too raw to shriek but still making a pitiful croaking noise. She was a celestial with her wings hacked off, yearning to soar to the skies but rotting alive with diseased stumps. The all-consuming fury was there,

there...but out of reach. Her skin crawled and twitched and she jerked helplessly, as if drowning in the mass of imaginary insects. Then all was dark.

———————————— • ● • ————————————

PERI WOKE, COMPLETELY SOAKED WITH SWEAT. SHE jerked, remembering the terror of not being able to escape her own body. At some point, she had drifted into nothingness. The panic was gone...for now. *What are they doing to me? Are they...filling me with poison?* Acid rose from her stomach to her chest, under her collar bones, in her throat.

Something shifted in the whiteness. A door. She had not been able to see its outline earlier. She lifted her head with great difficulty and saw Genjiro slip in, great urgency on his face. She wanted to snarl, growl in anger, strain against the manacles, demand an explanation. But she was just tired and hurt. *So hurt.*

"Why?" she asked. "Genjiro, why?"

"Peri, listen!" he said. "Don't attack me!"

"How the fuck would I attack you, strapped into this thing?" she replied, welcoming the spark of anger.

"I've come to set you free. We need to get away quickly," Genjiro said, starting to undo one of the manacles. His fingers worked dexterously. The calmer part of Peri's mind—the one that had left her bucking in terror and taken off when she had been injected—noticed the skill, the familiarity. *He is not just a trader...and, as he is not a locksmith, he is a burglar and a thief. Chalk that up to another thing I didn't know about him.*

Peri flexed and extended the numb fingers of her newly released hand. Her grip felt weak, but she grabbed Genjiro's arm. "If this is another mindfuck…," she growled.

"No mindfuck. Peri, these are dangerous people! Let me finish!"

"No shit, really?" Peri snorted. But she let Genjiro's arm go and lay still as he finished releasing her and helped her up. Peri stumbled as she put her feet on the floor but felt a surge of strength, being able to move freely again. She found her stride and followed Genjiro, slipping through the door.

The corridor they entered was still white, but the glaring overhead light was gone. The pale glow of the afternoon sun entered from behind half-closed blinders. Peri followed Genjiro, who pushed open a door at the end of the corridor. They entered a marshy shoal. Straw-colored weeds grew everywhere. In the distance, there was a flock of unperturbed flamingos standing in the shallow water. There was nothing but weeds and shallows as far as the eye could see. The ocean glinted in the far distance, and Peri couldn't tell if there was a coastline in the horizon. She glanced over her shoulder. The whitewashed house they had just exited had a flat roof and square windows. It blended into the grayness of the surroundings.

"I drugged them, so we have some time," Genjiro said in a low voice, leading Peri behind the corner. "Come, I saw them put your sword here." They entered a small shed with some firewood, coils of rope, and farming tools. Peri grabbed her sword and turned to face Genjiro. The look in his eyes chilled her to the core.

"Peri, if you ever felt a shred of friendship for me…please have mercy. I need your help."

Peri snorted, gripping her sword, her senses on high alert. She wondered how much time was of the essence. But the house was in the middle of nowhere, and she would be easily spotted no matter which way she ran. At least in the shed, they were hidden. She'd hear Genjiro out. Then she'd kill him.

Genjiro looked down, closed his eyes. "I worked for them the entire time. I sought you out and pretended to be your friend." Genjiro spoke as if it physically pained him, then opened his eyes to face Peri.

Peri glared. "Well, it worked."

"I had a sister in Morishima. It is thanks to her that I live. She saved me from the consequences of my own actions. I returned to my carefree life of *ukiyo,* while Tomoe fled to the West in disgrace."

Peri inhaled sharply. "Tomoe! I never thought anything of it...there are so many Morishimans in Wallila Gate, and we worked for them all the time."

Genjiro nodded. "Tomoe had gifted me back my life, but sake tasted like ashes, women left my blood cold, music was loud and unpleasant in my ears...*ukiyo* no longer lifted my spirit. Joy was gone from me. I had to find her and forge a new life for us both. A better life. More honorable life. I journeyed through Feng Guo, traversed the Shimmering Sands, saw many wonders. But I arrived too late. She was dead...by your hand."

"She left me no choice! I *begged* her not to fight me! But she insisted! You *know* this, I have told you the tale!" It was inconceivable. How could Genjiro blame her?

"I know, Peri, I know. But I did not know that when I got involved with Darien and the Esquadron. I felt hate, the righteous kind of iron-hard hate that drives vengeance. I learned the truth when I came to know you better, but..."

"Well, why didn't you just tell me the truth, and we could have screwed the Esquadron?" Peri snarled. They could have worked together, protected each other. *Why?*

"Do you know what a geas is?" Genjiro asked quietly.

Peri grimaced. She did, all right. It was the fundamental blood oath that, if broken, would condemn the culprit into eternal torment worse than anyone could imagine. It was said that you could hear souls of geas breakers scream and howl in the wind when the Wild Hunt sweeps across the skies on stormy winter nights. Something dawned on her, and her eyes widened. "You...reneged by freeing me, and now you are geased again?"

Genjiro nodded, suppressing a tear. "This is why I need your help and beg you not to leave just yet."

"What can I do? Nothing is as strong as a geas—which is why you never, ever agree to one."

"Perhaps that is so. But I carry the blood of an ancient samurai family in my veins, and with that, the traditions of an ancient nation. There is no more powerful action of atonement than *seppuku.* Do you know what a *kaishakun-in* is?"

Peri's stomach lurched. "No...but I do know what *seppuku* is—as in, suicide by ripping your own guts out."

"It is my only hope, Peri," Genjiro said. "In Morishima, it can restore honor even after the most dastardly deeds. But I need an assistant. A *kaishakunin.* When I have offered my soul—the organs that sustain my life for the judgement of fate and the *kami*—you must sever my head with one forceful blow. To witness my atonement, to help me have courage..." his voice trailed off and blood drained from his lips, "...and to end the agony."

Such a gruesome act. She should have offered protestations. *There must be another way. It can't be what the gods would want. Suicide solves nothing. I can't be part of something like that.* But she understood. There wasn't another way, and if she had any compassion in her heart for Genjiro, she would do this. *You don't play with a geas.* She nodded grimly and touched his arm.

"I...don't even know if it will work," Genjiro said, tears flowing from his eyes in spite of his efforts to stay stoic. "We don't have a katana." Peri glanced at the sword in her hand as Genjiro continued. "The swords of the West are not like katana. Katana are not just swords. They are divine beings." He wrung his hands, contorting his forehead. "You have no blood of the samurai...you have not been trained for this, never seen it done. Maybe we are just two misfit criminals making a mockery of a sacred act. But I thank you for your compassion, Peri. We must try."

Peri quietly mouthed Eoghain's name, to give her courage to do her part without faltering. She watched quietly as Genjiro knelt down. His face was as white as the building they had exited, and he wept soundlessly. "Like with everything else back home, there is an elaborate ritual to this," he said. "A pristine white kimono. A blade that will be used just once. Four sips of sake...Peri, I'm terrified. Tomoe would not be. She would not hesitate."

Peri thought back, remembering Tomoe's determined face and sad, wise eyes—the posture of a noble warrior. *No, probably not.* She put a hand on Genjiro's shoulder. Her heart thumped too hard in her chest, but she had to be strong. She was not the one about to slice her own belly open.

"I am a coward. There is no more contemptible thing

where I come from," Genjiro continued.

"Not wanting to die—by ripping your guts out no less—hardly makes you a coward," Peri said. "You came to free me in spite of the geas, too." True, it was Genjiro's fault that she had been captured and tortured in the first place, but she didn't want to remind him of that.

"When you see me in agony, or hesitating, strike with full force. Samurai are trained to do it so that one strip of skin keeps the"—he swallowed—"head attached. So that it won't roll away. But...it's difficult."

"The spectators will have to live with the disappointment," Peri said dryly.

"They say you should think about the cherry blossoms when you do it...I haven't seen them in a long time," Genjiro said, eyes closed, his white knuckles gripping the hilt of his knife.

"Then think about them, and let that image lead you to light," Peri said, now crying silently, too. She knew she had the strength to sever his head. Her sword may not have been a divine katana, but it was sharp, well balanced, and a familiar companion to her. She focused. Like in combat. Closing everything but Genjiro's face out of her mind.

Genjiro's hands trembled. Hers did not. Nevertheless, Genjiro inhaled and thrust the blade in his belly, gritting his teeth and yanking sideways. What blood was left on his face seemed to drain away at the moment the blood spurted out and pooled at his knees. He made a motion as if to yank the blade upwards, and blue intestines began to spill out. A moan escaped his white lips and his hands let go of the blade.

Peri struck. The head rolled, spraying blood, and

Genjiro's moan was cut short. The sudden silence felt suffocating. The faint wind carried the scent of salt. A bird made a cawing sound somewhere in the distance.

Peri watched as the bloodied torso slumped. This had been Genjiro just seconds ago. His warm, lean body she had hoped to curl next to earlier that night. Now it was just another carcass. Peri walked to the head and picked it up. The lips were peeled back, the expression one of utter terror. The face was one of a kind. Genjiro. Peri picked it up. The bastards would not have his face—his eyes—even if Genjiro himself was gone.

———————— •●• ————————

PERI DRUDGED ALONG THE MARSH, SWORD AT HER WAIST, Genjiro's head cradled in her arms. One step, another. *Squish, squish, squish.* Spongy ground, salty water sloshing under her feet, tufts of weed. She would eventually reach the ocean. Then she would follow the coast and find her way back to the main road to Wulani. Find Ewynne. Her party.

But not Genjiro. She would never again find Genjiro.

A part of her was still spurred by that sharp, cold clarity that had overtaken her as soon as Genjiro released her from the manacles. But another part of her seemed to be shimmering outside of her body, as if her arm was *kind* of her own, but not really. As if it was a disembodied arm moving through the air. But also, she was moving it, like always. Both at the same time. It felt like her head was vast, and all the shoals and marshes and open skies were inside of it. But also, her head was tiny—tiny in the middle of all the grayness and below the vast sky, and full of pressure, hot. Both at the same time.

A group of people emerged from the shoal, advancing on her. They wore gray camouflage, blending into the surroundings, but she could see them. Feel them. She walked as if unaware of them, but when they were within hearing distance, she spoke in a low, growling voice. "You motherfuckers, I see you. I know you're armed. Probably one or two of you are spellcasters. You motherfuckers tried to keep me strapped down. You pumped poison into me. And now I have no pity and I'm going to kill you all."

They drew their weapons, initiated their chants.

Peri gently set Genjiro's head on the ground and drew her sword in one fluid motion. Someone flew through the air, slicing, striking, her hair flying, laughing. Peri watched that reddish-brown whirlwind of murder with dispassionate interest in the vastness of her own head. She felt a terrifying, glorious clarity and power enter her, a violent rage, an insatiable lust for destruction. It was as if she could hear an underground river flowing, echoing in her heartbeat. Mowing the faceless fighters down, spilling their blood. It sustained her, rendered her immortal, invincible, omnipotent! The Edge beckoned her. *Come to glory! Come to divinity!* But she didn't need it. Not now, not yet. The gifts from her blood were enough to destroy these insignificant beings that had the temerity to assist in keeping her trapped.

When it was over, Peri drew breath and wiped her cheek. She was covered with hot and slippery blood. She picked up Genjiro's head and held it to her chest. How many dead? Twenty? Thirty?

MY DAUGHTER! EMBRACE THE POWER OF YOUR BLOOD, AND NO-ONE WILL EVER TRAP YOU AGAIN!

SAVOUR YOUR TRIUMPH, THE ETERNAL STEP OF YOUTH AND VIGOR! YOU HAVE PROVEN YOUR WORTH.

Peri nodded. The underground river was flowing. She was still filled with the terrifying, glorious clarity. She was alive, her muscles surging with strength, breathing easily, just enough out of breath to know that she had exerted herself. She was so very alive, and they were so very dead.

Peri saw the red-haired, blood-covered girl standing down there. *Wait a minute? Is that me?* The Peri down there was getting smaller. Still holding Genjiro's head.

Peri looked up and saw the glorious, golden celestial with flaming red hair rising. Flying. *What is happening?*

And Peri saw them both, two versions of herself, from both angles, at the same time. As if she was a disembodied vast thing watching them both. She felt faint. And transparent. And then she was somewhere else.

18
DIMITRI'S SANCTUARY

"Hello, Velimir—you who once carried Dimitri's blood in your veins."

Velimir gasped at the unexpected company. He had been playing rock, scissors, and paper with Casimir, who, after three hundred rounds, was still just as fascinated with the game as he had been when they started.

The creature in front of him pushed a dark hood off its face, then dropped its cloak and flexed a pair of shiny, white wings. With a single smooth gesture of its hand, it held a crystal emitting a blue glow. Its hair and skin were of luminous, golden hue, and its voice was like a hymn emanating from a temple of a serene, benevolent god. *A celestial. A creature of Yonder in the bowels of hell. Intriguing.* Velimir could feel its extremely powerful aura, and tension immediately flooded through him.

"A celestial in the depths of the Abyss. You are far away

from home," Velimir said.

"I am called Irina, and I am sent by Cijeli the All-Father," the celestial said. "I managed to come here unobserved by hostile forces, but it was not easy. The Three have an interest in the fate of Dimitri's children, and I have a reason to want to assist Peri of Eilean de Taigh-Sholais. I believe you will help me with this."

Velimir was immediately irritated at its presumptuous manner. He was about to say as much when Casimir nudged him and made huge, pleading eyes. Maybe reacting too abruptly wasn't the best of ideas.

"I see. And how will I do that?" asked Velimir, trying to keep the annoyance in his voice to a bare minimum.

"She will be drawn here shortly. She has been subjected to devastating horrors which have heightened her abilities and, unfortunately, her divine sire's sway on her. She is lost, separated from her companions. But she will be able to summon them here if the correct Vysokian words are spoken. You will tell her the correct phrase." While Irina spoke, she was serene and almost indifferent, as if she believed that by her merely stating something, it had already happened.

"Why don't you tell her the phrase yourself? It's not like I have nothing else to do. I'm positively burning to get on with our three hundred eleventh round of rock, scissors, and paper," said Velimir. He still resented the unfairness of the situation. The prophecy and uppity divine beings now centered around Peri. His chance for greatness was over.

"Poor, tortured spirit, so ready to throw freely-given aid away in your pride. My presence here means that the All-Father is taking a chance. And you seek another chance, too, do you not? This way you can aid your sister, and thus she will be more willing to help you. It is our hope that you two will work together, despite your previous animosity." The celestial was unprovoked by Velimir's anger. She had a kind and pitying look in her eyes. This irritated Velimir even more. He growled in discontent.

"Eee...Velimir had a very very very difficult life and Velimir all suffer suffer suffer in the Abyss. Oh yes, and he's me'se new best friend and he's really nice, oh yes! Please Irina not be angry with Velimir! I'se can makes you pancakes," interjected Casimir in a panicky voice.

"That will not be necessary, Casimir," answered Irina. She kept her eyes fixed on Velimir.

Velimir had to admit that the celestial had spoken the truth. "It is unfolding in earnest, then. The Edge. Her mind at work here. And now a celestial taking an interest in her." How it hurt that it was happening, and that he wasn't at the center of it!

"So it is, and you have a role to play," said Irina. "You two are the wildcards of fate—the ones that were not supposed to live. She, the free spirit, you, the creature of will. Mongrels, as the Esquadron would call you. That is why we must hope that you two—creatures of chance and chaos— will tip the scales for the greater good. The Esquadron are set on creating an evil force powerful enough to rival Cijeli and threaten the whole creation. They seek to produce an entire race of terrifying beings. Peri is now their rival and archenemy, but you, too, have your own destiny to face yet. Will you cooperate?"

Infuriating as it was that Peri still had the chance for glory and Velimir didn't, he could not deny that the celestial talked sense. If he could offer assistance to Peri, he could persuade her to return the favour. If the celestial court wanted to assist Peri in order to hinder her enemies, Velimir might as well be a part of it. His ambitions may have died a bitter death, but he had always been resourceful. He would find another way to wield power and discover his way to glory. "I will assist my sister," Velimir said, making sure it sounded like *he* was the one doing a favour here. Casimir snuggled next to him, and Velimir forgot to flinch. *Must try to keep that pride and temper in control, especially when facing Peri.*

"Good," Irina said. "The phrase is *'cramma noch veala'* recited upon the correctly drawn runes which you will be familiar with. She will be here in a moment."

And then she was there, covered with blood and carrying what looked like a severed head. Velimir observed Peri from the shadow of an obsidian column and smiled wryly, feeling something akin to appreciation. *Looks like she* has *embraced the wrath in our blood.* He stepped out of the shadows, looking directly at Peri from his full height. He was not the one with the upper hand here, but he would be damned if he sniveled or groveled because of that.

"So. You have finally arrived. I have been waiting," he said.

Peri arched her eyebrow. Velimir could not read her expression at all.

"If I recall correctly, I killed you the last time I was here. You also were more opaque then," she said, waiting for an explanation.

"You did, indeed," Velimir said. "But it was you who dragged me to Dimitri's former realm. As you will recall, your mind holds sway here, whether you are able to control the process or not. Our battle undid all my hard work of gaining a corporeal form." As he spoke, Velimir fleetingly wondered where Casimir had gone. Probably hiding in one of the alcoves high in the lava rock wall of the cavern.

"That was pretty suicidal of you, brother. You deliberately coaxed me into turning into the Edge." A few drops of blood dripped from Peri's sleeve and plopped to the sulphury ground, causing a little puff of ash and a faint echo.

"Let's just say that I got a bit carried away. But enough about the past. Let's dispense with the pleasantries and discuss my deal," Velimir said.

"Your deal?" Peri's voice was flat, her grayish-green eyes regarding Velimir.

"My ambition of becoming the Lord of Wrath was everything to me. After the loss of my divinity, my hopes died. But the time of the prophecy is upon us, and the prophecy still holds true for you."

"And? I wish I had nothing to do with the damned prophecy," Peri said. "I have no interest in becoming a god, even if such a thing is possible."

Velimir felt a flash of powerful resentment. The ungrateful, pampered brat whom fate lavished with an endless cornucopia of chances and incredible fortune, while he had fought tooth and nail for everything he ever had and lost it all! And there she stood sullen and resentful, as if she wasn't the luckiest person alive! But Velimir kept his face impassive, his voice steady. This time he wouldn't let his emotions get the better of him.

"That may be the case, but it doesn't matter. You have no choice," Velimir said. "You will have to deal with it, as I am sure you have already perceived. And I know more than perhaps anyone of the Vysokian prophecies. Instead of you stumbling aimlessly around, I plan to inform you of them. For starters, I will tell you how to get out of here."

Peri seemed to consider this, then nodded. "What would you want in exchange for your help? I doubt you'd be helping me out of brotherly love and the kindness of your heart."

"What do you *think* I want?" The sneer almost made its way to his voice. "I want to live again, sister. And you can make that happen."

Peri contemplated for a long time, Velimir keeping on that impassive mask a lifetime of playing the dutiful son to Radek had trained him so well for. Then she spoke. "I see. Then there are but two questions. One. What will you do if you get your life back? Two. How do we make it happen?"

"What will I do? I don't know, not yet. I will find my destiny. I want to live again. I know that much. And how? By you willing it to happen. Here, in this old sanctuary brimming with Dimitri's latent energies, your will alone could make me alive once more."

Peri looked skeptical. "I have no doubt that pretty wild stuff can happen here…but just like that? I can resurrect people now?"

Velimir uttered an impatient sigh and looked down at Peri from his height. "Not normally. But you are in the Netherworld, where reality shifts, in the place where Dimitri had his last stand. I don't know what scene of slaughter you have just arrived from, carrying a severed head, but I wager you have arrived at another phase. The last time, you were whisked here uncontrollably, when extreme circumstances destabilized you. This time, you retain your form. Perhaps you are more capable of controlling yourself now."

Peri frowned. "I felt the Edge beckoning. But I didn't need it. I was able to take them down without it. And the next thing I knew, I was here."

"Yes. Your blood and the prophecy intensify. Fates are playing dice, and you are in the thick of the game."

Peri shrugged and tucked the dark bundle deeper in the crook of her arm. "Looks like. So…You want to live. You intend to find your own fate. Not a problem for me, as such. Maybe you don't deserve to live, but then…do I? Many are dead that deserved to live, and many undeserving keep on living. Fine. We'll do it. In return, you'll tell me more about the fucking prophecies and help me find my way back to my friends." Peri looked Velimir in the eye, now fearless and resolute. "What do I need to do?"

"Heart is the seat of a soul," Velimir said, "so put your hand where my heart would be."

Peri stepped forward and craned her neck, looking up at Velimir, gliding her hand along his shadowy outline. "Weird," she said. "I can feel you even though I can see through you. But then, everything here is weird. Next step?"

"Repeat after me," Velimir said. He was pretty sure that it would work, but he still felt an apprehensive tightness in the pit of his stomach. "I, Peri of Eilean de Taigh-Sholais, daughter of Dimitri the Fallen…"

"I, Peri of Eilean de Taigh-Sholais, daughter of Dimitri the Fallen…"

"…call forth the spark of life within you, blood of my blood…"

"…call forth the spark of life within you, blood of my blood…"

Velimir felt a faint bumping in his chest.

149

"...in the name of he who raised this sanctuary, in the name of my indomitable will and his."

"...in the name of he who raised this sanctuary, in the name of my indomitable will and his."

The bumping grew stronger, and Peri gasped as a golden shape of a physical heart started to take shape inside of Velimir's shadowy form. He closed his eyes and savoured the essence of life, the essence he could feel tingling in the electrified air between them, the essence he fervently believed had power here, the essence Peri let freely flow into him. His shady incorporeal form started to solidify, to gain substance...a strong, real body, like the one he had in life. His lungs started to draw air. Triumph filled his heart, a joy so powerful that only the mightiest of efforts prevented him from weeping. *Mother, I did it! Mother, I live again! Mother, thank you for being there for me, even in the land of death!*

"I...live! I LIVE! I swore on the ashes of my mother that I would scratch and crawl my way back into the world of the living...and now I have!"

———— • ● • ————

PERI WATCHED THE JOY AND TRIUMPH ON HER BROTHER's angular face, trying to figure out what she was feeling. Did she still resent Velimir for killing Connor? When her brother had taunted her with that beloved name, she had lost all control and embraced the wrath inside of her. But now...she didn't feel the same anger. She had seen somewhat through Velimir's strained manner. *He must have suffered a lot during the time that had passed in the land of the dead.* She doubted he would admit it if asked about it.

"I am pleased. Thank you, sister," said Velimir. His golden

eyes brimmed with sincerity.

"Anytime," said Peri. "So, tell me what you know."

"First off, I can help you to summon your companions here. If they willingly respond, you will be reunited with them."

Peri's eyes lit up. "That *definitely* would be a good place to start."

"Furthermore, in my youth, I spent much time studying the ancient Dimitrian cult and the Vysokian prophecies. Wulani and Yalifa are already running red with blood, yes... but the battles will culminate in a besieged city of Shinaris at the edge of the desert. It is there that you must go, where the first step of the prophecy will unfold." Velimir leaned back on a jagged obsidian formation and crossed his arms.

Peri blew out a long breath. "You are right. Best take the fight to them. I did try to hide and blend in when I was in Yalifa. They found me. And they will come back." Razeem had said as much. According to travelers from Wulani, the war had escalated—Dimitri's offspring hunting each other, some of them trying to protect themselves or hide, others on the offense.

"Getting out of here is not that simple, though," Velimir said. "Dimitri has seen to that. The way to Shinaris from Dimitri's sanctuary goes through the Theater of Time. It is a place where time and space distort. A place that catches the Dreamer's wayward thoughts, forgotten dreams, and memories lost in time, making them physical reality. 'The infinity is but a stage, and all the Dreamer's children merely players,' it says. Dimitri constructed the place before his fall. Now it serves as his gateway to the Hereworld."

Naturally there had to be some obstacle in their path.

"Okay, well, let's worry about that once my friends are here. Ewynne will come, and the paladins, they swore an oath to me..." Peri bit her lip and her eyes welled. She glanced at the head cradled in her arms. Genjiro would never come to her again.

Velimir smirked. "A trophy?"

His amusement irritated Peri. "It is no trophy! I just...it's none of your business. I didn't want to leave.... him for them to find." She whispered the last words and looked down at her boots. Then she tossed her hair behind her shoulder and stared at Velimir. "Let's do it, then! Call them here. Ha, they'll be surprised to see *you*!"

19
ASGARD

Jelena emerged from a crack in a rough, steep cliff. Just moments ago, she had stepped into a hidden cavern behind a waterfall where the primordial elven forests of Silva Lunari merged with the ocean and the Otherworld. She knew she was far, far away from Silva Lunari and even farther away from the Valley of the Lilies of the Elysian Fields that she called home now.

Before reaching the elven lands, Jelena had journeyed on River Vuolas through the Plains of the Eternal Hunt, trading her services as a healer and a priestess. She had made exhaustive inquiries among the elves and finally been able to find her way to the secret passageway to Asgard—the home of these 'Northmen' whose magical tree she hoped had given Kiril his magic back. Otherwise, her lover was most likely a listlessly shuffling shade. Anxiety nipped at her, but she firmly told it to go away. She had found her destination, and if Kiril had gotten the message, he might be somewhere here, too. Now was not the time to wallow.

The scenery was breathtaking. The wild nature was sharp in its clear contrasts. Steep mountains with snowy tops, dark narrow fjords and grassy fields bathing in the sharp light of the midsummer sun. The clank of weapons, the roar of the fighters, and the thud of the feet on the ground could be heard everywhere. She even heard curious sounds echoing from somewhere—a rapid succession of loud, sharp pangs, accompanied by screams of pain and rage.

Jelena frowned. Who was fighting here? Was Asgard under assault? The fighting seemed chaotic, with no clear purpose or sides, just small groups of warriors fighting each other gleefully with intense vigor. Some of the warriors wore familiar armor and insignia. Jelena thought she spotted the ragged battle standard of Lughani Vos and the uniforms of a Varidomoan mercenary company the Stribog Citadel had employed to supplement its own forces with on occasion. There also were warriors donned in Morishiman gear, like Tomoe's familial armor, and wielding the narrow skillfully crafted blades—katana. Most of the uniforms and weapons, however, were completely unfamiliar to her.

Nobody paid attention to her in the midst of the roaring and the clatter, so she quietly walked to the edge of a tall spruce forest. She touched the dove amulet hanging overtop her sand brown clerical robes and mouthed Milostra's prayer. *"Mir. Samilost. Oprost."* Not only did the shadow of the spruces shield her from attention, it was also pleasantly cooling in the midday heat. Not long after, she spotted a person cautiously advancing at the edge of the forest. *Could it be…?*

The small, gaunt man was awkwardly holding a cross-bow that was loaded but pointed to the ground. Jelena stopped in her tracks and got tears in her eyes, a huge wave of relief washing over her. *Kiril! Beloved!* But she dared not shout. The fighters didn't seem to discriminate. The invaders would assume that Kiril and Jelena were among the denizens of Asgard, while the defenders would probably assume they were the enemy. It was heartbreaking to see Kiril so hesitant. There was little left of the sleek, sardonic confidence he had radiated in life that had been so attractive to her. *Obviously, he hasn't got his magic back. It's almost as if a limb has been amputated from him.*

In moments, Kiril noticed her. The crossbow dropped from his hand, and his mouth hung open. Jelena threw all caution to the wind and ran to him, taking him in her embrace. Kiril fiercely hugged her back, pressing his face against her chest, inhaling deeply. Then he looked up, laughing and shedding tears at the same time.

"You found your way here," Jelena said. "We are together now. All will be well. Velimir—"

A shadow crossed Kiril's face, and he averted his eyes. "You...know everything, don't you?" he whispered.

"I know, beloved," Jelena said. "I have been watching when you were thinking about me. Or trying not to."

"Jelena..." Kiril said, face still downcast. He hesitated for a moment, looking for words to explain himself and failing. "I just...I just didn't want to be so *hurt*."

"I know. Listen, we—"

But before Jelena had time to finish her sentence, somebody leaped from a depression behind the spruces—a huge man, wearing a bearskin on his shoulders and waving a bloodied war axe.

"Ha! Assassins! Spoiled your ambush! Meet true steel!" the man bellowed. He charged and slashed the blade at Kiril.

Kiril instinctively tried to launch a spell trigger but realized his mistake and grabbed at the dagger at his belt, trying to dodge the blow. It was too late. The axe cut Kiril's neck clean, nearly severing his head. His body slumped to the ground. Both Jelena and the large man stared at it in disbelief.

"What a slow assassin," the berserker warrior said, frowning. "How curious."

"You...you!" Jelena shouted, reaching a point of rage she had rarely felt. After being accepted as a favoured devotee of Lord Milostra, she had served as an initiate in the planar monastery of the Order of the Palm. Milostra's clergy didn't believe in violence, but they needed to be able to defend themselves and the defenseless.

The bemused berserker was still frowning and looking at Kiril's lumped corpse, so Jelena punched him in the throat with far more force than would be necessary to render the target helpless. The small spot was directly in the junction of the body's energy ways. Her punch knocked the berserker backwards, and she kicked him in the groin.

"Why did you have to kill him, you bastard?" growled Jelena, grabbing the man's hair and punching him, again and again, unleashing her fury on her own cold-eyed sneering father, on Radek, his superficial glib charm that so quickly turned into cruelty. She punched and punched while hearing nothing but the roar of her own blood in her ears. She continued long after the man was quiet, his face a raw, bloody mess.

Jelena didn't spare another look at the fallen berserker but threw herself over Kiril's dead body, weeping her eyes out, clutching Kiril's shoulders. Some of Milostra's favoured devotees knew how to resurrect if the soul had not departed too long ago, but she didn't have that kind of power yet. She wondered where Kiril's soul was now. *In Manala, alone and lost?* Despair gripped her, and she wallowed in it when someone tapped her shoulder. A freckled blonde girl of perhaps sixteen, wearing a too big horned helmet askew on her head and wielding a too long spear. She held the reins of a beautiful winged horse which snorted behind her. The girl had already hauled the raw and bloodied body of the berserker onto the horse's back.

"Excuse me. I am here to collect the dead!"

"Over my dead body are you taking him!" Jelena snarled, tears still flowing down her cheeks. She gripped Kiril's shirt with her numb and bloodied fists.

"But...he was slain here. I will take him to Valhalla. No big deal. He'll make it to dinner." The girl looked quizzically at Jelena. "You don't know where you are, do you? I hear it often happens to souls that are drawn here, but they...never look like you."

Jelena tried to piece together the girl's words. "I confess I sought Asgard out, but I swear we had nothing to do with the invasion."

"Invasion?" The girl frowned. Then she smiled and extended her hand to Jelena. "There is no invasion. People here attack everyone, because that's what we do. We live for the joy and glory of war! Anyone slain on these fields in battle will be taken to the halls of Valhalla and resurrected good as new. That is my task, mine and other Valkyries. I am Auri."

Resurrection? Hope sprang to Jelena's mind. She clambered up, smoothing her blood-soaked robes. *What a sacrilege, my Lord! Forgive me!* She helped Auri haul Kiril's corpse up. "Where did all these fighters come from, then?"

"Lord Odin welcomes all who loved war in life to Valhalla. They seem to find their way here naturally," Auri said. "But anyway, there is a festive meal on the schedule, and your man will be in perfect health to attend. Jump behind me and hold tight!"

20
DIMITRI'S SANCTUARY

EWYNNE WAS BITING HER FISTS, HER CHEEKS WHITE AND tear-stained. The candle on her nightstand was about to sputter out. Kauno, who was sleeping in Peri's bed, had suggested she try to get some rest. But Ewynne could not. Today, Ewynne and Kauno had waited in the inn in case Peri and Genjiro found their way back, while the paladins had searched from the surrounding hills, using their *plavosvetljo* spell. They had returned empty-handed and exhausted and were now sleeping. Peri and Genjiro seemed to have vanished into thin air.

Suddenly Ewynne heard a disembodied voice.

cramma noch vae bzzzt

Crackling and hissing noise. It sounded like Peri's voice?

cramma noch ve...fuck! bzzt

An exasperated, deep and resonant male voice spoke. "*Cramma noch veala.* It can't be that difficult, can it?" it said.

"Well fuck you too. I never studied Vysokian! But... Ewynne! Ewynne? Can you hear me?"

The tension on Ewynne's face erupted into a joyous smile. "I can! Peri! Is it you? You are alive!"

"It would appear. But I'm...in the Abyss...again. Listen, would you guys come to me? I know where we need to go!" Peri sounded manic, speaking faster than usual.

"Come to you? To the Abyss? What the hell, Peri?"

"Well, I'm in a place that is safe for now...I can summon you here if you are willing to come. If not, though...I'm not sure if I can get out of here on my own."

"Of course. Of course we'll come. I'll gather the others. Wait."

Ewynne roused the others, explaining what had happened. They asked no questions. The paladins were soldiers, trained to act without question when there was urgency required. They wordlessly grabbed their gear and followed. Kauno, though still wearing her slippers and nightgown, took the news in stride, like she took everything.

"*Cramma noch veala*! You still there?"

"I'm still here." Ewynne could see the mix of relief and puzzlement on her companions' faces.

Peri's voice came through once again. "So, everyone, listen. Deeply appreciate it if you came to join me in the Abyss. This place is safe for now, and with your help, I'll get out...and more. You have to accept the summons, and it will work."

Razeem had cast *plavosvetljo,* mouthing the words soundlessly, while the others gathered their gear. He nodded his satisfaction. "No illusions or deception. It is Peri's voice, and I detect no hostile intent. Peri, I will come to you, as

160

I've pledged."

"As will I," said Jussuf.

Kauno shrugged and smiled. "Kauno is curious to see where we end up this time."

"And I will always come when you need me, Peri," said Ewynne.

"Okay, great, but there's just one—"

But the disorienting vortex had already sucked them in.

———————— • ● • ————————

RAZEEM AL-FAROUQ HAD SEEN HIS FAIR SHARE OF DE-mons, walking dead, and illusions created by skillful magicians. He had traveled through portals—stationary ones, as well as those conjured hastily in the thick of combat. He was familiar with the momentary disorienting lurch in the stomach caused by teleporting through space. Neverthe-less, he had never left the Hereworld behind and liked to think of himself as a down-to-earth, practical man. He spe-cialized in counter-magic techniques, but as any seasoned paladin, had sweated and bled in battles against creatures from the Abyss. However, this time he would enter hell it-self—or at least a secluded pocket of it where Peri's unsta-ble divine essence held sway.

After the brief period traveling through space in fluid form at warp speed, the party materialized in a vast cavern filled with obsidian rock formations, furniture carved of rock, dry sand, sulphureous puddles, and ominous archways high up in the gallery. The cavern walls glowed eerily.

And there was Peri. She welcomed them with a bemused expression on her face—which, as well as her clothes, was completely covered with cracking dried blood. She cradled something dark in her arms and was accompanied by the largest man Razeem had ever seen. The man had bronze skin like most of the natives of Wulani. His head was bald, and he had sharp, angular cheekbones. There was a determined, triumphant smile on his face. His eyes shined like amber and gold, glowing in the dark. *Almost like the proverbial furnaces of hell.* Razeem shuddered. He knew who this was.

Ewynne gasped. "Velimir! Peri, what is this?"

Peri smiled awkwardly. "Well, I sort of resurrected him, and—"

"You did what?!" Ewynne interrupted, a terrified expression on her face.

"I had to! He helped me, otherwise I would be stuck here," Peri said, frowning. "And he told me what we need to do about the prophecy. He has studied them because he wanted to fulfil them."

Jussuf reached for the handle of his mace. "This…thing, this vile beast! It is not even undead…it is an abomination! Peri, what have you done?"

Razeem knew that Peri's volatility and comfort level with violence often shocked Jussuf, who was worried about what would become of her. Nevertheless, Jussuf, who before joining the Order of the Eye had an extremely formal and conformist upbringing, found the young woman fascinating, and, Razeem suspected, attractive.

"Do not call me 'thing,' paladin." Speaking in his deep, booming voice, Velimir stared the young man down, as if he wanted to make sure that Jussuf knew exactly how much taller Velimir was than he.

"But 'vile beast' is just fine, is it, brother?" asked Peri, a hint of a smile in her eyes.

Velimir's tension eased a little, and he almost seemed to smile.

"This…this body of flesh is moments old," said Kauno, reaching her arm towards Velimir, still wearing slippers and a night gown with a massive backpack slung over her shoulder. Her sinewy arms were surprisingly strong. "You were a wraith before, weren't you…Velimir?" Kauno's face only conveyed neutral interest, even though she knew well enough who Velimir was and of Peri's history with him.

"Indeed. All my hard work of reforming myself was undone after certain…unfortunate events," Velimir said.

"That is not what normally happens to spirits of Valkamans once they depart," said the frowning Kauno. "I believe your body must have channeled so much of your divine sire's power that it dissolved at the moment of your death."

"No matter," said Velimir. "Now it is back with all its vigor and strength!" He crossed his arms at the waist and smiled with narrowed eyes.

Ewynne had been blinking back tears, staring at the two in disbelief. Her eyes focused on the bundle in Peri's arms. "What is that, Peri?" she asked.

"That," said Peri levelly, glaring at the party, "is Genjiro's head."

"Genjiro?" asked Velimir with a sudden, sharp interest. "You are carrying the head of someone called Genjiro? Hanamori Genjiro?"

"That, apparently, was his last name," said Peri. "He sought me out, befriended me, and then betrayed me. He is dead now."

Velimir's eyebrows raised a little, but he remained silent.

"I always knew there was something not right with

Genjiro!" Jussuf exclaimed. "Something was *off*. He acted like a shady merchant, all his tales about the underworld... but he was highborn. It was in his gestures and speech patterns. Subtle, as the customs of Morishimans are different. But I had an upbringing like that, too. I just couldn't put my finger on it. By Juris!" He grimaced. "Had I only—"

"It doesn't matter now!" Peri snapped. "He is dead and gone, and I won't discuss it more than that. I will tell you guys what you need to know later. Not now. We need to go into some...theater that can fuck with memories and stuff, or something, and then there should be a means to get out of here. Velimir told me how to summon you here and about the theater. In exchange for that, he...no longer is dead." Peri shrugged, then glanced at Velimir. "So, I suppose this concludes our business, brother. If there isn't anything else—"

"As it happens," Velimir said. "I have something more to ask you."

"So tell me," said Peri, looking at him.

"Take me with you. To Valkama. To travel as your companion."

"Are you out of your *fucking* mind?" asked Ewynne. Unlike Peri, she rarely used profanity.

"You want *me* to take *you*...to travel *with* me?" asked Peri. "Why *ever* would I do that?" While the words were incredulous and indignant, her voice was not. There was a strange gleam in her eyes that had been there ever since the party had reunited with her in the Abyss.

Velimir straightened his shoulders, making him appear even taller. "As I said, I know more about the Vysokian prophecies than probably anyone. I don't think you want to waste time stumbling about when divine powers are playing dice with your fate. I could help you. And I am a warrior of no small ability. I have only grown stronger by my stay in the Abyss," Velimir said. He shrugged and half-smiled. "There's also that I doubt you will make it through the theater and to Shinaris without my help, unless one of you is an expert in Dimitrian lore, fluent in Vysokian."

Jussuf was about to open his mouth and protest, but Peri shot him a warning look. She started to laugh. "Hey, the more the merrier," she said. "Why not? You are a strong warrior, and you have everything to gain by being at my side."

Razeem spoke for the first time. "You...you would bring such a danger amongst us? When we don't even know what exactly the ritual of resurrection entailed—what he *is*? I find this alarming. How can you trust this man, knowing what he is capable of?" His deep and cultured voice brimmed with concern. Peri may have seen horrors and killed her fair share of men and creatures, but she also was barely grown up—younger than Razeem's eldest daughter. And, Razeem feared, liked to play with fire.

Peri averted her eyes and kicked a small rock. "I don't trust him. But it is entirely correct that he is the consummate expert about this motherfucking place and the motherfucking prophecy. Right now, we can use all the help we can get," Peri said.

"I have no intention of harming any of you," said Velimir. "On the contrary, I will follow Peri and help her."

The rest of the company looked less than reassured, but Peri skipped to Jussuf and yanked her backpack off his shoulder. "Oh, by the way...I have a little joining present for you, Velimir. Look!"

Velimir watched her unwrap an oblong object strapped

to the backpack. He gasped as he recognized it. "You kept it. My old sword."

"Yeah," Peri said. "Way too big for me, but I couldn't bring myself to get rid of it. Catch!"

"It would appear that introductions are not necessary on my part," said Velimir, enjoying the weight of his old brutal greatsword like a friend's embrace. "But what should I call the rest of you?"

"If you must address me, you may call me Jussuf. Jussuf al-Rasid," said the young paladin, through gritted teeth.

"And my name is Razeem al-Farouq. Well met…Velimir," said the older one. Having expressed his concerns, he decided to default to courtesy.

"And Kauno…is Kauno!" said Kauno and took a few twirling dancing steps. "Kauno's little friend here is called Varpu." The bird glanced at Velimir, then continued to indifferently perch on Kauno's shoulder.

"Is he now a powerful Dimitrian spawn again?" asked Ewynne, eyes still dark and large, staring at Peri. "I know that you needed his help and we had no idea what we were doing, but still…I can't *believe* that you did this."

"You can, and you should, address me directly, little sister," said Velimir. "And no, it did not return my divinity. It was a breath of life, made possible by the power of hers." As ecstatic as he was about getting his life back, there was pain, too. His goal of ascending as the Lord of Wrath had been everything to him. Indeed, it had seemed like his sole reason to live, but apparently, it wasn't quite that simple. He had pursued living again as relentlessly as he once had pursued godhood, purely out of instinct. Now, Velimir had no idea of what would become of him and what would be worthy of his efforts.

Peri seemed to read his mind. "Look, Velimir, if it is any consolation, I would trade places with you anytime," she said. "Well, at least in that you could have all the divinity I have. While I think your plan to start the war was raving mad, I really don't care. I don't see it as my grand duty to stop you or anything. I just want to be left alone."

"And this is where we disagree, lady," said Razeem.

"Yes, Razeem," Peri answered. "But Velimir, the reasons I ever wanted to stop you were strictly personal. What I'm trying to say is…ah, I don't *know* what I'm trying to say! The bottom line is that I'm trying to make you realize that having this divinity is not worth being jealous of."

Before Velimir could reply, the nervous Casimir appeared from behind a stalagmite and started to fidget and tug at Velimir's sleeve.

"What is *that?*" asked Peri. She and the rest of the crew stared at the imp.

Casimir seemed even more nervous because of the attention and made anxious eyes at Velimir, tugging at him intently.

"Me'se talk a little with me's best friend, yes?" the imp said, glancing fearfully at Peri.

"Um. Can I have a moment with…Casimir here?" said Velimir as nonchalantly as he could manage.

"Casimir." Peri's expression was blank.

"I'll introduce him in a moment," Velimir said, realizing that he was now associated with the silly imp and gritting his teeth in annoyance.

"By all means," answered Peri, smiling a little.

The imp and the large, golden-eyed warrior took a few

steps aside. "The new master's here now, and Casimir all shy and scared and what if the red-head kick and hit poor Casimir and not like Casimir?"

Velimir felt the headache again. The evil, intimidating Velimir was supposed to be reassuring and comforting to a silly imp because it was afraid of his sister? But the pleading look in Casimir's eyes was just too much to ignore.

"Casimir, I'm sure she will not be like that. She is actually nicer than I am—"

"Oh no, oh no! No-one nicer than Velimir! Velimir me's all best friend in all world forever, oh yes!" Casimir hugged Velimir.

Velimir gritted his teeth. "Casimir, perhaps you could introduce yourself to Peri—"

"Wait wait wait! Is me'se birthday! Me's made a big big big cake all 1347 candles, yes! Me'se give everybody cake and then everybody likes Casimir, yes?" His eyes were so full of hope.

Velimir sighed. "No doubt they will."

"And me makes pancakes, too, yes?" The imp seemed to be his happy self again.

"And the pancakes, too," answered Velimir in a mild voice, in defeat.

While the imp went to hassle with his conjurings, Velimir addressed the perplexed group, aware of the blush on his cheeks.

"Before you ask, that...imp was Dimitri's 'faithful companion.' He has been waiting for Dimitri to come back ever since his last stand," Velimir said.

"An imp for a companion," Peri said. "Makes sense, I guess. They do have demon blood."

"Since you have a sufficient amount of divine essence to remind him of Dimitri, I guess you are his new master now. His name is Casimir. Oh, and he has a birthday today. He has already made a cake with 1347 candles. And he is busy conjuring pancakes. He is capable of conjuring food and other material things while in the Abyss," explained Velimir in a monotonous voice.

"Birthday? That is ridiculous!" exclaimed Jussuf.

"Awww, Jussuf. I think it's kind of cute," Ewynne said.

"We are supposed to eat a…birthday cake of that ridiculous creature?" continued Jussuf, as if looking for something he would be justified to be indignant about.

"You are far more ridiculous than the imp, paladin!" retorted Velimir. "And surely it won't hurt too much to eat the cake and pretend to be grateful? He's actually a pretty good cook." His face warmed, and he pretended to cough. What was he doing? Defending the stupid imp to Peri's group?

"Kauno would never say no to a birthday cake and pancakes," Kauno said. Her sparrow friend seemed to nod in agreement.

When Casimir arrived with the mighty cake, levitating it, Peri spoke to him. "Hello, Casimir. I wish you a happy birthday. Um, how do you think we are going to blow out all those candles?"

"Great one! New master, maybe? Casimir littlest companion!"

"Yes, I know. Velimir told me. Want me to help you blow them out?"

"Yes, oh yes! You'se nice, too?"

"On occasion." Peri smiled with a gentle look in her eyes. If a cake could be divine, this one met the mark. And the birthday was excellent, considering the circumstances. Everybody eyed Velimir warily, and he sat away from them, but at least Casimir seemed happy.

PART THREE
PERI AND VELIMIR

"We are the Pilgrims, master; we shall go
— Always a little further: it may be
Beyond that last blue mountain barred with snow,
— Across that angry or that glimmering sea,
White on a throne or guarded in a cave
— There lives a prophet who can understand
Why men were born: but surely we are brave,
— Who make the Golden Journey to Samarkand."
— James Elroy Flecker, *The Golden Journey to Samarkand*

21
THE THEATER OF TIME

"*Va gremaccha stuggyocha rach, thea lagramas cha ra sammarach*," Peri recited. She kept glancing at Velimir for affirmation. A stone slab slid away with a grinding noise and revealed an ominous archway into a winding corridor. The others startled, but Velimir clapped his hands and nodded.

"Here we go!" he exclaimed. "'The infinity is but a stage, and all the Dreamer's children merely players.' Gods know I kept trying out the phrase while waiting for you, but the passageway must have remained dormant, because Dimitri's blood is no longer present in me. But now…we are ready to proceed to the Theater of Time!"

Peri glanced at Razeem. "Do your thing, will you? Is this real?" Whenever they had encountered magic in any form in the past, Razeem's ability to discern illusions and counteract magic had been invaluable.

Razeem cast *platosvetljo*. He uttered the phrase and waited for a moment for something to materialize from under dispelled illusion. He frowned. "It is...but it is not," he said.

Peri rolled her eyes. "How very fucking helpful."

"I suspect this has to do with the nature of the Abyss," Razeem continued, ignoring her. "Illusions and conjurations are easier to detect and neutralize when reality is as solid as it is in the Hereworld. Here, matter works differently. There is little I can do with this."

Peri bit her lip. "Yeah, that makes sense." She paused. "Sorry, I was being an ass. You came to the fucking Abyss when I needed you, and nothing here works as normal. I guess there is little to do but to just walk in then. Be on guard, everyone."

She started to walk, sword drawn, aware of her companions at her back. After a few minutes of walking down the corridor, it took a sharp turn to the left. They stood in front of a heavy purple velvet curtain. Peri pulled it aside.

They entered a stage with a dusty piano pushed to one side. A few books levitated in midair, pages fluttering idly, specks of dust circling around them. Someone had tossed a bunch of chess pieces onto the stage. The place where the audience should be was pitch dark. The party took a few hesitant steps. A bright spotlight lit a seat in the audience, and a shadow stood. It was vaguely man-shaped and started to advance. As it approached, its face became more corporeal, gaining more character and features. It was a middle-aged man, flushed face, thick eyebrows, and a crooked smile.

"What do you want?" Peri asked.

"You don't even remember, do you?" said the thing, its

voice sounding metallic and muffled at the same time.

"Should I?" Peri asked.

"Why should you—that is the question," the man said, gradually becoming more solid. "Why should you, you who spread death and misery in your wake? But we all have to start somewhere..."

It stepped back in the shadows, and a luminous and transparent scene started to play out in front of the party's eyes. A younger Peri, her face softer, unfinished. Her step light, the familiar glossy veil of reddish-brown hair bouncing behind her back. She skipped on a dwindling alleyway in the outskirts of Lughani Vos. The city gate loomed in the distance.

"The carnival day, a bit of wine and fun, on your own in the big city...a lass of sixteen years," the muffled voice sneered from the darkness.

"Silas the Slick," Peri said, her jaw stiffening.

The scene, frozen in the air, started to unfold again. Peri stopped by a lone street lamp, waiting in the shadows. The man from the audience that had been the wraith moments before, his step unsteady from drink, stopped to urinate. Peri swiftly stepped next to him, bringing her dagger to his throat. "Enough," she said in a low, quiet voice. "You'll feed the alley rats now." She slit the man's throat and laughed in delight. Her soft, young face looked harder and older as her eyes flashed red. She sat on the fallen corpse and *hacked hacked hacked* the chest, plunging the dagger *again again again.* The blood sprayed on the cobblestones and on the wall of the adjoining shack and on her clothes and face. And she laughed.

Peri scoffed. "Motherfucker, you so had it coming."

"Did I? Perhaps I did," laughed the gleeful ghost. "That's what you told yourself, but didn't it feel wonderful to murder me? When you slipped by the pier for a swim and washed the blood away, stole a gown off a laundry line, and took the boat back to Eilean de Taigh-Sholais, didn't you savour the memory? Weren't you, secretly, grateful that you had found someone loathsome enough that you had an excuse to savagely murder him?"

"You beat the hookers black and blue! You branded them with iron! You knocked their teeth out! You severed Liseanne's arm from her body when you found out she was moonlighting! You'd buy girls as young as ten years old from desperate mothers!" Peri shouted, her hand gripping her sword.

"I did, I did," the ghost laughed. "You should thank me for giving you permission to do what you had always wanted to do, always dreamed of doing."

"As. I. Said," Peri spoke through gritted teeth, "You. Had. It. Coming."

"He did! No question about that, Peri of Eilean de Taigh-Sholais." A female voice, echoing like howling wind in a narrow corridor, rang from the gallery. The spotlight focused on a wraith of a woman. As she advanced towards the stage, her visage became more corporeal, but it still was gaunt and pale, the eyes sunken in the face. The woman wore rags and only had one arm. "But did *I* have it coming?"

"Liseanne." Peri stepped back. "We were…friends…and when I saw what he had done to your arm, I couldn't tolerate it anymore."

The woman uttered a sharp little laugh. "*You* could not tolerate it? *You* felt angry? So, then you went and butchered him and rowed back to the island of abundance, to your loving family. You never saw me again. You never sacrificed another thought to me, did you?"

"I...you weren't around anymore..." Peri's posture sagged a bit.

"See, Silas was a monster, but I was completely dependent on him! What do you imagine a one-armed hooker does for a living once she loses her only protector? There are no freelancing hookers in Lughani Vos. And what of the other girls? Another man took Silas' place, and he was even more cruel. Me, he cast away. I sold myself for scraps of food to those who would still have me when I was diseased. I starved, wasted away!"

The ghost woman was right. The thought of consequences had never even occurred to Peri—before or after the so very satisfying murder of Silas the Slick. Peri didn't know what to say. 'Sorry' seemed insulting.

Liseanne shot Peri a look of utter contempt. "So many dead because of you! Tejero's enemies! Highway bandits! Bounty hunters! Dimitrian spawn! Beasts, monsters, cold-blooded killers, what does it matter? You murder as others breathe!"

There was a murmur of near silent death rattles emerging from hundreds of throats, like a giant wave approaching from the distance, steadily getting louder. The full audience glowed eerily now, a wraith sitting in every seat. They rattled. They started to rise. They approached as a wave. Hundreds of them.

Peri's band of fighters hacked and slashed. Peri darted back and forth, her clever feints wasted on the mass of wraiths. Velimir laughed and roared, mowing the things with his greatsword. Razeem kept slashing at them from behind his shield with his scimitar. Whenever the wraiths brushed by, there was a numbing chill and a sapping feeling, as if Peri died a little, as if they had nipped and stolen a bite of the time she had left, hastened the death and decay hiding in any living thing's bones. The enchantment in her blade caused the shades to diminish, and eventually evaporate, but there were so *many* of them! Occasionally, a fleeting memory jolted her. Some of the faces were familiar. Ewynne did her best to hinder the wraiths and encase the warriors with her protective spells. Peri fought and fought, but her arms finally started to wobble, and the chill from the brushes with the wraiths crept deep in her marrow. There was no end to the things. They just kept coming. A blind, red rage tugged behind her eyes.

Then the sun seemed to rise behind their backs and filled the room, illuminated every corner of it. And with it, the wraiths disappeared. Peri panted and kept blinking in the light. The piano, books, and chess pieces were gone. There was just the empty stage and the gallery.

"Whoa," she said, letting the sun warm her. "So that's the incantation you told me about, Jussuf?"

The young paladin nodded proudly, sweat pouring down his forehead. "Invocation of the Dawn. It is an exhausting ritual, and we have used it to clear undead-infested places... but nothing like this."

"Good job having prepared it," Peri said.

"We had no idea where you were," Ewynne said. "We tried to prepare for anything. Undead, mages, demons...you name it. But I admit, I wasn't prepared for *this*."

Kauno walked to Peri and touched her arm. "You are

quite drained, honey. We all are. It seems our valiant crew has passed a trial of some sort. But healing and recuperating before moving on would seem prudent. And lucky for us, we have our camping gear with us, and Casimir is capable of conjuring food in the Abyss."

Velimir flexed his fingers, eyes alight. "The joy of combat! I am of true flesh and blood!" Then he frowned. "During the fight, I felt the creatures sap my life force, as undead do... but I feel drained no longer. The fatigue is gone!"

Peri arched her eyebrow. "Huh. I'm as knackered as ever after dealing with undead."

The siblings' words seemed to alarm Jussuf and Ewynne. But Kauno just smiled. "The ritual of resurrection—a willingly given breath of life in the heart of your divine sire's domain—who knows what it has begotten? It remains to be seen, and Kauno certainly is curious."

———————•●•———————

"YOU NEVER TOLD ME THAT YOU KILLED THAT PIMP," Ewynne said. It was hard to tell if she was offended by the fact. She hadn't smiled at Peri once since being summoned to the Abyss. "I remember when it was—that time when you went off on your own after the carnival."

"It wasn't something I wanted to advertise." Peri kept fiddling with the buckle of her boot while everyone was making themselves as comfortable as they were able to on the floorboards of the Theater, spreading bedrolls and leaning on abandoned stage props.

"You can tell me anything. Actually, until now, I always assumed you did." Ewynne didn't sound angry. More dejected.

178

Peri wanted Ewynne to understand. "It...it's not just that I did it. You would have understood why. Knowing what he had done, how he reveled in his cruelty. It was that I loved it so much." Peri shrugged. "Oh well, not like I haven't killed a shit ton of people since. Which is, I guess, what this meta-physical mindfuck place is trying to hint at, or something. But what is the point?"

Razeem spoke up, having only been listening thus far. "I'd wager that it is about the gravity of taking life, Peri. You have killed many...I have as well, in your service and other-wise...and we will have to answer for it in the end." His kind eyes regarded her. "It might have been the right thing to do, or just the only thing to do in order to survive, but there are always consequences. No blood is shed without the multi-verse taking note. Taking a life—even as vile a life as that of the pimp you murdered—creates a ripple in the pond and has unforeseen consequences."

Jussuf had been crouching next to Razeem, muttering his healing spells above a frostily glowing scratch a wraith had left on Razeem's forearm. Razeem's healing skills were rudimentary—he had dedicated himself to countering mag-ic—while Jussuf had pursued healing and repelling undead. The younger paladin spoke up. "But surely sometimes it is the just and righteous thing to do! Slaying the truly evil is what must be done."

"Yes, sometimes it is necessary. But it is never a thing to be taken lightly, or a thing you should be happy about. It is a solemn duty," answered Razeem, sadness in his eyes.

"I hate killing," Ewynne said and shivered. "I have gotten more used to it, maybe...but it doesn't get easier."

Peri guessed it didn't at that. The adventure part of their

life Ewynne liked almost as much as Peri did, but violence was another matter.

"Your Dimitrian blood doesn't run as strong," Peri said to Ewynne, then glanced at Velimir and smiled a little. "You did an impressive job out there, brother. Not that I suspected any different."

"Thank you, sister," said Velimir, trying not to sound too grateful. He felt the tension and suspicion in the group, but Peri seemed to react amazingly well to him. Of course, she didn't trust him—why ever would she—but she was courteous and even joked a little here and there. What was her angle? Was she trying to get him to feel comfortable, perhaps reveal more of himself than he had intended, make himself vulnerable or dependent on her? He would of course assist Peri as their interests were aligned for now, but he'd not volunteer information or insight until it was prudent to do so. Peri may have led a sheltered life, but clearly Velimir had underestimated her. She had been capable of keeping secrets long before Velimir had shattered the idyll of her existence.

"Hopefully, nothing too fucked up happens when we sleep here. Not that there's a choice. We need rest after that battle. Is anybody hungry?" Peri asked.

As several of her companions nodded, Casimir started to conjure tea and sandwiches, fussing and humming out of tune so badly, Velimir started rubbing his forehead.

"My lady? May I have a word with you? In private?" Jussuf asked Peri.

The paladin's expression was hard to read. She nodded, and the two of them retreated off to one side. Velimir watched them, straining his hearing in curiosity. He couldn't hear the words, but the discussion seemed to be intense.

Peri looked somewhat anxious, and increasingly angry. They talked rapidly, waving their hands and frowning. When they came back, both stared straight ahead and ignored each other.

"My lady." Velimir grimaced in distaste. The way the paladin kept looking at his sister...well, why wouldn't the git be impressed with the daughter of wrath—Velimir's fellow "mongrel"—one of Dimitri's true progeny? Velimir had no doubt who he liked the least in the group. It also was surprising that Peri was traveling with two paladins. While the old man wasn't nearly as irritating as the younger one, he likely had a rigid mind and limited imagination. The eccentric with a sparrow perched on her shoulder seemed harmless—even silly—but Velimir could tell that she had power and wisdom. While the other party members had seemed wide-eyed and overwhelmed with the hellish realm, for Kauno it seemed to be just another location, just another campfire or crossroads inn or walled city. Her attitude was that of open-minded curiosity. So far, she didn't seem to have a problem with Velimir's presence.

And then there was Ewynne. Her Dimitrian blood was the result of a mating with a mundane woman—thus she was not remarkable as such. But she was important to Peri, and if that was the case, there probably was more to her than met the eye. Ewynne had shown nothing but courage in their battle against the wraiths. Velimir wished she wasn't so hostile to him, and then berated himself for feeling so. What did he care what some goody-two-shoes lesser sibling thought about him? But the feeling nagged all the same.

Casimir's conjured flames died down, and the group started to retreat to their bedrolls, but Velimir could not get to sleep. He sat alone, staring ahead, viscerally grateful for living again but feeling such a confusing turmoil inside. Casimir hovered nearby, shooting worried glances at him but opting to be quiet. Suddenly, Peri tossed her blanket aside and walked to Velimir, sitting across from him. She frowned slightly and gazed at him with eyes like the sea on an overcast day.

"Brother, did you...did you really enjoy killing Connor?"

Velimir's first instinct was to say that he did, to keep his facade. But another part of him wanted to be truthful, to get closer to Peri.

"Truth to be told, sister...not at all. I thought that I would, but I didn't." He hoped the answer would not make her consider him weak. It was unnerving that she even asked the question. Again, it felt like she could see much more than Velimir was comfortable with.

"Well, you paid the price. I will not hold it against you anymore. Though I hope you'll one day understand what a horrible waste of a great life it was." There was no venom in her voice. It sounded like a heart-felt truth.

Velimir could not come up with an adequate response, so they sat quietly for a while. He wondered what Peri would make of his pathetic attempt to save her when they both were just infants, she just a babe in arms. Amusement? Disdain? Pity? None of those were something Velimir cared to be on the receiving end of. She was too young to remember, and Velimir was not about to remind her of another thing he had failed at. Nor did he have proof, in case she suspected him of manipulation or garnering of sympathy.

"The young paladin. Is there going to be a problem?" Velimir then asked.

"I don't know. Look, Velimir, I know he seems like a pompous ass. But that is not all there is to him. There is decency, and courage, and genuine willingness to do the right thing even when it's inconvenient...but, what I came to say to you in the first place was that don't sit alone, apart from the others. If you are part of the group, I don't want you singled out. Goodnight, Velimir."

And with that, she walked away.

— • • —

STILL GROGGY FROM SLEEP, THE PARTY HAD EATEN A conjured breakfast, gathered their gear, and started to explore their environment further. At the end of the gallery there was a narrow door. When Peri opened it, they were greeted by the sight of a wide chasm and an oppressing heat. Deep below flowed steaming and hissing lava alongside obsidian rocks. A rickety, translucent bridge traversed the chasm, obscured by shadows in midair.

Peri glanced at Razeem and grimaced. "This would be when I would ask you to cast *plavosvetljo*...but since we are in the Abyss, it might not reveal anything."

"I have a *feather fall* spell prepared," Ewynne said, "but floating down there would still be...a problem."

Jussuf swallowed nervously and straightened his shoulders. "This is my sworn duty," he said and stepped forward. "I—"

"Whoa, hold on," Peri said, gripping the young man's arm and stopping him. "Just because you pledged—well, I know how you paladins are, but nope. Hey, all kinds of crazy stuff happens to me all the time, so how bad can it be?" She leaped over the edge, onto the translucent bridge. It held

183

steady under her feet. "Look! It's fine!" She spread her arms, grinned, and waved. Then she started to skip ahead, towards the murky area in the middle. The others shrugged and followed. The bridge felt like thin air, but it supported them. As they reached the shadowy center, they stood for a moment in pitch darkness, then they saw light entering through a narrow opening. They made their way toward it and followed Peri, who had already disappeared into the crack.

They were greeted by a sweet-smelling meadow of soft grass and a gathering of narrow birches with small gossamer leaves. In the distance, there was a bubbling stream flanked by gently swaying willows. The light was soft, and though the sun was shining, there was a hint of chill in the air.

Kauno smiled. "Kauno's homeland in early summer. Balatsky Taiga. Whatever is at work here must have picked some of Kauno's memories for decoration."

Velimir felt a faint pang of pain, a distant memory of a dream. A new life in Balatsky Taiga, a home in the land of forests, meadows, and lakes. *No matter.* Dreams of the powerless met cruel ends, and now he was on his way to finding power again, one way or another.

There was a big ornamental metal cage with a lever inside. Outside the cage there was a plaque carved with scribbly runes. Peri knelt to observe the plaque. "Velimir, is this Vysokian?"

"It is," he answered and crouched to take a look. "The prophecies say that a leap of faith paves the way to the besieged Shinaris. I never assumed it would be this literal. As for this device...it must be a dormant one-way portal."

"So...I suppose we go in, you recite the runes, and then we pull the lever and hope that this is not some sick joke that turns us all into minced meat," Peri said and grinned.

"I wouldn't think so," Velimir said. "Our divine sire would have better use in mind for a child who survived the Theater. Be prepared for a battle."

"Hey, aren't we always," Peri said and stepped into the cage. The others followed.

Once everyone was inside, Velimir straightened his back and started reciting the runes. *Valkama, witness my triumph! Back to the world of the living, to power, to glory! Even the Abyss is no match for the great Velimir!*

22
VALHALLA

"Let me get this straight." Kiril tried to get his customary collected posture back but was still shaken, even though a friendly maid had carried a plate of cold meats and cheeses and a pitcher of crystal-clear water to him, arching her eyebrow only slightly when he declined the mead. "That psychopath nearly severed my head because we were in an area where everybody wants to fight until death, for no particular reason? And this is his idea of a desirable afterlife?"

Jelena shrugged and nodded, a smile of creeping amusement on her lips. "I killed the lout myself. I guess my Lord's teachings of compassion and forgiveness weren't the first and foremost thing on my mind at the moment—"

"I should hope so—Wait a minute. *You* killed him?" Kiril took a long look at Jelena—her round, soft shoulders, her gentle smile, her feminine body unburdened by any sort of armor, just a simple robe becoming her curves. Nor did she carry a weapon.

Jelena smiled a little helplessly. "I got a bit carried away. I thought your soul was lost in Manala, and I would have to do gods know what to find you—Oh! You mean how did I do it? I must show you a thing or two about planar martial arts. Any favoured devotee of Lord Milostra goes through a training in the Way of the Palm. There are monasteries in the Yonder, too."

Kiril arched an eyebrow. "The martial art that Milostra's wandering clerics train at before they start their itinerary life, I recall. Only I seem to remember something to the effect that it can only be used defensively."

Jelena wrung her hands. "Well...it is more like it *should* only be used defensively." She blushed slightly and fiddled with a stray blonde lock. Kiril remembered how she used to do that in life and felt a warm, disarming jolt of awe and vulnerability—a sudden outburst of the love he had denounced after losing her. Like then, it felt both wonderful and terrifying. He drew breath and reached his hand to hers, feeling the soft skin, the warmth of another person.

"Now we are together," Jelena continued. "That is all that matters. We have to look for Velimir—be a family again, put things right. I have my Lord's blessing. I told you how I felt him praying to me in a great distress." Jelena had explained to Kiril how she had channeled her Lord's power and done her best to send Velimir strength. "Was it truly him? What is he thinking? What are his goals?" Jelena paused and spread her hands. "I don't know. I only know that he has suffered and draws strength from me at his greatest hour of need. I have no idea if he heard me when I prayed for him, but he is my son. You are my man. We will be a family, and we will find him. Dimitri's blood is no longer present in him. Perhaps the madness has faded."

Kiril sighed and looked down at his plate. "I really did my best to accelerate the madness, as you know. I—"

Jelena grabbed his arm. "I know. But right now, we have to focus on finding this priestess. Unless…I hear that Lord Odin's sacrifice was a harrowing experience. And he is a *god!* And, well, I just demonstrated I am not defenseless. Perhaps we don't need your magic. Perhaps—"

"And have me hiding behind your skirts, following you like a puppy, useless?" Kiril said sharply. "*No.* I am…a man. My intellect, my mastery of the Art is what makes me someone. I wanted to be a man worthy of you, a man that does… good." The notion still felt as odd as it had in that short, sweet while in life, but he had been willing to listen to Jelena then. He certainly hadn't succeeded fabulously by reverting to his old ways, so he would listen again. "My intellect, my mastery of the Art, make me what I am," he repeated. A passerby bumped into Kiril while trying to dodge brawlers, and some ale spilled on his clothes.

Jelena nodded slowly. "I can understand that. And it is certain that your magic will be a great asset to our quest. The Three seem to think that Velimir still has a role to play in the future. Then it is a matter of fulfilling your promise to the ladies. I think I know how the elf is hiding."

"Really?"

"My grandmother told me stories about elves when I was a girl. She was from Balatsky Taiga."

That had played a role in their decision to seek a new life in the vast land of forests, meadows and lakes beyond

Leshenkaya. Kiril sipped from his cup and strained his hearing in the midst of the clatter of tankards and the raucous singing and laughter.

"People of Balatsky Taiga have to take care not to get covered by the forest," Jelena went on. "There are spots in the forests where the veil between Hereworld and Otherworld is thin, and time and space distort. You can become trapped in the Otherworld, and never find your way back. When the forest covers you, familiar places look off, colours and shapes different. Birds fall silent, and the trees hum ominously."

Kiril had spent very little time in the forest in life, born and bred at the dull, muddy outskirts of Oligorsk inhabited by skilled labourers and low-level scribes and officials as he was. "Does that happen naturally or is it something the creatures of the Otherworld do?" he asked.

"Humans don't know for sure," Jelena said. "But elves, whose ancestors still live in the primeval depths of the forests—they can intentionally cover themselves with forest. That is what they do when they wish to avoid confrontation. They call this phenomenon *silva stragulum.* My grandmother was lost in the forest once as a child, and an elven woman took her home and told her this."

Kiril recalled the vast forests surrounding the chaotic battlefields around Valhalla. "But if she is covering herself with forest, how could I possibly find her?"

"*Silva stragulum* is highly resistant to high magic," Jelena said, "but there are folk traditions that help those who have been covered with forest to see clearly. Wearing your clothes inside out helps. It doesn't really do anything about the forest cover, but it jolts your brain out of its familiar mode of perception and may help you see through distortions. Drawing blood and painting a heart on a stone may also help anchor you, my grandmother said." She shrugged and bit her lip with a worried expression.

The two turned their heads as they heard a creaking sound of the massive oaken doors at the end of the hall. Several winged horses rode by with blonde warrior women carrying slain warriors into the hall.

"That's how we came in, too," Jelena said. "There is regular traffic. The ladies patrol the fields and haul the dead here, and then the dead are resurrected."

Indeed, a warrior priest sporting a red beard, benevolent smile, and a horned helmet was already resurrecting the first warrior, who shook himself, smiled a thanks, and headed to the bar for a full tankard.

There was a rowdy game of dice, a brawl with gamblers making their bets, and a few skalds singing about warriors and their deeds in another corner of the large hall.

"And this is what they do? Day after day? Fight, die, get resurrected, get drunk, play dice..."

"That is what I gathered, yes," Jelena said.

"What about improving oneself? Gaining new knowledge? Intellectual exchange? Experimenting? Books?" Anger stirred in his veins. Grimnir, he recalled, had been a man driven by curiosity and wanderlust. But there was no trace of any intellectual or mystical pursuits in this hall. Impressive as the massive hall was, complete with golden shields for a ceiling, the atmosphere didn't differ much from any tavern frequented by soldiers and mercenaries.

"Why not? Whom do they bother here, aside from hapless wanderers from another universe like us who weren't exactly invited?"

"They come here and are quite happy with this and themselves for all eternity?" Kiril's frown deepened. As happy as he was to be reunited with Jelena, it bothered him that she had suggested foregoing the ordeal to get his magic back. As if it was somehow optional, a luxury. As if restoring him as a whole man was not much of a priority.

"Would you rather them be unhappy? Have you never met a mercenary before? You are just upset because you got killed," Jelena said, now frowning, too.

"Pardon me for overreacting," Kiril muttered dryly.

Jelena burst into laughter. Seeing the jolly creases around her eyes made Kiril's frustration dissipate. She kneaded Kiril's palm with her thumbs. "I didn't mean to sound dismissive about your magic," she said. "A warrior would want a missing limb back, wouldn't he?"

The doors opened again, and a tall armored figure entered the hall. A woman with flowing blonde hair, broad shoulders, thick calves, built like a brick, stalked swiftly towards Kiril and Jelena's corner of the room. Jelena squinted at the smaller figure scrambling after the armored woman. "Auri...?"

The large woman glared at Jelena with narrowed steel-grey eyes. She jabbed her finger at the dove amulet hanging from Jelena's neck. "So, it is true! You have brought—" she spat at the smaller girl "—*her* here! To *Lord Odin's hall!*" Her voice rose in crescendo. The chatter and singing in the background died down, and heads turned.

"I swear I didn't know!" the young Valkyrie Auri wailed. "I didn't know that she is a...a *pacifist!*"

"A what now?" muttered someone.

"She follows a god who denounces war," the hulking Valkyrie said, and the crowd gasped. "Who denies the right of conquest and the glory of battle!"

Jelena could not argue with that. *Do no harm. Do not injure, abuse, oppress, enslave, insult, torment, torture, or kill any creature or living being*—that was the command of Lord Milostra. "I…meant no offense," she said feebly.

"How could you not have meant offense?" demanded the angry Valkyrie. "Your very presence here is sacrilege! You brazenly carry the symbol of this…pacifist god over your robes!"

Someone approached from the bar at the back of the hall. "Whoa whoa there!" said a shirtless, wild-haired berserker. Jelena recognized the man she had earlier beaten to a pulp. She offered him an awkward smile. The man paid her no heed. "Now that 'pacifism' sounds like a load of crap. This lady surely is no pacifist! She did some sort of trick, then beat me to death with her bare hands! Feisty! I'd be interested myself but she seems to be taken with the little assassin!" the man said and winked at Jelena.

"I'm not actually an—" Kiril tried, but nobody paid attention.

"That *is* true," Auri said. "She can beat a man to death with no weapons! Surely, it can't offend Lord Odin to have such a fury here?"

"On my honor," said the berserker, "I vouch for her. The little assassin is a lucky man."

"Very well," said the hulking Valkyrie. "You have been spoken for. But you are not taking another step in Asgard."

"We are on a mission. For the ladies—the Norns—who guard the Yggdrasil," Kiril said.

"Are you now? Yes, I heard that some petitioner was sent to do an errand," the Valkyrie said. "But having a...*pacifist* traipse around our holy grounds was not part of the bargain. No, she stays here. Under lock and key." She looked directly at Kiril. "Do as you were told—deliver the elf to her jailors—and then we'll deliver your pacifist to you, and the both of you can sod off." She put her gauntleted hand on Jelena's shoulder.

"It is fine," Jelena said and squeezed Kiril's hand, searching for something to say that would hold any weight with warlike people. "I trust you will treat a hostage honorably. I request permission to talk strategy before he leaves, however. I may have knowledge to impart that would help him succeed in his mission."

The Valkyrie shrugged. "Permission granted. Pacifist or not, you have guts. Have your talk. But we will watch you the entire time and then take you away." She backed off with Auri, and two other Valkyries stepped forward to flank her.

"Don't be distressed, beloved," Jelena murmured. "This is a setback, but I have an idea."

23
SHINARIS

THE PARTY EMERGED FROM THE PORTAL IN FRONT OF what looked like an entrance to a castle. An angry mob was milling about, and the guards seemed ready to attack at any minute. There were arches of palm trees, some of which had been toppled over by catapult shots, and sand swirled in the midday heat.

The group had little time to take their surroundings in, however, as a tall, unsmiling woman noticed their appearance. The woman had combed her sand-colored hair meticulously and pulled it back in a severe single plait. She wore a gray tunic and pants, no jewelry, and had sandals on her feet.

"What is this?" she exclaimed, articulating in the exaggerated manner some adults feel children should be spoken to. "Children of Dimitri appear out of thin air!"

"I really don't like her voice," muttered Peri.

Velimir silently agreed. It sounded harsh and grating.

"Intruders! The wall has been breached! Kill them!" a guard shouted. The guardsmen, wielding scimitars and wearing Wulanian armor, looked unlikely to be swayed by a diplomatic approach.

"Wait! They might not be enemies!" said the gray-clad woman.

"Nah, don't fall for their tricks. Just kill them, and let the gods sort them out!" grunted an orc apparently in charge of the guards.

That was all the permission Velimir needed. He welcomed the short-lived battle, rage and power flowing through him. The guards were powerful warriors, strong, well-trained, and tough, but they were no match for Velimir, nor for Peri's other companions. In minutes, they were taken down, blood covering Velimir's chest plate. His eyes were shining, and from the corner of his eye, he could see that Peri's were, too.

When it was all over, the woman walked over to their group. "Hello, Peri. I am Tamasin," she said. "A friend. It is a pity that your welcome to Shinaris was this violent."

Peri shrugged and eyed the woman with intense suspicion.

"I'm pretty damn used to that kind of thing already. How do you know my name, and how do you know that I'm a Dimitrian spawn?"

"I have been keeping track of all the progeny of the fallen celestial, and you are one of the most powerful who remains. So many of your kind have been slain over the past few months. Wulani is, indeed, running red with blood."

"What is your interest in this?" Peri obviously didn't trust the woman who knew far too much and was far too eager.

The woman gave a slight bow. "I am acting as a protector of Dimitri's innocent offspring. I am somewhat familiar with the Vysokian prophecies, and recent events suggest that they contain a fair amount of truth. By taking an interest in Dimitri's offspring, I aim to prevent the ascent of a new god of wrath," Tamasin explained, like a governess addressing children.

"Uh huh. And you have no intention of harming these offspring?" Peri remained unconvinced.

"I am not your enemy, Peri. And anyway, unless you can teleport around the planes at will, I fear you are trapped in this besieged city just like the rest of us. A Dimitrian spawn named Darien has gathered an army and is bombarding it, intent on destroying everyone who carries Dimitri's blood in his—or her—veins." As if to corroborate Tamasin's words, a rock was hurled from beyond the city walls and thudded into the already splintered mosaics covering the plaza in front of the castle. Tamasin didn't startle.

Peri scowled at the rock, then at the woman. "Let me make an educated guess. For some obscure piece of information that may or may not be completely useless to me by the time you are willing to part from it, you want me to get rid of Darien and end the siege," Peri said. That was, in her experience as a sword for hire, how these things generally went.

While Peri looked only grim and annoyed, Velimir felt like sniggering. *You tell her, sister!*

"Well, that is one way of putting it," said the unprovoked Tamasin, blushing a little. "But I assure you, my information will be useful. However, before you can do anything about

Darien, you need to deal with Shermag, who now is the leader of Shinaris. Shermag is also a child of Dimitri. The celestial mated even with orcs, as he believed that their race had unique gifts worth cultivating. Shermag—half orc, half celestial—is a general from further east. I brought him and his men here to protect Shinaris and the Dimitrian offspring I had gathered." Tamasin paused for a moment, a dissatisfied frown on her face. "But Shermag has gone mad. He has barricaded himself in the castle throne room, and his troops are getting restless, running amok through the city. This has caused dissent in the city, and supplies are running low, so things are falling apart."

"Not a nice guy then, this Shermag." Peri uttered a prolonged sigh and shrugged in resignation. "All right, as it seems that the only other option would be laying down to wait for death, I guess we go after the mad general then."

"And saving the innocent citizens is, of course, the right thing to do," Razeem spoke up.

"I am assuming you will need a base of operation and a place to recuperate before you make your move. Walk down the main boulevard, and you will find the last tavern still in operation, called Twin Scimitars. Farewell for now, Peri. We will meet later," Tamasin said and walked away.

"Really, Peri, you could work on your diplomacy skills," said Razeem, wiping sweat off his forehead and squinting at the road leading to the city through swirling clouds of dust, debris, and toppled over palm trees. "I realize we can't trust just any stranger who claims to be a friend, but this lady could be a valuable ally."

"It's not my diplomacy skills that have kept me alive so far," Peri snapped. "And I don't like her. I don't trust her."

"You don't like anyone who acts in an authoritative manner," Razeem answered.

"You are right," Peri admitted with a hint of a smile. "Still, I reserve the right to make my own judgement. Anybody want to dodge some more catapult shots, or do we go to the tavern?"

After collecting anything of value from the corpses, the group made their way toward the tavern. Everywhere they saw scared, starved, and distrustful faces. Catapult shots had splintered mosaics, palm trees, and benches. There was debris everywhere, and scavengers scurried about, looking for anything of value.

Velimir decided that the trek to the tavern was as good an opportunity as any to approach Ewynne. "Dear sister," he said, "I can see that you have developed quite a skill as a magician." He remembered the shaky, panicky incantations of a pale, wide-eyed slip of a girl in the abandoned temple where he had met his unfortunate end. It was a far cry from this calm, determined spellcaster who kept her head in the middle of violence and chaos.

"I've had a lot of practice since...you died," answered Ewynne, her eyes still hostile and her voice uncharacteristically flat.

Velimir chuckled. "Now there's a comment you don't hear from a member of your adventuring group every day," he mused, hoping that Ewynne would warm up a bit. She did smile a little but didn't answer. It was better than nothing.

⸻ • ● • ⸻

THE ONLY SURVIVING TAVERN IN THE CITY HAD MEAGER offerings, but there was ale and simple soup available.

Razeem and Jussuf discussed tactical maneuvers, Ewynne looked bored, absentmindedly hovering an apple-sized sphere of rainbow colour for Casimir's delight, and Kauno rubbed the neck of his sparrow with his index finger. Velimir looked at Peri, who sat beside him. Indeed, this was odd—she had been the object of his envy and hatred, his sworn enemy—but now they traveled together as allies. Velimir realized that he felt a budding respect for Peri.

"So, you have welcomed me by your side," he said. "I must say that your courteous treatment of me...pleases me, sister."

Peri shrugged. "Either you are part of the group or you are not. And I treat my group as well as it is in my powers to do."

"But you don't trust me yet," Velimir stated.

"You can't be surprised at that," answered Peri, arching her eyebrow.

"But...why didn't you try to bind me in any way, then? An oath, a pact...In Dimitri's former realm, it might have bound me just like a geas." Velimir had mulled the question over in his mind for a time now. Peri clearly wasn't as naïve and guileless as he had formerly thought. He grinned wolfishly. "Too late for that now."

Peri ignored his grin. "I would never enslave anyone to my will. Never. And...I hope I will be given a second chance when I need it. Use yours well, Velimir," she said, looking him in the eye, dead serious.

Velimir was taken aback by her earnestness and intensity. He didn't know how to respond. "I..." He settled for, "I will think about what you said."

Kauno kept glancing at Velimir. The attention made him

want to squirm in his seat, but he said nothing.

After Kauno quietly finished his meal, he spoke. "Kauno has been observing you for a while now, Velimir. Kauno wonders how you feel about your new life."

"Are you wary of my presence, mystic? You saw my blade speak for its allegiance earlier today."

Kauno bowed his head and consulted the sparrow nestled in his hands. Velimir rolled his eyes. Then Kauno lifted his head and looked at Velimir with his frank, watery blue eyes.

"Varpu agrees with you. Varpu reminds Kauno that your blade may be the only way to speak for yourself that you are comfortable with, as of yet."

"Your deluded comments are unnecessary. Peri will lead, I will follow," Velimir said. True, he didn't intend to be a follower any longer than he had to, but for now, it rankled him less than he had anticipated. Observing Peri and her fate unfolding was intriguing, and envy didn't burn him as he had assumed it would. The idea of her as the reigning god of wrath started to feel less and less distasteful to Velimir. If it could not be Velimir himself, who could be more deserving?

"Kauno is impressed by your humility. Varpu has faith in you, too."

Velimir was about to angrily retort that he cared little for the opinions of avians, but something about Kauno's honest and kind expression made him bite his tongue. "I think I will go…sit alone awhile," he said instead in a strained voice. "I have a headache."

When Velimir was sitting alone next to the dying log fire, trying to sort out his confused feelings about the mystic's commentary, he heard footsteps. Peri.

She sat next to him. "Don't worry, brother. There is no danger of excess humility in your makeup," she said.

"He...showed acceptance to me. But then, he *is* insane," Velimir said.

"Maybe—though I would probably call it eccentric, if there's a difference. But he is also one of the kindest and gentlest people I know," Peri said.

"Is that a good thing?" Velimir frowned. "Those can be exploitable weaknesses."

"No. I will never be trusting, good and kind," Peri said. She leaned back in her chair and crossed her ankles, gazing at the flickering flames. "But I know enough to appreciate it when I see it. It is something Connor taught me by his example."

It did sound odd to Velimir. He could not imagine what it might be like—wielding power without control and intimidation. He had always assumed that it was the way it was. Velimir's underlings at the Stribog Citadel had either been terrified of him or admired him blindly, just like his gang of street children before being adopted by Radek. But perhaps there was something to Connor's and Peri's way. Peri's group was disciplined and efficient when needed, and they were dedicated to her even though they were not fearful of her. They saw her as a flesh and blood grinning, sweating, and farting girl—flawed but important to them all the same.

"I...observed you once," he said. "In the monastery garden at Eilean de Taigh-Sholais. You were describing a dream to Connor, where you rode a skeletal steed and beheaded people, laughing. And the dead joined the chorus of the previous dead."

"I remember that one." Peri shivered. "Of course, it was

not just the dream that I was upset about then. Connor was trying to stress to me that dreaming of murder didn't make me a murderer. But I had killed Silas. I couldn't bear the idea of him knowing. I bet you have had some bad dreams, too."

Velimir blew out a long breath. "I have dreamed of murdering before I knew what it meant. And I saw all kinds of visions, and Dimitri always talked to me...more and more until...the end."

"I think you were badly in his clutches, brother." Even though it was hot in the tavern, Peri added another log to the fire. "What was your stepfather Radek like?"

"He was a bastard." Velimir didn't want to talk about Radek. He didn't want Peri to think he was asking for sympathy. "What was Connor like?"

"He was what kept me from going insane." Peri's voice was oddly dispassionate. "Imagine a five-year-old girl feeling an urge to murder, and still he made me feel like I was not a freak, but a real person. A person worthy of love. I loved him, and he made me appreciate the kindness and goodness I do not possess myself. When you murdered him, I shattered inside," said Peri, now facing Velimir, her eyes glinting like steel.

Velimir wanted to say he would want that undone, that he would want Peri to forgive him. But he couldn't. Just couldn't. There was a tense silence. Still, Peri didn't avert her eyes. Still, Peri didn't leave.

"So, what do you plan to do with me once this is finished? Once all this prophecy is over and done with, and you have found your destiny in it?" Velimir asked.

Peri seemed to find the question strange. "It is not my place to say. You will have your own destiny to find then," she answered.

Velimir's life had not prepared him for communicating with someone like Peri. In his experience, even allies had, in some way, been opponents. He was used to gauging the balance of power, anticipating the angle the opponent was working, debating the strategic value of revealing any information. But Peri seemed entirely uninterested in such designs.

"Even if I planned to do evil? Even if I planned to do something like that again?" Velimir insisted.

Peri laughed. "I often don't even know what evil *is*. And even when there is no doubt, I am no glory hound. I just don't see the point. Evil can never stop being part of the world, in one way or another. Don't get me wrong, if evil comes close to those I care about, I fight the fuck out of it. But I don't go out of my way to be a hero. You can do what you want to do. I would do something worthwhile if I were you."

Velimir nodded, deep in thought. Peri touched his arm briefly. The soft, light touch caused a sudden jolt of emotion—as if his heart became too large in his chest. It startled him, but he kept his face impassive.

"Goodnight, brother."

"Goodnight."

• ● •

As Peri was about to wrap herself in her blanket, Ewynne tiptoed next to her bed and sat down. Her expression was uncharacteristically serious.

"You were talking with Velimir again," she said.

"So I was," Peri answered.

"You seem to be getting along awfully well with him. You

203

two even…laugh together, like you have some secret joke nobody else gets."

"Perhaps we do, though I'm not sure it could be called a joke."

"Peri, he killed Connor! I am sure you haven't forgotten that."

"And it is damn good that you are sure, because otherwise I would get really mad at you," Peri growled. Then her face softened, and she took Ewynne's hands in her own. "But you don't understand. No-one does. Velimir is proud—he doesn't want any of you to see that he feels any weakness or need for approval. But I can tell he really has suffered. He has literally been through hell. He doesn't tell me, but I feel it. I feel *him.* He has paid for it. He has suffered more than I have," Peri said, looking Ewynne in the eye. She wanted Ewynne to understand, to not judge her for wanting to connect with her brother.

"And so he should! The last time I checked, you didn't plan to start a war to kill thousands of people because of some mad plan to become a god." Ewynne looked a bit angry now.

"You…you don't know what you are talking about," Peri said. "You have no clue how the blood calls. Velimir was mad, completely in Dimitri's clutches, and I would have gone down just the same way if it hadn't been for Connor. Velimir doesn't tell me much about his life, but I have an idea it has been hell."

"I don't believe this. You are defending Velimir to me." Ewynne sounded wounded.

"Wyn, you are the most important person to me. You *know* that. But please don't blame me for wanting to know him better. He is the only one who...knows." Peri's voice quavered a little and her eyes welled with tears.

Ewynne remembered the countless nights when there were two small girls sharing a bedroom. When Peri woke up panting and moaning, her eyes wide in fascination and horror. Her describing the dreams with hot, steamy streams of blood, disfigured corpses beckoning her to dance, gallows everywhere and her splitting skulls, drinking blood, slicing throats. Finally Ewynne had to close her eyes and ears, unable to take it anymore. Connor would come and calm the frightened, desperate child, soothe her, convince her that she was all right, that there was nothing wrong with her, that dreams did not count, but what you actually did mattered. Yes, Velimir probably was the only one who knew.

"Sorry, Peri. I...I just worry that you will become like him. That he gives you some kind of mad ideas and you start to...He coaxed you into turning into the Edge, dammit!"

"Ewynne, he is not the same man anymore. He doesn't quite know who he is or what he wants yet, or what he will do...but the madness is gone. He's just desperately clinging to his dignity, trying to drive everyone away. I don't hate him. Not anymore."

"Just be careful, Peri. Reserve your own judgement. Don't trust him too much."

"I won't. Goodnight, Wyn. I love you," Peri whispered.

Ewynne hugged her sister and slipped under her own blanket.

———————————•●•———————————

IT WAS SO EARLY THAT IT WAS STILL COOL IN THE COURT-yard of the inn where Peri sat alone, eyes closed, leaning on a still standing palm tree. Kauno approached Peri, carrying a bundle in his hands. He sat next to the brooding girl and put it in her lap.

"Kauno embalmed the head and treated it with herbs. Then he wrapped it in a cloth of brown silk. Now you can carry it as long as you need to," he said.

Peri opened her glistening eyes to look up at him and smiled wanly. "Thank you," she said and pressed the bundle to her face. She inhaled. It smelled of eucalyptus and thyme. "Is this the silk you were going to make into a cape?"

"Kauno was happy to use it for this purpose, honey," said Kauno. He was wearing none of his wigs—his hair was a tangle of thinning unruly tufts. He crouched and watched, hand on Peri's shoulder, as Peri averted her eyes and sat in a brooding silence. He cleared his throat. "Peri...would you like to talk about it? Kauno knows you cared for Genjiro. Sometimes talking helps."

Peri's lips thinned, and her jaw stiffened. She spoke without looking up. "I'm grateful—really grateful—that you treated the head, Kauno. But you need to understand something. Genjiro betrayed me, but regretted it and set me free. He is now dead. That is all you—any of you—need to know." She pressed the bundle against her heart and swallowed a sob. "I will carry the head with me until such time that I can release it to the waves, so that Eoghain can help bring him home. And now that you have all the information you need, I don't want to hear his name mentioned, and I don't want to hear any questions. Ever. Do you understand?"

Kauno sighed and patted her arm, then stood up and walked away. He found the others inside the tavern, where they were breaking their fast. "She doesn't want to talk," he said. "She made that very clear. She doesn't even want to hear Genjiro mentioned. She wants to put the pain neatly in a box and hide it in the attic, pretending it is not there. For the time being, there is nothing we can do to help but to be there for her."

"She has always been like that," Ewynne said. "Most of the time she doesn't want sympathy. She says that sympathy doesn't change how things are and only makes her feel pathetic."

Razeem sighed. "She refused to tell us any details. They tortured her, we know this much. We don't know how Genjiro died or what exactly they did to her."

"Ever since the Abyss, she has been...giddy. Speaking fast, grinning all the time. Reckless. I mean, more than usual," said Ewynne. "And now, suddenly, she wants to be alone and is quiet and miserable."

"That is not such an unusual reaction to trauma," said Razeem. "Whatever happened must have been devastating. Reality sinks in with a delay."

"I worry about her judgement," Jussuf said. "That she resurrected...him...is one thing. But she allows him to travel with us!"

Velimir, who was sharing the table with them but sitting a bit apart, drew breath and turned to face Jussuf.

Razeem raised his hand. "Jussuf! We may question the wisdom of it, but it was her decision to make, and we have pledged ourselves to her service. So have the courtesy of addressing Velimir directly, like a man. We are brothers in arms now, no matter how tenuous our alliance."

Just then, Peri entered the room. All heads turned to her.

"Stop looking at me like that," she said. "We have a job to

do, and we need to concentrate on that. I did some recon before dawn and I know how to get in." She stuffed the brown conspicuous bundle deep in her rucksack, hands and lips trembling as she did so. Then she leaned on the table, and some of the maniacal gleam of the past few days returned to her gaze. "We can break into the castle cellars and find our way to the throne room. Instead of drawing all the guards in combat, we might be able to infiltrate the castle and take the general by surprise. Or at least eliminate the guards in a few patches."

"Anything like wards?" Ewynne asked.

"Nah, I already picked the lock. Easy peasy. Let's roll." Peri jerked her head.

• • •

RAZEEM HESITATED FOR A MOMENT, THEN ADDRESSED Peri. "Forgive me for intruding, but are you sure that you want to confront the general now?" he asked. "You have suffered devastating losses, been whisked around in the Abyss, and experienced mind-boggling things. I can see that dealing with Genjiro's...remains upset you." He glanced at the rucksack.

"In case you haven't noticed: besieged city. Catapult fire. No time to sniff the flowers," Peri said tersely. "Give me some credit."

"You refuse to discuss Genjiro's death and what it means to you. Or the details of what you went through during your captivity. Are you sure that is wise?" asked the older man. He had expected Peri to react with hostility, but her act of having it all together seemed to be wearing thin.

"Why is everyone so damn interested in what I am feeling

or not feeling?" Peri asked and flipped her hair behind her back. "We have a job to do and it has to be my first priority, no matter how much I ache inside..." her voice trailed off.

"Forgive me, Peri," Razeem said.

Peri nodded with thinned lips and quickened her pace. The others lagged a bit behind, but Velimir's stride matched hers.

They walked quietly for a while. Velimir could not begin to guess what she had felt for Hanamori Genjiro. Something akin to what he once thought he felt for Tomoe? But she did not let sorrow consume her. First and foremost, she was the leader. Focused. Purposeful. A true daughter of Wrath. His sister...

Velimir decided to speak up. "Sister, for what my opinion is worth, you are doing as a leader should. There is no shame in that. Ruminating and indulging in one's feelings is a luxury those who carry the burden of leadership often do not have."

Peri turned around to look him in the eye, surprised.

"Thank you, Velimir. I do feel...a lot. But my feelings are not a performance they can demand of me, to determine if they approve, if they are what a normal person is supposed to feel! Those memories are jarring. But private, and mine alone," she said, eyes grim and narrow.

"I respect that," Velimir said.

"I appreciate it that someone does," Peri said. She seemed to want to add something, but didn't, and the sister and the brother continued their journey.

THE GUARDS IN THE CASTLE CELLARS WERE QUICKLY DISposed of. They were ordinary hired help, something Velimir and Peri didn't have to break a sweat with. No spellcasters either. Apparently, the general didn't consider the cellars themselves worth protecting. A staircase led upwards. Peri took a look at her companions. They were still worried about her, she knew. But Velimir had shown her acceptance and respected her wish not to share. In combat, her brother was just like her—wide-eyed with pleasure, savage, so alive. The Dimitrian blood may have been gone from him, but he still found glory in fighting. Killing, even. But then, so did she.

She shoved her musings aside. "There is a narrow doorway on the top of the staircase. For all we know, they are guarding the entrance. We have to take care not to get hemmed in—that would make us sitting ducks. Ewynne and Jussuf stay back. I go in first and charge in case they have archers. Then Velimir kills everything that moves and keeps them off our spellcasters, and Razeem goes after the mages. Got it?"

They nodded, Velimir still regarding her with that appreciative expression on his face. Jussuf and Ewynne cast protective spells on the warriors to their best ability. Ewynne wrapped Casimir in *Svetilje sphere* so that no harm would come to the imp. Razeem cast a more powerful version of the *plavosvetljo* spell that would remain in effect around him for minutes. That would help them to see through illusions and detect anyone that had been rendered invisible with magic. Then up they went.

Peri saw that she had been correct—the force stationed in the hall guarding the entrance of the staircase as well as a large doorway was considerably more powerful than the one in the cellars, complete with two battlemages. However, they were no match for the group, as Razeem was dealing with his specialty: counteracting and eliminating magic. The defenders had been counting on illusions, invisibility, and confusion spells. They had considerable arcane firepower, but they didn't last long thanks to Razeem's abilities. The elemental damage was mitigated by Jussuf's and Ewynne's protective spells.

"This seems like an entrance hall," Peri said. "Those doors must open to the throne room. Shall we go on? We are on a roll!" The others nodded, so she continued. "Looks like we are going in, then. And I don't think they had time to sound an alarm."

As they opened the doors, ready to fight, they saw everyone in the throne room paying attention to a heated exchange between the gray-clad woman, Tamasin, and a huge orc sitting on the throne, his eyes gleaming with an expression between exhilaration and dread.

"Your guards threatened me, but know that I came of my own volition," the woman said. "You should know that I don't take kindly to threats, Shermag. What is it you want?"

Peri again gritted her teeth at Tamasin's voice. She noticed that the woman sounded far less phony when making a threatening statement.

"Shermag knows that the famous Peri has come to Shinaris," the giant orc said. "You must think Shermag is too stupid not to remember there is no way in or out of the city?" The orc stroked his impressive tusks as he spoke.

"Paranoia has addled your brain, Shermag! Peri may be our only hope of escaping this siege alive!" screeched

Tamasin.

"Bah! Shermag knows the truth!" snorted the orc. "Shermag is no idiot! Tamasin has brought Peri in to kill Shermag! Darien is Dimitri's child, and he wants Shermag's head, too! Tamasin is plotting against Shermag. Tamasin is plotting the death of all the children of Dimitri!"

Actually, that would kind of make sense. Peri trusted Tamasin just about as far as Ewynne could throw her, and the orc didn't seem stupid. It would certainly pay to hear his side of the story.

"You are mad, Shermag. Mad! Have I not always aided you and all the other children of Dimitri? I brought you here to a sanctuary. It was your paranoia that brought Darien upon us!" said Tamasin.

"Mad? Paranoid? Maybe, but that doesn't mean Tamasin isn't out to get Shermag! Shermag finally understands that Tamasin lied! Tamasin lured Shermag and all the others into a death trap! Guards! Take her away!"

Tamasin tried to protest, but it did no good. The guards hauled her away.

Peri approached Shermag, hands visibly off her sword.

"And now the murderer arrives!" growled Shermag. His bodyguards formed a shield wall around their leader.

"Shermag! I have no intention of killing you! I would hear your side of the story!" Peri shouted, hoping that Shermag's praetorian guard also paid attention.

"Shermag been fooled one time too many!"

"Listen to reason, orc, and you may live to see another day!" Velimir snapped.

The orc's frown deepened at seeing the giant of a man at Peri's side.

"Please! I don't trust Tamasin either! We could work together!" Peri said.

The orc seemed to be thinking hard, unable to decide what to do.

"Let's say you are correct—she has lured the Dimitrian spawn here into a death trap," Peri ventured on. "Do you suspect Darien works for her? He definitely is a threat. He is bombarding the city as we speak."

"Shermag does not know if Darien work for her," the orc spoke grudgingly, "but Shermag suspects it is so. Perhaps Tamasin is fooling Darien too. But even if that is so, everybody is trapped in Shinaris. And Darien is invulnerable."

Peri looked skeptical. "I have no doubt he is powerful, but he high-tailed it when I...went mental and butchered his goons."

"No, he really is. Has been for a while. Many have tried to slay him, but no magic, no enchanted weapons, nothing harms him. His army has seen him survive many assassination attempts, and believe him a god already. How he has achieved it, Shermag does not know."

"Well, isn't that just great? An invincible Dimitrian spawn with an army of his own who wants to kill all his siblings. And I should dispose of him," Peri sighed.

"Sounds kind of familiar, doesn't it?" muttered Velimir.

"Mister 'RAAGH, feel my unholy wrath'..." Peri said, and both started to chuckle.

"Wait," Jussuf said, looking to the right of Shermag's throne. "There is a...disturbance. *Ponishtiti.*"

A figure materialized at the orc general's side.

"Connor!" Peri gasped. Indeed, the old sage stood in front of them, looking much as he had in life. The simple monk robes, the greyish-blue, inquisitive eyes, the white hair. But instead of kindness, his face conveyed deep disappointment, even anger. He gazed at Peri, the accusation in his eyes piercing Peri's heart.

"Yes, it is me: Connor. It seems you have forgotten me, child." Profound disappointment. Pain of unreturned love.

"It is not true, Connor! I have not forgotten you at all!" A few hot tears spilled over to her cheek. The accusation hurt.

"No? I sheltered you with unconditional love. But even as I consoled you in my naivete, you were already a cold-blooded murderer! I educated you, equipped you for a life without the burden of the taint in your blood. I *died* protecting you! And what do you do? You resurrect the one who killed me. You hail him as a brother in arms!"

"But...I still love you. I do! I just...need Velimir! He is not the same man anymore..." Peri tried to explain, infuriated about losing her cool in front of the group and Shermag.

"What garbage!" Connor said. "That fiend is a slave to his ambition and greed, just like he always was!"

"Leave my sister be, old man, or I will kill you again," Velimir said.

"And what about Ewynne, my other daughter?" Connor was now looking at her, the same disappointment in his eyes. "With Peri, I tried my best, but she was clearly a wasted effort, a bloodthirsty killer to the bone. With you...I would have expected better from you, but you follow and enable her, a callous murderer every bit as much as your more flamboyant sister! Filth! I should have let both of you die, help me gods!"

"No, Connor! No! We have tried! We have only killed when we had to!" Ewynne was also crying, wincing in pain.

Connor laughed cynically. "Rubbish!" He casually threw a lightning bolt in Ewynne's general direction, causing the girl to reel and whimper in pain.

"Halt! I sense evil! This cannot be the wise and gentle stepfather you have told me about!" Razeem shouted. "This is some sort of cunning, evil creature!"

"Razeem is right!" Peri shouted. "Connor would never be this cruel! Stop tormenting us, whatever fucking thing you are!"

And suddenly Connor was Connor no more, but a creature of chill and void, a towering shadow of stealth and inertia. Gone was Connor's voice, and instead there was a chilling sneer.

"How...cunning. The disgusting paladin helps Dimitri's fool child to see through my manipulations. No matter. Slay them, my minions!"

And suddenly they were surrounded by countless shadows, wispy replicas of their master, eager to drink their life force. Shermag's guard stayed in formation around their leader, and the orc observed the fight, unable to decide who or what was a threat to him. Ewynne, with tears still in her eyes, tried to take down the magical protections of the master shadow. The warriors kept hacking at the shadows just as they had done at the Theater of Time, Jussuf chanting and calling holy sunrays to dispose of the undead, again and again. Kauno called dusty winds from the towers to spur the melee fighters on as the chill of the shadows slowed and weakened them. Thanks to Jussuf they were prepared for a battle with undead and were finally able to dispose of the lesser shadows. Nevertheless, the battle had been hard due to the sheer number of them.

Finally the rest were defeated, and the master shadow was alone, bound by a luminous cage of positive energy Jussuf channeled while sweating profusely.

"Where do you come from? What are you doing here?" asked the young paladin.

"I am doing the same thing I've been doing ever since the orc barricaded himself in this castle," answered the shapeless shadow's chilling sneer. "Spying. Keeping an eye on him. But you revealed my presence, so I defended myself."

"Who sent you?" Jussuf asked.

"Majsilaa the Great. The rightful high priestess of the new lord of Wrath!"

"Majsilaa?" Velimir spoke up. "She was a high-ranking priestess of Cijeli, who denounced the All-Father and followed Dimitri to exile. So, she is not just a legend, either... but she can't be alive. She would be hundreds of years old!"

"You'd be surprised, child of Dimitri."

"Show us the way out of here, shadow. The paladin will compel you," Velimir said.

"Very well. Perhaps my mistress can do business with you. Walk through the rift I came through, and you will find your way to an ancient seat of power." The area where the shadow had appeared shined with dim purple light.

"Begone now," said Jussuf and recited a few syllables. The shadow hissed and blinked away. The cage of light was gone as well. But the dim purple portal remained.

"Wow. What did you do to it?" asked Peri.

"I exorcised it," Jussuf said. "A creature like that does not truly die. It is a concentration of negative energy that, when dispersed, goes to other planes of existence. Its mistress, however, will not be able to call it to her service."

"Good job," Peri said. "But I...I am very drained, and I expect the rest of you are too. Whatever lies beyond that rift, we must face it in better shape. Let's rest and recover our strength and spell power. I trust you have no objection, Shermag?"

"Shermag knew it! A shadowy spy been lurking behind Shermag's back all the time! Mad, they said...paranoid, they said...but nay, Shermag nay has an objection. Why, he'll serve a meal for his brother and sister for helping to dispose of the thing!"

While Shermag went to raid the wine cellar, everyone sat forlorn and quiet.

Peri felt like she was spread quite thin, barely containing the maelstrom of bad stuff she had been hiding under her devil-may-care bravado. It was not an act *as such*, it *was* her nature...but it was also something she chose instead of dwelling on whatever troubled her. That didn't mean that the troubling stuff wasn't there, and there had been quite a shitload of bad stuff as of late. Judging from the others' expressions, she guessed she looked quite wild and haggard.

"Don't look at me like that," she said, offering a reassuring smile for her companions. "I will be all right. Think of this as a warming act before going to meet some immortal evil priestess!" But nobody answered the mechanical grin that didn't quite reach her eyes, and she felt that she had exhausted her reserves of being uplifting. She walked to a dimly lit corner of the throne room and sat alone, head buried in her knees. She should go see Ewynne, but couldn't muster the strength. Then she felt someone join her.

"Sister, I...I happen to know about creatures that do that. They see in your soul and draw your worst fears and all that is forbidden to the surface, torturing you with them," said Velimir. "And it has nothing to do…with reality. They can just play with what is in your mind. The thing could touch your memories, but not what Connor truly was."

Peri nodded, touching Velimir's arm.

"I…I wonder if he feels anger for…I don't know." She just kept looking at Velimir.

"I…wish to…" but whatever Velimir had wanted to say seemed to be stuck in his throat. "Oh, sister. Never mind."

Peri nodded again, never taking her hand off Velimir's arm, and they just sat together quietly for a long while.

THE COLD MEATS WERE SERVED ON THE FINEST CUTLERY of the castle that had once housed the grand duke of Shinaris. The wine also was excellent. Peri didn't remember drinking anything that good in a long time. Yet the meal had been a quiet and solemn affair. Shermag and his men as well as Peri and her companions were too occupied with digesting all the new information they had learned to bother with small talk. She had put on a brave face, but when everyone else retreated to their bedrolls, she finally felt free to wallow in her torment.

Connor, I loved you like I never have loved anyone. You were my salvation. You were the one who helped me to battle that horrible lure in my blood—somewhat. Your guidance taught me that there is another kind of power besides that of an oppressor, an iron fist. Peri had to know. Was it wrong that she traveled with Velimir? Was it wrong that his support and understanding meant frighteningly much to her? Had she betrayed Connor and his memory? *As bizarre as it is, he is now the only person who can help me with my darkness, like you once were. Like we are two pieces of the same soul.*

There was no answer. Then she saw Razeem approaching. Peri frantically wiped her eyes, tried to stiffen her shaking shoulders and swallow her tears. Alas, when Razeem approached her with a kind and worried look in his eyes, she lost the modicum of control she had managed to muster.

Razeem sat next to the pale and scowling girl and put his arm on her shoulder.

"Peri...I feel tempted to call you 'child,' but that would undoubtedly irritate you to no end. You may be the leader of this group, and a strong leader you have been, but you are also very young and must battle a frightening inheritance. You are not made of steel. That shadow was a creature of pure evil. It hit you in the worst possible way."

"Do you...do you think I have abandoned Connor?" she asked. "Do you think it is wrong that I get along with Velimir?" She clutched the bedroll with white knuckles.

"Obviously the reason you get along with him is not that you wouldn't care for Connor. And, if Connor is the man I imagine he was, he would probably be proud of you. It is a noble thing to do to give a second chance to another. Just guide Velimir in the right direction."

"You and Jussuf! You always are so damned sure about the right direction! I don't even know what it *is*, most of the time."

Razeem knew as much and hoped that he had been able to be a good influence. The battle was by no means lost. There was much good in Peri, too. "You *are* in great danger of becoming cynical, but you do have principles and courage to act on them. I believe Velimir still clings to his old, power-hungry ways…and power-hungry is something you are not. Help him see the folly in that."

Peri bit her lip, sighed, and nodded. Then she curled on the bedroll, tried to make herself comfortable and closed her eyes.

Poor child, Razeem thought. *She is trying so hard to put on a brave face and be strong for the group. By Juris, she is barely older than my daughter, and already she has battled demons, been tortured by madmen. I do not deny that the instant connection between her and Velimir could be dangerous, but that is where I come in. I must do my best to guide both of those young, proud souls, the strongest among the children of Dimitri. Juris, give me wisdom to find just the right way to do that.*

24
ASGARD

Kiril carefully planted his foot on a moss-covered rock and shifted his weight once he was assured that the spongy moss would not slip from under his foot. A bird chirped lazily now and then, but it seemed that the deeper he ventured in the vast forests surrounding the fields of Valhalla, the quieter it got. Jelena had told him to look for a spot where the forest seemed unusually odd, silent, or ominous. He tried to listen closely, to determine if the birds and humming insects made sounds less frequently. But soon the only thing he could hear was the thumping of his own heart.

Indeed, in his limited experience, forests had always seemed slightly ominous. He had on occasion accompanied Radek in the high society hunting events, in the manicured and frequently logged forests with their wide paved pathways. This forest was a far cry from those tall, neat, uniform rows of lumber littered with scenic spots for the visiting gentry. This forest was vast and deep, and every tree seemed ancient and unique. The crooked old pines leaned on lichen-bearded spruces. Their crowns spread and mingled wildly in a chaotic fashion. There were spots where a massive trunk had tumbled down and now lay falling apart, covered in moss, lichen, and fungi, and sprouting new growths. At such spots, the sun made its way to the forest floor.

Kiril swatted an insect off his sweating forehead and stopped to remove his clothes and turn them back the correct side out. As soon as he managed to yank the clothes over his clammy limbs, he undressed yet again, turned them inside out and started the process anew, feeling more than a little stupid struggling with the scratchy linen with dangling privates harassed by tiny insects. Jelena had assured him that it was necessary to repeat the process every so often. Otherwise, your brain would get used to the inside-out state of the clothes, she said, and then you would no longer be able to see through *silva stragulum*.

While Jelena was just as much of a born-and-bred city-dweller as Kiril, she had grown up listening to her grandmother's stories of the Old Country, the vast and wild Balatsky Taiga where the grandmother as a little girl had befriended the folk of the forest, picked spring flowers, and built a secret hut in the shelter of spruces. For Jelena's grandmother, the forest had been a friendly refuge and realm of magic, while for the adults it had commanded respect and offered sustenance. That was how Jelena had wanted Velimir and Tomoe's children to grow up, and Kiril had not objected. At the moment, however, he felt uncertain that the forest could be a benevolent force in life.

Just as his weary eyes passed yet another moss-covered, rocky formation, it seemed as if something...shifted a little. As if the air was liquid and flowed gently. It was suddenly very quiet. A silvery outline flickered in the air and pulsed a few times. Kiril knelt down in the depression. *Is this now the* meaningful *ominous silence as opposed to the* regular *ominous silence?* He pulled his dagger and drew blood from his already scratched and aching palm with thinned lips and hissed as the skin split and spilled a few red drops. He wiped moss off the nearest rock to create a more or less flat surface and painted with his finger, with his own blood. *Why am I supposed to draw a heart? That is not even what a heart actually looks like. What if I drew a liver? Or a pancreas?* Kiril shoved his doubts away. Jelena had been adamant that folk magic, the most ancient and obscure kind of magic, was what worked where his own complex and logical high magic would fail.

The crudely-drawn heart glowed crimson. Kiril stood up abruptly and took a few steps back as the silvery liquid out-line materialized into a humanoid shape. He was looking at a crouching elf with a rough, bloodied club in her hand. She had silvery hair pulled in what had once been a neat plait, but now greasy, dirty, and tangled hair stuck out from her head. Wild and wide grey eyes stared back at Kiril from a pale, dirt-spotted face. She had the lithe but strong body of an elven warrior, but her face was gaunt.

"How?" the elf said, rage and frustration playing across her face. "How did they know to send a Valkaman hound after me? I was sure *silva stragulum* would keep me hidden!"

Kiril shrugged and wrapped his hand around the rune-inscribed stick of wood and bone in his pocket. He had found what he was looking for. Now it was the simple matter of using the beacon the Norns had given him in order to summon a patrol of warrior spirits.

"I have no quarrel with you, human," the elf, Vallara Silverbond, said, "but know that I'm not going back there. I am here for a reason. I have killed many that wished to live for that reason. Your death, while regrettable, won't make a difference."

Kiril squeezed the beacon, and it throbbed. "This is nothing personal," he said. "I need something from them, and I made them a promise."

"I was a warrior priestess of Lord Ortus," said the elf. She stood up and held her club as if it was the finest mace of elven craftsmanship. "It is true Lord Ortus no longer answers my prayers." She bared her teeth. "But I am a warrior still."

Kiril sensed the teleportation magic before the warriors actually materialized. This was high magic, and he still was able to sense the subtle signs even though he was cut off from its source. The Norns had assured him that the ten warriors would be fine and proven. They certainly looked the part when they materialized out of thin air. They roared and clanged their shields with their axes, then charged. Kiril watched as they descended upon the elf, who cursed and smashed them with her club. Fast as wind, furious and desperate, she was able to cut down six of the warriors before they overwhelmed her and held her down, face in the moss. When it was all over—when Vallara realized that she had lost—she ceased struggling and let the warriors stand her up.

"Valkaman man! You don't know what it's like! You can't imagine—" she tried, staring at Kiril, but the leader of the remaining warriors punched her in the gut so that she retched, then gagged her. "Shut up, *alfr*," he grunted. "The little man did his part, and you are going back to where you belong." He grinned at Kiril and patted his back. "Well done! Perhaps you are worthy of attention from the Yggdrasil. Now let's start our trek to the tree."

Kiril followed the jubilant warriors and the elf. He kept glancing at Vallara. She had implored him, her look full of despair. Now she just stared ahead, eyes dull as marbles. He wished he was not so aware of her, hearing her steps, seeing her subdued form in front of him, the living reminder that the price of his and Jelena's dreams was someone else's despair. *It will be all right. Once I have my magic back, she will be just a distant memory. What's one more person suffering because of me? Soon I will have a chance to become a whole man again.*

25
RUINS OF A DIMITRIAN TEMPLE AT THE EDGE OF THE DESERT

ONCE RESTED, THE PARTY PREPARED TO ENTER THE PURple glowing rift, knowing only that it would lead to "an ancient seat of power." The morose Shermag and his men followed the preparations.

"How did Tamasin convince so many Dimitrian spawn to follow her here? She seemed to *assume* that I would trust her," Peri asked, frowning.

"Many have," Shermag grunted. "Tamasin a leader of a great monastery in the East. Monastery that has protected the common folk of Laipa for centuries. Many Dimitrian spawn panic, seeing the stronger ones butcher and hunt their kin down." Shermag shrugged. "In more peaceful times, before Darien, Tamasin teach orc children to read. Many folk think orc no more than animal. That's why Shermag, too, first trusted her."

Peri smirked. "No wonder she talked to me like a child. She actually *does* teach children. Good for me, I'm a brat who doesn't like to be told what to do, so I distrusted her immediately. While we don't know what Tamasin is up to, we *do* know that Darien will flatten this place in days, and we'd better come up with a plan to defeat him. Tell you what, Shermag. You keep Tamasin locked up, and we'll find out how to defeat Darien. Sound fair?"

"Shermag no trust you, but Shermag trust Tamasin less."

"Good enough." Under the circumstances, she couldn't ask for more. And then she took a step into the faint purple light.

The scenery awaiting them at the end of the rift was very different from the dry dust and palm trees of Shinaris. The ground was swampy, and a half-crumbled temple, forgotten and moldy, loomed in the distance. Poisonous mists swirled about, and the humid air sapped all strength from the party's limbs. As they advanced with caution, they discovered the temple yard was drier but no less hostile. The trees were dead black twigs, and the ground was completely barren, the cold stone of the temple wall seeping latent death and hatred. Velimir shuddered.

"What?" Peri was surprised. Velimir was not easily shaken.

"Just…bad memories. Perhaps I will tell you about them one of these days, sister."

"I hope you will. Whoa, this place makes my blood feel… heightened. The Edge stirs." She lowered her voice. "Velimir, it feels *good.*"

Velimir nodded. "Your blood is calling to you, sister. This was, after all, a place dedicated to our father. Let us approach."

On high alert, they traversed the barren yard and peeked into the darkness of the inner sanctum. A faint clatter of bones cut the silence. Only thin rays of the pale sun penetrated the damp darkness. Something stirred by the altar.

"It is master! Master come again!" The croaky voice belonged to a rotten corpse, the remnants of a festive cleric robe still covering it. It was surrounded by other walking corpses in various stages of decomposition, wearing the rags of less ornamental robes. The other undead clattered closer, enthusiastic.

Then the same former priest of Dimitri changed his tone, his rotten face twisting in rage. "No, it is but a vessel of his power! Kill it!"

Peri charged, her reddish-brown hair like the mane of a warhorse, her eyes wide with anger. "I am not a *vessel* of anything, you disgusting fanatics!"

You certainly are more than that, sister, thought Velimir, and threw his blade in the mix. These undead horrors, still waiting for their master, were akin to the psychopaths who had tried to murder him and Peri in the very beginning of their life. Velimir hacked, rage and joy mixed in his heart. At moments he was again in the other stone temple, small and helpless, running for his life from an overwhelming enemy that didn't think him worth anything. Now he had a chance to get back at them.

"V...Velimir? VELIMIR!" Peri jerked his arm with all her might.

"Huh?"

"Um...they are down already. Have been for some time...you are hacking a heap of bones." Peri's expression was compassionate.

"O...oh," he said, aware of the rest of the group staring at him.

"The bad memory again?" Peri asked, so quiet that the others wouldn't hear.

Velimir nodded.

"We'll talk about it another time. Look, there is someone over there." Peri gestured towards a female figure standing by the altar, rigid and tall.

"Razeem?" Peri called, not taking her eyes off the figure.

The paladin bowed his head in prayer for a moment and then shook his head. "I don't sense a hostile intent from her."

The group cautiously approached the woman. She was thin and pale with white hair, though not feeble with age. Her skin was unnaturally luminous and smooth, her eyes large and dark. She wore a sapphire-embedded silver collar and high-heeled boots. Her dark clerical robes, like her boots, were of good quality, but worn and dull.

"You have disposed of my guardians, Peri. No matter, they were mindless and unruly. Useless. They perished in the time of Dimitri's fall and have been waiting for him to return ever since. However, you also exorcised my spy. Now that was unkind."

Peri shrugged. "It attacked us. And you would be Majsilaa?"

"That is correct. And *you* are here because of my son."

"Your son is Darien?" Velimir arched his eyebrow. "If you are the Majsilaa of legend, you can't have given birth to him."

The woman laughed harshly. "Oh, I gave my fertility as well as my heart away when the great Dimitri fell. I was a high priestess in this temple when the All-Father cast his favourite son away. I followed Dimitri to exile, for I loved the son more than the father. I vowed not to perish until my beloved Dimitri ascended to godhood, to be ready to serve as the first among his clergy, his high priestess! And so, I turned to the art of lichdom. To gain eternal life. But…Darien was my darling. My everything. I devoted myself completely to him, for he was the one I sponsored to ascend to godhood. He was the one who would embody my beloved Dimitri."

"So why do you want to kill him, then?" Velimir asked.

"Because he is a filthy traitor! He and the whole Esquadron! He cast me away, to rot here in this forgotten temple, with only the dead as my companions. But now, thanks to you…" she paused to smile, her incisors like fangs, "I have a chance to destroy him!"

"What is it they are after?" Peri asked. "Darien, and another one—Rajsa—had a chance to kill me. Instead, they kept me alive and injected me with something."

The others shared glances behind Peri's back, but she didn't notice.

"When they learned that you had manifested as the Edge, they devised an ambitious plan. When your body's natural alarm system—fight-or-flight response, as it is called—is triggered, your divine essence springs into action. But they learned of chemicals that can inhibit this process. If they can make your body think it is in mortal danger, while keeping you constrained, they can drain and harvest this divine essence."

"What did they plan to do with the essence?" Velimir

asked.

"They plan to create an entire race of celestials with Dimitrian blood. A race that will dominate the entire Valkama and destroy other life forms unless they can be of service. I objected to that, for it is a sacrilege. A clone, an artificially created celestial...blasphemy! The creation in its imperfection and Dimitri's dominion over it, the Esquadron as his elite guard and demigods...that was the original plan. That was the plan we should have stuck with." Majsilaa's eyes gleamed like the surfaces of a dark pond on a starry night.

"So how did you lose your power?" Peri asked.

"Darien used the love I have for him against me!" Majsilaa said through thinned lips, her hands balling into fists. "He accompanied me here to discuss how we would restore the temple once Dimitri ascended, and he took my original heart that I wore as a talisman, leaving me here to rot! Because my natural lifespan is long spent, I would perish without the latent Dimitrian energies sustaining me."

"Ambitious priestess, who once loved Dimitri so fiercely...what circulates the blood in your veins if Darien has taken your heart?" Kauno asked.

"As I said, my heart was removed by the time of Dimitri's fall. The ancient Anubian masters of Siri removed and embalmed it, replacing it with a mechanical heart, my life blood with fluid that nourishes the flesh. And the heart in which my life force is stored became an artifact of immense power. Now, without it, I am helpless." Majsilaa's jaw stiffened and her eyes narrowed. "Darien, I believe, has taken it to Siri to be imbued with his own blood, to render himself invulnerable. As long as it is stored with the old masters, no harm will come to him. Go to Siri. Find them. Do whatever you have to do to bring the heart back to me." Majsilaa adjusted her sapphire collar. "And once you do, I will destroy it, and you, in turn, can destroy him. He'll never see it coming."

"Gods willing," Peri said. "He thinks we are trapped in Shinaris with the rest of the Dimitrian spawn."

Casimir had been hiding behind the backs of the party, but somehow he summoned up the courage to speak. "Great Majsilaa! Is maybe the dogheads still in Siri make things go whirr whirr whirr?"

Majsilaa raised her eyebrows. "Casimir. Are you not such a..." —her voice turned cooler— "'faithful companion' after all?"

Casimir flinched. "Casimir wait wait wait and master not come...The redhead also nice maybe?"

Majsilaa uttered an exasperated sigh. "Oh well, perhaps it is Peri here who shall have the honor of ascending as the reigning god of wrath, though she is ill prepared for such a destiny. But I can see why you would choose to follow her, Casimir."

"Is also Casimir's all verybest friend in all the world, oh yes! Velimir!"

"Is he now?" Majsilaa chuckled and glanced at Velimir, who scowled. "Yes, one of the two wildcards of fate, the ones that were not supposed to live. He disposed of one of the chosen ones, Kazumi...but now his opportunity for greatness has passed. As an answer to your question...yes, 'the dogheads' are still 'making things go whirr whirr whirr' in Siri, as far as I know. The ancient masters of life and death, smiths of wondrous machinery. But they possess little power and little interest in it, since the civilization they performed burial rites for and traded with is long dead."

Ewynne wondered how Casimir had ended up being Dimitri's "faithful companion." She had taken quite a liking to the imp, and wondered why he liked Velimir so much. She had to admit that Peri was right about many things she had said. Ewynne wanted to hate Velimir, to keep him at the longest possible distance, and had rebuffed her brother's attempts to approach her. But Ewynne had always been easily tuned to others' feelings, even when they did their best to keep them unexpressed. Velimir was hurting; he had suffered much, even though he did his best to hide it. Ewynne had always been compassionate—much more so than Peri— and she could not be unmoved by such suffering. But the feeling threatened her very perception of reality. There was Connor and the island, the safety and happiness they represented, smashed to pieces by Velimir, and after that, only the life on the road with its threats and its pains—a clear-cut divide caused by an evil enemy—and if she started to feel sorry for Velimir, she didn't know what to think about anything anymore! She shrugged. She would be damned if she let Velimir see she was wavering.

"The forgotten road to Siri is full of dangers. Djinn, dust devils, demons of old," Razeem said.

Majsilaa shrugged. "That is not my concern. You were capable of exorcising my shadow spy. You must have a trick or two up your sleeves. Head west, to where the wetlands and the dry river bed turn into a desert, and at the edge of a windswept gorge descending to the valley, you must make a secret call. Otherwise, you'll be lost in the sands, following an endless maze of narrow pathways carved into the rock. Only by calling 'alriyah walriyah' will you find Siri and whatever lives down there."

"Is that the Sjenka's shadow path thing?" Peri asked.

"Ah, you have heard *that* theory," Majsilaa said. "Nothing to do with Sjenka, but people conjectured that the lady of shadow must be responsible if winds keep spinning you so that you find your way to the hidden city. And we let them keep thinking that and chasing, literally, shadows. This magic is much older, lost when the last civilization of Siri fell. No-one left to call the birds...but I digress. It will serve to take you where you need to be."

"'Alriyah, walriyah' and brace for being spun around. Got it. Sounds like your average day as of late," said Peri.

"Farewell, Majsilaa," said Velimir. "We shall return with your embalmed heart and bring the fight to Darien!"

Majsilaa smiled her cold, thin smile and nodded courteously, turning her back, staring at the remnants of the temple like she had been doing when the party entered.

As the group prepared to make their way to the west through the wetlands, Razeem spoke up. "Peri, that woman was...*still* is a servant of Dimitri! How can we trust her?"

"Oh, for gods' sake," Peri snapped. "Don't you realize trust is a luxury I don't have anymore? The prophecy is unfolding, and I have the most powerful of the remaining Dimitrian spawn after my ass! And Darien seems pretty troublesome. If you need extra convincing, feel free to take a stroll in Shinaris!"

Razeem bit his tongue, taken aback.

"Peri is right," Velimir said. "The prophecies talk about...a betrayer. I don't know who it might be, but if Majsilaa betrays us, we must just deal with it. If Shermag is to be believed, this is our only hope of defeating Darien. We have escaped Shinaris, but Darien will be after us as soon as he realizes Peri is not there."

Razeem nodded. "I cannot argue with that. Allying with a force of evil makes me uncomfortable, but let us hope that her desire for revenge will keep her on our side for good. Lead on, then."

26
SIRI

The dry river bed descended to a wall of pale rose-colored rock. It was split by dozens of steep cracks. "So, this is the place," Peri said. "I guess I'll do the honors. Saying...the thing is supposed to take us to the right one. Be prepared." She took a wide, steady stance, cleared her throat, and called, "Alriyah! Walriyah!"

Nothing happened.

"Fuck. Did we just walk through all the goddamn sand for—" She stopped as she heard a faint murmur in the distance, but she could not tell where the sound was coming from. It rapidly grew louder, like a huge ocean wave gathering strength. Soon the sand was whipping as dozens of little eddies in midair and the hiss had grown into a deafening roar. She had to close her eyes as the sand got in her face, into her nostrils. Then she was whipped around, spinning, spinning, pelted with sand...until the spinning stopped.

Peri blew dust from her nostrils and squinted through the settling dust. Everyone was wiping dust off their faces and clothes, trying to reorient themselves. The dizzy travelers found themselves standing in a narrow gorge split in the steep rock—one of the dozens of corridors they had seen before making the call. Behind their backs, it reached beyond where the eye could see. The party peered deeper into the gorge. They saw swirling colors of ochre, pale rose, and pearly blue in the rocky walls and heard ominous wailing.

"Must be the wind," Jussuf said, straightening his shoulders, glancing at Razeem.

"It may be more than that," the older man replied. Jussuf's expression suggested that the thought had occurred to him as well. "The descent to Siri is flanked with cavernous tombs and shrines. Dust devils, djinn, and demons roam the desert. Many may have settled in Siri after its fall."

"Treasure hunters sometimes try to enter the valley. None have returned. Their bones likely lie somewhere in the sands," Jussuf said.

"Or worse," Kauno said and reached to adjust her curly chestnut wig. "The living have left Siri centuries ago...but the dead can be vengeful if disturbed."

The winding path through the crack descended slowly to the valley. It felt as if someone was watching them from the darkness of the cavernous openings. "Peaceful dead," Kauno said, "but they keep watch. They will let us pass if we don't disturb them."

Ewynne spotted a bleached skeleton holding a rusted sword and a splintered shield. It was half-buried in the sand. She nudged it with her boot. "Someone didn't get the message, I guess," she said.

Peri shrugged. "We didn't come here to loot tombs."

The colorful walls of the gorge were so tall that the sky was just a dusky ribbon high above. A hawk circled, whistling and starting to descend. "A messenger," Kauno said. "Our arrival will not go unnoticed."

The chasm finally began to widen. Ewynne felt the sand whipping at her face and wrapped the hood of her traveling cloak tighter around her head. A plain stretched before their eyes. At the other end of it, there was the entrance to the lost city—arches of pillars and flower garlands towering over the stairs. Two hawks and an ibis watched over the stairs, all hewn in the pale rosy stone.

Peri drew a breath. "There it is. The ancient people had bird mages who watched the skies from their laboratories. The mages commanded birds. Birds were holy to them."

Kauno nodded. "The art of bird magic is long lost in time. But the bird gods remember wherever they are."

"Fascinating to be sure," Velimir said, "but it looks like there are some restless creatures blocking our way."

Shafts of shifting sand whirled in the distance. They howled and whipped the dirt, flinging grit and dust in the eyes of the approaching party. Dozens of distorted faces flickered in the middle of these small tornadoes.

"Dust devils!" Jussuf yelled and drew his mace.

They approached, bracing themselves against the gusts of the wind. The dust devils circled around a man who had drawn a glowing sword—a sword that sparkled icy blue and emitted glittery steam.

Kauno raised her hands and called out in her native tongue, *"Haje!"*

The circle of the dust devils started to expand, as if an

invisible centrifugal force was spiraling them to a trajectory. They seemed agitated and tried to resist. They stirred sand such that it got into the party's nostrils and eyes, and tried to blow them off their feet as their cloaks flapped like battle standards in a storm. But Kauno's spell steadily pulled the dust devils apart, and soon, they gave up and went their way, aimlessly milling about the dust field.

Peri stopped in her tracks. "Samir Arakelian."

The lean and long-cheeked blue-eyed man gave a little bow, adjusted his iridescent cloak, and tucked the sword into a luxurious-looking purple sash. "If it isn't little Peri from Eilean de Taigh-Sholais!" he said. "Looks like ye made yer way to Siri after all, lass!"

"You didn't pay your tab in the inn," Peri said. "And your crew was drinking *a lot*."

"Ah, don't be like that, lass," the man said. "Ye were their darling. They wouldn't mind if yer friends…borrowed a little." He brushed dust off his red and green silk vest that seemed to be embedded with magically enchanted elven metal thread.

"They did mind. You also stole a silver chalice from the lighthouse. That was a real asshole thing to do. They keep it open because it's a cathedral and meant for all travelers in need of protection."

"Come on…we *were* travelers in need! Needed all the silver we could get."

Peri's chest puffed indignantly. She was about to retort something when Velimir spoke up. "Peri," he said, "please enlighten us as to who this man is."

"I told you that I had planned to join a pirate crew to see the world," Peri said. "Well, here's the pirate. Don't see a crew, though."

"Ah, well, ye see…kind of an accident happened to the latest crew," said Samir Arakelian. "Rather recently, in fact… which is why it is excellent that ye are here, lass! I am in need of some assistance, as ye can see."

"And what would you give us in exchange for assistance?" asked Velimir. The pirate wielded a sword that looked like a priceless artifact, and though his clothes were colorful, like the feathers of a peacock, they were magically enchanted, and Velimir could spot the shape of a high-quality chain shirt under them. The man was more than a harmless ne'er-do-well—which meant that he might have something to offer.

"The pleasure of me delightful company, of course!" said the pirate and grinned, then paused as if waiting for applause. No-one smiled back, so he continued. "I could act as a guide, as I've been studying and exploring Siri for a while. And…I may be willing to part with this sword, should ye help me to get out of Siri safely."

Peri glanced at Ewynne. "It *is* a nice sword," Peri said.

THE WINDING CORRIDORS, FLANKED BY HIEROGLYPHS and pictures of birds, snakes, and other animals seemed endless. Peri had lost track hours ago. Occasionally, the party could spot a slithering shape in a shadowy corner, a rat prickling its ears or a scarab or a scorpion scampering across the corridor. When the party could see a few rays of light from behind the corner, a jackal appeared and cocked its head, regarding the party with its dark, inquisitive eyes. Then it threw its head back, howled, and ran away.

The corridor opened to a courtyard. The sky peeked out high above the galleries which were hewn into the stone overlooking the plaza. There was a wide dry depression in the middle, a bridge crossing it to a dusty marble gazebo flanked by the familiar figures of the two hawks, the ibis-headed figure regarding the courtyard from the roof of the gazebo.

Peri smiled. "The book I read in the library back home—*A Pilgrim's Memoirs*—mentioned a floating island. They knew how to preserve water and create lakes, rivers, and gardens here. This used to be the heart of the city."

"Well, there's yer entrance to the Anubian kingdom," said Samir Arakelian. He pointed at a narrow opening framed by polished gray rock. The steep stairs descended into the darkness. Statues of two creatures with human bodies and jackal heads flanked the entrance. There were hieroglyphs on top of the staircase. "Ye do yer business with them and come back up. I'm not going down there." The pirate crossed his arms, dropping his calculated manner of ease.

"Is there something you are not telling us?" Velimir asked.

"No, just they don't have any treasure, and they are not too fond of visitors, so I'm not risking annoying them for nothing," the pirate answered.

Peri and Velimir looked at each other and shrugged.

"There are no spirits of the dead here," said Kauno, "that Kauno can tell, at least. They all seemed to live in those cave tombs around the city. This city is full of life—animals of the desert—but the people who built it are long gone. Their spirits are not here. As for demons or djinn, if there are any, they are hiding."

"So…we'll just go down there and see what they want," Peri said. "I don't need to tell you spellcasters to be on alert for anything weird. Let's hope they are not hostile. What *are* they, anyway?"

"No-one is entirely sure," said Kauno. "The Anubi are an ancient race—older than the people who built Siri. They speak human tongues but are much more intelligent. They lived harmoniously with the citizens of Siri and performed their burial rites. Since then, they have kept their peace. They have no interest in the outside world."

So Peri and Velimir, weapons drawn, led the party down the stairs in the faint light of *virvatuli*—Kauno's spirit ally from Balatsky Taiga. It was a pale ghost light that often wandered the marshes. Once the spirit of an unborn child that a desperate mother had buried in the swamp, it was now lonely and confused. It had been luring travelers into the bog to be its companions. But Kauno had asked it to come with him, and it had found peace.

As they descended, Razeem glanced at Velimir, hesitated, then decided to speak up. "Velimir," he started, a pensive look in his eyes, "maybe you don't care what I have to say, but—"

Something about the paladin's questioning eyes and deep gaze reminded Velimir faintly of Brother Connor. "You are right, paladin. I care not even a little bit what you have to say," he said, eyes hard as flintstones.

But Razeem was not easily discouraged. "Spit venom if you feel the need," continued the unprovoked Razeem, "but I think you would do well to appreciate that you have been given a second chance. Your power-hungry machinations sent you to the Abyss the first time. How did the power and riches you had amassed serve you there?"

"My will and fervour served me well in the Abyss," Velimir answered, scowling at Razeem from his greater height.

Razeem nodded. However, he was not done with the subject. "But those qualities are not what took you there. There are many men of will and fervour who will not end up in hell."

Velimir turned abruptly to face him. "I couldn't care less where I go if I fail again, you senile fool! If that happens, nothing matters anymore!"

"Senile I am not, and I don't believe you mean that. Besides, there is also this life. It can be more worthwhile than your first one," Razeem said.

Unexpected tears sprang to Velimir's eyes, but he held them back. He tried to scorn the pompous paladin in his mind, but his heart was not in it. The eyes...The way he talked to Velimir...

"I...I...Go parrot your pious platitudes to those who can be redeemed! For me it is far too late!" Velimir said, almost choking. He scowled in anger to hide it.

Razeem sighed and quickened his pace, leaving Peri and Velimir behind. She had not commented on the exchange.

"Take it this way, Velimir. Razeem sees something worthwhile in you," Peri said quietly.

That didn't make it any easier. Velimir nodded curtly and continued in silence.

———————————— · ● · ————————————

AFTER A LONG WHILE OF DESCENDING IN SILENCE, THE stairs ended into a small antechamber in front of a stone slab carved into a similar gray stone as the entrance to the staircase. There was a polished brass door knocker attached to the slab in the shape of the head of a jackal with a lolling tongue. Peri glanced at her companions, who just waited.

"Go ahead," Velimir said then. "I have your back."

Peri knocked. In a short while, the slab slid aside and revealed a creature who looked like the statues that had been guarding the entrance to the Anubi kingdom high above. He pricked his large ears and tilted his head, regarding the visitors with his bright eyes. "Furless. Again," he said. His words were clipped little yips. His pelt had a rusty red hue, and his body was lean but muscular. He was barefoot, and his nails looked like those of a dog, sharp and curved.

"Well, sorry to disturb your peace, but this is important," Peri said.

"Of course, of course. Always important. Furless are so very important. But, of course. Have to be hospitable." The creature extended his hand that was human-shaped but likewise had sharp and curved nails. "Name is Kurra. Your is?"

"It is Peri. Peri of Eilean de Taigh-Sholais," Peri said, shaking Kurra's hand. It felt warm. Coarse, short rust-colored hair covered the back of it.

"Welcome, welcome. You want to drink water? We will serve." Kurra, who was wearing a short skirt made of plated shiny metal, gestured for the party to follow. The underground lair seemed cozy. There were small alcoves and shelves everywhere, full of jars, implements, complicated clockwork mechanisms, and small statues depicting humans and animals. There was also a little garden with flowering cacti and a few bushes of herbs. An Anubus sprinkled water on the bushes from a small earthenware jar, drop by drop.

There were animals everywhere—snakes, jackals, scorpions, scarabs, rats, spiders. There was even a vulture perched next to a narrow shaft carved in the ceiling. The animals seemed to feel safe and at home. There were also other Anubi, who nodded a greeting as the party passed by, then continued with whatever they were doing. Some had pelts that glinted iridescent blue, others with an emerald hue. Yet others were jet black. There were alcoves covered with sliding slabs. "Homes," Kurra said. They passed a group of Anubi working on a jackal that seemed to be sleeping on a large stone table. One Anubus covered the animal with a luminous shield emanating from his hands, while another worked on it with a scalpel. There were tiny cogs, gears, and screws spread on the slab. The jackal's paw was completely smashed, a raw red mess.

"There!" Casimir interjected. "Is dogheads making things go whirr whirr whirr, just like Majsilaa said!"

"We help," Kurra said. "We helped the furless of Siri, too, but they went away."

"A wild jackal that can't hunt or scavenge..." Peri said. "Seems like a quick and painless death would be the only help for it."

"We make new paw!" Kurra said proudly. "Look at my hand." He spread and extended his fingers. The joints had a faint metal glint to them. "With these, flesh not gets old and decay." The Anubus bent down and offered his open palm for a rat that had been observing them. The rat climbed in his hand and snuggled cozily. Kurra gently extended the animal's tail. It, too, was made of tiny metal particles lovingly knitted together.

"Amazing!" said Ewynne. "You...you can make new limbs

for injured animals!"

"That is true," Kurra said. "Time comes when things decay, go to other place. We did services for the furless of Siri. But sometimes the animals stay. This rat—I call her Amili—is hundred and eighteen years old, in furless numbers."

"This is kind of what we wanted to talk about," Peri said.

"Yes, talk. Sit, sit." Kurra had led the party to a long table with a group of goblets and a large pitcher. They sat on the benches and gratefully sipped their water. Velimir only moistened his lips. The water storage down here in the bowels of an abandoned desert city must have been scarce and precious.

"Your kind eat this?" Kurra offered a plate of roasted crickets. He saw Ewynne's horrified expression and said, "No worry, they went to other place. No more here."

"Thanks, I'm good," Ewynne said and smiled feebly.

Kauno picked one and sucked it. Velimir's jaw stiffened, and he crunched on one, swallowing it with a quick gulp. Jussuf looked green and Razeem said, "Thank you, but we… are not accustomed to such a cuisine."

Peri was already on her second cricket. "Hey, this is not bad! And let me get this straight. You make new limbs for animals so they never die?" Peri asked, licking cricket crust from her fingers.

"Sometimes, yes. But animals not afraid of other place. We just ask for some to stay, to be our friends. Many others go to other place."

"But you didn't do this for the people of Siri."

Kurra shook his head. "Didn't ask them. The furless… have cubs. A lot of cubs. And if they come and ask to stay… too many stay. That cannot be. Not enough food, water. This is why we not have cubs. We stay, can't have cubs." Kurra stood up and filled the goblet from an ornamental little faucet depicting an ibis that was embedded in the wall. There seemed to be some sort of water reservoir built in it.

"But you did make Majsilaa a lich. Back in the day," Peri continued, moving the conversation in the right direction.

"A...lich? We helped Majsilaa to stay. She said that it is important. She had to stay to help Dimitri!"

"Wait," Razeem said. "You...wanted to help Dimitri?"

"Yes. Dimitri was very kind. He comforted the ones who cry when someone goes to other place." Kurra's earnest expression grew wistful. "Then Dimitri had quarrel with his father, poor young man. We helped Majsilaa."

"Um...okay." Peri raised her eyebrows and paused for a moment to digest the information. So, they thought Dimitri was a good guy? "But Majsilaa's heart is here now, isn't it? Her adopted son brought it here so that you'd make him invulnerable."

"Yes, that young man!" Kurra's expression brightened. "Your friend, maybe? You furless are having family trouble? He said it was important. He protects the animals in Wulani from evil furless who kill. Majsilaa sent him, remembered we help."

Peri sighed and closed her eyes. "Kurra..." she said in a wavering voice, "you have been lied to. Big time."

Kurra frowned. "Lied? That is...when you say things that are different from real? Yes, the furless do that. Very confusing."

"In fairness, according to old scripture that the cult considers apocryphal, Dimitri's compassion was his downfall," Velimir said. "He 'grieved with the grieving, cried with the crying.'"

"Yes, he did!" Kurra said. "That is why we helped Majsilaa to stay. Dimitri was very kind."

"He is…not anymore," Peri said. "Majsilaa betrayed you. Dimitri changed."

Kurra digested the information, following a skittering scarab with his bright eyes, petting the rat curled in his palm. His lip trembled. "But…why? We remember. He *was* kind."

Velimir pushed aside his goblet and leaned forward. "Dimitri was angered because the All-Father allowed all the suffering, or so it says," he said. "True, the cult considered that origin story blasphemous, unworthy of the unadulterated wrath in Dimitrian blood. But my mentor said that from a scholarly point of view, it was a sound one."

For Velimir himself it had always rung true, perhaps a cautionary tale of misplaced passion. Perhaps, indeed, Dimitri had entertained such notions before seeing the error in his ways. He and Kiril, too, had been swayed by Jelena's cherished notions of compassion and decency before realizing they were traps and tricks of the more powerful and the indifferent multiverse.

"Yes…" Kurra said slowly, "I do remember. Dimitri was angry, shortly before Majsilaa came for help."

"Dimitri embraced his wrath, for it was all that was left for him, and the power in it intoxicated him," Velimir said. It must have been so. That very intoxication had carried him all his life and fought his way out of the Abyss.

Peri reached her hand out and grabbed Kurra's. "Majsilaa's son wants to do something very bad. Kill thousands of people. Animals, too, will die. They will…create a race of evil celestials. Cruel ones that will kill all the creatures that are not useful for them. The rest will be their slaves."

Kurra covered his muzzle with his hand. "That...that is very bad. Oh dear. We had no idea."

"Kurra, we can stop him. Give Majsilaa's heart to us, and we will take away its power," Peri said and held her breath.

Kurra hesitated. "But...will you hurt Darien? That would be bad. He was such a nice young man."

"By Juris! Darien is—" Razeem started, but Peri touched his arm and looked Kurra in the eye.

Peri's eyes brimmed with tears. "Kurra..." she said, her voice quavering, "your people possess the secrets of immortality. You can make people invulnerable. Do you understand what...what any number of powerful people would do to get their hands on you? They might try to bribe you, trade with you. But most likely they'd just capture you. Keep you slaves, force you to work for them. You'd never be free to live here with the animals again. They'd destroy you. They'd kill anything to get to you."

Kurra shook his head several times. "Oh no, that would not do at all," he said, squeezing Peri's hand. "This is our home. The animals of desert are our family."

"Yes." Peri paused and held Kurra's hand to her heart. "And I want to keep it that way. When all those people who believe Darien is invulnerable see him...well, die, they'll believe the rumors are false. And...you should not help anyone but animals that way anymore, no matter what they say. Okay?"

Kurra nodded several times. "Oh dear. It seems that furless feel strongly about it. Yes. Thank you for telling us. You can take the heart, but spend the night, please. It is a long way back. Very nice of you."

They were led to a dormitory that was illuminated by a few ornate lanterns hanging from the ceiling. When Kurra had bid them goodnight, promised breakfast, and left from earshot, Velimir spoke. "That was easy. How refreshing! The naivete of these creatures is remarkable."

Peri nodded, still looking bewildered. "He...he just took me for my word. Like he took Majsilaa. Like he took Darien. I could have told him any number of lies, and he just promised to hand the heart to us."

"The notion of lying seemed to confuse him," Kauno said. "They have never developed the need or the will."

"Yeah, that is something all right," Ewynne said. She lifted the corner of a sheet on one of the beds and inhaled the faint smell of herbs. "These beds look really nice. Been a while since I slept in one. And it's nice and cool here, but not cold. I'll go to sleep now."

As she snuggled under the sheets, the others followed suit. Only Velimir stayed up, sitting on a cozy chair carved into a globe-shaped rock and cushioned with velvet and something soft. What Peri had said had him thinking. It was true that the possession of the secrets of life and death were priceless. They were of use even to divine beings. It was true that these creatures seemed defenseless and easy pickings for anyone powerful enough to make their way to the abandoned city and brave dust devils, djinn, and other dangers. Thus, it would make sense to capture and enslave them. But the very idea seemed to be an affront to Peri. Kurra's trusting naivete had rendered Peri different. None of her usual wisecracks and profanity, no sardonic grins. Instead, she was wide-eyed and touched.

And the thing was, it had an effect on Velimir, too. The

idea of harm coming to the creatures made him feel…uneasy. Like there was something wrong with it. It was as if Peri was in possession of some intuitive knowledge he could vaguely sense but could not make sense of. It stirred memories. Something was moving in that dark fjord where everything he didn't want to think about was lurking underwater.

———————— •●• ————————

RAZEEM COULD NOT SLEEP. HE COULD NOT FORGET VELImir's intense reaction to Razeem's attempt to approach him earlier in the day. The old paladin had seen enough to understand that Velimir was not nearly as unaffected by it as he had claimed to be. He had been angry and confrontational—that was how people usually reacted when they felt threatened.

He could sense that Velimir still was evil. He was obsessed with power and still perceived compassion as weakness. But Razeem also felt the turmoil this tormented soul was in, and the remarkable strength of will the man possessed. Velimir had seen the depths of the Abyss, he had experienced first-hand the folly in megalomaniacal plans. Razeem could sense the pain the proud and unrepentant facade was trying to cover. As a paladin, it was his duty to try to guide this soul into changing his outlook and ways. But how should he approach Velimir further?

He could see Velimir brooding and keeping his own company, his expressionless face and golden eyes fixed in thought. He decided to try again.

"Can I sit next to you, Velimir?"

"Do as you wish, paladin. I do not own this place," Velimir answered, the venom in his voice gone.

Razeem sat for a while, wondering what Velimir had gone through in his first life.

"Has anyone ever shown you kind guidance, Velimir? Anyone strong who was not cruel?"

Velimir hesitated, but then scoffed. "Indeed not, old man. You apparently are still under the illusion such a thing exists."

"Such a thing exists. And once you are able to see it, you will have learned much," answered Razeem calmly. He adjusted the lantern so that he could see Velimir's face more clearly.

"Whatever lets you sleep at night." Velimir kept speaking in that dismissive tone, but his face had tensed, and he was unknowingly squeezing the fabric of his undertunic in his fingers.

"Do not try to drive others away when they are trying to include you."

"I do not ask for pity!" Velimir snapped. "I plan to earn my place by being useful and competent!"

"Being kind and appreciating your usefulness don't have to be mutually exclusive," Razeem said, keeping his voice even and soothing. This was much like trying to pacify a jittery animal.

Velimir was quiet for a long time, and Razeem had no idea what he was thinking. Finally, Velimir spoke. "Paladin. You have traveled with Peri longer than I. Can you explain to me why she is so shaken now? What is it that bothers her about these creatures so much?"

Razeem rubbed his forehead, giving it some consideration. "The idea of being constrained, of lacking freedom, is anathema to her. You should know, Velimir—against all caution she refused to even contemplate binding your will because doing so would have been unholy to her. She must see these creatures as something pure, something that has been spared the corruption of humankind, and the idea of them being so guileless and defenseless terrifies her." Razeem smiled to himself. In his estimation, it was a good sign that Velimir was interested in Peri's reaction.

"There is much power in her blood, but she doesn't seem keen on pursuing it," Velimir answered.

"That power is tainted, Velimir," Razeem said, allowing a bit of intensity in his tone. "The Edge is powerful indeed in terms of raw destruction. But every time she uses it, it... diminishes her. Erases some of her humanity. She is aware of that, though no doubt she is tempted at times. Perhaps you should discuss it with her."

Velimir nodded, deep in thought. "I apologize for calling you a fool, paladin," he said then. "Whatever I think about your fool god, you are a useful member of this group."

Razeem smiled just a little. That was certainly progress.

"Thank you, Velimir. So are you. Goodnight."

———————————•●•———————————

PERI'S STEP WAS LIGHT AS THE PARTY STARTED TO AScend the sloping corridor back to the abandoned city square. She felt the shriveled heart pulsating faintly against her bare chest. It was dry and warm and tingled with magic. Kurra had attached it to a thin silver chain, and Peri had put it around her neck, hiding the heart under her chain shirt.

"Now the heart should be safe. No-one knows we have it," Peri said. "I wonder if we should return to Shinaris briefly and inform Shermag of what we have learned. Then we could coordinate the attack on Darien better. But Shermag is also very unstable. If he decides he doesn't trust us after all, it would be disastrous to part with the information. And I would avoid Tamasin for now. Deal with one problem at a time."

Velimir nodded, arms crossed at his waist. "I advise against involving Shermag. Too much of a gamble under the circumstances. His armies are already worn by the siege. We are capable of taking Darien down by ourselves."

"And Darien's army?" Razeem asked.

"It will be of no consequence once their 'invincible' leader is removed," Peri said. "They are fanatics, believing him a god. If they see him fall, they will quickly lose their morale. Ewynne and Kauno have a few handy spells to deal with masses so that we can hinder them before Darien is killed. We'll just have to get to him quickly. Shermag said that he holds command at the center of the siege camp. It's not as if he's trying to hide."

The party arrived above the ground and found Samir waiting at his camp, sitting on his bedroll. "Me lass! Took yer sweet time, ye lot did!" the man said.

"You could have followed. They were very hospitable. Offered us roasted crickets and everything," Peri said.

"Uh," the pirate grimaced. "Ah well, if yer business is done, I suppose it is back to the valley, aye?"

"It is," Peri replied. "Lead on."

"Here, lass, take the sword," Samir said. "Ye have earned it. I prefer to use a rapier to match my wit, and it is too fancy for me, anyway."

Peri accepted the sword and immediately felt the cold

emanating from the sparkling blade. "Wow. This has a powerful enchantment," she said.

"It does indeed," said Razeem as he watched Peri unsheathe the sword and take a few tentative stances with it. "It is imbued with elemental frost that, naturally, counteracts elemental fire. It offers protection from natural heat, too. And there are more enchantments that I don't recognize."

"I find it curious that you would be willing to part from it, pirate," Velimir said, regarding Samir from his full height.

Samir shrugged. "I value me life. I could not make me way out of Siri alive with me crew gone. And beautiful as it is, there is more treasure stored in me ship."

The dust devils approached when they exited the city, but Kauno was prepared and was able to chase them away easily. They were about to enter the narrow gorge when they smelled smoke and felt a wall of oppressive heat.

"You shall not leave Siri." The voice boomed and crackled like fire. A human-shaped creature of shifting smoke and smouldering flame towered before them. Three smaller creatures of living flame, faces shifting in the middle of the pillars of fire, stood at its back. It had black shining wings, like the luminous white ones of a celestial.

Casimir uttered a little whimper and flapped behind Velimir's back. Razeem crossed his arms and spoke in a loud, resonant voice. "Ifrit. Begone. You have no dominion over us. Avenging spirit, you have no authority to raise your weapons against those who have committed no wrong."

The ifrit laughed ominously. Its mouth was wide, and its teeth were sharp and long.

"Um, about that." Samir Arakelian smirked and pointed at the sword at Peri's waist. "Here's yer thief. She has taken the sword of the Shandalar family, and I'll...get going. See ya, bye!" He produced something from his sash, tossed it to the ground, and vanished in a cloud of smoke.

"What the—" But Peri had no time to worry about Samir. The ifrit charged at her, roaring like a furnace. "Hey, listen, we didn't—"

"Save it, sister!" Velimir yelled and drew his blade. He charged at the smoke and heat, praying that Jussuf had spells available that would mitigate the fiery damage the creature could cause. He observed the ifrit's limbs, knowing that the fire elementals were bound to it and would orchestrate their movements in harmony with it. He had encountered ifrit in the Abyss. Avenging demons who punished oath-breakers and those guilty of sacrilege, they were creatures of order and enemies of the free-roaming demons he had fought for in the Demon Wars.

The ifrit was pure fire, heat, flame, consuming rage, but it also had human limbs and skill and accuracy with the fiery blade it wielded. Every time one of the fighters managed to hit the creature, they took a good amount of fiery pain. The ifrit hissed and emitted steam every time Peri's sword cut it, and the fire elementals shied away from her. Still, the blistering pain in Peri's skin was maddening. She started to feel the unreason, the all-consuming rage, the alluring presence inside her tugging, straining to get out of control.

"I HATE these things! Hate them! Hate them!" she growled, hacking away.

Velimir recognized the red flash in Peri's eyes and remembered the feelings that accompanied it. The flickering madness, hate, rage, lust of power, the intoxicating *invincibility*. But then he remembered Razeem's words about how turning into the Edge would diminish Peri. True, the Edge was a glorious avatar of power, once Peri learned to command and control it, but that was not the case yet, and she had shown little interest in learning. Actually...he liked Peri just the way she was, flesh and blood, her smart-aleck wit, her disarming spontaneity and recklessness, her sudden bursts of overflowing emotion. She could not afford to be diminished. The idea of her fading away made Velimir's throat constrict.

"Peri! Don't give in! We will kill it regardless! It is not worth it!" he shouted.

Peri glanced at him, slightly annoyed, but nodded and concentrated. *No rage, no lust...can manage...will not lose control.* Ewynne pelted the creatures with a miniature blizzard. It dissipated rapidly in the desert heat, but the creatures grew weaker, emitting clouds of steam. Velimir growled and roared, pushing himself to ignore the blistering pain. Jussuf's healing rejuvenated their boiling bodies. After a while, the ifrit roared for a last time and disappeared in a flash of smoke, like the final spark of embers of a cooling campfire in the night. Now there was nothing left of it but the burned skins of the fighters.

Velimir put his hand on Peri's shoulder. "Sister...I know how it calls. But it would consume you. Razeem spoke of it. And I...I don't want that," he found himself saying.

"I just...I hate them! I have always hated heat. There is something *malevolent* in it. Those things didn't even have proper bodies!" She was still pacing, eyes flickering nervously, even though the battle was over.

"An ifrit and three fire elementals bound to its service." Velimir took her hands in his own. "A powerful creature, but nothing our team couldn't handle. Jussuf will heal you. It will be all right. Let us just cross the gorge, call the winds to spin us, and then make a camp at the river bed."

Peri still looked wide-eyed and shaky, but she squeezed Velimir's hands before letting go of them, picked up her gear, and started to make her way to the gorge. Ewynne approached Velimir, Casimir perched on her shoulder and a puzzled expression on her face. "Velimir, you...helped her not to turn into the Edge. Perhaps...perhaps you have changed."

For a moment, Velimir's surprised face looked soft and unguarded. A tiny smile made its way to the corner of his mouth. "Perhaps, little sister," he answered. Ewynne offered him a tepid smile and shrugged, and the party uneventfully traveled through the gorge, leaving the watchful eyes of the ghosts behind.

27
A CAMP AT THE DRIED RIVER BED

LATER IN THE CAMP, WHEN JUSSUF WAS DONE TENDING Peri's blistered skin and had moved on to Kauno, Velimir approached Peri.

"Peri, sister, may I have a private word with you? About a thing I have given much thought to as of late?" he asked.

"Sure. Have a seat." She made space for Velimir on her bedroll, hugged her knees, and smiled at her brother.

Velimir sat down and faced her with great intensity. "The end of the prophecy is drawing closer. Disposing of the impostor Darien will be glorious, but it is only the beginning." Velimir made an emphatic pause. Velimir's eyes were so intense, his face so full of purpose and enthusiasm.

No wonder he had fought his way from the very Abyss, Peri thought. She felt a flash of deep appreciation, something easier to accept now after praying to Connor and talking with Razeem.

"My ambition to become the new Lord of Wrath was everything to me," Velimir continued. "However, it died with the loss of my divinity. My opportunity for *that* greatness has passed, but I have spent some time in your company now, sister…" Velimir paused, the appreciation Peri had just felt reflecting back in his eyes, "and I have come to…really value you. A true leader, a fearsome warrior, a courageous soul, a woman of character and spirit…I can, without resentment, say that you are worthy of the divinity in your blood, which is no longer present in mine. And this is what my proposition relates to."

"Go ahead." Peri opted to say nothing more, even though Velimir's words touched her deeply.

"I don't know what you plan to do, but the time of the prophecy is nigh. In one way or another, you are one of those epic people who forges the fate of the very Valkama. Take my old goal, sister! Become Lady of Wrath, for I cannot imagine anyone more deserving! And I will pledge to stand by you, to always have your back, to be your right hand! Imagine, sister and brother in arms, all the multiverse in awe of us, even the gods themselves trembling as we go by, ruling over—"

"Velimir…*Velimir!* Valkama calling! Down here!" Peri waved her hand in front of Velimir's eyes.

Velimir stopped talking, and a nonplussed frown started to spread on his face.

"You *still* don't get it, do you?" Peri was incredulous, shaking her head.

"Get what?" Velimir seemed genuinely puzzled.

"I have no such plan. I do not want to become a god at all, much less one as nasty as a god of wrath," Peri explained, articulating clearly, as if talking to a child.

"But...why? *Why?*" Velimir was frustrated beyond belief. "It is all within your reach...rule over lesser men and your own destiny, the real power to make the world bend to your will instead of you bending to destiny!"

Peri slowly shook her head. "I don't want to be a tyrant, lording over others. There are no 'lesser men,' though I will always stick by the ones I call my own."

"But if you were a god, you could do *anything* you wanted. You would have the ultimate freedom, the very freedom you love so dearly!" It was beyond Velimir why she wouldn't want the thing he had died for.

"You...you still believe that? You are very intelligent, Velimir, but you have some astounding blind spots. It is *such* arrogance to think extreme power doesn't corrupt and take away one's own will." Peri paused and exhaled, shaking her head again in frustration. "It molds, it lures...for the Yonder's sake, *you* should know! Dimitri played you like a violin, and you ruined your own life, along with countless others. Do you ever think about Tomoe?"

Velimir jerked as if Peri had slapped him across the face. "What happened with Tomoe?" His voice was quiet now, his expression wary and taken aback.

"I was forced to kill her, Velimir. She wouldn't have it another way. She said she would have lost her honor if she didn't fight to protect you. Such love, and you spit on it because of the madness you wallowed in. She died for you."

Velimir felt as if he was punched in the gut. The same expression had been in Peri's eyes when she had tried to reason with him in the old temple, before his death. The penetrating, demanding look that didn't wish him ill, but that felt extremely threatening. The idea of godly glory felt like a mirage, like the artificial surge of euphoria the first few drinks of alcohol produced.

He realized in retrospect how joy had slowly faded from Tomoe's eyes and been replaced by suffering during the last years. He tried to evoke the idea of Peri's glorious ascension, but it had lost its appeal. Peri had managed to puncture through beliefs that had protected him for a long time, yet she made no move to harm him. Such anger he had felt about Tomoe's betrayal...but did she do it for *love?* Because she knew Dimitri was manipulating him. Velimir was suddenly gripped by the pain of knowing he'd never hold Tomoe again. *Because of Peri!*

"YOU!" Velimir glared at Peri.

Peri dipped her chin and blankly stared back, not saying a word.

Her direct gaze made Velimir's anger melt away. *It is so much better to always blame someone else, isn't it?* "No...of course," Velimir said and looked briefly away, then returned Peri's gaze. "It was I who drove her away. And, of course, she fought. She was a samurai. Fallen from earthly grace, true, but that was her core. Her honor was the thing defining her. She...she always was worried about dying on foreign soil. Said her spirit would not get peace if she was not buried in her ancestral lands." Velimir felt all strength sap from his limbs, his heart beating too fast, his head spinning. He felt swept away by a roaring stream of murky water. There were so many thoughts he had hidden deep in the fjord of the things he didn't want to think about, but they wouldn't stay hidden anymore. Velimir's face trembled as he struggled against tears. So much locked inside of him. So much he had not dared to think about. Tomoe—forever lost to him. How much he had wanted to control his destiny, and yet he had been but a puppet to the malevolent one who knew where to hit him. He clenched his jaw, hands trembling.

Then he felt Peri's arms around his shoulders.

"Brother...She is buried close to the waterline near the temple where we had the final confrontation. I arranged a proper burial for her. There is an urn and her weapons. If we survive, once all this is over, I promise to show you where they are."

"I, Velimir, child of Dimitri the Fallen, swear..." Velimir placed his hand over his heart. "I swear that I will travel to Morishima, if I only live to do so, and bury you in the soil of your ancestors, my love. I swear, Tomoe...and forgive me." *And your brother is dead, too, thanks to what I set in motion. Whether he betrayed Peri or not, she cared about him.* Velimir sat in solemn silence, Peri's comforting arm never leaving his shoulders.

After a few moments, Peri squeezed Velimir's arm and cleared her throat. "Velimir, I'm beginning to see a glimpse of the man Tomoe loved. What I said to that wraith is true— you are not the same man anymore. Don't ruin your second chance with dumb-ass goals. I...I care about you, brother."

"Thank you." Velimir put his arm around Peri's shoulders as well. They sat quietly, comforting one another.

Afterwards, when everybody was already retreating under the starry desert sky, Velimir's visibly shaken state left the others quiet. He did his best to carry himself in his normal proud and determined manner, but something of the turmoil he was in was leaking through. It was as if bringing up Tomoe had toppled a dam inside his soul, and the murky water was roaring as an unstoppable mass. Allowing himself finally to think about her—allowing, because there was no going back once the dam was broken—brought up other things, too. Kiril, who always had stood by him, protected him when he was but a child and believed in him... and whom he had stabbed and left for dead. His mother, the gentle, lovely woman who held him together before her death...how had he honored her memory? What would she think about his aspirations? Yet she had sent him that message of love in his moment of greatest need.

Peri's eyes regarded him with quiet compassion. Once the group retreated to sleep, Peri spread her bedroll next to Velimir's and took a long, hard look at the group, daring them to comment upon that. When no-one did, she took Velimir's hand into her own and simply bid him goodnight. As their palms joined, Velimir knew Peri had accepted him. He *must* apologize to her for killing Connor...but how did one express such a thing? *"I'm sorry that I killed your stepfather, whom you loved dearly. And sent assassins after you."* Pondering this and other things pouring into his mind from the dark recesses of his soul, he felt something unfamiliar, something he didn't much care for. Guilt and shame. He wanted to harden his heart, to tell himself he had done exactly what a strong-willed, exceptional person should do. But there was no going back now that the dam was broken. Velimir drifted asleep.

In his dream, he was walking in the surroundings of the old Dimitrian temple at the outskirts of Lughani Vos again, amid the forgotten tombstones and ruins. The temple was still there, but the latent power seeping from it was gone. It was just a stone building, without a life of its own. Velimir recalled faintly how he had felt looking at it in those days... powerful, exhilarated, full of mirth of the coming ascension. He had felt his divine sire's promises and power radiating from the stone, similar power flowing through his veins. Was it but poison? At least Dimitri's promises were nothing but lies.

Velimir knew where to go. He walked down to the marshy waterline of the ancient dead dark sea, its bottom littered with bones and the barren beach with dried driftwood. She waited for him. She wore her full battle gear, the Hanamori dark blue colors. She was pale and transparent, gliding over the ground. But her eyes were just as deep, dark, and lovely as they had been in life. Velimir couldn't read her expression. She just watched him. She did look a little sad, but then she always had.

"Velimir. You have come to me. I didn't know if you would."

"I...am I dreaming?"

"In a way. Who is to say what dreaming is? In Morishima, the Dreamlands—Yume-Do, as we call it—is just as real as the world of waking. We are really meeting, and you will remember."

"Tomoe...I mistreated you so..." Velimir whispered.

"Shh. I heard you before. Your sister has taken you back to Ningen-Do, the realm of mortals. Listen to her. She will be your salvation, and you will be hers."

"Are you not angry at her? For killing you?"

Tomoe's translucent brow furrowed briefly. "Of course not. I went down in honor, as a samurai is supposed to do. She fought me in honor as well."

"And me? For treating you so badly, for not listening to

you?" Velimir could feel the weight of his sins on his shoulders and lowered his eyes.

"There was some...bitterness," Tomoe said. "My soul is bound to this wretched place now, the few people who come here whispering about me. I am a lonely, sad ghost. But I consider it my own failure as well. I could not make you realize that you should seek salvation and redemption. I fell in a battle against that fallen celestial." She glided a few inches closer and touched Velimir's cheek with a cold, shadowy finger. "The poison burning in your veins is no longer present. You should be pleased, beloved."

"I fought my way back into the land of the living. I was so proud, so determined to find another way to make a difference, to have power again. And now...I don't know what to think anymore." Velimir hesitantly extended his hand towards Tomoe's face. There was nothing to touch, yet her eyes sparkled in the ghostly face, dark and alive.

"You ought to be proud. Not many could have achieved that, as Peri well knows and respects you for that," Tomoe said. "I do not know what your fate is to be, but I do know that there are always many paths through a vast forest, not all of them the obvious ones. Always listen to Peri. Be there for her, and she will be there for you. Your souls are linked." A crow cawed somewhere and a mild wind made the surface of the ancient sea ripple.

"Tomoe, I swear I will do anything within my power to bury you in Hanamori lands. And if you ever can forgive me..." Velimir's voice, already a whisper, trailed off.

"I have already forgiven you. This was fate. It was a sadder one than what I anticipated, but perhaps one day I will go to Takamagahara, to join my blessed ancestors in their glorious halls. Farewell, beloved. Remember what I said to you about Peri."

And then she faded away.

"Tomoe, wait!" Velimir wanted so much. To hold her, to make love to her, to beg forgiveness for every time he had cheated on her or acted cold because she wouldn't put up with his plans. To ask so many questions, to hear all her untold stories. His chest ached as he realized he would have heard them all and much more had he but listened to her and lived a life, a mortal life with her, adventuring, having children, growing old together.

He woke up, realizing he was crying in his sleep. Peri was facing him. Her eyes were open, and she was still holding his hand.

"You are crying," she whispered.

"I met Tomoe in my sleep," Velimir whispered back. "She was haunting the temple yards, like she said she would be if she was not buried in her ancestral lands."

"We will get the urn and the weapons. We just have to deal with this prophecy business first."

"Sister...can you tell me what happened to Kiril?" Velimir asked in a strained voice.

"I finished what you had started so that he wouldn't suffer."

Velimir winced. "There is no end to my wrongdoings," he sighed. "Tomoe, Kiril...and Genjiro, too."

Peri bit her lip. "Please, calm yourself. After Majsilaa performs her rites, we have Darien to confront and a siege to lift. It will be all right. Eventually."

Peri didn't know if it would, in fact. But she wanted Velimir to believe that.

28
YGGDRASIL

Kɪʀɪʟ sᴡᴀʟʟᴏᴡᴇᴅ ᴀɴᴅ ʀᴀɴ ʜɪs ꜰɪɴɢᴇʀ ʟɪɢʜᴛʟʏ ᴏᴠᴇʀ the tip of the spear he held in his hand. It was fine dwarven craftsmanship—the dwarves of Asgard were master smiths just like the dwarves of Valkama—and glittery runes adorned the tip. More to the point—a hint of a grin formed on his face at the pun—the tip would pierce his heart before sundown.

"It is not the actual Gungnir, of course," said Skald. "Lord Odin keeps Gungnir with him wherever he goes, concealing it as a staff when it suits him. But we felt that you deserve a well-crafted replica, attempting something only a god has done before. Master Fjalar gave it his best."

"Give him my thanks," Kiril said and smacked his dry lips.

"We will," said Urd and sat at Kiril's side at the rough-hewn bench of their outdoor dining table. "I confess that this worries me. What if he can't withstand the ordeal?"

"Then he will die, the elf will still be in our custody, and we will have to send another petitioner to deliver her to the House of Apathia," Skuld said. She walked across the table to look Urd in the eye. "This is what he wanted. It is also necessary that he gets his powers back in order to make the journey. He won't renege—his woman is a hostage to the Valkyries."

"I know, but..." Urd shrugged as her voice trailed off and she lowered her eyes.

"He is right here, you know. Don't talk over his head," said Verdandi, who had nimbly been tying a hangman's knot. She turned to Kiril and lightly touched his arm. "No mortal has tried this before—and if you fail, we are talking about a more final death. Your soul will be drained, dissipated. There will be nothing left to reappear on any of the myriad lands of the dead. But you know this. You must be a very brave man."

I'm not, though. For a fleeting moment Kiril felt that being a helpless man in his woman's capable protection wouldn't be so horrible after all. He would still be able to enjoy her presence and all that the afterlife had to offer. What if he could not withstand the ritual? What if the tree rejected him as unworthy of its attention? What if a mere mortal emulating a god's sacrifice offended it? What then? *A final death, not a reassemblage. A black, cold hole of nothing.*

Kiril tightened his lips in resolve. Without magic, he was not a whole man. Not worthy of Jelena, not worthy of a second chance.

Urd smiled ruefully and put a hand on Kiril's knee. "I know that Hildur was quite furious about your pacifist lady, but...I can't hold it against her in my heart that she came up with such a bold scheme to find her love in the land of death."

"You have always been too soft-hearted for your own good, Urd," said Skuld, arms crossed. She glanced at the giant ash tree looming over the cool and dark pond, the longhouse, and the table they were sitting at. A few dark clouds slowly drifted over the pale sun.

"Age softens the heart," answered Urd, the oldest and most matronly of the Norns. "You see countless lifetimes come and go, and you can't judge the little mortals so harshly. The young don't see shades of gray."

Skuld scoffed. "I am older than humankind, older than elvenkind or dwarves of the mountains, older than Lord Odin himself, older maybe than this Valkama of his."

"Yet you always will be the youngest sister, the spirit of things to come, eyes keen on the horizon," said Verdandi.

Skuld shrugged. "His lady has courage. That counts for something."

"You have no idea," Kiril said. "She grew into a courageous woman of conviction from a meek, abused shadow of a person. She is…the only light I have ever known. I will do what I must, hold my end of the bargain and return for her. I will be worthy of her love."

Verdandi put her hand on Kiril's shoulder. "It is time," she said. Kiril stood up and handed the spear to Skuld, who accepted it with a grim nod. He followed the three silent sisters, gusts of the rising wind whipping his hair. The Yggdrasil groaned in the breeze. The wind rippled the surface of the pond—the well of Urd, the Norns had informed Kiril—and the two swans glided farther away from the approaching company. The wind picked up and howled.

Verdandi placed the hangman's knot on Kiril's neck. It felt unnaturally heavy and almost sentient, as if a snake was resting on his shoulders. Verdandi hoisted the rope over a sturdy branch reaching over the pond. She touched Kiril's arm and went to stand behind Kiril's back with Urd, ready to pull the rope. The youngest, Skuld, remained facing Kiril, holding the spear, gazing at him with her steadfast gray eyes.

"*Yggdrasil, life-giver, friend of the clear sky,*" Skuld recited. The wind picked up a few leaves that spun in the wind.

"*May this petitioner's sacrifice nourish you and please you,*" said Verdandi. The trunk of the Yggdrasil creaked.

"*May it be so. May it echo Lord Odin's offer,*" said Urd.

Kiril felt the noose tighten around his neck. His heart wanted to thump its way out of his chest as the fibers of the rope chafed and scratched, then ever more persistently and painfully dug their way under his skin and against his windpipe. He started to choke and stood on tiptoe, trying to escape the terrifying pressure. Soon his eyeballs and temples seemed to burst, and he felt a flailing panic, but could do nothing, as his body, heavy as lead, was slowly lifted and twitched suspended at the end of the rope. The agony and panic were maddening. The rope seemed alive. It stopped choking Kiril just short of entirely squeezing the life out of him. The tiniest flow of breath passed through and he hung, spinning in the wind.

Suddenly, the Norns let the rope loose for a moment, and Kiril was hurled against the spear the expressionless Skuld held steady. He had been wounded by swords, maces, spears, and the like before, but never had his entire body weight been helplessly impaled by a cruel spike. It was like an explosion of fiery pain, then just a stunned smarting feeling, with him barely able to see from under his drooping eyelids. He was hoisted over the dark waters of the well of Urd again, impaled by the spear, blood slowly dripping down his legs, a shadow of breath keeping him barely alive. He felt very thirsty, but he knew the rules. No water. No food. Or the sacrifice would be forfeit.

As Kiril's vision dimmed, he felt like he was adrift in a lake of blood. It pulsed and hummed. His ears roared. In a momentary flash, he could see the translucent form of Grimnir reflected in the darkening clouds. The man grinned and winked and was then gone. *Ygg...dra...sil...*Kiril found that he was able to produce a sound resembling speech inside of his mind. The syllables floated on the surface of the pulsating blood waves, made of shadow, buzzing and reverberating.

*Ygg...dra...sil...*Kiril called again, sent more shadow syllables to float on the surface of the pulsating blood. He heard a howling wind but saw nothing but dark skies above. For a moment the surface of the blood ocean was still. Then he felt as much as heard a voice. A vast voice that permeated the entire blood ocean, Kiril just a tiny speck in it, a voice that was a pulse rather than a sound.

"Yggdrasil? ...yes, that is what they call me. Those ones. Many have given me other names. Meru. Asvattha. Valandor. Kunlun. Lakiri...but for you, Yggdrasil will do."

Kiril tried to form a reply. But no words came to mind. He felt completely empty of meaning, of anything to think or say. A vague panic took over, but he didn't have the words to express even that.

"What was lost can be restored," vibrated the voice. "But before you can be whole, you can no longer hide from the truth. You must *see*."

See what? Tell me more! But the Yggdrasil remained quiet. Kiril writhed in agony. The dark clouds gathered, and the winds howled. Kiril hung in the wind-swept tree.

29
RUINS OF A DIMITRIAN TEMPLE AT THE EDGE OF THE DESERT

Majsilaa studied the faintly pulsating, shriveled, dark thing in her hand. "Hello there, heart of mine," she murmured softly. She extended an alabaster finger and followed the contours of the organ, soft and light as the paws of a cat on a prowl. "The blood of my betrayer son imbues you, rendering him invulnerable...but not for much longer." There was nothing warm in the deeply satisfied smile on her lips. Her pupils were large in her bright, dark eyes. Her face was pale like the moon above on a cold, starry night.

Peri smiled uneasily. "Well, there it is, then. Once you do...whatever it is you have to do, we can kill Darien...hopefully before his forces overrun Shinaris."

"Don't just snipe him down. When he dies, I want him to know that it is I who took back the invulnerability he stole from me." There were snakes with kinder eyes than Majsilaa's.

Peri pursed her lips. "I don't usually go for theatrics. Quick and easy is the best way to kill," she said. "But yes, his followers need to see him as a false god, an impostor. And they will. Don't worry, he'll be quite pissed off, I imagine... shortly before he dies."

Majsilaa pulled her shiny silvery strands of hair behind her shoulder. She started to squeeze the heart in her hand and chant in Vysokian. Small streams of blood flowed from between her long, elegant fingers. She opened her palm and ground with her thumb what was left of the heart. A rosy tint colored her skin. The pale face was replaced with a softer and rounder one. She had wide, green eyes. Her lips were like rose petals. Her hair became wavy and thick, the color of chestnut. The matte black worn robes strained at her chest as her breasts and hips enlarged. Majsilaa breathed lightly, staring bemusedly at the ground remnants of the heart in her hand.

"I...used to like colorful robes," she said, glancing at the matte black ones she was wearing. Her voice was different, too. The chill was gone. It was a melodious voice of a young woman who probably could sing beautifully. "I...loved things. Life..." She sounded puzzled.

"I imagine you did," Kauno said. "You loved Dimitri, the most beautiful and compassionate celestial of them all so much that you renounced your position as a high priestess of Cijeli, and instead followed Dimitri into disgrace and exile. You sacrificed your youth, beauty, and fertility so that you could be with him forever. It changed you."

"I started to remember when I devoted myself to Darien. He was such a beautiful little boy. Smart, charming…I chose to mother the one who would embody my beloved Dimitri. I remember guarding his sleep, watching him smile, supporting him as he took his first steps…perhaps I pampered him a little," Majsilaa said, a drowsy smile on her full face. "Oh, how I loved him."

"Alas," Velimir said, "that time is long past. Darien will pay for what he has done, and you will have your revenge, so we'll—"

"No!" Majsilaa gasped, her green eyes widening. "You are planning to *kill* my Darien!"

"Well, *yeah!* That was the idea," Peri said. She stared incredulously at Majsilaa's deepening, increasingly angry frown. "That's what you wanted!"

"No." Majsilaa's eyes darkened and she clenched her fists. "No no no."

"If this is because you have rediscovered your capacity for love," Razeem said, "then think about the countless lives Darien seeks to destroy. Think of those the Esquadron will enslave and murder. What of their lives? What of their loved ones?"

Majsilaa hesitated. "I…" But then a stubborn expression set on her face. "No! I care not! You will not kill my Darien! I will see anyone, *everyone,* destroyed before I let harm come to him!"

Jussuf scoffed. "That, fortunately, is not in your hands anymore. We are done here. Let us leave this place."

"*Rechala va staccha!*" Majsilaa screamed and raised her hand. She seemed to squeeze something invisible in her hand, and Jussuf stopped in his tracks, raising his hand to his throat. He coughed, and his face started to turn purple.

"Stop it!" Peri yelled, lunging for the priestess as Jussuf's coughs intensified and his eyes started to bulge.

Majsilaa took a few steps back. "Mists of the past, vapors of this desecrated place! Rise, defend me!"

Sickly green vapors emerged from the dark corners and started to close in. Peri sneezed and coughed. The burning sting reminded her of how the manacles had bitten in her wrists when she had strained and bucked against them, strapped on the gurney with a needle stuck in her arm. She roared and charged, slashing a wide arc with her sword. The upper part of Majsilaa's torso was split open and her arm almost severed. Peri's sword stuck in the lower ribs, and Majsilaa collapsed in a pool of blood. As she hit the ground, her mouth and eyes were still wide open.

Now freed from the dead woman's grasp, Jussuf gasped and hyperventilated. Peri slammed her boot on the corpse and pulled her sword off with a grunt. It made a squelching sound, and more blood gushed out. "Now that didn't go smoothly," she said dryly. She crouched to search the corpse and grimaced in distaste. "Bah, nothing but this crappy silver collar. It's not even enchanted. Maybe we can sell it for some coin."

Razeem sighed and stroked his stubble for a moment before speaking up. "Peri, even though this woman was a servant of Dimitri, you shouldn't be so casual about killing."

"Oh, for fuck's sake, the river of blood we are spreading in our wake...Razeem, I do like you, but right now I don't need your lectures. I'm pretty damn pissed off as it is, and I don't remember you complaining about the food, lodging, and equipment that selling loot has bought us," Peri said, straining not to snarl.

"But..." Razeem wanted to explain that attitude shaped people and their futures, but also sensed that it would be a losing fight. *Forgive me, Juris. It is always a fine line for a paladin, the one between being a realist and getting results, and not straying.*

"Velimir, what is it?" Ewynne asked quietly. Velimir hadn't commented on anything that had happened, just stood there, expressionless, a tiny squint of tension around his eyes.

Velimir looked at her quizzically. The girl, apparently, was capable of spotting subtle reactions. He saw no reason not to indulge her. "Ewynne...I don't know if you remember Tomoe."

"I remember her," Ewynne said. There was a modicum of warmth in her eyes for the first time when looking at Velimir.

"The last thing she ever said to me was that she didn't believe I had a heart anymore," Velimir said in a pained, strangled voice.

"And now, Majsilaa was all for killing Darien, but when she got her heart back, she attacked us to protect him," Ewynne said, nodding in understanding.

"Yes. It brought back the memory. Little sister, I know you don't care much for me, but I wish you would at least believe that I have no intention of harming you or Peri."

"Perhaps you have got your heart back too, Velimir. I don't feel the kind of connection with you that Peri does, but I...have noticed things. I still don't trust you and I'm still so mad that you took Connor from us..."

Velimir tensed as Ewynne said that. What could he ever

offer to either of them but his pain?

"I...I don't enjoy that you are hurting. I know that you are, you know," Ewynne continued, voice quiet, face downcast. "I...ah! Just...you helped Peri with the ifrit. I want to thank you for that, but I still haven't forgiven you. But I don't want to see you suffer either..." Ewynne's eyes darted around. She seemed unable to make up her mind as to what she wanted to say.

"That suffering is all I can offer you," Velimir answered. "I can't bring Connor back."

"Just...take care of Peri. I'm scared...she is more and more gone. The closer the prophecy comes, the less I can reach her. But the other day you helped her...it means a lot." With that, Ewynne ran away. She had felt an urge to comfort Velimir, but doing so would be like spitting on Connor's memory. While Peri had loved Connor just as much as she did, Peri had always been reserved and had trouble expressing her feelings. Ewynne had made the old sage laugh with her pixie-like antics, while Peri was often withdrawn and sullen.

"Ewynne? May I have a word?" Jussuf asked, his gray, honest eyes intent on her.

"Sure, Jussuf." What did he want now?

"What is this all about with Velimir? You know...I worry about Peri. I might be able to be a good influence on her, but she is confused about Velimir and him joining our party. It all started when the...fiend came along! He is stirring up all that tainted blood she is fighting so hard to resist!" Jussuf said.

"Jussuf, it started before that. Velimir is certainly affecting her profoundly, but are you sure you are not just making it an excuse to blame him?" Ewynne tried to sound neutral and adult, but Jussuf's eyes still darkened in anger.

"You are too close to her to see! Of course she will say that! She doesn't want to see what that demon-spawn is doing to her! Oh, I'm sure he can dress it up in pretty words and acts of understanding. But that call of murder is not something to be understood!" Jussuf paused and continued in a softer tone after seeing Ewynne's expression. "I don't condemn her. She didn't choose to be born with the Dimitrian essence. But she should fight it, seek to purge herself of it. It is not a part of her. It is an alien presence! As a paladin, I would help her with that...but instead she wants me to empathize with how it feels. No, that cannot be. It is the way of succumbing to the taint. And Velimir, I am sure, is just another step in that downward spiral." Jussuf looked so angry, so grim, so bitter.

"You are starting to scare me," Ewynne said, keeping her voice mild and kind. "She doesn't wish the Dimitrian essence upon her any more than you do. But it *is* a part of her as a person, her history. You never were there when she was but a small child and woke up, telling me how she would love to murder someone who deserved to die...how her blood was soaring in her veins when she imagined cutting a throat and feeling the warm blood gushing on her hands. Stuff like that. All the time. When we were like five."

Jussuf's lips paled. "She...has never told me."

"She wouldn't," Ewynne answered. "But you have to remember, Velimir knows how it is. Of course, she wants to form a bond with him, because no-one else knows what it is like." Ewynne realized she was defending Velimir and felt claustrophobic. "I...am tired of this discussion. See you, Jussuf."

30
SIEGE CAMP BOMBARDING SHINARIS

"Dude is prancing in the middle of the camp like a peacock," Peri said. "It's almost like, I don't know, a battle-field temple. He has built an actual *throne* under the canopy and they kneel before addressing him instead of saluting."

Kauno nodded while smoothing dust off her tunic. "Kauno borrowed the sight of a helpful and friendly rat. They seem to revere him and he welcomes it." The two had returned from a scouting mission where they'd been covered by Ewynne's *shifting shadows* spell, but had still given a wide berth to Darien. The man was a stealth specialist, possibly able to see through such measures, and they hadn't wanted to take chances.

"No doubt he already considers himself a god, seeing the ascension as mere formality," Velimir said. "He imagines Majsilaa's heart keeps him from any harm that might come to him."

"Shinaris is all but finished," Razeem muttered, shielding his eyes and gazing at the smouldering remnants of the city. The catapults were still bombarding it, but the screams and wails were fainter and less frequent. The others paid no attention, their eyes intent on Peri.

"There's only a small squad of battlemages and clerics, by the looks of it," she said. "They have been laying a siege and are now finishing it, bombarding a dying city to rubble. They haven't been expecting resistance, much less magic, for a while."

"There are no guarantees that this state of affairs will continue," Velimir said. "It is likely that Darien has skilled magic-users at his disposal and will rely on them if he expects to be attacked by a Dimitrian spawn of equal power." A slow smile started to form on his face, and he chuckled deeply. He could see where Peri was going with this.

Peri bounced on tiptoe, tossed her hair behind her shoulder, and grinned widely. "I think we should just walk right up to him! Once we are in the range for him to see through the spell, he'll think himself untouchable and, probably, gloat. But the army is only paying attention to the Shinaris direction. Ewynne and Kauno can hinder them with their mass effect spells until we finish him."

Ewynne didn't share Peri's enthusiasm. She drew breath and glanced at Razeem, who stood with his arms crossed, a grave look upon his face. "I don't know, Peri…" she said. "We don't know what exactly he's capable of doing. Yes, our spell capacity has increased at an abnormal rate being around you, but what if it's not enough? What if our spells run out before he dies? What then?"

Peri shrugged and smiled. "Well…I guess then we will be fucked." Only Velimir smiled back. "But we'll try to take full advantage of the first strike."

Razeem let out a long breath and shook his head. "It is one *hell* of a gamble, Peri. But it is true that we have the element of surprise on our side, and we may not get another chance to confront him when he's not surrounded by magic-users."

"Okay, so here's the plan," Peri said. "Ewynne and Kauno: hinder the incoming troops with mass effect spells. Jussuf: keep healing and shielding us as best you can. Razeem: do whatever you can to keep Darien in our line of vision. Everyone else: single-minded focus on taking him down. Don't let anything distract you. I'm telling you that all efforts will be futile until Darien is down. But once he is, the army will scatter." She regarded the group calmly, hand on the grip of the Shandalar sword which emanated glittery frost from the scabbard.

"How do you know that, Peri?" Jussuf asked.

"I know about fanatics, and I have this feeling in my gut," she answered, frowning slightly. She didn't like to be questioned in a situation like this, but she wasn't infallible. If her followers could bring up points she might have missed, it would be a bad mistake to discourage them from speaking up.

"I agree. Gut instinct is an important thing. All good military leaders have some, and it is a grave mistake to ignore it," Velimir said. Razeem, a veteran of many campaigns, was nodding.

"Let's go, then. If this goes south, Kauno will cast *wind spurs* on us and we'll run like hell," Peri said.

———————————— • ● • ————————————

DARIEN WAS TRIUMPHANT AS HE SPOTTED PERI. HIS sallow skin had a lustre now, and he moved precisely and sharply, a spring in his step. His cloak sparkled with tiny diamond shards and shimmered with enchantments. His dark, wavy hair glinted in the sunlight, and he magnanimously flashed a set of perfect teeth.

"Peri, Peri, Peri!" he said. "You are resourceful for a mongrel, but then I knew that already. You butchered quite a few of our people at the experimental house of the marshlands. I redoubled our efforts to crush Shinaris when I heard you were trapped in there, Butcher of Yalifa…only to find you gone!"

"Butcher of Yalifa, eh? That's a new one for me." Peri grinned humorlessly. "Well, shit happens, Darien."

"I thought I would have to content myself with slaughtering Dimitri's weakling progeny and forget about you for the time being. But you—" he laughed, eyes alight, a provocative grin on his face, "—you just walked right in. I kindly thank you for volunteering, but now, if you'll excuse me, I must destroy you." He leaped at Peri with remarkable speed, drawing a dagger that had a glowing, black blade that seemed to be covered with red veins.

When Darien's feet hit the ground, Peri dodged and Velimir slashed his old, brutal blade at the man. He scored a perfect hit, a nerve center that brought massive damage. Velimir smiled like a predator as he saw blood drain from Darien's face, his expression changing from triumph to incredulity.

"What…? No! NO! Majsilaa…somehow…sound alarm! ALARM! TO ARMS!" The familiar rage both Velimir and

284

Peri recognized shined in Darien's eyes. The blow of Velimir's blade would have finished any ordinary man, but Darien became transparent for a moment, and in a second there were five translucent copies of him, all bouncing around without a moment of stillness, slashing at the party with remarkable speed. Razeem's *plavosvetljo* flashed and flickered. Jussuf kept shielding the fighters with all his might from physical harm and mental confusion.

There was a roar of approaching steps as the catapult crews started to pour in, drawing their weapons. A few mages were pelting the group with lightning that kept dispersing into a shield Ewynne channeled over them. Kauno was singing to call the wind and rising gnarled roots from the ground to entangle the assaulters. Peri and Velimir kept dodging and grimacing and grunting whenever Darien's and his copies scored enough damage to bypass Jussuf's protections. The spellcasters kept chanting, their voices hoarse.

A few men from the vanguard, all wearing exquisite enchanted armor, managed to break through Ewynne's channeled shield. The one leading the assault was wielding a blade that seemed capable of cutting through it. The men sprinted and roared, beelining towards Velimir and Peri, who kept attacking Darien copies—he a spinning whirlwind of murder, she ducking, sprinting and poking, feinting and retreating, going relentlessly for the gaps, preying for a false step or a moment of hesitation.

One of the attackers was zapped by a stray charge of lightning Kauno had called from the skies to pummel the area where the army was trying to get through. The rest continued, roaring their battle screams even louder. Another man's ankle was grabbed by a vine sprouting from the ground, and he fell on his face. The moment he hit the ground, Peri leaped to impale him with her sword. The remaining fighters faltered for a moment, and that was enough for Velimir to shred them in pieces. Blood sprayed on his face and he roared with laughter and joy.

Kauno stopped chanting for a second, bringing her hand to her throat. Ewynne tossed her a water skin, and she guzzled the water. The lightning stopped pelting the ground, but no more men seemed eager to try to come through. Soon Kauno resumed the chanting, and the army remained behind Ewynne's barrier, staring at what was taking place at the front of Darien's command center.

One of the copies of Darien managed to make it to Peri's flank and stabbed her in the ribs. She stumbled, and the wound started to emit noxious fumes and turn purple and sickly green. She shivered, barely managing to roll away as Darien struck again. For a moment, the air around her oscillated and wavered in golden waves. Her eyes turned red and an alien croak emerged from her throat. Jussuf promptly aimed his palm at Peri's side and called something. Blue and white creamy light streamed into Peri's wound. The red color of her eyes faltered and the golden waves grew fainter. The poison burned and fought the light, Peri hissing and panting, but soon the venom was gone, and Peri found her rhythm back.

Finally, the profusely sweating Velimir was able to decapitate the last copy of Darien. It collapsed to the ground, leaving a very real, beheaded, soiled corpse. The real Darien. No more copies emerged. The corpse dissolved and disappeared, and there were a few moments of silence.

"Noooo! No! Lord Darien! Dead! This is impossible!"

Pale and confused faces, a few glances at the enormous, bald man with eyes glowing like living fire, covered with blood and laughing wildly.

"Fear me, for I am Death! From the pits of the Abyss, I have fought my way! Your false god has been struck down! You have awoken the wrath of the rightful ones! You pathetic worms!" Velimir bellowed. The men of the vanguard stopped in their tracks, dropped their blades, and ran. The remainder of Darien's army started to retreat in panic, glad to get out without attracting attention. The catapults stood silent witness to the destruction they had brought while the party cheered, while a spinning vortex appeared in front of them.

31
THE THEATER OF TIME

Peri lurched through time and space. She was no longer at Darien's siege camp. After the ever more familiar disorienting lurch, she found herself standing at the stage of the Theater of Time. This time there was a gallery of mirrors; Peri could see an infinite number of Peris with their grave, pale faces in the dusky green reflection. She wasn't alone with the mirror images. A glittering, ethereal female celestial smiled at her.

"Greetings, Peri of Eilean de Taigh-Sholais," said the celestial. Her voice was like a hymn emanating from Cijeli's temple. "I am Irina of the Celestial Court. I have gone through a great deal of trouble to be able to talk with you."

"Your timing is not very convenient," Peri answered, sheathing her sword.

"The Yonder and the Nether are in turmoil, for a big shift of transcendental energy has occurred. That is why I have been able to make my way here to the Nether. Dimitri spread his essence all over Valkama with his seed. One of the strongest in the Dimitrian essence—Darien—is dead by your hand. Now, all that simmering murderous potential is ever more condensed. Every death in his name increases its potency, every death of his spawn increases it hundredfold. And the death of the progeny of his willing acolytes—thousandfold. Among those left who could hope to contain that potential without being incinerated and perishing, you remain among very few," Irina said, ignoring Peri's annoyance.

"Yay." Peri crossed her arms at the waist.

"As you knew would happen, Darien's army is scattering and running," Irina continued. "The forces in play now move swiftly toward fulfilment of the Vysokian prophecies. Tell me, Peri...what do you know about your origins? What do you know about your birth? What do you know about your mother before Connor brought you to the safety of Eilean de Taigh-Sholais?"

"Nothing." Peri had wondered about that, but sometimes, when the urges and the dreams were at their worst, she thought she was better off not knowing.

"The stakes for you and the whole Valkama are higher now. Everything that ever happened and everything that ever will swirls around in the ether of the infinite planes. The Dreamer has always been dreaming. But this place can capture those impressions and give them form, as I imagine you discovered on your way to Shinaris. Now watch your past unfold. It is time you learn the truth, so that you will be able to handle the stakes of the future."

A translucent woman appeared at the stage, wearing simple robes, indifferently holding an infant in her arms.

Peri recognized the glossy hair and the strong body build—the familiar features that stared back at her every time she glanced upon a mirror. But the woman's eyes were different from hers. The feverish exhilaration, the steely purpose. Burning fanaticism Peri had never experienced, but had always been able to recognize. The woman nodded and smiled at Peri.

"The sole purpose of your life was to be sacrificed in a ritual," the woman explained. "A mass slaughter of children willingly sacrificed by their mothers, to call our beloved Dimitri back to this world as a god. I would murder you, my child, so that Dimitri could ascend." The voice was so feminine, so dreamy.

Peri's mother faded away, and another shade appeared. *Connor!* Peri's heart jolted. She tried to talk to him, but she was frozen in time, not able to move or speak.

"We—a group of Eoghain's devout—had learned of this sacrilege," Connor said. "We stormed the temple where it was to take place. We interrupted the ritual and slayed many priestesses. We managed to thwart Dimitri's ascension, but still we were too late. Most of the children had been slaughtered."

"But not all of them." The speaker was a small boy, perhaps four or five years old, his voice holding bitterness and pain much older than his years.

"True. Not all of Dimitri's children died that night," Connor said. His voice was very sad, defeated. He bowed his head and looked down at his feet.

"I tried to use the chaos to escape," the child said. His posture was rigid, his eyes burning in a strange hue of gold and amber.

"I was able to save only one child," Connor said quietly, face downcast.

"He saved you, leaving me behind," said the boy, such anger and resentment in his eyes. The scene flickered momentarily before Peri's eyes: the little, terrified boy dragging a screaming baby with him, Connor taking the baby and the boy's hand, and the hand slipping. The little boy was left lying on the ground, Connor running with the baby.

"And so I fled on my own, survived in the streets until I was adopted and raised by Radek Rosinin," small Velimir said. He paused to take a few shuddering breaths, lip trembling. "I didn't care. I killed Connor in the end."

The heartache. The bitterness in the voice of a small child. The shades vanished, and Peri was left feeling dizzy, tears flowing freely, not bothering to try to gain control.

"And that is how you came to be and survived. Your mother, who only gave birth to you in order to murder you, was killed by Connor," Irina spoke. There was the smallest hint of compassion on her face.

"Connor never told me any of this..." Peri whispered, her head humming. *How unlovable am I when my own mother wanted to murder me?*

"And what of your brother, Velimir? What if Connor had raised him rather than you? Would you have become as he was?" Irina asked.

Peri started to choke on silent tears. She fell to her knees and buried her face into her hands in gripping sorrow. "Yes. Without a doubt," she said.

"You have welcomed him by your side, and you call him brother."

"He *is* my brother. And...I love him." Peri gulped. It felt bold to say it. But it was true.

Irina didn't seem to mind. She smiled and nodded. "Now you have learned the truth about your origins. Your companions will be here in a moment. You will be challenged by the Theater before you can proceed back to the Hereworld. When great shifts in the reservoirs of transcendental energy occur again, I will be able to contact you. The Dreamer's ways are inscrutable, but the Three have an interest in thwarting my fallen brother's monstrous plans. Farewell for now, Dimitri's child," Irina said and started to fade away.

"Wait! Irina!" Peri called after her. "Can I...meet Connor? Here? Can he, too, come from the Yonder? If there is some disturbance or shit so that it's easier to travel?"

Irina seemed to consider this for a moment. "He does not reside in the Yonder. He would have been welcome to the Elysian Fields, but true to Eoghain the Wanderer, he chose the Blessed Isles of the Otherworld as the place to dwell. But...due to the fluid nature of the Otherworld and the current instability of the planes, I believe I could get a projection of him here. I will consult with the All-Father and send Brother Connor to you," she answered and faded away.

———————— • ● • ————————

THE PARTY, STILL TRIUMPHANT, MATERIALIZED TO THE stage. "Eek! Is back in the Abyss again! You'se okay, yes?" Casimir said, fussing around Peri. Peri's face was very pale and streaked with tears.

Ewynne rushed to her. "Peri! What happened?"

"There was a celestial here...Irina..." Peri answered, her eyes fixed on Velimir.

"Sister, has she harmed you somehow?" Velimir asked.

He knew that celestials were among the most powerful beings in existence next to the gods themselves, but still the mere idea that one had threatened his sister made his hand unconsciously reach for the hilt of his blade.

"No...we'll talk later...but be ready! Something's about to happen," Peri said, scanning the environment with wild eyes.

"Are you fit to fight?" Jussuf asked. It was not often that he had seen Peri so shaken.

"I'll have to be," Peri said, gripping the arms of Ewynne and Velimir. The mirror gallery had vanished. In its stead, the city walls of Lughani Vos now loomed over the stage.

At the bridge leading to the gate, two entities faced the party, looking every bit as corporeal as any of them. One of them looked like Velimir in his days of riding high on the Dimitrian fever dream, wearing his hideously buffed armor and wielding the massive blade. Only the height and the hue of the eyes from behind the visor revealed that the apparition wasn't Velimir, but a copy of Peri. The Peri-apparition was accompanied by Tomoe. Shiny black hair cropped short, determined mouth, sad and wise eyes ready to fight as she drew the thin, curved blade of her ancestral katana. She looked dangerous and elegant, as breathtaking as she had been the first time Velimir saw her and had been instantly smitten. He stared at her with a clenched jaw and gripped his blade with white knuckles.

The apparitions glared at Peri, advancing steadily. "I fought tooth and nail for everything I ever had! Anything good in my life was taken from me!" snarled the Peri-apparition from behind the visor. "How I despise you and your blind luck, the way you were protected and pampered without a care in the world. I would have given much for what you had and took for granted."

Peri tried to think of how to respond to the alternative version of herself as the thing approached with a steady and light step.

"I will crush you. Like I will crush anyone standing in the way of my immortality and ascension," growled the Peri in Velimir's armor, voice flat with hatred and menace. Then both apparitions—Peri and Tomoe—attacked. There was not much to do but to fight back, and hard.

Tomoe flashed her blade at Velimir, who did not try to defend himself. He dodged the blow halfheartedly, and it drew blood. The pain from the wound made the pain crushing his chest a bit easier to endure. Tomoe was deadly, agile, and fast, but Velimir only retreated, parrying and getting more cuts.

"Velimir! Why don't you fight?" shouted Ewynne.

Tomoe-apparition lunged and spun, ending at Velimir's blind side in a maneuver he would normally never have fallen for.

"Tomoe...just kill me," Velimir whispered and dropped his blade with a clang. He dropped to his knees. Tomoe made to slash her blade at him, but Ewynne's spell knocked her back, holding her momentarily. Ewynne wasted no time but cast the *Svetilje sphere* on Velimir. For the rest of the battle, Velimir just hugged his knees inside the sphere.

Then the battle was over. As corporeal as they had seemed and as deadly as had been their blades, the phantoms vanished immediately as they were vanquished. The sphere protecting Velimir blinked and dispersed, but still he made no move.

Ewynne approached and put her hand on his shoulder. "Bro, dumb...it wasn't really Tomoe. You should know by now that this place is full of mind games," she said gently. Velimir realized that it was the first time she had called him brother without venom.

"It...it looked just like her...I couldn't hurt her...anymore..." he whispered, bleeding from the cuts, not noticing.

"Yes, they know how to play those games well," Peri said. "And I must say, your buffed armor still looked like a bit too much." But Velimir was too deep in anguish to answer with a grin or mock-indignation.

The dizzy group was gathering its breath at the stage, when suddenly a glittering celestial and a kindly old monk appeared to greet them. Jussuf and Razeem went down on one knee in front of the celestial, their faces awe-struck and joyful. Connor looked like he had in life, but was glowing and smiling gently.

"Connor!" Ewynne shouted, then glanced at Irina. The celestial's nod was enough to convince her it was the real Connor this time.

"This is a family matter. You will have some privacy," Irina said, and with a gesture of her hand, all three siblings and Connor were teleported into a cavernous space glittering with multi-colored jewels.

The girls hugged the old sage. He squeezed back. Velimir kept his distance and watched, still bleeding from his cuts.

Connor spoke. "You have both been so brave, fought so hard, not only survived, but resisted the taint of your sire."

Peri felt uneasy and bit her lip. When Darien wounded her during the fight, she had almost released the Edge again. Only Jussuf's healing grounded her enough to resist the temptation. *And it felt glorious.* "And sire is all he ever was," Peri said. "You were our father." She felt a faint nudging at her heart as she said it, but the peace emanating from Connor calmed that murmur.

Connor nodded, then glanced at Velimir.

"Your brother was less lucky," he said in a pained voice. "As you know, the Theater stores memories. Watch..."

And then a vision depicting Velimir's life flowed before the eyes of the girls. The translucent events unfolded in the midair, just as Peri's murder of Silas the Slick had before. Velimir's flight from the priestesses, the cold and horror of the streets. The child that only knew danger and hostility, always so afraid, always so angry, his divine sire giving him false succor and promises. They saw Velimir live under Radek, felt Velimir's very fear of death by his hand, the overwhelming pain and bottled rage accumulating with every beating. They saw how Velimir shattered inside when he found Jelena murdered, the gripping, shredding horror of it so much like the one they had felt when Connor was slain. And how Dimitri leapt into that void. How the madness burned in Velimir's veins, how he fell from the height of chaotic haze of megalomania and pain, how he wandered the pits of hell determined to live again.

Ewynne ran to Velimir and threw her arms around him.

"Why didn't you tell me?" she sobbed, her face pressed against the broad chest. "I would have treated you much better!"

Velimir held her shoulders and locked her gaze with his. "I murdered your father! What else is there to say?" he said, barely daring to look at Connor.

"I never forgot the little boy I left to die," Connor said.

"I always worried what became of him…and at the moment your sword split me, I knew. You deserved better."

Velimir braced himself and dared to look Connor in the eye. He saw only patience and kindness. What had humility ever meant to him? Succumbing to the whim of someone able to assert their will on you. A fate worse than death. A fate reserved for the "pawns" like he and Kiril had called them, a fate deserved by those who didn't have the power to resist the likes of Radek. He had been forced to show humility to Radek, and every time had gnawed at him and increased the intensity of the burning reservoir of rage simmering at the core of his being. What he was about to do he would previously have found next to impossible to endure. But now that he chose to do it of his own free will it felt appropriate. He knelt in front of the old man and bowed his head.

"I beg your forgiveness, Connor," he simply said. No elaboration was necessary. Connor already knew everything there was to know about the circumstances.

Connor put his hand on Velimir's head. A warm, kind hand.

"You are forgiven, child. Help my daughters. Be helped by them. There is a good man inside of you whom you can grow to be."

The girls put their hands also on Velimir's head. He felt sheltered by love and forgiveness. He realized that before this moment, he had never even momentarily felt safe.

"Now is the time to heal old wounds," Connor said. "You will need each other's help against the hostile powers seeking your destruction." He started to fade away.

"Will we see you again?" Peri asked, gripping his beloved hand that already was half translucent.

"These are volatile times, and the veils between the worlds are thinner. Anything is possible," the old sage answered, before leaving the three behind.

———————— • ● • ————————

THE SIBLINGS OF THE DIMITRIAN BLOOD VANISHED AND materialized back at the stage of the Theater of Time, looking bewildered and overwhelmed, each one of them crying.

Jussuf and Kauno stepped towards them, but Razeem stopped them. "Let them be," he said. So they kept their distance, watching the three.

"I don't wonder that you hated us so much," Peri said. "I mean, it was, of course, not Connor's fault, but still. I could so easily have been the one living through that hell..." Peri held Velimir's arm.

"And you tried to save Peri, even though you were just a small boy," Ewynne added.

But Velimir shook his head. "No excuses. I resented, I coveted, I was bitter. I placed blame upon those who had none. As for grabbing the baby...well...It just felt natural to me to try to take one of the babies with me. There were so many, and I could only take one..."

"Just like Connor," Peri said. "And he had to remember forever the little boy whose hand slipped and was left to die."

Velimir nodded. "He forgave me. I physically felt it. He didn't hate me. He felt sorrow and gentleness and let it flow into me. He didn't forgive me because he had to or because it was a bargain. He did it because he had compassion in his heart and he saw me as worthy of it. I...I thought there is no such thing..." His voice choked with emotion again.

"Now you perhaps understand why we loved him so

much. Why we hated you for taking him from us," Peri said.

Velimir winced. "If only I could bring him back..."

"He is somewhere else now and belongs there," Ewynne said. "For a long time, I just wanted that everything would be like it was before...that we were just children and could play at the island without a worry, giggle about boys, play pranks on people, and I hated you, thinking it was all your fault that things had changed. But it is not true. This thing would have found us; it is bigger than any of us. There is no going back."

Velimir embraced both of his sisters. He felt a powerful, uncontrollable force crushing his chest, pleasant and frightening at the same time. Yes, it was true. He loved them. He didn't know Ewynne that well yet, but he loved her all the same, because he loved the idea of having a little sister, and he loved her as an inseparable part of Peri and her history. He loved them with all his heart. He would die, he would give up his hard-won life, to protect them. Love—the force he had renounced together with Kiril—was back in his life, and it was devastating and fierce. But it was joyful. He was reborn.

"I love you, sisters," he whispered. "I will dedicate my new life to making up for my previous one."

———————————•●•———————————

Jussuf could no longer contain himself. He approached the group and spoke to Peri. "What is it? What has happened to you?" he asked. Velimir's arms were curled protectively around the girls, as if the man had earned the right.

"We know the past now. We know how we came to be," Peri answered in an even, colorless voice. Jussuf noticed how she sought Velimir's hand in her own and squeezed it.

"And? What about it? Tell us what you learned!" Jussuf demanded. Peri had always been kind to him, in her profanity-laden way, but she had always kept her distance. And now she shared intimate gestures with the man who had killed her protector, who shared—and stirred—her demonic blood!

"Nothing about it," Peri said, an edge creeping into her voice. Jussuf's interrogative tone seemed to get under her skin. "What makes you think it is your business somehow?"

"Peri." Ewynne shot her a disapproving look and aimed a kinder one at the young paladin. "Jussuf, it would be wise of you to give us time to take it in. Peri's mother was a psycho who wanted to kill her own child in a ritual intended for Dimitri's ascension. And that's just the beginning of it."

Razeem put a restraining hand on Jussuf's arm, but the young paladin shook it off. The way Peri stared at him as if *Jussuf* were her enemy! The way she stood as a unified front with Velimir as if they belonged together!

"And what about you, fiend?" Jussuf snarled at Velimir. "I bet you are using this information to pressure and influence her even more."

"I assure you that is not the case," Velimir said coldly. "Lay off her. We all have learned much today and can't be bothered with you."

"Enough!" Peri said. "This won't do. Darien may be dead, but we can't have this friction. In all probability, this is just the beginning. He wasn't the last of the powerful spawn, and…the fewer that remain, the more shit will get real. We must deal with the rest, one way or another."

Velimir nodded. "The prophecy talks about a secret

300

pact. That probably means the Esquadron. There is also something about a traitor. But it is so vague that it could mean anything."

Razeem smirked. "That, I fear, is the way of prophecies."

Peri took a few steps on the creaking floorboards of the theater, focusing on the next step. The magic battle had demolished what was left of Darien's siege camp, but it was too late—the city had already been bombarded to rubble. "Oh well, seems that Darien flattened Shinaris. Too bad about Shermag...Once the Theater spits us back to Valkama, perhaps we should go and examine the carnage. See if there are any survivors who would have something interesting to say. Or other clues."

"Peri, does it not bother you at all that hundreds if not thousands of people are dead? It is not your fault, but it was done in your name, to get to you," Razeem said.

Peri stopped her pacing and sharply turned to face the man. "Frankly, Razeem, no." She stared at him with hard eyes. "I didn't know them, and I kind of have other things on my mind now. I am used to dead people I didn't know. Pretty damn used to it, in fact. And now I feel that it would be most counterproductive to start to whine over something like that, especially as there is nothing to be done for them anymore. Further questions?"

Razeem lowered his gaze. "No...I am just trying to help you. To keep your heart from hardening, to remember what is important and right. So that the taint won't gain you little by little."

Peri strained as to not snap. "Fine. I get it. But spare me today. After what we learned, I have enough to deal with."

A small vortex started to hum and gyrate at the stage

and quickly grew larger. And as they expected it would, it sucked the party in. After spinning them around for a few seconds, it released them with a plop.

32
THE RUINS OF SHINARIS

THE GROUP FOUND ITSELF BACK AT THE SIEGE CAMP, next to the smoking ruins of Shinaris. The smell of death permeated everything—charred flesh, the rich iron odor of blood, smoke, the sand still swirling in small clouds generated by the explosions. With a chill, Peri realized that the smell made her spirit soar. As if every dead person killed in her name made her more alive and powerful. *Well, I suppose it does.* Irina had said as much.

Velimir noticed. "You feel it, don't you, sister? The exhilaration," he said in a low voice.

Peri nodded miserably.

"It doesn't come from you, you know. It is our father's essence calling to you. It has nothing to do with what you believe is right and would choose to do. It is very much a tangible, physical thing—borne in our blood."

Unable to find the right words, Peri gripped Velimir's hand.

They walked the demolished streets to the palace under the scorching sun, corpses and rubble everywhere. They started to examine its shattered ruins, careful of the collapsing structures. Shermag lay there with his elite troops, the madness and paranoia still etched on his face.

"Poor brother," Peri said to him. "Rest in peace." Shermag's breastplate was dwarf-forged and enchanted with powerful runes. As Shermag had been an orc, it was large enough that it could be fitted for Velimir with a little work. "Let's take his breastplate. He won't need it anymore."

The disheveled Tamasin appeared from between blackened and broken pillars, brushing dust off her clothes, a few scratches on her face.

"Peri! I'm so glad to see you alive!"

"I bet," Peri answered. "I, on the other hand, am surprised to see *you* alive."

"Once I was able to escape my cell, I tried to get Dimitri's children out alive, but it was too late. Darien's armies had already destroyed the city, and my own escape was a close thing."

"What do you want?" Peri crossed her arms at the waist and stared at the woman with narrowed eyes.

"I can tell you are still suspicious. Please believe me, I have only your best interest in my mind. Yours, and the whole of Valkama."

Peri was buying none of it. "You wanted me to kill Darien and Shermag, too. Now they both are dead, and I am out of Shinaris without your help. I don't see you holding too many bargaining chips under the circumstances."

Tamasin adopted the expression of a patient, beleaguered schoolmarm. "Understand that Darien was but the

304

beginning. Mighty forces are moving, and you will be in the center of the events, whether you like it or not. I felt loath to involve you in a problem that is partly a result of my own naivete, but the circumstances leave me no choice. There is another powerful Dimitrian spawn still alive. I believe now she is part of a coalition called the Esquadron, like Darien was. Her name is Rajsa."

Peri's face jerked at that, and though she tried to suppress her reaction, it didn't go unnoticed by Tamasin.

"Like so many other persecuted Dimitrian spawn, Rajsa came to me for help. I knew she was a cleric of Stribog, but harsh as the god is, he has always been on the side of legitimate order. Rajsa asked for a sanctuary in the monastery I used to lead before taking up the role of protecting Dimitri's offspring." Tamasin paused and looked far to the east, over the mountains. "I foolishly offered her a sanctuary, believing she would use her skills as a priestess for fulfilling the monastery's duties in the service of the city of Laipa, take care of things in my absence. But now she has closed all access to the monastery and uses it as her base. She has converted the monks to her cause. I believe she was working together with Darien."

Razeem arched his eyebrows. "The Sentinel Monastery of Laipa? Monks trained in the ways of the Austere Fist? This is most concerning!"

Peri sighed. "And the Austere Fist is…?" she asked wearily.

"A martial art Master Lin of legend brought from Feng Guo to the independent city state of Laipa a thousand years ago," Kauno said. "By the means of extreme austerities, the monks gain the ability to manipulate time and gravity. The

Sentinel monks are the only non-Feng skilled in this art. Masters of Austere Fist were feared even by horselord Ulagan's armies when he set out to conquer Siri."

"Splendid," Peri said. "And I suppose those fuckers are also immune to magic or something, because of course they are."

"Not entirely," said Tamasin, "but extremely resistant to it."

Velimir hazily remembered when a Zmaj-Vostokan Dimitrian spawn had tried to murder him, only to find Velimir immune to her sorcery. She had been able to instantly disappear and reappear without using high magic. Kazumi was her name—a member of the Esquadron, as the party had learned from Majsilaa. At the time, Velimir had assumed that she had been under some sort of prearranged enchantment, but perhaps she had been trained in the way of Austere Fist instead.

Tamasin smoothed her hair and adjusted her plait. "For centuries, the monks have used their skills to protect Laipa and travelers. How Rajsa controls them I don't know, but she may either have persuaded them, or use some form of mind control. She is, after all, a Dimitrian spawn and a powerful priestess." Tamasin pointed over the mountains. "At any rate, Peri, you must traverse the desert to Laipa and confront her."

"Oh yeah? Or what?" Peri knew she was being churlish and childish, but something about Tamasin really got under her skin. She had never got along with women who tried to tell her what to do and pretended to mean her well, regardless of what she wanted. Or men, for that matter, but the worst offenders she had met had been women.

Tamasin closed her eyes briefly and sighed, then looked

Peri in the eye again. "It is to your own advantage to act as a force of good in this matter. I don't know how many of the Esquadron are left. They are out to destroy you and much else, perhaps the whole future of Valkama."

Peri was annoyed by her condescending manner but said nothing, just nodded wearily. The woman walked away with no-one sparing her another glance.

"That bitch is phony beyond belief," Peri said. "But might as well check this out. It is not as if we have any better ideas. The Esquadron will not rest until every Dimitrian spawn is dead. And I refuse to die without a fight." Peri stuffed her sword deeper into the scabbard. "Off to save the world. Yay."

33
YGGDRASIL

KIRIL HUNG IN THE WIND-SWEPT TREE.

In truth, he was not entirely sure that he really did. Had he already failed and ceased to exist, this flickering suffering just an echo that would soon blink out and fade into eternal oblivion? Most of the time, his emaciated form seemed to float adrift in the crimson blood ocean, occasionally baking under the scorching sun in darker, denser, and partly coagulated black puddles at shallows by barren obsidian cliffs jutting from it. Then, the tide would wash him away again, and he'd drift, drift, drift...unable to move a muscle. Occasionally he had a moment of lucidity, regained his sense of direction, and was able to pry one eyelid ajar. Beyond the yellowed film of his retinas, far below, glinted the dark waters of the Well of Urd, with the white strands of foam and the two indifferent swans. Yes, he hung in the Yggdrasil.

The hunger pangs he no longer recalled. Thirst had

turned into nausea, then throbbing panic, then the exhaustion of listlessly nodding on and off to the shoreless blood ocean. Kiril had tried to implore the Yggdrasil, to talk to him, to show him the truth it had said he would have to face. But the tree ignored him. Yet Kiril didn't perish. He hung in the tree.

Suddenly the Yggdrasil throbbed. The blood ocean vibrated. *Hmm, where was I? Oh yes, the truth. One who keeps looking away can't go further. Witness the truth. Know it.* For a moment, even the blood ocean disappeared. Everything was absolutely still. There was nothing, yet the nothing shone brightly.

And then Kiril started to experience events. It was not that he *saw* them, as closing his eyes or looking away was not an option. The images flickered at the stage of his mind, the sensations and sounds shook his body from within. He saw families. Families in their everyday activities, sharing tender moments and familiarity, inoffensive ordinary men, women, and children. Kiril vaguely recalled faces. Uneasily, he realized that these were families of those he had casually murdered for business reasons. Soon he came to know what it was like to have grim-faced messengers telling you that the person you loved, the person you curled next to each night, would never come back, was lying somewhere slaughtered by a few *crn-prasak* spells so casually tossed by none other than Kiril himself. His body and mind relived their debilitating pain, the despair, the gripping in the chest. Even when the loss of Jelena had rendered him similarly gasping for breath, feeling the loss of his loved one like a loss of his own vital organ, he had not in retrospect made the connection to the loss he had caused in the past.

Then Kiril shrieked in a pool of his own slippery sweat and burning urine, desperately trying to scramble away from the pummeling fists, the slicing knives and...*no, NO! THE MAGE! The acid and flames he summons out of thin air, the black slimy tentacles and gnawing rodents he can conjure in my soft viscera!* Through the panicky, concussed tears, he saw his own hardened, locked-up face from the perspective of so many he had tortured. He had always found torture distasteful, but never truly acknowledged the terror he willingly had inflicted on other human beings. The abject horror of helplessness he now felt himself, of being at another's mercy and not being able to do a damn thing about it. The same loss of agency, the powerlessness he realized now that Velimir had done everything in his power to escape. Helplessness and physical pain were one thing. Another was seeing the unfeeling faces of the torturers, the way they refused to allow humanity to reflect back in their eyes. One could scream and scream, and it made no difference at all.

Me? I did this to someone? I, who always despised petty, sadistic people like Radek and his ilk? I told myself it was necessary, that it was business as usual...that they knew the risk when they robbed our caravans or burglarized our headquarters...but if someone did this to anyone I love, would I accept that as an excuse?

Kiril saw that the idea of who he had been, what he had ever believed in, was just a shallow lie. He detested the man he had been, the smug magician who used his intellect to wound and scheme, who scorned those with more courage, yet clung to his illusory superiority to openly sadistic thugs like Radek.

There was no denying what the Yggdrasil was showing

him. This was who he was. There was no way that worthless man was worthy of Jelena's love or a second chance. Kiril tried to moan but didn't have the strength. The images faded. He still didn't perish.

Kiril hung in the wind-swept tree.

34
A CAMP IN THE MUSAHARI DESERT

"Mmmh?" Velimir felt an anxious presence and stirred in his sleep, carefully opening one eye. His bedroll was next to Peri's. The two slept side by side these days. Peri was fast asleep, hands protectively curled around the backpack she used as a pillow. Her cheek was pushed against the conspicuous bump that was Genjiro's head. Velimir was pleased to notice that tonight she was not moaning and flailing in her sleep.

Casimir fidgeted next to Velimir and kept glancing at him, but didn't seem able to look him straight in the eye. "Velimir? Me'se very worried and can we'se talk?" Casimir looked sad and somewhat guilty, as if he had just snatched the last piece of sugar candy. "Please please please?"

"Mh. All right. Give me a minute." Velimir gently

adjusted Peri's cape to keep her warm, then yawned and stretched and walked to the remnants of the campfire with the nervous imp.

"I hope this is something good. It is the middle of the night, and we have a long trek ahead tomorrow," he irritably added, then regretted it immediately as Casimir's large and pleading eyes saddened even more. "I am sorry, Casimir. Of course it is important, if you are in distress," Velimir said more softly. The imp had that effect on him.

"You'se think...can have many best friends, maybe? Not only one best friend, no, but also one two three four—" Casimir started to babble, avoiding Velimir's gaze.

"I get the idea," Velimir interrupted. "As an answer, I think the concept of a 'best friend' loses something essential if you can have an infinite number of them, but I think it is perfectly possible to have a few you cannot put in an order of preference."

"Velimir really thinks so? Not just saying it is all good good good can have many best friend so that me'se all happy and then Velimir really crying all sad sad sad and think Casimir not his best friend anymore and not like poor Velimir and—"

"Casimir! I rarely lie to others in order to make them feel better. I gather you have a new best friend now?" Velimir had an idea who it might be. Casimir spent more and more time perched on Ewynne's shoulder when he wasn't cooking or fussing around the party members.

"Oh yes oh yes! But Velimir still also me'se best friend in all world and Abyss and Hades and Gehenna and Tartarus and Manala and Naraka and—"

"Casimir."

"Cause greenhead is really really really nice and greenhead hug little Casimir and greenhead spells say all ooooooomph and Velimir not cast spells at all and imps can be special friend to a magician but Casimir still wants to be Velimir's—"

Velimir raised a hand to halt the imp's babbling. "I believe you. It is perfectly all right if you want to be best friends with both me and Ewynne, with the additional responsibility of being Ewynne's familiar," he said. Skilled mages often formed a bond with a magical creature, such as an imp or a pixie, and the creature augmented and assisted their abilities. More irascible mages might be abusive and bind the creature by force, while the creatures voluntarily formed a bond with a mage they liked. This was presumably what Casimir was talking about. Velimir recalled how he had asked Kiril why he didn't have a familiar. The man had just said that he'd always been a loner, and let's leave it at that.

Casimir's anxiety was gone in a second. The imp's face was alight with joy, and he started to sing out of tune, dancing a little jingly dance.

"Meeee'se the happy happy imp, meeeee'se can coooooks a spicy shrimp, meeeeee'se pour me'se friends some self-made meaaaaad, along with some..."

"Casimir! You'll wake everyone up!"

Velimir scowled, but the overjoyed imp hugged him, flapping his leathery wings. Glad that no-one was there to witness the indignity, Velimir hugged back. Come to think of it, Casimir was probably the first creature he had started to treat decently. Or perhaps it had been Myra, the vampire he had plotted to escape the Abyss with. He wondered what had become of her.

After retreating to his bedroll, Velimir couldn't sleep. If someone had told him when he was at the height of his madness that he would care about the feelings of a silly imp to the extent that he'd let it interrupt his sleep and still comfort the thing, he would probably have split that person in half for the mere insult. Yet...it didn't make him feel weak anymore. Ewynne cared about others' feelings, and she wasn't weak. Granted, sometimes his little sister chirruped like a little, exasperating bird, jumping about and interrupting his moping and thought processes...but that was who she was. *Little Ewynne.*

Velimir drifted asleep and found himself in the gardens of Eilean de Taigh-Sholais. He was aware that this was the Dreamlands, yet the dream seemed very vivid and visceral, just like the dream of the Dimitrian temple in which he had met Tomoe. He was wearing his old Dimitrian armor. In the old times, he had felt safe inside of it, but now it felt like a prison around him. He walked to the bench on the sunny side of the library, the one he had seen Connor and Peri sitting on. The old sage sat on the bench, his gray-blue eyes looking expectantly at Velimir.

"Take off that armor, Velimir. You don't need it anymore," he said in his gentle voice. "No-one will hurt you."

Velimir stripped off the chest plate piece by piece. He felt the sun and the gentle wind on his bald head and marveled at the beauty of the garden. Connor gestured to him, beckoning him to sit next to him on the bench. Velimir lowered himself, hesitant and almost shy. Connor took hold of his hand.

"You have come a long way, Velimir," Connor said. "And now I have something to ask you."

"Anything," Velimir said.

"I'm asking you to help Peri. She is still much influenced by her divine sire. More than she knows. The blood is so strong in her—so strong now that all these murders of Dimitri's offspring have distilled its potential. Things will not be easy for any of you, and she *will* be tempted by Dimitri's power. She may delude herself into thinking she can handle the taint as her power grows. She listens to you like she listens to no-one else. Velimir, watch my daughter's step."

Velimir hesitantly put his hand on the old man's ethereal knee. It touched him that the man would ask for his killer's help. But Connor was right. He was closer to Peri than anyone else—even Ewynne. "You have my word. Nothing would please me more than to be able to give back something," Velimir said.

Connor nodded and held Velimir's hand for a while. Then his dream faded into surreal, unrelated images.

35
MUSAHARI DESERT, AN OASIS ON A TRAIL BETWEEN SHINARIS AND LAIPA

"You know, I think I would be perfectly happy if I never saw another grain of sand in my life," Ewynne said after a long, silent trek in the desert.

No-one answered.

"I mean, it's so dull to look at! Before the desert, at least the scenery was pretty," she continued.

"Yeah. Well…Look, there's something!" Peri pointed, squinting her eyes.

"An oasis? A Bedouin village, perhaps?" Velimir said.

"Let's get drunk!" Peri immediately lightened up. She had been far too long without the mellowing buzz of alcohol. *It quiets down Dimitri's voice, too.* As well as the disturbing awareness of the bulging bump in her backpack. At times, she wanted to throw it away. *It's just a...dried carapace, right? Genjiro left the building long ago.* But in her heart of hearts, she knew. Connor and the monks had taught her that rituals and respectful treatment of the remains of the departed mattered. No matter how many soiled corpses she had left lying about without a second thought, she had to give Genjiro a proper burial. *Like I gave to Tomoe.*

The party approached and was able to see a gathering of tents next to the oasis that shimmered in the heat. There was a military troop standing in a formation next to the tents. They wore enchanted, masterfully crafted equipment—chest plates emblazoned with Cijeli's emblem: the open sky. These were elite soldiers, led by paladins—and backed up with several platoons of battlemages and clerics.

Peri slowed down. "I have a distinct feeling that this is not a Bedouin village where we could get drunk," she said in an emotionless voice.

"By Juris! They have a significant portion of the Eastern Wulani battalion here!" Razeem exclaimed.

"Perhaps we should try to sneak past them using *shifting shadows*?" Ewynne suggested.

"Won't work," Jussuf answered. "With that many clerics and battlemages, they are bound to notice, and then we will be in an even worse position."

Peri nodded. "It is likely that they are waiting for us. A question or two about Shinaris on their mind, perhaps. And, if there is another way to Laipa, they have most likely blocked that as well."

"We should go and talk to them," Razeem said. "Cijeli the All-Father is an honorable deity—an ally to Juris—and these are good and just officials. I'm certain we can explain the circumstances to them."

"I wouldn't bet on it," Peri said. "But you're right. Let's go and have a chat with them. It's not like there are many other options available."

Peri walked with her head high, like a woman with nothing to hide. Without looking at her side, she knew Velimir's stature matched hers. As the two approached, the commander of the army swallowed nervously and glanced at the troops behind him. He took a deep breath, brandished a scroll, and read from it with a determined look in his eyes.

"Peri of Eilean de Taigh-Sholais, otherwise known as the Butcher of Yalifa, your execution has been ordered and will take place immediately. May Milostra have mercy on your soul."

"May I inquire what she is being accused of?" Razeem asked, anger lacing his deep voice.

"She is a spawn of Dimitri and a mass murderer! She has destroyed a whole city and all its citizens!"

"I suppose you decided to dispose of those little bureaucratic formalities like an investigation or a trial?" Peri asked, the venom dripping from her voice.

"You don't even deny it! That is all the proof that is needed!" the commander shouted. "Attack!"

"No! This is not right!" Razeem shouted, then barely dodged a crossbow bolt.

There were a lot of women among the soldiers—faces tense and serious, neat, immaculate plaits down their back. Religious orders recruited more female warriors than armies of lesser wealth—they could afford enchanted bracers and the like to compensate for what promising warriors may lack in natural strength. Following the volley of crossbow bolts, the young, serious, and determined soldiers of the vanguard charged into the melee. *"Neka svane zoraaaa..."* echoed Cijeli's battle cry, and while the voices were tense and on the verge of breaking, it seemed to bolster the soldiers with courage.

Fighting off an army! A more disciplined one than that of Darien's. These were well-trained, honest, patriotic people believing in protecting their homeland from something evil and dangerous, and having the right to do so. Still, it meant little to Peri. What meant anything now was staying alive, dodging, slashing, beheading, cutting, ducking...dealing death. She found herself laughing gleefully as she noticed that Velimir's whirling blade was moving faster than he had been capable of before Darien's death, just a gray glinting blur spreading pink mist in the midst of screams of pain and dismayed chortling sounds. She herself was faster, too. *Way faster.* The soldiers might as well have run face first into a giant mechanical shredder. *I'm fucking INVINCIBLE!* She was born of wrath, born to do rage and murder. And at the moment, she reveled in it, feeling the underground river throbbing in her too-hot blood.

Velimir fought with vigor too, feeling only slight regret at dealing death on a large scale yet again. He was too angered because of the unfounded accusations, the fear and group-think that made these sanctimonious fools attack his sister, thinking it their right to kill her. That they wore the symbols of legitimate authority and believed themselves to do the right thing meant little to him. In fact, it made them even worse in his eyes. Velimir might live for redemption now, but he was none the worse at dealing death for his change of outlook.

Ewynne's eyes widened as she witnessed her siblings do their dual act—Velimir spinning his blade and mowing down everything with his superior reach and strength, Peri darting in and out from behind him, lunging and rolling away, preying for a misstep. They had been a terrifying sight before, but now they seemed to have transcended humanity. They were faster and stronger than vampires! The second line of attack faltered as the troops witnessed their companions slaughtered helplessly before their eyes.

But what good did it do if the battlemages incinerated or electrocuted the party? Ewynne had never worked as part of an entire troop of mages—but she knew that they were formidable when coordinated. The platoons of mages in their golden robes were chanting in unison, and a roaring firestorm started to form over them. The mages looked blurry as they were sheltered by the *ethereal armor* spell, conjured and channeled for each one by the clerics at their side. If Kauno conjured a thunderstorm, the lightning would not get through—at least not fast enough. The fiery tornado started to expand, belching smoke and cinders, rolling Peri's and Velimir's way. Ewynne raised her hands and kept chanting. The sphere of her protective shield hovered and shimmered. But there was no way her shield would absorb all that, or that Jussuf's divine healing or Kauno's rejuvenating nature magic would heal the party fast enough. She braced herself, hoping for a quick death in the explosion. Imps could not be harmed by fire or lightning—perhaps Casimir would live.

The maelstrom of fire engulfed Peri and Velimir and exploded, a smoky column reaching for the sky. And then...

nothing. Ewynne's heart thumped in her chest. Peri's sooty face grinned through the swirling smoke. Velimir's eyes glowed as if he had just stepped from the Abyss through the flames like a demon lord in a summoning circle. Ewynne's mouth hung open. Peri whooped. "Fucking MENTAL!"

The low rumble of thunder Kauno called grew louder. A mass of dark clouds obscured the sun, and for a moment, it was almost dark. Then a network of silvery strands of lightning flickered above. A bolt zapped the column of mages. But instead of absorbing the bolt, the shimmering shield channeled over the mages simply dissipated in blue smoke with an enormous crack. The lightning jumped, forked, and multiplied. The rows of mages and clerics jerked and buzzed, then collapsed as cooked and blackened husks.

The party stood watching in stunned silence for a moment. Kauno's thunderstorm retreated with a few faint cracks and a quieting rumble. The last stray currents sizzled among the blackened heaps of corpses and died down.

Peri sprinted to the edge of the carnage. One mage who had been stationed farthest away from the point of impact was still alive, groaning with tears swimming in his glazed eyes. Peri poked him with her boot. "How'd that execution idea work out for you?"

The mage opened and closed his mouth a few times, trying to form words. He blinked. "...mercy..." he croaked.

Peri uttered a silvery laugh of a young child and patted the man's cheek. "Nah, I don't think so," she answered and squeezed his throat. She didn't have to squeeze for long. The man's eyes rolled back and he died. Peri jumped up and paced around, whooping once more. "See?" she said to the others, gesturing at the hundreds of dead, the masses of corpses. "See!? We did this! Irina wasn't lying. Offing one of Dimitri's pedigree spawn really makes me like a thousand times more powerful! Like a fucking god! And it rubs off on everyone around me! We can fell *armies*! Fucking epic!"

"But Peri..." said Ewynne quietly, "don't you see? That must be true of the rest of them, too. These poor sods didn't have a half-celestial channeling Dimitri's essence around them. But the Esquadron will. And they are coming for us."

That sobered Peri a bit. She pursed her lips, then flicked her hair behind her shoulder. "Point taken. Well, fuck them. We'll deal with it. Let's see if they have any good loot that hasn't burnt to a crisp."

Razeem bowed his head, hiding his face in his hand.

"What is it, Razeem?" Velimir asked.

"I...I truly was sure that they would listen! They were not evil. I could tell that by the power of my god! I would never have thought that people would be capable of such miscarriage of justice unless they were evil. How can Cijeli—or my own patron, Juris—let this happen?"

Velimir shrugged. "Why do gods let anything happen? They are not omnipotent. And...people are panicking. An entire city has been reduced to rubble. I...exploited people's fears in my former life. I am not surprised by this, only disgusted."

Razeem nodded. "This weighs heavily on my heart."

"Then perhaps this will lift your load a little," Velimir said. "I want to thank you. I always despised your kind, but when I still was wallowing in bitterness and megalomania, you talked to me as if I was worthy of your efforts. Even though I insulted you. It was one of the things that has led me to change my outlook and assume new goals."

A small spark of light appeared in Razeem's eyes, and the tension on his pained face eased somewhat. "That means a lot, Velimir. Even as I grieve for the loss of these souls led astray, I take solace in that the soul of a great warrior has been turned to light."

To light? I'm still drenched with the blood of brave men and women. But Velimir kept his disquiet to himself and smiled and nodded at the paladin. Razeem wanly smiled back and sighed, gathering his gear for camping.

36
LAIPA

Laipa's city gates were flanked by high and narrow towers with blue spiral stairs surrounding them. The city wall ended abruptly into the steep cliff on top of which loomed the monastery. High atop the narrow tower, a lookout sounded a horn and after a moment the gates were pushed open. A man wearing a pragmatic, sand-colored uniform and a Bedouin headdress appeared, a platoon of scimitar-fielding infantry at his back. His unsmiling hawk eyes regarded the party scornfully.

"Peri of Eilean de Taigh-Sholais. The sacred laws of shelter apply even to you," he said. "You will be allowed in Laipa to recuperate and buy supplies. But cause no trouble."

"Whoa. While I appreciate the no small talk approach, I was hoping for a bit friendlier welcome," Peri said. "I *have* come in peace. May even be able to help you with the monastery situation." Peri, half-amused, arched her eyebrow.

The man didn't share any of her humor. "I have heard reports of the destruction of Shinaris and the butchering of the Eastern Wulani battalion. You should be grateful to be let in at all."

"It was not exactly like we had a choice," Velimir cut in, annoyed.

"The reports conflict, and I can't spare the resources to examine the truth now," the man said. "But I recognize you, Velimir Rosinin. The fact that your sister has resurrected you and hails you as a comrade suggests that she is a force of darkness."

"You are the captain of the city guard, yes?" Razeem said, and as the man nodded, the paladin continued. "The Laipan monastery used to be on good terms with the Three. I am a devoted servant of Juris, and I can vouch for Peri and the company she keeps. She is being attacked by those who seek the destruction of all children of Dimitri and has only been defending herself."

The captain was not impressed. "I can see you displaying the symbol of the Order of the Eye. You match the description of Sir Razeem al-Farouq, so perhaps that *is* the truth. I already said that I will allow you in. I do not trust your intentions, but with the monastery cut off and having abandoned its role as the defender of the city, I prefer not to waste resources in confronting you. But make no mistake—I will, if you give me cause. Men!"

Without waiting for an answer, he gestured to the platoon, who made a sharp turn and followed him to the streets, marching in formation, slowly disappearing out of sight while raising a cloud of dust.

"Obstinate fool," Velimir spat.

"Perhaps…but he is no coward," Peri said, watching the disappearing soldiers. "He has heard what we are capable of, yet made it clear he is willing to attack us if needed."

Razeem adjusted the scimitar at his waist with sweaty palms. "He has reason to worry, that is for sure. I just wish he had listened to us, as we could have helped with the monastery situation."

Laipa was dusty, hot, and paranoid. Hollow-eyed peasants stared ahead, while bragging and staggering mercenaries lorded over them in the streets. Once in a while, robed monks and nuns, their eyes cold and aloof, patrolled the streets but seemed to care little about what was happening.

It didn't take long for the party to find the tavern, a pleasantly cool white-washed building painted red and blue. Peri waved for two ales over the busy counter, welcomed them with a satisfied sigh and started to quaff. Ewynne ordered a sweet pink monstrosity called "Sunset at the Shimmering Sands," while Razeem and Velimir settled for chilled wine. Kauno only wanted water.

"Another city with starving children and suffering, poor people no-one cares about," Razeem sighed. "Why the monks have abandoned their role as the protectors of the people, I don't know."

"They are doing whatever Rajsa tells them to do. She couldn't care less about the people of this city," Peri said. She hastily gulped down the dregs of her ale and waved to the bartender for more.

"That makes sense," Velimir said, "but something is off about this whole situation. I wish I could figure out what is going on. I don't like this. I have a feeling that we are playing into someone else's lap by going after Rajsa and whoever else is left of the Esquadron."

"Yeah. The problem is, there is not much alternative. They are out to kill me. I guess we'll just have to play along until we figure out who the famous traitor is." Peri popped a few olives in her mouth to go with the ale.

"Kauno is so happy that Velimir is no longer feeding angry and fearful spirits!" Kauno said. Today he wore a simple desert-dweller's garb, the weather having taken precedence over his preference for playfulness. "Friendship and love between sisters and brothers is how it is meant to be. Varpu says so, too. He is happy with Velimir's progress."

"Oh, do be quiet, Kauno!" Jussuf said, his temper flaring after being kept under a lid for days. "He is deceiving you because of your kind heart! Only I would have imagined that your vaunted wisdom and affinity to the spirits would allow you to see more clearly. Yes, Velimir, everyone can see that you have changed. Why, you seem to have charmed even Ewynne! Only I wonder if this is not some sort of act for Peri's benefit."

"It is no act, paladin. It is also none of your business." Velimir stood rigid, eyes cold and hard.

"On the contrary!" Jussuf exclaimed. "Out of respect for Peri, I have kept my concerns to myself, but your manipulation of her has become too great a danger to keep silent. In the name of Juris the Ever-Vigilant, I have sworn to protect Peri with my life, and I wonder about your fiendish motives."

"My motives may not be as transparent as yours, fool, but they are also not as superficial," Velimir said, holding back his anger. He was aware that the bond between him and Peri caused Jussuf distress. That, in and of itself, didn't give him pleasure. But how dare the paladin comment on things he knew nothing about?

"Well? Go ahead, impress us all with your depth. What is it you hope to gain by ingratiating yourself to Peri?" Jussuf sneered.

"We, fool, are bonded by blood," Velimir said. "In a manner you can't begin to comprehend. As for what I hope to gain: redemption."

"Redemption? *You?* You must be joking." Jussuf snorted and mustered a sarcastic laugh.

That was all it took. Velimir snapped. He hauled the paladin up by his collar.

"Redemption. Among other things," he snarled, then shoved Jussuf back. Jussuf was red with rage, his hand reaching for the mace at his waist.

Peri leapt between them. "Stop it, this instant! Both of you! Jussuf, you had no right to say that."

"You are being manipulated by him!" Jussuf said. "By Juris, if it wasn't so filthy and unnatural, I would suspect you two of being in love!"

The flustered men glared at each other, neither willing to back off. Peri was quiet for a moment, then spoke in a calm voice. "Razeem and Jussuf, come with me. We'll talk outside."

The men followed her to under the welcoming canopy, Razeem grim and worried, Jussuf pacing and agitated. Peri's expression softened, and she sighed. "You must leave, Jussuf. The group is not working anymore. You two will come to blows. You are unhappy, and it is only getting worse. And if this means that Razeem will leave too...I will just have to accept that."

"Why is it I who must leave, and not Velimir?" Jussuf

asked. "I have served you far longer than he has."

"Not only is Velimir the one I want around, not only is he my brother, but it is also what Connor said. That we need each other. Frankly, I don't appreciate you trying to think for me and being so overprotective."

"You were clearly out of line, Jussuf," Razeem said. "Are you sure this is even about him? That this is not about something else entirely? About you?"

Jussuf scoffed. "Oh, I know what you are insinuating. And perhaps you are right! It doesn't make any sense, I know that. Me, the scion of the al-Rasid dynasty! Me, the pious Jussuf, the son who would join the Order as is customary, the prude my brothers used to laugh at behind my back! That I would...court a foreign mercenary, a demon-born woman of no breeding, with coarse manners and an irreverent nature. What a joke! Yet...it is what it is." He swallowed an angry sob.

Peri blinked a few times, speechless.

"Oh, no need to mock me, Peri! I know well enough that you could never love anyone with 'a stick up his ass' as you would put it, who actually takes tradition and his religion seriously, who...yes, I *know* we are not matched!"

Peri frowned. "Mock you? I wasn't going to mock you! I just...had no idea, is all." Peri bit her lip and looked at Razeem rather than face Jussuf's resentful gaze.

"I will leave, then," Jussuf said, starting to loosen the straps of the enchanted breastplate he was still wearing with jerky, abrupt motions, hands trembling. "I suppose you want this breastplate back, as it was payment for clearing that restless ancestral tomb back in Yalifa."

Peri shook her head. "You were part of retrieving it!

Keep it as a thank you for being a faithful companion for so long." She turned to face the grave-looking Razeem. "Will... will you leave too?"

Razeem shook his head. "I pledged myself to your service until such time that the Vysokian turmoil has played itself out. It has not yet. You are dismissing Jussuf, so I, too, will release him from the role as my second hand and wish Juris' blessings upon his journey."

Jussuf's face crumbled at that. A tear spilled over the rim of his eye. He angrily wiped it away with the back of his hand.

Peri winced and closed her eyes for the duration of a fragile inhale. Then she steeled herself and looked Jussuf in the eye, hoping to convey respect to him. "Jussuf...," she said, "I hope you will find it in your heart one day to believe that I wish you well."

They shook hands, and Jussuf walked away with a determined step, not looking back. Peri struggled against tears as she walked back inside with Razeem, but gained her control before showing her face to the rest of the group.

"Where is Jussuf?" Kauno asked.

"Gone." Peri's grim look dared the group to say something. They didn't respond, just looked at her expectantly. "This couldn't go on anymore. He was bitter and unstable, and the friction was only getting worse."

Razeem nodded. "The situation had escalated beyond my ability to influence him. It is regrettable, and I hope he will find peace. He is the son of one of the most prominent families in Wulani...a lot of pressure is upon him. But Juris will watch over him as long as he remains true and prays. His faith will protect him."

"Couldn't be helped. His skills with dealing with undead and healing will be sorely missed, though." Peri shrugged off her gloomy mood and lifted her tankard. "Fortune favours the bold, right? Drink hail!" She slammed the tankard down so that some of the ale foamed onto the table.

After that, the evening took a lighter turn. Velimir didn't say much, just observed the group. He was tempted to think of them as his friends, though such a word, uttered without sarcasm, hadn't belonged to his vocabulary in a long time. Peri was getting more and more drunk, steadily determined to do so. Ewynne was giggly and starting to nod off, Kauno drinking only water. Velimir and Razeem drank slowly, sipping their wines.

Finally, Ewynne fell asleep, head pressed against Velimir's shoulder and feet in Kauno's lap. Velimir felt a strange tenderness, an emotion he had never experienced before. *Little Ewynne. Little sister.* She might have been sweet, sunny, and happy, but she was not frivolous. She was brave in and out of combat, strong in her own way.

"Kauno will take Ewynne to her room and then retreat to sleep himself. Varpu needs his beauty sleep," Kauno said, supporting Ewynne with his strong, sinewy arms.

"You do that, Kauno. I would shudder to think what would happen if your avian friend turned less attractive by lack of sleep," Velimir said. "Goodnight."

"I will leave you two to it, then. Goodnight," Razeem said.

So Velimir was left with the visibly drunk Peri. Her eyes shone and her speech was slightly slurred. Her hair was swimming in a puddle of ale she had spilled on the table, but she didn't notice. Velimir himself wasn't that drunk. He still associated excessive consumption of alcohol with Kiril's misery and the soggy, sweaty days of madness and guilt in Simune's bed.

"Sister. Will you tell me what happened at the marshlands?"

Peri averted her eyes and was silent for a moment, as if trying to decide whether to open up or not. Velimir waited. It was, as always, her choice to make. Then Peri spoke.

"I have never been so helpless in my life. They had me literally—" her voice cracked "—strapped down. Manacled on a gurney. There was some acid in the manacles that burned my wrists when they jerked against it. I was in a room that was just...white. There was nothing in it. Just a sick, glaring rod of unnatural light that penetrated everything. A hollow voice speaking to me from somewhere behind the walls. They had stuck a needle and a hose in my arm, and I could hear a *clang* somewhere behind the wall. And then...then some purple liquid started to come through the hose...it burned my veins and then...*it* started."

Peri's voice trailed off, and a lonely tear welled in her eye. She angrily wiped it away. Velimir took hold of her hand and wiped her cheek, and involuntarily she shed a few more tears.

"You have seen me crying, too, and offered me comfort," he said. "Go on."

"The weird thing is that it didn't hurt. I was not in pain. But my body was in utter panic. I could not make it stop panicking. Normally, you know, you can just make fear an icy lump in your stomach and steel yourself. Call bravado and bloodlust and even enjoy it. But not then. I would have done anything, absolutely anything, to be able to escape my body. I was jerking and bucking and shrieking, and it made no difference at all. I felt like my mind would fall apart. Like I was being eaten alive by millions of squirming bugs..."

"As I understood from Majsilaa, this would normally have triggered the Edge, but they devised a way to harvest the produced transcendental energy instead. Material for their artificially created celestials," Velimir said.

"At that moment, if I had known for certain that I'd lose myself and rage as the Edge forever, I would not have cared one bit. If I had known for certain that I'd forget all I ever was, I would have done it in a heartbeat. They...they meant to keep me like that for the rest of my life. Draining me, filling me with panic, keeping me in that room where there was absolutely nothing so that my mind started to fall apart and create horrors of its own."

She paused for a moment, then looked up to him with a challenging look in her eyes. "Why did you want that, Velimir? Great as it felt at the time, the Edge is...just fucking dangerous. Like shinedust, only worse. It made it so crystal clear that I would lose everything I am, everything I believe in, just to get some more of its poison. And the few times that I've gone there have worn me thin. Why did you want to lose what you were and turn into a monster—little more than a vessel channeling Dimitri?"

"I...all I ever saw was that there was no mercy or love or gentleness," Velimir said. "Or if there was, like in my mother, it got crushed and stomped by those who had none. I hated Radek so much. I had no choice but to let him beat me, to humiliate me and laugh at my pain and powerless anger. To hear him rape my mother and not be able to do a damn thing about it...I wanted no part of being that weak creature."

Peri staggered next to him and put her arm around

his shoulder.

"You were not weak or pathetic, bro," she murmured. "You were a child. Dimitri offered you what you wanted most—escape from that powerlessness. He offers me things, too. He...knows my heart. So often I can remember how it felt to be the Edge. That nothing can stop me. That nothing can stand in my way. That I can just mow down everything that pisses me off. But you were right. I *was* pampered and protected, taking it for granted. I didn't grow up good, like Ewynne. But I listened. And it made an impact. So, I can see through Dimitri's shit...most of the time." Peri snuggled her chin against Velimir's shoulder and squeezed him, and he returned the gesture. Her eyes, while a bit unfocused because of the drink, were intent upon him.

Velimir steadied Peri in his arms. "I see my folly clearly now, and it is you who made me see. I will do anything to protect you and Ewynne, and if it means giving up my life and returning to the Abyss, so be it," he said, jaw firm, his eyes burning with emotion.

"Velimir...I am not a cleric or paladin, but you wouldn't go to the Abyss again. I'm sure Razeem would agree. But I don't want you to die...I want you to live and to travel with me. What Jussuf said about us...the part with us being together..." she struggled to get her thoughts into a proper order.

Velimir waited, stroking her arm.

"I do love you. But not like he meant. Like another half of my soul."

"I know," Velimir said. "I have never felt so...understood. By another who really knows. In a way, even if we were not siblings, we would perhaps be too close to each other for a romantic relationship."

Peri was quiet for a while, resting her head against Velimir's shoulder. It felt good to have her near, in the same way it felt having his mother or Kiril hug him when he was a child.

"Genjiro traveled with us for rather a long while. He was my friend for even longer. Wyn and I did some protection stuff for him when we stayed in Wallila Gate. He was lodging in the same inn as us. He was a merchant of Zmaj-Vostokan imports. Well, he never spelled it out, but I soon figured out he was a smuggler."

Velimir felt dizzy, conversations and tales from long ago flooding his mind. "That is not surprising. Tomoe's brother was involved with illegal activities back in Morishima, with the clan's tacit approval. But he was expected to accept his execution when he got caught. Tomoe could not stand that. She threw it all away to save him."

Peri nodded. "She threw it all away to save you, too. She died for you. I know it is a harsh truth to hear, but—"

Velimir raised a hand and interrupted her. "You, my dear sister, punctured my armor of lies. What was Genjiro like? Tomoe only remembered him as a very young man."

Peri closed her eyes and smiled wistfully for a moment, thinking back. "Superficially, he was a charming rogue, a bit of a flirt. But there was a sadness in him I never was able to reach. He took life like I do...like it is and not like it should be. He wanted to...see everything and be on the road like me. I...I almost thought myself in love with him..." Peri sobbed a bit, "and I thought he at least considered me a good friend..."

Velimir squeezed her hand. "What happened? How did Genjiro die?"

"Did Tomoe explain to you how *seppuku* works?"

"She did. It is hard for outsiders to understand, but it is something they are well prepared for. The samurai start learning about it, practicing it even as children."

"Genjiro thought it was the only chance he had to escape the fate of a geas breaker. He didn't have the training, as he was not chosen to be a warrior, but he was of a samurai bloodline. We did our best with what we had, mimicked the ritual, with me having no clue what I was doing—"

"You were his *kaishakunin*?" Velimir remembered Tomoe's explanations about the elaborate ritual.

"If it can be called that. I did take his head off with my sword. He was terrified that we were just making a mockery of a sacred ritual...When the blood and the guts spilled out, he turned so white. And it was so silent after the head rolled away. And, you know, it was so sudden—that he had been someone I maybe loved, and now, a second later, it was just a carcass. Gods know how many people I have killed. But this was different."

Velimir continued to console her by stroking her arm.

"Veli, he was terrified. And I have no idea if I did it right at all...the head is not supposed to roll out, but it did. And it was no katana, and we didn't have any of the stuff they have there in Morishima...what if I even offended their *kami* or something? His face was frozen in horror..."

"My beloved sister, we will lay his remains to rest. We will find a way. We will."

Peri's sobs intensified. Velimir led her to her bedroom, and she didn't resist. She passed out in seconds. Velimir, heart full of emotion, covered her with a blanket and curled up to sleep by her side.

---•●•---

Peri groaned and slowly opened her eyes. The sun was high already, but as the plan had been to get drunk, no-one was expecting her to turn up early. She felt the rancid smell of pub air in her clothes and her hair, which was glued into sticky strands by spilled ale. She groaned again. She remembered how Jussuf used to cast a soothing spell on her on occasions like this. He didn't approve of women drinking, but when he had mentioned this, Peri had told him to get stuffed in no uncertain terms. *Poor Jussuf.* So concerned with what was proper and expected, so pompous...a gentle, wistful smile formed on her face.

Velimir entered the room, looking annoyingly vigorous and healthy. Peri remembered hazily how she had broken down, talking about Genjiro, and ...*probably?*...passed out in Velimir's arms. The latter didn't embarrass her, but the former did.

"Good morning, sister. I have brought you a big mug of coffee, a pitcher of cool water, and toast with scrambled eggs. They will bring a tub for bathing in a minute," Velimir said, arranging the food on the nightstand.

"Wow. You know how to treat a damsel in distress," Peri managed. "How come you are so perky and fresh?"

"I didn't drink very much. I rarely do."

"So, you...remember everything? Me whining about stuff?" Peri asked, blushing a little.

Velimir stopped what he was doing and sat next to Peri, looking her in the eye. "Yes, I remember everything, and I'd like to think that you do as well. I wouldn't categorize it as whining. You cried because you have been subjected to

338

diabolical torture, and because you were worried about the fate of a person you loved. I see no weakness in that."

"It was a relief to be able to let go a bit...to be emotional," Peri said, her blush deepening.

"With me, you are always allowed."

Peri squeezed Velimir's hand briefly, then stretched and yawned.

"Eat, Peri. It will get cold. I will go now so that you can bathe in peace." Velimir left Peri alone and went downstairs for his own breakfast.

The others were already waiting. Even Ewynne was less chirpy than usual, shuffling her food around with a fork.

"Is Peri in good enough shape to lead us?" Kauno asked. "Kauno wonders why people must drink bad-tasting liquid that makes them first silly and then ill."

"She will be soon," Velimir answered.

After a while, Peri descended the stairs, looking much better. Her hair was shining again, and her mood had also improved with clean clothes and a bath.

"More. Coffee." She went to get some before uttering another word. Just as she was about to gulp down a large sip, they heard a commotion. A young woman stumbled into the tavern, shooting a fearful glance at the party, and grabbed the proprietor's arm.

"They are coming! They are on their way!"

"Who?" asked the man, frowning.

"The monks! They mean business. There are several platoons! They want...her." She glanced again at Peri.

The proprietor turned pale. "They...they didn't use to harm civilians..."

"They do now! You know that! Last time they came for a

Dimitrian spawn who put up a fight, near a hundred people died! They didn't give a damn! Since Tamasin left, they have been monsters!"

"Fuck." Peri rubbed her temples. "No chance that this is a coincidence and they are, in fact, *nice* harmless monks that scribe scrolls and tend to libraries, not some weird killing machines controlled by Rajsa. If they attack us, we don't have a chance against that many without using area effect spells—or even mass effect ones. That means collateral damage. Buildings will collapse. So, let's skedaddle if we can."

She leaped up and approached the proprietor, who involuntarily took two steps back.

"Dude!" Peri said. "I'm not going to hurt you! We'll leave, so the monks will leave you alone. Is there a way out of here? Quick!"

"K…kitchen…go to the kitchen, ask the cook!"

Razeem shoved the man a few coins as they rushed through the door behind the bar, already hearing the shuffling of dozens of determined feet from the street.

The cook, a middle-aged woman with a pasty complexion and squinty eyes, dropped her pan with a clang at the sight of the armed party.

"Tell us how to get out of here quickly, woman," Velimir said.

The woman didn't hesitate. "Jump down this pit. It goes to the sewer, and it comes out by the sea, beyond the high cliff, at another side of the mountain range."

They jumped down into a sloping chute where there were traces of food and other decomposing material. Even though it seemed to be regularly flushed with water, the smell of decay was everywhere. Smelly brown water splashed when they made it to the sewer. A rat squeaked and scurried to the darkness of a bend in the tunnel.

Ewynne gagged. "I have a hangover!" she groaned.

"You are not the only one," said Peri. "And, of course, I didn't even fill the waterskins. I was so excited to start boozing."

"Worry not. I did," said Razeem. Thankfully, the man had seen to it that everyone's gear was good to go.

"Look at the bright side, sisters. We managed to evade the monks. Cheer up! If we follow the sewers, we will eventually make it to the other side of the mountain range, to the shore. Then we can start planning how to infiltrate the monastery."

37
YGGDRASIL

Kiril hung in the wind-swept tree.

Time had stopped having meaning for Kiril. He lingered in a haze of pain and weariness. At times, the parched drifting of the blood ocean seemed like a relief compared to witnessing the unstoppable stream of wrongness he was guilty of. Yes, he was a bad man. If he ever was released from this lingering between life and death, it would always gnaw at him to know what a worthless man he had been. *But others have done the same. Others have done worse.* Kiril tried to reassure himself, but it sounded increasingly hollow in his own ears. And these memories, or echoes of memories... were not the worst. He had done his level best to kill that tiny spark of vulnerable awe inside of him after Jelena died, and the rest of humanity had paid the price. As he hung from the tree, there were times when he wanted to succumb. To blink out of existence. To fade away. But the Yggdrasil didn't let him. He squirmed and writhed. He hung in the tree.

Then he felt a soothing, pleasant coolness. The coagulating blood retreated, and a wave brought Kiril to a sandy shore. He closed his eyes and enjoyed the breeze, rejuvenated by the air that didn't stink of sulfur. He felt a soft, loving hand caressing his forehead and opened his eyes.

"Jelena?" he croaked.

"It is me," she said, with a dreamy smile. Her eyes were blue as the sky and full of love. Her voice was soft and musical. "I know what you are afraid of. What you think you will see next. But I have come to release you from the Yggdrasil. It is enough. You had a business ethic. You only hurt those who were involved in shady activities and knew the risks."

"Well, not exactly," Kiril said. The words throbbed and pulsated around them rather than being formed by his parched throat and cracked, dry lips. "After you died, I turned my back on the whole idea of having such constraints. Chess pieces and all that. The bandit companies we employed in our schemes to gain control of Lughani Vos and capture Dimitri's offspring—"

"Shhh," Jelena said, pressing a soft finger on Kiril's lips. "You didn't know. We can leave now. It is all right."

She's right! I didn't know. We are done here! That was what Kiril's mind immediately yelled. A bit too shrill, a bit too fast, a bit too eager. Indignant, even.

He closed his eyes for a few seconds, biting his lip. Then he faced Jelena's eyes, bracing himself. "I didn't *not* know that those bandit companies enslaved children. I suspected, but looked away. Didn't want to know. Washed my hands of it. Like a true hypocrite."

Jelena smiled dreamily, as if Kiril had said something

amusing. "How could it have been your fault when you didn't know? And besides...others have done worse."

Kiril tried to collect himself, to resist the balmy feeling of her cool, comforting hand that called him so strongly. "You..." he managed with difficulty, "you don't sound very much like Jelena."

A tiny line of irritation appeared between her eyebrows. Her soothing hand slowed down. "How can you doubt me? Do you not love me?" She sounded wounded.

"I..." Kiril croaked, finding a semblance of his own voice though he was vaguely aware that he was at the same time hanging at the end of a rope, "I don't love whatever creature you are. The Yggdrasil said that I must witness the truth before what was lost is restored. So I must."

Jelena's forehead burst open and from it sprung a giant flesh-colored worm. It shrieked and raked Kiril with needle-sharp teeth. It was painful, but he had been lingering in pain for a long time. "Go away," he again vibrated with his mind. "You cannot harm me."

———————— • ● • ————————

THE CHILDREN TOILED AWAY, GRAY AND LISTLESS. EASY to control, small enough to crawl into cramped spaces, and expendable, in lawless lands they made the perfect labor to finance Kiril's schemes. Some of the bandits abused them for sport—others showed paltry kindnesses. In the end the children all perished, disposed of as if they were garbage.

Kiril remembered how mad he had been when Radek had beaten Velimir with the horsewhip. He had shaken with fury, straining not to finish the man with a sequence of flaming arrows. And yet...he had simply refused to think about where their goods came from—about who was toiling for the power and resources they had amassed. The children worked their little bodies into exhaustion, coughing their lungs out, feeling the whip on their narrow backs. They sank to their knees, died, and were tossed in a pit with a few shovelfuls of dirt over their faces. If he had thought about them at all, what would they have been for him? Tools? Pieces in the chess metaphor he had been so fond of using? No different from Velimir and the other infants had been to the priestesses of Dimitri.

Others have done worse, Kiril Belaja. And that matters not one bit. The deep rumble of the Yggdrasil vibrated Kiril's writhing, emaciated body.

No, it did not. It should have been him who died nameless, face in the dirt, not an innocent. *No more...no...*

But Kiril continued to see. Kiril hung in the wind-swept tree.

38
THE MOUNTAIN RIDGE BEYOND LAIPA

"Finally!" Velimir was the first to step out of the darkness of the seemingly endless sewer tunnels. The strong current swiftly carried the dirty water to the outer sea. A bright salty breeze welcomed the party to the light of the sun glittering on the surface of the grayish-green sea. *Like Peri's eyes,* Velimir thought. *She grew up at the holy island of the god of favourable winds and seafarers. Let us hope that Eoghain the Wanderer is watching over her—these waters, Eoghain's Deep, are named after him.*

The shore reached to the distance and there was an abruptly rising, steep cliff high above. Waves lapped gently, and the gulls mewed up at the tiny ledges in the face of the cliff. Peri smiled. "Fair winds and following seas, Voyager," she whispered. She spoke up, addressing her companions.

"Been a while since I've seen the ocean. I feel restless when it's out of sight."

"Aren't you always restless, Peri?" Kauno asked. "Wanderer spirits, hungry and curious spirits, are drawn to you."

"True enough," Peri said. "But when I see the horizon, I feel like there is always an escape available. That there is vast space to go and see what lies beyond. Even as a kid I used to look at maps in the library of the monastery, and I wanted so badly to go to the uncharted places with only dragons drawn on them."

Razeem was shielding his eyes from the glaring sun with his hand and scanning the skyline, then pointed at the silhouette of a fortress-like building at the highest cliff overlooking the bay. "The monastery is up there. Not for nothing is it named Sentinel. It is a very strategic location. They can see anyone approaching. Laipa is at the other side of the mountain range."

Velimir nodded. "Trying to frontally assault it would be risky at best even with all the firepower we have available. Who knows what Rajsa has at her disposal, how she has warded it against attacks? We should follow the shore until we find a way inland, then camp and make a plan for our next move."

After a trek of a few hours and losing the monastery from sight, the party reached a place where the face of the cliff was broken by a gorge where a crystal stream tumbled down from the rolling hills. They slowly traveled uphill on the slippery stones. As they were approaching the end of the gorge and the entrance to the flat grassland, they spotted a man wearing a simple monk's garb. He was tattooed and stood proud, obviously waiting for the travelers.

The group stopped. "Razeem?" Peri asked.

Razeem prayed to Juris and concentrated. "Yes, Peri. I sense a hostile intent from him."

"Surprise, surprise…" Peri sighed. "Either some aspiring hero with a death wish. Or something worse. Like more Esquadron. In other words, prepare for a fight and stay in formation."

As the party approached the man, he spoke.

"I have been waiting for you," he stated in an ominous voice.

Peri burst into a giggle. This seemed to annoy the man, who frowned. Many had come after her head and announced their intent both more and less pompously—and been unceremoniously disposed of. Bounty hunters and glory hounds didn't quite grasp the magnitude of what Dimitri's offspring were capable of—especially now that his essence was distilling and magnifying.

"A dramatic, ominous greeting," Peri said. "You auditioning for a mummers' show or something? We've heard it all before. Tell me, is it that you will free Valkama of my evil in the name of your god? Or is it that you will crush me like the insignificant bug I am, like a good megalomaniacal villain from a trashy knight romance?"

"Let's see how amused you are when I collect your Dimitrian essence to fuel my ascension!" said the tattooed monk.

"Another of the Esquadron?" Velimir asked.

"Very good!" the man said brightly, his round, heavy-lidded eyes flashing momentarily. "*I* am the great Hesyeth, and it is I who shall ascend. Rajsa has foolishly sent her monks to search after Peri here, and once I've disposed of all of you, I will take the essence from Rajsa, too!"

Peri grinned. "Well, well. A backstabby lot, the Esquadron."

"Rajsa aims to embody Dimitri as an ally to Stribog—ever the strategist, that one. But the great Dimitri—and me, the new god, his worthiest son!—don't need Stribog. Don't need any of the old guard. An era, a new era, will start, and I will be its herald! My holy fleet of celestials will fly the skies and spread terror to all the spheres beyond the very Valkama!"

"Hesyeth," Velimir said, "I've been where you are. I have felt the throbbing of my blood, the glory of Dimitri's promises. They are nothing but lies! He will cast you aside, like he has cast anyone who is not of use to him anymore! You are of our blood. Trust us, you don't have to die here today."

"FOOL!" yelled Hesyeth, his scream echoing in the canyon. "It is you who failed great Dimitri. You have been thorns in our side, true, but in the end, you have played the game just as we intended. Did you really think Tamasin was a protector of Dimitrian offspring?"

"No. We really did not." Peri's voice was flat and tired. "Neither did Shermag."

"Yet he perished neatly with the rest of them, just like we wanted. Tamasin has planned this for a long time, you see…ever since she established herself as a philanthropist in the monastery, so that she gained the trust of the Dimitrian spawn fleeing persecution. And now, she will be the general of my celestials, my right hand! You, and your brother, you mongrel mistakes, don't deserve glory! I will see to your deaths now, and not a moment too soon!"

He chanted to call a gust of wind to the gorge. It swept its walls with a wailing sound and tossed the party around. They screamed in pain as their energy drained and shriveled.

This was a formidable mass effect spell that drained humidity from the bodies of those it affected, and it tore effortlessly through the defenses the party had prepared. Kauno hurried to call something in a singing tone. Faint grass started to rise from the ground and the party could feel a soothing, calming balm easing the pain and dryness in their bodies. Nevertheless, they struggled.

They advanced to hack at the man, who was protected by shimmering layers and spheres. Razeem had prepared a trigger for a persistent *platosvetljo*, so they were able to dismiss the projected copies of Hesyeth that appeared. The triumphant Ewynne called a *prism of cancellation* to remove the spell protections. Taking his cue from her, like so many times before, Velimir was about to finish the man with a devastating strike. Just before his blade found its mark, Peri felt an unpleasant apprehension in her gut. Surely it couldn't be this easy? And indeed…

"Fools! Did you really think I would go down that easily? More proof of the inferiority of your puny race!" Hesyeth bellowed, and was gone.

"Er…Razeem? Another *plavosvetljo* sound like a plan?" Peri suggested, knowing that the persistent *plavosvetljo* pulsed and renewed itself, but the delay might be too much.

The ominous silence had everyone on their toes. Razeem started to call the syllables but didn't have time to finish before the earth trembled and knocked everyone off their feet and tossed them sprawling in the distance. Razeem and Ewynne lost consciousness, while Peri and Velimir struggled to get back on their feet.

Facing them stood a five-headed emerald-green hydra, who stomped the ground and was aiming one of its heads at the fallen party.

"Coveeeer!" Peri screamed, ducking the acid shower. She shot a quick look at Velimir, who nodded in understanding, proceeding to protect Kauno so that he could keep the party rejuvenated enough not to succumb to the hydra's attacks. Both of them knew that hydras could turn invisible at will, spit cones of acid, and cause the earth to tremble by stomping it.

The party tried to get to the hydra and avoid the acid, only to be tossed sprawling in the distance whenever it stomped the ground. Velimir had lost count on how many times he had been sent reeling backwards and lost consciousness, then staggered back upwards thanks to Kauno's frantic healing. The grass in the gorge seemed to wilt and the tumbling spring to dwindle—Kauno's rejuvenation spells drew moisture from the environment. *How long before it runs out?* The projected animations of various elemental monsters the spellcasters summoned lasted their time and then were slain. Fortunately, the hydra was starting to take some damage as well. At one point, it was positively bleeding and staggering.

"We'll get him! Quick, Velimir, finish him! He is toast!" Peri panted, and Velimir charged to do just that.

But before he managed to strike, the wyrm turned invisible again and disappeared. With an audible groan, they recognized the familiar incantation they had heard so many times from Jussuf. It was healing itself back to full health in the sanctuary of invisibility. Whatever magic Hesyeth was using to conceal himself while healing, it was resistant to Razeem's *plavosvetljo*.

Peri fought off the staggered feeling of concussion and

struggled to her feet. Ewynne pummeled the hydra with her remaining spells that barely singed it. Velimir hissed in a pool of green acid, scalding and burning his calves. Kauno kept a worried eye on the yellowing grass and drying twigs of the nearby bushes. Razeem had run out of spells and struggled to get to Hesyeth, managing an inefficient slash before the beast's stomp sent him reeling again.

Casimir, who was immune to acid, got close to one of Hesyeth's heads. He sank his teeth into the scales. The needle-sharp adamantine teeth punctured through. Hesyeth roared and swatted the imp aside, but the acid cone went astray and missed Velimir. Velimir lunged under the hydra's belly and thrust and sliced with his sword. As the hydra groaned and faltered, the rest of the party descended upon it. The acid burned their skins, their bodies were battered from flying backwards, but they wasted no time lest Hesyeth recover. The hydra bled black blood and shivered, eyes glassy. Ewynne sighed and collapsed on the raggedly breathing Razeem. Kauno reached for his water skin, and Velimir wiped goo and blood off his scalp.

"Now it looks dead. I will sever its head. And if it sprouts two new ones and attacks us again, I'm going to scream," Peri said in a flat voice. She severed the head, and they waited. After a few seconds of nothing, Hesyeth's body dissolved and disappeared in a blink of golden dust. Peri sighed in relief and collapsed to her knees. "Gotta hand it to him—that one had something to back those brags up with," she said.

"Indeed. It seems that Dimitri mated with a shape-shifting reptilian," Velimir said.

"And an orc." Peri nodded. "Dude was not prejudiced. Have to give him that."

"He set out to engineer a progeny that would transcend the existing races," Razeem said, leaning back against a rock and smiling at the sunlight on his face. "And now, the Esquadron have taken that plan even further—to entirely bypass the role of gods and nature in the creation of life. A sacrilege indeed. Even Majsilaa was capable of seeing that."

"Hesyeth foolishly bragged about Tamasin's deception and about backstabbing Rajsa," Velimir said.

"Dude was just too proud of the plan. Couldn't bear the idea of us dying and never knowing how clever he was," Peri said. "Mental note for all of us when appropriate: don't gloat, just kill."

"True—but this means that there are not many left in the game—and soon the prophecy will be drawn to the conclusion. We have to get into that monastery," Velimir said. "However, I wager that we will be sucked back to the Theater of Time before too long. That happened when you killed Darien."

Indeed, a translucent pillar of hovering air emerged, glinting in the colors of a rainbow in the sun, and the party was sucked into a vortex.

39
THE THEATER OF TIME

Again, the party found itself on the stage of the Theater of Time. Irina was waiting for them, glittering in the midair, her luminous wings idly fluttering now and then. Now there was a stone altar in the middle of the stage. A toppled chalice had spilled its contents—blood—all over the altar and a bloodied knife. Of whatever had been sacrificed, and of who had performed the ritual, there was no sign.

"Hello again, wayward child of celestial blood," said Irina in her serene voice. "And your faithful friends."

"Hi there...aunt? I guess that's what you are," Peri said. Celestials were all children of Cijeli, so Irina must be Dimitri's sister. "So, now we've offed another of the Esquadron, and that caused enough of a transcendental disturbance that you were able call us here? I'm beginning to see a pattern, you know."

"Commendable," Irina said, her benevolent serenity not the slightest bit disturbed by Peri's smart-aleck tone. "This time, there is someone who wants to meet you before I assist you with moving forward. He, too, has taken advantage of the disturbance." She nodded at a man that had appeared next to her, her face tensing slightly as she did so.

The man was lean and rather small in stature. His hair was shiny black, his features a perpetual snide smirk. He wore all black, his hair pulled back in an oily ponytail.

"Well hello there, spawn of the upstart intent on usurping my power. Do you know who I am?" the man asked Peri, his voice matching his expression. It was slightly nasally, smug, and oddly refined.

"Judging by the phrasing, you must be Veit," Peri answered. What Dimitri stood for—wrath and destruction for their own sake—were closest to Veit's dogma, such as it was. The god's followers were fanatics and arguably insane, able and willing to murder indiscriminately. "This is getting interesting. Gods are seeking audiences with me now."

Ewynne glanced sideways. "He doesn't look much like a god."

"Oh, and what should a god look like then?" Veit retorted. "Gods look like whatever it pleases them to look like. Many of my faithful are assassins, so it amuses me to appear like a stereotypical one portrayed in the ghastly knight romances you are so fond of consuming, Ewynne dear. Let's dispose of these…friends of yours, Peri. This is a private matter."

In a flash, Peri found herself standing in a dimly lit shack, with the windows covered by sackcloth, facing one of the mightiest gods of Valkama—the great Veit, the god of murder, strife and deceit—alone. She reminded herself that the Theater of Time did not function like the Hereworld and that the eyes of the multiverse and its more benevolent forces were upon her as they spoke. Still, she felt uneasy.

"Being the reigning god of murder, I have an interest in what you plan to do with the powers of your dead sire, Peri. There are not many players left in this game, and it is very possible that you shall emerge as the winner." Veit's eyes were gleaming black pinpoints.

"Would you believe me if I said that I intend to take the power, but turn it into the force of righteousness, and come down on you and your ilk like a light of blinding vengeance?" Peri asked.

"I suppose I must give you a little more credit than that," Veit said. "However, I do not know what you intend. I am not willing to share any of my power with an upstart goddess. You should know that much."

"Well. You are a powerful little godling, aren't you? Why don't you just kill me? Why haven't you done so already?" Peri asked. Back in Yalifa, she had been hired to wipe out a nest of Veit cultists that had been slaughtering local smallfolk in their rituals. It had been a hell of a fight, and Jussuf had needed to consult with several temples of Milostra before he had been able to cure the lingering poison Peri had contracted from their blades. And those were just unremarkable mortal agents of the god himself.

Veit smiled thinly and closed his eyes, sighing theatrically. Then he opened those focused, piercing pinpoints of hatred again. "Oh, if it only was so easy," he said. "Alas, the Dreamer, in its mysterious ways, has designed the universe so that we cannot directly smite anything that possesses transcendental energy. I rather am interested in hearing what you plan to do should you win."

"I think that your divine bickerings are vastly overrated, and the job is all yours if you are so keen to keep it," Peri said. "I really don't give a damn. I want to follow the road to the unknown, see what happens next, once this stupid prophecy gives me the opportunity to do so."

She felt the Edge *nudge* her, a surge of intoxicating pleasure and a sensation of omnipotence. But she knew it was poison. It had destroyed Velimir in his first life.

"Hmmm. Can one so powerful in divine essence truly display such a lack of vision, or do you intend to deceive me?" Veit pondered. "No matter. Like I said, I can't attack you, but I can…assist you a little with testing yourself, as is apt in this place. See how you will fare against a few of my favoured devotees!"

And then the god was gone. Peri flashed back to her friends, but there was no-one else to be seen.

"Razeem. *Plavosvetljo*," Peri said right away. The favoured devotees of gods were mortals given great powers from their divine patrons. As Peri had anticipated, Veit's turned out to be assassins, waiting to stab them from the safety of invisibility. Their blades glittered sickly glowing ichor, their black leather jerkins were adorned with Veit's emblem—the blood-shot eye ripped out of its socket. 'Blimey!' one assassin had time to croak before Velimir decapitated three of them with a swirl of his blade. Peri stabbed the remaining one in the heart, rolling from behind Velimir's back at the same time. The assassins had not anticipated a spell as powerful as Razeem's masterful *plavosvetljo*.

Peri felt her blood throbbing. YOU WAYLAY THE MINIONS OF A GOD THAT WOULD DEFY YOU! YOU

MAKE ME PROUD, DAUGHTER. She found herself uttering a shrill giggle. "They went *splortch*," she said.

Veit blinked back to visible. "Tsk. I was curious if they
would be able to hide from the pally. Guess not. Oh well. By
the way, dear Peri, you *do* know that your facetious brag-
gadocio is incredibly tiresome and unbecoming to one of
divine blood, don't you?"

Peri extended a middle finger to Veit's general direction,
but the god of murder, strife, and deceit was gone with one
final snide smirk.

"Gotta hand it to you, Razeem," she said. "That spell has
been a lifesaver. Can't imagine how any high-rolling adventuring party manages without paladins."

"The most basic versions of *plavosvetljo* are the very
first magic skills that aspiring paladins learn," Razeem said.
Then he frowned. "These assassins...they were Veit's own
favoured devotees, weren't they? Dedicated to him, and he
casually let them be slaughtered here, for no good reason?"

"Yep. Veit is an asshole. Not that I doubted it, but our
little chat confirmed as much," Peri said.

"What did he want of you, sister?" Velimir asked.

"He was worried about the potential competition."

"What did you tell him?" Kauno asked.

"I told him that being a god sucks, and the job is all his if
he wants it," Peri said.

Velimir nodded. So far, Connor's fears of her being
tempted by the power didn't seem to be coming true.

Back at the stage of the Theater of Time, Irina addressed
the group. "Now you have learned the truth about Tamasin's deception. Part of the original Esquadron, she sowed
the seeds of the plan long ago. She trained in the ways of the

Austere Fist and established herself as a community leader as well as a religious devotee in Laipa. Thus, she was able to emerge as a protector when the Esquadron and others started to persecute Dimitri's offspring. Her former good deeds and reputation helped her to convince the Dimitrian spawn to gather in Shinaris for protection—only to be slaughtered by Darien's army."

"So, I suppose they are holed up in that monastery with Rajsa, seeing as they are part of the same team?" Peri said.

"That would be my guess," Irina answered. "And though I can't directly assist you, I can offer you advice. There is a secret way into the monastery. Close to the rocky arch at the beach, there is an entrance to a hidden city of smugglers and others who live in Sjenka's shadows, called Gallant's Cove. It is a network of caves that is partly submerged during the high tide and covered by an illusion during the low one. Under there, there is also an entrance to the monastery. Your old…acquaintance holds court there and could perhaps be persuaded to let you in. Seek the stony arch during the low tide. And hope for the best. My brother will destroy much, should his ascension succeed."

"Casimir sad for old master," Casimir said, his lip trembling.

Irina put a faintly glowing hand on the imp's tiny shoulder. "Casimir, I know that at one time he was kinder to you than other celestials," she said, smiling wistfully. "That was Dimitri—compassionate to the core. He befriended a diabolical creature that the rest of us regarded with suspicion. Though imps are amoral, child-like creatures—others with a mean streak, others less so—they do possess demonic blood. But Dimitri saw them as worthy of compassion and friendship as any other creature. So, I can't blame you for thinking kindly about him, Casimir. It is just…he seeks to destroy too much."

Ewynne had been poking the fallen chalice with her dagger, sniffing the blade. "How did he change so much?" she wondered. "If he used to be nice and kind, how did he become a monster?"

"Dimitri…could not accept that there is a greater truth," Irina said. "That things don't always go as we wish they go, that there is not always a happy ending, a hero coming for rescue. He wanted the All-Father to be all those things—to 'make it so.' He was angry about life's inherent tragedy and Cijeli's refusal to interfere."

"Well, maybe he *should* have been angry! Maybe he was right!" Peri said. "Don't get me wrong, he's as bad as they come, but isn't it just awfully convenient that it's 'oh well, shit happens, no can do' when…when people and animals suffer and die, and assholes just ruin everything for everyone, and no-one can stop them and they are even respected by polite society!"

Everybody stared for a few moments in stunned silence. Then Irina spoke.

"That is, in essence, what Dimitri thought," she said, looking Peri in the eye, grave and serious.

Peri scoffed and looked away, tossed her hair behind her shoulder. "Enough of this crap. Let's go back and camp at the entrance of the gorge."

40
AT THE SHORE OF EOGHAIN'S DEEP

THE PARTY WATCHED PERI RUMMAGE IN HER BACKPACK while the last remnants of sun disappeared behind the cliffs. The constant murmur of the ocean echo could be heard through the gorge.

"Full moon," Peri said. "And low tide now. I'll go for a walk, find that stone arch Irina mentioned." She looked up, and her face was pale and grave in the moonlight, eyes dark. She glanced at Velimir. "Brother...I'd like you to come with me."

"We could all—" Razeem started, but Peri interrupted him.

"No. Just him. Please," she said. "We'll go together at the next low tide."

Velimir walked next to Peri, sheathing the sword he had

been tending to. Peri had pulled Genjiro's silk-wrapped head from the backpack and cradled it tenderly in her arms. The two walked away from the camp without speaking, leaving long shadows. Where the gorge met the pebbly shore, the murmur of the ocean was louder. Moonlight glistened on the waves that had retreated far away towards the horizon. There were outlines of driftwood and other debris carried by the ocean visible on the sand under the eerie moonlight.

"Thank you for not saying anything or asking anything," Peri said.

Velimir nodded and touched her arm.

They didn't have to walk for long before they found the stone arch. It emerged abruptly from the waves, reaching all the way up to the cliff, beyond where the eye could see. Now, at low tide, there was ample space to walk under it. At high tide, water would no doubt roar under it as an unstoppable mass.

There were a few wispy shades wandering at the shore end of the arch. Peri and Velimir could hear faint singing—a monotonous tune with an air of inevitability to it. The kind sailors would sing while heaving the heavy, wet ropes or scrubbing the decks. "Ghosts," Peri said. "Drowned sailors, maybe?"

"Perhaps, sister," Velimir answered. "These treacherous waters must have claimed the life of a great many."

"Sailors lost at sea will drift to the Otherworld," Peri said. "But sometimes you can pray for them and keep remembering them, call their spirit home. Eoghain's clerics help with rituals like that. I know that Genjiro is not welcome to his own home…that he is damned as a geas breaker. And I don't know if what we did helped at all. But if I pray at the edge of the Otherworld—all oceans are at the edge of the Other-world—maybe Eoghain can help."

"I...was not brought up with religion," Velimir said. "Anyone can witness the power gods grant to clerics and paladins—but a life of devotion is alien to me."

"That's another thing of value I took for granted," Peri said. "I was always bored in Eoghain's services that Connor dragged me to...smart-ass when Connor and the monks taught me about the faith. Later though, I'd regularly go to the midnight service to please Connor, and because I am a night owl by nature. But something has stuck. I felt the Voyager noticing me when we came out of the sewers and saw the open horizon. When I see the ocean before my eyes, I feel at ease within my own skin."

"Peri, my beloved sister. There is nothing I can teach you about faith and the ways of the gods. My mother revered Milostra, but she never spoke about it, for Radek had forbidden it in his house. But I have witnessed the infinity of the planes—how much there is beyond Valkama, beyond life and death, even. I will join you in prayer, for even if I don't know Eoghain the Wanderer, I know you. And my love for you, my desire to make up for the evil of my former life, will add to the potency of your prayer...I hope."

Peri swallowed a few tears and leaned her head against Velimir's arm. "I'm so tired of this all," she whispered. They stopped to remove their boots and walked barefoot to the water's edge. Peri kneeled on the wet sand. Velimir followed, wrapping his arm around her shoulders. Peri set Genjiro's head aside and started to dig a hole. The water lapped back and forth, but she managed to dig a depression deep enough to set the bundle inside. Then she filled it back up and patted sand over the mound.

"Eoghain the Wanderer, Beloved of Zephyr, the Blessed Voyager, the Calm Within the Storm," she recited. "I have not been faithful to your teachings. I have never been pious. I am wrathful and cynical. I often just don't care. But I have always carried you in my heart, felt you in the breeze, seen you in the open horizon, heard you in the creaking of the ropes in the wind. When my heart starts to sing when embarking on a new adventure, I suppose it sings for you. I chase the unknown, and when I do that, I worship you in spirit. In the name of Brother Connor of the Blessed Isles, I beseech you to release Hanamori Genjiro of the geas that evil people lured him into, so that his spirit may move on and find peace. When the waves wash his remains to the outer sea, likewise invite his spirit to the Otherworld. So says Peri of Eilean de Taigh-Sholais, child of Dimitri the Fallen, ward of Connor."

Peri pressed her face against Velimir's chest, and he held her silently for a long time, feeling the hot tears against the cool of the night breeze. He stroked his sister's head gently as she wept.

"Velimir," she said then, "I have been thinking. When this is all over, I want to come with you to Zmaj-Vostok. Genjiro told me so many stories about his journey. I want to see the Steppes and the horsemen. Feng Guo and the Wall of Sunset. All the temples and walled cities and bamboo groves and jungles and crystal rivers he told me about."

"Truly? Nothing would please me more, Peri!" Velimir said, a spark of enthusiasm in his eyes. "A solemn journey in honor of the dead, to be sure, but also, an adventure! And no doubt opportunities to seek redemption."

"Genji told me about the yakuza families with their colorful animal tattoos and games of entertainment. They become family when they get those tattoos, and though they are criminals, it ties as strongly as a samurai bloodline. There are smuggler captains with *wako* fleets preying on merchant ships around the port...and illegal gambling houses in the back of fine restaurants, and secret societies, and ninjas, these shadowy assassins you can contact in shrines of certain kami...Veli, I want to see it all." She wiggled her toes in the wet sand.

"It seems Genjiro's tales have a more urban flavour to them than Tomoe's. I suppose that is fitting—he spent much time in the capital city, while Tomoe, being part of the clan's military, lived in their *shiro*—the castle—in the countryside. She described sharp, volcanic mountains rising abruptly from the sea. Pine forests covering the slopes of the snow-capped mountains, rice pads, and plains. And once a year, the cherry trees blossom for a very short time."

A shadow crossed Peri's eyes. "That's what they are supposed to think about...when they...you know. I said to Genjiro to think about them, but I don't know if he was too terrified."

Velimir squeezed her shoulders. "It is in Eoghain's hands now. So let it be decided! Let us be resolute and survive this prophecy, so we can journey to the other side of the Shimmering Sands."

Peri nodded. "There nothing for me here, and even less for you. You, the Dimitrian madman of Lughani Vos. Me, the Butcher of Yalifa."

"Some would call you a hero, sister."

"Don't give a shit. Don't want to be a flaming hero either.

Don't want any stupid statues of me or anything, people wanting me to solve their problems. And heroes always get the stupid, pompous lines in Wyn's knight romances. There, nobody will have heard of us. We can be whatever we want to be."

The two started to walk back towards the beach. When they stopped to pull their boots back on, Peri could have sworn she saw a lone pink flower floating on the waves towards the outer sea.

41
YGGDRASIL

Kiril hung in the wind-swept tree.

His skeletal form swayed in the wind as he continued to float above the crimson ocean. Then suddenly, something was different. There were now tiny black figures, like ants, scrambling on the ocean's surface. At once, the crimson ocean dried and shriveled into cracked orange wasteland. The tiny figures were tin soldiers forming armies, marching, razing and looting, leaving toppled fortresses, ruined fields of wheat, and ravaged towns behind. Lands burned in their wake. Ethereal flames danced in the background, and ominous organ music played as the armies marched on.

There was a balcony of obsidian rock watching over the armies laying waste to the dry, cracked land. Kiril—or a vaguely humanoid empty and translucent form occupying space around him—floated over there, to watch the armies march. On the balcony, a few demons chuckled at the process. A small, gaunt man sat in front of a desk, unaware of the presence of the demons, a pile of well-worn books and a chess set in front of him. He was fingering the shiny obsidian knight. He watched the armies' progress with a furrowed brow and a smile of grim, joyless satisfaction. *Me,* Kiril thought. *This was me, though years ago.*

For a moment Kiril felt a great urge to slip into the familiar form of the man, like a hand sliding in a well-worn glove. It was not just the shape of his body that was familiar—it was the fortress formed by his elaborate thoughts, defenses, arguments, rationalizations. Those were like iron constructs, chaining the man in place, yet he was unaware of being chained. The essence of this prison of cogitation around the bitter, cynical mage was determined in its misery, but it was misery he felt he was in control of—a misery that he imagined made him invulnerable. *But...he understands nothing. The Black Knight—another chess piece in this game he imagines he is playing—is none other than the boy he loved. In the end, the boy, too, will be sacrificed, all so that he won't feel pain. And as he watches this sordid little display of a megalomaniac's imagination, he imagines* that *is what war is. No, I do not want to go back.*

While hanging in the wind-swept tree, Kiril had already seen far more than the man sitting in the prison of his own thoughts ever had been willing to see.

The humanoid shape occupying space around Kiril floated to a field of mangled bodies, the scene of another skirmish in glory of this or that, a god, nation, religious order, adventuring company, or ruling family. The last cries of the dying had ceased, and the black coagulated blood stained the trampled ground. Torn out legs and arms, puddles of intestines collecting flies, young, soft faces frozen in horror. Perhaps some of them had fought for something worthwhile, something they believed in. All the same, their corpses lay side by side with those who had no say in their fate and would rather have lived to a ripe old age. Naturally, Kiril had seen and brought about a lot of death in his mortal life, but the *scale* of war was different. It ravaged entire nations and generations. *Which was exactly why we planned to start a war. For the very reason of this ugly carnage and the destruction.*

The formless humanoid shape flew over the war-torn lands at the speed of wind, as it had no flesh body to slow it down. It witnessed a mother wailing for a lost son—her handsome soldier son who had been so eager to fight in the war and lost his life in his first skirmish. Forlorn families leaving their destroyed homes behind, children keening in desolate sorrow for the animals that had to be killed so that they would not starve when abandoned.

There were survivors of war, too. Some witless, waking screaming every night, staring hollow-eyed at horrors forever imprinted in their brains. The crippled, the blind, once proud and able-bodied men now pitifully dependent on the goodwill of others and resentfully aware of the fact. Others had been decent people before the war awoke the beast in them and offered an excuse to feed the beast. Then, when they returned to their peacetime lives, they found that they had grown to like the beast.

It was intolerable that the bitter, cynical man at the balcony, undeniably, had been the architect of such a thing, yet somehow considered himself superior to others. Like any living being—as Kiril had come to realize hanging in the wind-swept tree—he had wanted to escape suffering and had done what seemed the best way to do just that in the confines of his mind.

But the mage on the balcony didn't understand that the pain of all those living things he sought to hurt to escape the pain of his own was no different from his own pain. Their pain *was* his pain. There was just one huge primordial pain that all living things shared and radiated. Kiril floated farther and farther away from the confines of what he thought of as 'me.' He floated above the war-torn lands. He was everywhere and nowhere at the same time. He was every trampled little insect, every dead young soldier, every orphaned child, every crippled youth, and also Kiril, the evil, cynical mage—the entire multiverse—all at the same time, radiating the same pain, the separation between everything just an illusion like a shadow in the mirror.

The hangman's knot, which chafed at the skeletal mage's neck, disappeared, and he fell from the tree. He fell through darkness and stardust and moons and planets. He fell through hellish lava realms and radiant celestial rainbow-lit palaces. He fell through a thick coat of clouds, through canopies of trees, through mountains and ravines. As he tumbled through Yggdrasil's branches and leaves, he screamed—not a scream of fear, but a scream of joy and freedom. He plunged into the cool, dark waters of the Well of Urd, then sank towards the bottom, where glittering runes beckoned him. His mind filled with their song as he surfaced with a splash, startling the two swans. He climbed up and instantly recognized the familiar hum he was able to call to his fingertips.

The magic was back. He was whole again.

42
THE GALLANT'S COVE

As the party approached the stone arch, the ghosts milling underneath it shied away. This night was cloudier than the one before, and the party couldn't see very far. There seemed to be a campfire in the distance. The ghosts sang a raunchier tune this time, laughing once in a while. It was hard to tell if someone had built a real campfire, or if it was a ghostly mirage.

"Here. An entrance, covered by a rather complicated illusion," Razeem said. "And warded, too. Ewynne?"

Ewynne concentrated, frowning, reciting syllables, wiggling her fingers. With a final word, the illusion dissolved. She nodded with satisfaction. "It's like picking a lock, only it is made of subtle matter."

"Good job," Peri said. "They are probably not expecting anyone, but no doubt they still have some protection. Plus, we can't exactly have a huge magic battle in the caves. Let's just be on our guard and...ask nicely? We have gold. We can pay them for using the passage."

Obscured by the *shifting shadows*, the party tiptoed into the narrow rocky passage. The stones were wet and cold; the passage would be underwater during the high tide. Kauno touched Peri's arm, and the party stopped, waiting as he leaned on the wall and closed his eyes. He was communicating with an animal, asking to borrow its senses. That was how the party did close range recon with targets that might be able to see through magical invisibility.

Kauno waited for a few minutes. A bat flew toward them from down the tunnel and ascended to the darkness high above. "Now Kauno will have to ask the *virvatuli* to blink out, or they will see us coming. There will be torches and a few guards who seem pretty relaxed. Kauno believes this place has never been infiltrated. It is well hidden. But better surprise them anyway."

The party formed a line, the sure-footed Peri first, each holding a hand on the shoulder of the person before them. She reached out with her arms and took a careful step, taking her time, shifting her weight every time before stepping forward. In this slow manner, they advanced to the range of the torchlight and the two guards who were playing cards, their backs to the tunnel, swords set aside. Peri smiled and shook her head. She crouched, then kneeled and advanced on all fours until she was close enough to see the soft fuzzy hair on the nape of the neck of the guard closer to her.

She drew a dagger and, in a flash, placed it on the man's throat. He gasped and almost squealed, but thought better of it when she nudged the blade. "Hello there," Peri said in a low voice. The man could not see her, but his card-playing partner and fellow guardsman could. He could see Velimir's enormous form and glowing eyes, too. The man was on the verge of panic, raising his hands slowly to cover his mouth.

"Don't worry," Peri said. "We're not here to harm you. We just didn't want you to get jumpy and start anything. We've been informed that there is a way to the monastery through these caves. That's all we want. So, take us to your leader, and we'll do business with him."

Peri kept her blade against the small of the back of the guard, while Velimir walked next to the other one. The guards led the party through a dimly lit corridor that opened into a cozy inn in a large cavern. Someone was playing a violin, and there were men and women relaxing, drinking ale and wine. A girl and a boy of perhaps twelve years were dancing, bungling the steps, collapsing into each other, and bursting into laughter. "Um, boss...," said the man who could feel the point of Peri's dagger in the small of his back.

A man in a shadowy corner turned to face the party. His smile froze into an awkward grimace. "Peri! So glad to see ye, lass!" he croaked.

"Samir Arakelian." Peri's voice dripped icicles. She stared flatly at the pirate. Velimir glared from his massive height, his golden eyes bright in the torchlight.

"I see ye still have that nice sword with ye...," Samir said feebly.

"Indeed, it was not snatched from her dead hands by a raging ifrit," Velimir said. "No thanks to you, pirate."

"Come on...I knew ye'd kick its tail easily! And the sword's enchanted with elemental cold. Do ye think I'd ever have set ye against an ifrit if not?" Samir said, spreading his arms in a placating gesture.

Peri glared. "Yes. I think you would have."

"Uh…I see ye're still a bit sore…but, ye're in my city now. I know ye lot have a lot of powers…but ye wouldn't start a fight here. Could take casualties. And there are children here! Ye wouldn't harm them." Samir pointed at the pale and silent children who had stopped their playing, aware of the tense situation.

"I wouldn't? I WOULDN'T?!?" Peri's voice rose. "A thing or two has happened since you knew me as the carefree and restless lass on the island, Samir! I am the blood of Dimitri the Damned, Dimitri the Destroyer! I walk the edge of wrath and euphoria every living moment! You have no clue what you are dealing with, you two-bit scoundrel!" Her eyes started to glow red, and she seemed to grow taller, her outline shining in the dark, her voice deeper and echoing in the caverns.

Samir became white as a sheet and took a few steps back, gnawing his lip. For a moment Peri stood there glowing, like an ember in a campfire. Only the faint drip of water from a stalagmite broke through the nervous silence. Then Peri deflated somewhat and looked like her usual self again. "I am called the Butcher of Yalifa by some, Samir. Try to pull anything with me, and you'll find out why."

Samir stopped holding his breath and exhaled. "Uh…is there anything I could do to…make amends?"

"Why, there is indeed!" Peri said, grinning maniacally. "So glad you asked! We happen to know that there is a way to the monastery within this mountain. Take us there, and I'll get over it."

"Hmmm," Samir said, color returning to his face. "We could, indeed, do business. Let us retreat to my private

374

office." Samir started to walk towards a torchlit corridor, and Peri shoved the guard she had been restraining aside. Samir glanced at the crowd. "As ye were, the rest of ye! This is just business! Drink! Dance! Rejoice!" he barked.

Samir's office turned out to contain a more or less round table skillfully crafted from driftwood. There were cabinets and shelves spilling over with assorted valuables. There were chests and crates, too, cargo from ships the pirates had been preying on. "As it happens," Samir said, his face eager in the light of an obscured lantern on the table, "I may have been a bit of an informant for the ladies now running the monastery. Well...more like I am the head of their intelligence in Laipa. Spymaster, they fancy calling me. Had a well-established network in place long before they turned up. And there has been a long-running...business relationship with some...practically minded monks. A handy way of distributing goods to Laipa, ye see. And these ladies have been intent on finding ye, Peri. Waiting for a word on how their lizard-boy Hesyeth fared against ye. Still waiting..." The man motioned with his hands, looking at Peri expectantly.

"So...if you tell them I am dead," Peri said, "they'd drop their guard, and I could ambush them."

"You could tell them that both Hesyeth and Peri died of wounds received in the combat," Velimir said. "Do your part convincingly, and we could throw a good amount of gold your way on top of letting the ifrit incident go."

"Aha! I knew we could all be friends!" Samir exclaimed and grinned. No-one grinned back, so he continued. "Well, anyway. Truth to be told, those ladies are too zealous for my tastes. I'd rather see the power of Dimitri in the hands of someone more...level-headed. A reasonable person, such as ye, lass. They're expecting me to report tomorrow at noon. Ye could stay the night here. Excellent wine and ale available!"

Peri nodded. "Very well. Show us a nice dry cave to get some sleep in. But I don't think we'll drink anything you have to offer."

"Ye *wound* me, lass! I would never—"

"Silence, fool! Do not try our patience!" Velimir growled. Samir swallowed and fell silent.

Kauno smiled at Samir and patted his arm. "Don't mind Velimir. Of course, you would never. But just to be on the safe side, my bat friend will keep you company for the night." A bat descended from the darkness above and landed on Kauno's shoulder.

"That's better," Peri said. "And before you get any ideas, we have a night watch system. We always do when on the road."

"I would never! Please follow me. I will show you a nice and dry cave to camp in."

———— • ● • ————

THE DISMAL CAVE WAS CHILLY, BUT CASIMIR CONJURED a magical fire. The embers glared orange and the ethereal flames flickered blue. The party huddled around the fire, nibbling at their stale rations. "Too bad we aren't in the Abyss," Peri said, then laughed. "I can't believe I just said that. I just meant that Casimir could conjure proper food for us if we were." She gnawed at a strip of dried meat and shrugged. "It is what it is. But guys...this is *it*. Once we enter that monastery, it is likely we won't leave before the final showdown. There's only Rajsa and Tamasin left of the pedigree spawn, and who knows what fucked up thing happens when only one of us remains?" She paused to look everyone in the eye, one by one. "If any of you want to leave now, you would be well within your rights. It is my blood they want."

"Out of the question," Razeem said without pausing to give it a thought. "I have sworn a solemn oath. And besides, if this isn't something a paladin of Juris should partake in, then I don't know what is."

Peri nodded and took a sip from her waterskin. "I could never be a paladin, but...maybe I have started to understand them a bit while traveling with you. Wyn and I used to make fun of them when we were kids. But for you...doing good, serving your god...it's like being able to follow every road and board every ship that looks like an adventure is for me. It's who you are."

Ewynne turned her eyes to Razeem, warming her hands over the steady orange glow. "But you have daughters, don't you? I would hate it if they lost their father because of us."

Razeem shook his head. "If they did, it would not be because of you, but because of the Esquadron. They have always known that their father is dedicated to fighting evil, like one man from every family of Wulanian aristocracy. It is a path I chose with pleasure. It was my childhood dream."

Kauno leaned back and smiled. She didn't seem too bothered over the prospect of a horrible death in the hands of megalomaniacal madwomen and the apocalyptic destruction that would likely follow. But then, very little seemed to bother her. "And Kauno...will just pick another costume somewhere else, if we perish! But Peri of Eilean de Taigh-Sholais should be adventuring all over Valkama for a long time still. That won't happen if we don't prevail. Also, it would probably be best if an immensely powerful new god didn't create an army of living killing machines bent on destroying and enslaving all other life forms, Kauno thinks."

Peri shrugged and thought about flashing the faithful companions her typical devilish grin, but only managed to muster a wan smile. "Well, goodnight then," she said. "Rest well, and know that if I go down tomorrow, I will be grateful to all of you for all that we have endured together. The rest of us will keep guard as you spell-slingers sleep. We'll doze off for a few hours before showtime."

Kauno shot Peri an enquiring look, and she responded with a small smile and a thumbs-up. Then Kauno retreated to her own corner. Ewynne knew she had to replenish her spell power by sleeping, but she lingered for a moment. "Peri…," she said, "You…you were bluffing earlier with Samir, weren't you? When you let him think you'd hurt the kids?"

"Was I, though?" Peri grinned, then shrugged. "I honestly don't know anymore."

Ewynne's eyes darkened, but she touched her sister's arm. "Goodnight, love you both," she said and squeezed Velimir's shoulders.

She went her way, and Peri and Velimir were left sitting around the faintly glowing remnants of the fire, facing each other. Peri glanced at Razeem, who watched them from a respectful distance, then dug something out of her pocket and offered the tiny object to Velimir. He squinted at the fragile, wispy ring and picked it gingerly up with two fingers.

There was something vulnerable in Peri's smile. She suddenly looked so young, almost a child. "It's a gift from Kauno. For both of us. She made a similar one for me. Look." She slid the wispy, flaky white thing on her finger.

"What *is* it?" The similar ring in Velimir's hand weighed nothing and tingled with magic. He was afraid that merely looking at it might make it disappear.

"It is a ring made of birch bark that Kauno brought from the Theater of Time. After fighting the shades and crossing the translucent bridge, we walked into an early summer day from Balatsky Taiga. It was made of the stuff of Kauno's memories—she's from there."

"There may have been more than that at play, sister," Velimir said. "I've never traveled to Balatsky Taiga, but...that was where we were to live as a family. Mother, Kiril, Tomoe, and me. It was our dream, and we often pictured how it would be. Perhaps the Theater picked up on that, too." Even after all this time, he felt a pang of pain when the memory of the brutal loss of that dream surfaced.

"Yeah, that must be it. Kauno said that everything was even more potent with magic at that spot, so she picked some grass and leaves and bark as spell components to study back in Valkama. At the time, we thought it was just some Dimitrian stuff related to the portal to Shinaris."

Velimir prodded the ring tenderly with his finger and frowned. "Woven from bark, and fit for my finger...a thoughtful gift, I suppose, but it won't survive in a mailed fist. So—"

"It's not supposed to. It stores an enchantment for this night only. I...I wanted to..." she swallowed and her eyes glistened in the glow of the enchanted embers. Velimir took her hand in his own and she continued. "I wanted to share with you what could have been. What *should* have been. If we die tomorrow...I want to give you what you should have had. Let's do this. Razeem will keep watch."

Velimir slid the wispy ring on his finger. With no more words, the two locked eyes. Multi-colored mists started to swirl around them like a mirage. The mirage turned into thick smoke as Peri and Velimir faded into shades in the darkness. A cacophony of voices, singing, preaching, laughing, arguing, echoed around them, and the smoke started to sparkle with countless fireflies. Then the voices gradually died down and the fireflies faded into the glow of a torch, unperturbed by wind. The torch blinked out, and for a moment, it was completely dark and silent, like a cloudless night sky. Then the skies cleared, and the sister and brother found themselves somewhere else.

43
EILEAN DE TAIGH-SHOLAIS

VELIMIR WATCHED THE WORLD AROUND HIM FROM THE level of the boy he had once been, but the ever-present sense of dread constricting his throat and chest was not there. Velimir felt a peculiar sense of lightness and freedom. He stood on a wind-beaten cliff, the waves crashing against a sharp jutting rock down the waterline. The sea glinted green, the seagulls laughed, the warm wind carried the scent of salt. Trees and rocks were full of color and texture, but transparent, as if made of rainbows. Everything was deep and sharp and vibrant. Velimir looked at his hand. It was translucent, too, but not like his shady form had been in the Abyss. It was radiant and iridescent. He was an empty form made of light.

"Come on, Velimir! What are you waiting for?" At the other side of the depression full of wave-beaten pebbles, a girl of perhaps eight glanced over her shoulder and grinned at him. Radiant and made of rainbow-light, as Velimir himself was. He would have recognized his sister anywhere. He jogged over as dignified as he could manage.

Peri handed Velimir a wooden sword. "A gift from Seamus."

Velimir frowned. The weapon was well made, as training swords go, but it was *small* and *light* and made for *children*.

Peri nudged his arm with her head. "Aw, don't wrinkle your nose at it, bro. I know you want a real one, but Seamus made this special for you as a favour for Connor. I have my own as well, look!" She proudly brandished a smaller and thinner practice sword. "You get to start training with a real one in three years. I have to wait much longer than that!"

Velimir deigned to smile. "I suppose I should appreciate the gift. And besides…it is entirely possible to kill with a wooden blade."

Peri's smile faded. "Or even without one. Why does killing feel so good in the dreams?"

"We are not like others, are we," Velimir said. Even though only Connor and Ewynne were privy to their dreams of violence and the alluring rage simmering in their hearts, everybody on the island seemed to sense it.

"Brother of my soul," Peri recited.

"Sister of my soul."

Peri took his hands in her own. *"As darkness closes in, I shield you with my love."*

"And as darkness closes in, I shield you with mine." Velimir remembered that in this vibrant rainbow world, Connor had taught them what to do whenever things got frightening. Peri hugged him, and Velimir hugged back. Her hair smelled of sea water and pine needles.

"Wyn has a surprise for us at the secret hut," Peri said. "What do you think it is?"

"She has been whispering and giggling with Connor and talking to the faeries," Velimir said. "So, I imagine something magical." The faeries of the remote part of the island didn't show themselves to adults, but they were particularly fond of Ewynne. One of them, Fionnuala of the Seelie Court, taught Ewynne simple charms and illusion magic. However, the fairies shied away from Peri and Velimir, as if sensing their nighttime dream revels of murder, the lurking darkness in their hearts.

Velimir followed Peri through the dense spruce forest, a forgotten footpath flanking an ancient, equally forgotten stone wall covered with moss. At the edge of the forest, a thicket of bulrush reached above their heads. As the children approached, the bulrushes made way to reveal a hidden pathway—a fairy path, Velimir knew. Adults didn't know of it and never ventured to the other side of the little overgrown bay.

At the other side of the bulrush thicket, the Secret Cove waited for them. The granite cliffs, smooth from the millennia the waves had been crashing over them, were warm from the heat of the sun. The sandy cove was sheltered by a few alders. In their embrace awaited the Secret Hut that the three charges of brother Connor had built and no-one else knew of. Well, the faeries did, but they kept their own counsel.

The foundation of the hut was the hull of a half-moldered wreck of an ancient war galley the children had found buried in the sands of the cove. Velimir and Peri had dragged it to the shore plank by plank, next to a whale skeleton that sang when the wind rattled it. Ewynne had covered the gaping holes with leather curtains she had fashioned, and stuffed smaller ones with dried seaweed.

Driftwood cupboards, a stone ring for a campfire, and logs to sit around it…the chest for their treasures, the little altar to Eoghain the Wanderer. There was no sign of Ewynne, though she had promised to wait for her siblings at the hut.

"Help me…help me…"

It was Ewynne's voice. Velimir and Peri looked around and drew their wooden blades.

"Is there no hero to come to my rescue? I'm a maiden fair, a damsel in distress!"

Velimir grinned at Peri and relaxed. A small part of him was disappointed that there was no danger. The momentary anticipation of it had made his blood soar.

A vibrating thing of purple light started to glide in their direction from behind the hut. It flickered and stuttered, but its outline was vaguely lizard-like. "Raaawwwwg," it squeaked. Peri and Velimir frowned and stared closer. The thing had eyes huge as saucers and a round snout that seemed to smile. It inefficiently flapped a pair of bat-like wings.

"Is that supposed to be…a dragon?" Velimir whispered.

Peri's mouth twitched. "It's not very scary," she whispered back.

The apparition opened its maw and belched out a tiny spark of flame that whizzed out. "Raaawwwg?" it said again.

"It looks like a cow," Velimir whispered. *No giggling. No giggling. This is Ewynne's surprise. How do knights speak in her silly books?* "Verily, a foul beast!" He struck what he thought was a heroic pose, puffing his chest out.

The apparition's eyes widened even more. "Meep?"

"I'll smite thee!" Velimir charged and slashed with his new wooden blade.

The illusion uttered an indignant "eeeek" and puffed out of existence.

Peri was rolling on the ground, laughing. "...*aaah*...smite is such a silly word...*wheeze*...it said eek..." She stopped for a second, biting her lip, then glanced at Velimir and burst into laughter again. Velimir couldn't help chuckling, too. He had done his best, but as sure as he was of his martial talent, he didn't quite seem to have the knack of pretending to be a knight.

Ewynne had come out of hiding and frowned at her siblings, hands on her hips. "You could at least *try* to pretend to be scared. I worked on the illusion for ages. Fionnuala helped." Despite her words, there was a creeping hint of a smile in the corner of her mouth.

Peri tried to look serious for a moment, but the laughter was still bubbling under. "I'm sorry, Wyn. It just...it...*chortle*...I mean, it said eeek...*khihihihi*...and he said smite..."

Ewynne and Velimir watched as she tried to recover from the laughing fit. They shared a glance and a shrug. "Perhaps it was not very scary, Ewynne...but it was surprising," Velimir said. "And that is what surprises are supposed to be like, aren't they?"

"Connor said that it's good practice for me, anyway," Ewynne said. "And it's ever so great to have help from a fairy. Someday, I want to have green hair like Fionnuala!"

Peri had recovered from her giggling fit and put her hand on Ewynne's shoulder. "Wyn, it was cute and funny. Like you. And surprising. Very surprising. Thank you."

"Brother of my soul, sister of my soul," Ewynne recited.

"Our sister, the light in our hearts," Peri and Velimir replied. The children formed a circle holding hands.

"As darkness closes in, I'll shine bright." There was some pain in Ewynne's eyes as she recited the line. She was well aware of the whispers and urges in the dark that her sister and brother heard.

"And as darkness closes in, we will shield you from the storm." Velimir didn't know when the storm would come. But he would be ready and would not let it at his sisters.

———————————— • ● • ————————————

SUDDENLY, A SURGE OF MAGIC PROPELLED VELIMIR ELSE-where. The surface of the salty water rippled, and the last remnants of the pale sunlight glowed on the horizon. This was still the vibrant rainbow world. He was still the boy made of light…but he was alone. It would be dark in minutes, and it was getting quite chilly. Velimir was in a small boat and…to be honest, he had no idea where he was.

He had only wanted to row to the Triplets, the group of three islands at the mouth of Austere Strait. He knew that pirates had a hideout there. For a long time, Velimir had nagged Connor to let him join the soldiers of the garrison when they patrolled the islands, but he was strictly forbidden from following adult warriors into harm's way. Velimir knew he couldn't take on the pirates by himself, but he'd at least scout and spy on them. Maybe, just maybe, Connor could be persuaded to let him do something heroic. Peri didn't care what the people at the island thought about her, she just longed to journey to uncharted lands. But Velimir would have liked to be seen as a great hero, a peerless warrior and not some...*child* in need of protection.

The sun disappeared behind the horizon, and Velimir shivered from the cold. He could hear the low rumble of thunder in the distance. The shore was far away and his boat was very small. Every so often, Eoghain's clerics and the monks of the monastery performed rites for folks lost at sea. Fishermen, sailors, warriors—indeed anyone who traveled by water—could fall victim to the capricious weather and treacherous waters. There was a marker at the monastery's graveyard where the distraught families who didn't have a body to bury could inscribe in the memory of their loved ones. Connor and other adults had—many times—forbidden Velimir from venturing too far on a boat, especially alone. But he had been so sure that he had figured it out correctly. He hadn't told even Peri, because he had wanted his scouting report to be a great surprise to them all. But somehow the currents had drawn the little boat farther away to the sea than he had anticipated, and then every islet and cliff and rock and island looked the same...and now that it was dark and cold and the thunder rumbled in the horizon, he had no idea where he was. *I'm not scared! I'm not!* Very little scared Velimir, but whenever he felt even a hint of fear, he easily transformed it into anger. A simmering rage fueled by the alluring violent presence of his dreams, held at bay as if it was a loaded crossbow. But the sea was vast, an alien kingdom down in the fathoms, cold and indifferent. Who would he unleash his rage at? The sea could swallow a mighty man-o-war in moments were it so inclined...

Suddenly, Velimir could see a tiny light in the darkness. It steadily approached as he shivered, lips blue. It was a lantern, attached to the bow of a boat, a bigger one than his.

The boat glided next to Velimir's, and he could discern Connor's shape in the dark. A soldier from the garrison was rowing and helped secure the smaller boat and keep it steady as Connor helped Velimir climb in. Velimir stared at his toes, shoulders hunched. Even though Connor tried to hide it, his hands trembled as he helped Velimir on board.

"We have been looking for you all over, Velimir. You scared the living hell out of me!" Connor said. He shook his head and closed his eyes for a moment, letting out a long breath. "Thank Eoghain the storm isn't here yet. Why would you do such a thing? Why would you disobey and endanger yourself? You are not stupid. You know how dangerous the sea is!"

Velimir tensed and gritted his teeth, still watching his toes. He felt so foolish—how he had imagined that he'd return a hero, bring important information to the garrison, and everybody would tell Connor what a brave and clever son he had, maybe even allow him to follow the soldiers as a trainee. He could tell from Connor's voice that his father, usually so calm and gentle, was rattled.

"Look at me, Velimir." There was just a hint of sternness in Connor's voice.

Velimir reluctantly looked up. He couldn't bear seeing disappointment in those kind eyes that saw the moody and easily angered boy as worthy of love as the sweetest and sunniest child.

"I...I just wanted to help the garrison. To surprise everyone. I swear I wouldn't have attacked the pirates, but I would have scouted and spied so I could be a hero. I didn't realize the currents were so strong. I'm sorry."

Connor's face softened, and a smile formed on his lips

that seemed somewhat sad. He moved next to Velimir and wrapped his arms around the boy. "You have the heart of a lion, Velimir. But you are still a cub. Cubs play around the den, protected by the adults, until they are grown. Please believe me that far too soon, you will be all grown, and then you may be a great warrior, protector of others. But not just yet."

"I'm sorry that I caused you to worry," Velimir said and inhaled the smell of old books from Connor's robes.

"You are my beloved son, and I will always come for you, no matter what. Just don't do something like this again. I couldn't bear losing you. Now, let's wrap you in a blanket. Peri and Ewynne will be delighted to have you back. They've been worried about you."

Velimir started to nod off as he gradually got warmer, snuggled in his father's embrace. He felt loved and safe. So very safe.

44
A DAMP AND DISMAL CAVE IN GALLANT'S COVE

VELIMIR BLINKED BACK TO THE SOLID AND HEAVY WORLD where he was flesh and blood. Peri was flesh and blood too, facing him with that childlike, vulnerable expression.

"Did it work?" she asked. "To me, it lasted only a few seconds, and it felt like having no body and being inside of a rainbow."

"Peri, it did work!" Velimir said. "It took me to another reality that was…well, as if made of rainbow light, but it was all there. You, me, Ewynne, Connor…in that reality, he had saved both of us. We had a secret hut at the end of a hidden fairy path and—"

"We did have a hut!" Peri said. "We built it under a whale skeleton, covered it with canvas from an old soldiers' tent! You saw it?"

Velimir nodded. "And made of the planks from the wreck of a war galley?"

Peri shook her head. "No. We thought about that, but we couldn't drag the planks to the shore on our own."

That made sense to Velimir. "I seemed to know that it had been quite an effort for both of us, even with our Dimitrian strength. You know, we also had a mantra Connor had taught us."

"A mantra?"

And so Velimir related his experiences to Peri. Many things were familiar to her, but others had never existed in the childhood she had lived.

"Huh. I think...it would have been different knowing that I'm not the only one," Peri said. "Weird how things work. Like there are infinite realities and they all are *somewhere*. They are just tangles of strings that end up in some realities and not in others. From every crossroad, a different string."

Velimir put his hand on her shoulder. "Thank you for the gift, Peri. Thank you. Part of me...longs for the rainbow world where I never was swallowed by evil. But then, who knows? Perhaps I would have been killed by the first Dimitrian spawn that came for my head. Perhaps you and Ewynne were, and I lost my way. But no matter. It can't be. I must live for redemption in this world of flesh and blood, and perhaps dream of a pure rainbow world, above all these tangled infinite possibilities."

"That's the spirit, bro," Peri said and fell silent, fiddling with the buckle of her boot. She appeared to be deep in thought, conflicting emotions dancing on her face, whereas Velimir enjoyed the remnants of the lightness and freedom experienced from the perspective of a child in the rainbow world.

"Velimir?" Peri said then.

"Yes?" The vulnerability was still there, but there was also a new feverish urgency, a steely purpose.

"Share with me. For real. Connor, or the theater, showed us, but it was kind of like watching a story unfold. Show me how it was to be you. Share with me what it was like to be a child and live in terror of Radek." The dying embers of the fire reflected in her haunted eyes.

Velimir teetered on the edge of uncharted territory. It was bad enough that Peri had witnessed his shame. If she was aware of the inner experience of it, that would be yet another matter. So, he said what he thought he should say. "It is in the past. I can't dwell on it. If it would be anything as vivid as what I experienced, I would not wish those memories on you." Yet he could not deny that part of him wanted to let Peri even closer.

Peri leaned forward, tears in her eyes. "But the past brought us here. There's a chance that we die tomorrow, be separated, go *poof* and *really* die if Tamasin wins. I want to know, truly know, in case we don't make it tomorrow. I want to feel in my bones the life you suffered. So that our bond will be complete. Share your worst memories with me. Please."

Peri's eyes were full of compassion and profoundly sad. Velimir felt a strange stirring in his chest, suffocating, threatening. Peri's invitation for him to let some of that pain go, to dilute its force by inviting some of it into her own mind, felt like a relief at hand.

He faced her sister, his golden eyes alight. "Very well," he said, feeling like he was jumping into a chasm, letting go. He unleashed his memories onto Peri's mind. They were of the same blood, two halves of the same soul, and this all was possible without words between them. He didn't hold back. For a few seconds, he was trapped in a word made of obsidian shadow, where the red outlines of translucent wraiths gathered around jagged, sharp rocks in a barren wasteland. A vague dread lingered everywhere, but before Velimir had time to gather his bearings, it was already over, and he found himself back in the cave.

Peri was crying—crying and gritting her teeth in rage. She hugged Velimir as hard as she could, trying to cease her frantic sobs. "I want him dead! I want him—"

"He is dead already. Tomoe killed him," Velimir said, stroking her arm.

"I know...I know. It is just that...a man like him, he is not an epic villain in a story. He is just a disgusting, evil, ordinary man. I have seen others like him...killed them...even *worked* for them. They always prevail, they are everywhere, smug and pleased with themselves. They rule this world, Velimir, they ruin all that is beautiful. They are the banality of evil."

"But unlike in the past, we are not powerless." Once upon a time that would have been all that concerned Velimir. But in the rainbow world, as a boy made of light, he had wanted to be a hero. Someone who protected the powerless. Who sacrificed his own needs for others. Velimir smiled as he was aware of Peri's own feelings about being a hero. But truly, she didn't mind doing decent things. It was the language about it that bothered her. And she didn't suffer demands made of her or which infringed upon her freedom.

So be it. Velimir would be a hero discreetly if they survived.

"Brother of my soul," Peri said.

393

"Sister of my soul."

"As darkness closes in—and fuck how it will tomorrow—*I shield you with my love.* We'll have to teach it to Wyn, too," Peri said.

Velimir frowned. "Shh, it's not finished yet!"

Peri slapped a hand over her mouth.

"And as darkness closes in, I shield you with mine," Velimir concluded. Now it was time. They went to rouse the spellcasters to get their few hours of sleep.

45
HOUSE OF APATHIA

THE LONG TREK THROUGH MANALA HAD BEEN UNEVENT-
ful. The shades had kept their distance, and no bile hag or
anything worse had attempted to attack Kiril or the sad,
gagged figure by his side. At any rate, with magic once again
at his fingertips, he would have been able to make short
work of the monsters wandering the gloomy region. Perhaps they sensed his renewed power, or it just was evident
in his determined gait and newfound confident radiance.

Finally, in the midst of the soggy fog, loomed a forbid-
ding cylindrical building. Even though there was no sun or
moon anywhere to be seen, the building cast a long shadow.
It was leaden gray, and there was a row of high, narrow windows near the roof. They seemed to watch the landscape like
a set of hollow eyes. There was a wrought-iron fence with
sharp spikes surrounding the building. It was the first thing
apart from dripping dead trees and cold rocks the pair had

encountered in Manala. *Here it is. House of Apathia.*

Kiril knocked at the gate.

A middle-aged man with a receding hairline, wearing a long white coat, came to open it. "A dead human. By the looks of it, a Valkaman. What is your business here?" the man asked. He glanced at Vallara's subdued form in a manner that suggested he had an idea what that business was, then returned his expectant gaze to Kiril.

"I am Kiril Belaja, here on a mission for the Norns of Asgard. I am returning your prisoner."

The man bristled. "There are no 'prisoners' here! This is a sanatorium. A place of sanctuary and healing. But I suppose you should follow me."

Vallara didn't react with any emotion. She followed meekly, staring at the ground, shuffling listlessly ahead like the shades of Manala.

The massive oak doors opened to a rotunda where a spiral staircase ascended to the six stories of cells facing the center. Kiril stepped over the threshold that was inscribed with dully glowing gray runes, and the invisible geas knot at his heart tingled. Yet as soon as Vallara crossed the threshold, he felt the knot loosen and dissipate. *So, it is done. Jelena is safe.*

In the middle of the rotunda, there were five stories of rooms with obscured windows facing all directions. Footsteps echoed in the eerie silence.

"The...uh, patients never know when they are being watched, do they?" Kiril asked in a silky voice.

The man's round, pudgy face brightened. "Indeed! That is the idea of learning self-regulation in a safe environment. Privacy is a privilege these unfortunate souls are not entitled

to as of yet. We live in the hope that the fear of being observed will transcend into internalized judgement and emotional regulation—sanity, if you will."

"And so they turn into paranoid wrecks. Or become
catatonically docile, like this one." Kiril indicated at Vallara,
who stared ahead with empty eyes. "When she realized she
couldn't avoid returning here, she gave up the fight and died
inside, all before you ever laid a hand on her. Brilliant, I must
say."

The man scoffed. "We would never lay a hand on a patient! Not unless they need to be restrained for their own
good, at any rate. We are far more enlightened than that
here."

Kiril shook his head and smiled with a steely glint in his
eyes. "You turn an individual's own mind into the jailor, the
oppressor. And it is not as if your prisoners are necessarily
criminals. What they are is inconvenient—or someone who
the plane of Panoptica disapproves of, for whatever reason."

The white-coated man slowed down and frowned. "How
would you know this, Kiril Belaja from Valkama?"

Kiril shrugged. "I couldn't resist asking some questions
from my prisoner...er...your patient. I've always had a curious mind."

"Oh, make no mistake, Kiril Belaja. Your...detainee is a
deviant. A breaker of the cosmic order. The gods of Silva
Lunari agree and have cut her off from the source of her
clerical powers. But worry not! We are healers! Learning
self-regulation is the way of healing...and isn't deviance a
manner of illness, too?" the man said. "It is an illness in the
body of the commonwealth—leviathan, if you will—and an
individual person is a miniature of that body. Just as this

sanitarium is a miniature of Ratas, the city of order within the chaos of the Nether. I find the alchemist principle of 'as above, so below' so fascinating!"

That was a lot of words—a lot of words that were cloaking something sinister that this man seemed to fervently believe in. Kiril shrugged again. "Alchemist principles are fascinating indeed. I have always been interested in principles for their own sake, as a matter of pure intellectual exercise. So much so that I never applied for the rank of archmage. I had contempt for the fools seduced by the pomp and glamour and ceremony that go with the rank, preferring my low profile."

The man glanced up at the obscured windows and nodded discreetly. Then he resumed his good-natured smile and turned his attention back to Kiril. "A man after my own heart! I, too, was always intellectually curious. Though, in our work as healers, I have found a practical application for my knowledge."

Kiril ascended the stairs in the man's footsteps. "I sneered at the rank and the mages seduced by it," he said. "In retrospect, it seems that it was my own particular brand of snobbery. I did, however, make certain that I had all the skills and knowledge required of an archmage at an exceptionally young age. And one of the demonstrations of skill happens to be building a simulacrum—a specific type of application of your alchemist principle, I dare say."

The polite smile on the white-coated man's soft, round face died down, and he started to frown.

"A simulacrum, 'that which is formed in the likeness,'" Kiril went on. "An illusion skillfully crafted of subtle matter, far more elaborate than a crude visual conjurer's trick." Kiril glanced at Vallara's subdued form, and the man followed his gaze. Vallara turned translucent and started to flicker. "A body double capable of manipulating all the senses, perhaps even simulating actions of its target. Warded against any crude methods of detecting deception, such as the wards at your gates, naturally."

The white-coated man's nostrils flared, and a simmering rage started to rise in his eyes as Vallara—or the simulacrum created in her likeness—disappeared in a blink.

"Your arrogance was helpful, of course," Kiril said. "You knew how well your methods work, so you never doubted that she would despair if forced to return here. You would expect a meek, walking corpse, which is easier to simulate than a living, feeling person."

The man's polite, scholarly manner was now gone. "I haven't the faintest idea why you would concoct such a deception, Kiril Belaja," he said, "but I can't imagine that the Norns would trust an outsider without securing your compliance. What have you done?"

"Oh, they do have leverage," Kiril replied. "They have someone I love as a hostage. But they are not aware of all the relevant circumstances. My love happens to be a favoured devotee of Lord Milostra. And she has a boon for her safety when she ventures away from the Elysian Fields. If she is in danger, she can teleport back to her Lord. It is not something that we desired, since that would undo all our hard work of getting together, probably irrevocably. But they will not be able to harm her. With that, I am content."

The eerie silence of the dark corridors shimmered, and dozens of demons with glowing eyes materialized to surround Kiril. The largest of them cracked his knuckles and narrowed its blazing eyes.

"How very foolish of you," said the man. "Did you truly imagine that we would let you leave once you deceived us and allowed a dangerous deviant to flee? There just so happens to be an empty cell. Another deviant will serve just as well. You will never leave this place."

The demons slowly advanced at Kiril, pushing him towards a dank cell with an open door.

"Oh, I know." Kiril swallowed and inhaled. He felt how the hum of magic was once again out of his reach, behind a barrier woven into the very structure of the building. As he continued, his voice trembled at first, but soon he regained his newfound serenity. "Thanks to my conversations with Vallara, I am well-aware of your nature. I would have loved nothing more than having a second chance, sharing the afterlife with my love. But not at any cost. Not by condemning another. I know why Vallara wanted to leave the elven heaven and go back to the world of the living. Her daughter is infatuated with the cause of elven supremacy. She wants to reclaim a mythical past of elven glory and rule, and put to sword anyone standing in her way. Vallara wants to protect her child from that folly, even if it means breaking the natural order and making a deal with a necromancer to go back beyond the veil. She wants to do the exact opposite of what I did. Offer guidance and wisdom to her charge and discourage her from a disastrous path. So yes, I let her go. And I wish her godspeed. I know you won't let me leave. It is no more than what I deserve, for reasons that have nothing to do with your philosophy of terror."

"Then get used to your cell, mage," the man snapped. "You caught us off guard, but from now on, you will be cut off from magic for good. I truly hope this stunt was worth it. You will find that there is a great deal of unpleasantness that can be visited upon you without laying a hand on you."

Kiril smiled at the closest demon and walked slowly to the hay-filled mattress. There was no window, just a dim torch illuminating the dank corner. He sat down and closed his eyes. It was unfortunate that this was to be his eternity, but while hanging in the wind-swept tree, he had found a spacious place of peace within. It would be a long eternity, but never before had he been so certain of having done the right thing.

46
THE SENTINEL MONASTERY OF AUSTERE FIST

THE TREK THROUGH THE NARROW STONY CORRIDORS IN-side of the mountain was finally over. The party has crossed rope bridges, climbed ladders and stairs hewn in the stone, passed by cozy little caverns as well as large halls. They even passed a magical laboratory and an ominous shrine—no doubt for the kind of people who wanted to "live in Sjenka's shadows," as Irina had put it. After climbing a final rope ladder, they emerged in an unremarkable tool shed. Samir pulled a crate over the hatch to cover the secret passage.

"There ye go," he said, rummaging through another crate. "Not all monks are privy to my arrangement with the ladies. One in particular, Tamasin's bodyguard, is a zealous dimwit. Here, wear these robes. Yer spell should be sufficient, but just in case, wear them over yer armor."

Peri glanced at Velimir, who was struggling with the largest robe. A man who was larger than most orcs, with eyes glowing like amber and gold, and who towered over everyone...Yeah, somebody might notice, whether her brother wore the gray robes or not. Velimir really wasn't cut out for undercover work, but hopefully the spell would be sufficient to allow them to ambush Rajsa and Tamasin.

Obscured by *shifting shadows*, they followed Samir through the monastery yard. There were a few chickens, a pig, and a goat. There were herb bushes and gnarly apple trees, but nobody was tending to them. The halls of the monastery were likewise abandoned.

"The ladies will be in the cliffside chapel," Samir said. "It is well warded, so ye'll not be able to enter without them noticing. But if ye go to the cloakroom, ye can hear me talking with them and plan yer entrance accordingly." He opened a door to a room that had chalices and other jewel-encrusted paraphernalia in it, stacks of lovingly scribed tomes, more gray robes hanging from pegs. "They'll be behind the curtain. But remember, as soon as ye touch it, all wards will go off, and ye'd better act fast, whatever ye do."

"Very well, pirate," Velimir said. "Do what you do best. Charm. Lie. Deceive. Do it convincingly."

Samir grinned and gave him a thumbs-up, then went on his way as the party stayed alert, listening. Soon, they could hear voices from behind the curtain.

"What news, spymaster Arakelian?" It was Rajsa's cool, crisp voice.

"Pleased to inform ye that Peri and her crew lie dead at the entrance of the gorge. Hesyeth ambushed them and took them down. However...he, too, died of the wounds he received in the battle against those five. Sorry for yer loss." Samir's voice was expressionless, with none of his usual swagger.

"Unfortunate, I suppose," Rajsa said. "Hesyeth was the most powerful warrior of us all, that is for certain. But he was also something of a braggart and a fool. Probably he couldn't resist giving Peri a pompous villain's exposition before attacking. No matter, both are dead now—and only we remain."

"Thank you, spymaster," said Tamasin. "You are in the big leagues now. As soon as Rajsa arises as the new goddess of wrath, your wile will serve a far bigger cause than merely amassing wealth."

"An honor indeed," Samir smoothly replied. "May me ships and me spies thrive under her banners."

"Finally, the moment we have been anticipating is here," Rajsa said. "This was the last morning I communed with Lord Stribog as a servant. After we conduct the ritual, I will be his equal and an ally! Lord Stribog is wary of the Dimitrian unadulterated wrath, but he sees the value of wrestling power from Veit with this alliance. And I have been training to harness that wrath with discrimination."

"And I will train all our celestials in the ways of the Austere Fist," Tamasin said. "It is a pity that we could not contain Peri while draining her divine essence to create an infinite number of them. But once Rajsa ascends, I am positive we will find a way."

"I always wanted to be a commander and a strategist," Rajsa said. "But to be that as a god—the very Valkama my battlefield!—is more than a childhood dream come true. Spymaster, you do not know what Tamasin sacrificed to get us where we are now. No-one could know, so that she could play the part of a protector of the panicking lesser Dimitrian spawn. We, the Esquadron, were raised in privilege, knowing that we were special. But Tamasin was sent away at an early age, so that we could use her to gain the public support necessary for bringing our plan to fruition. She never has uttered a word of complaint, but I know the austerities she suffered through nearly killed her."

"Can only admire that sort of devotion," Samir said. "I'm honored to serve the Esquadron."

"Go now, spymaster," Rajsa said. "We have a ritual to conduct. Be available tomorrow at noon, as usual."

"As ye command," Samir replied. As his footsteps disappeared, Tamasin spoke to Rajsa. "Allow me to wrap you in the ceremonial robe. All is ready for your ascension."

Amid the shuffling sound of silky garments, Rajsa said, "Even as I rule over the lesser, I will always remember your sacrifice and leadership."

"I know, dear Rajsa. And now, finally, you will get what you deserve." Tamasin's voice was soft and tender.

"A…akh…"

Peri frowned and strained her hearing. She glanced at her companions, who looked as nonplussed as she was. *What now?*

"Finally, my Lord!" Tamasin's voice erupted in rapturous joy. "The day I have been preparing for is here! I will serve you this one last time, and then—"

Just then someone barged in the room, interrupting Tamasin. The party could hear agitated footsteps and scuffling. A gruff, incensed voice spoke up. "Mistress Tamasin! Zalbov always said this man was up to no good!"

"Why do you interrupt, Zalbov? I told you not to disturb our peace!" There was a barely discernible tremble of the earth as Tamasin's shrill voice rose in anger.

"Zalbov very sorry, but this worthless man tried to steal our most holy relics!"

"Deal with him as you wish, Zalbov. I have more pressing matters to attend to now," Tamasin growled.

"Oh, Zalbov knows how he'll deal with the thieving bastard all right. He'll—"

"Uh, Tamasin! I may have told ye a bit of a modified truth! Peri, actually, is still alive, right there in the cloak room! About to ambush ye!" Samir said in his unmistakable drawl.

"What!" The man called Zalbov growled and took a few thunderous steps toward the curtain. The earth subtly trembled again. Peri immediately saw her arm and the sword fully opaque in front of her. The *shifting shadows* had been dispelled. She barged past the curtain, sword drawn, followed by her friends.

They emerged at a stage in front of an austere altar. Tamasin glared at them, a big orcish monk by her side. Samir had disappeared during the commotion. Of Rajsa, there was no sign—only a shimmering black and gold enchanted cloak in a bloodied pile on the floor stones. Tamasin was holding a bloodied dagger in her hand.

"I assume that Hesyeth couldn't resist bragging then," Tamasin said.

"I never bought your act to begin with, so it was not a huge surprise," Peri said. "But we sure did kill your pet lizard. And now *you* backstabbed Rajsa! I suppose her body dissolved like it happens with the pedigree spawn. You lot are nothing if not consistent."

"It wasn't like that!" Tamasin sharply exclaimed. Her eyes gleamed with determination.

"Oh *really?*" Peri's voice grew into a low growl and her nostrils flared. "You wanted me to kill them, and I have, for lack of other courses of action. Now there's only me and Ewynne's tiny Dimitrian stream, and you want the final showdown. To the victor go the spoils. Pray tell, what was it *like?*"

"I was part of the Esquadron, true," Tamasin said. "I did my part. I was sent away to study the way of the Austere Fist, and I gained a reputation as a philanthropist and a religious leader to be able to lure Dimitri's offspring into a trap." Tamasin's forehead was perspiring, and she had grown pallid. "But the mistake they made was that I got to know God during my training in the loneliness of the mountains! The evil of Dimitri's blood must never take the form of a new god of wrath. I will see to it that everyone carrying his evil in their veins is dead until I alone remain."

"How presumptuous of you!" Razeem exclaimed. "You think that you alone would be above reproach to the extent that you could resist the innate evil of Dimitri's blood and use it as a force of good!"

"Oh no, dear faithful of Juris. I have always known that when I am the last one, I will commit a ritual suicide. Which is what I was about to do—to go to the true god, the Void, before I was interrupted." Tamasin grimaced and leaned on Zalbov. There was a small red dot in her abdomen. It was spreading slowly. "I had no idea that our spymaster was such a treacherous weasel. But I suppose I must be grateful to that pirate that I didn't act prematurely. Now I will have to make sure I'm the last one remaining—that there is no chance that Dimitri's evil will threaten Valkama with its foulness."

"You would kill Ewynne as well?" Peri asked, starting to pale. "The sweetest and nicest person there is, just because she has some Dimitrian blood in her system?"

"Regrettably, yes," Tamasin answered.

"That we will not allow," Kauno said. There was no anger on her face. She was merely stating a fact.

"I'll show you regret!" Ewynne snarled. Tamasin didn't even look at her.

"You are not a big believer in free will, are you?" Peri said. "You think you are good because you are willing to kill yourself and give up the godhood?"

"I must bear this burden because I am not willing to be a god," Tamasin said. "It should be telling what kind of person wants to be a god. Hesyeth. Rajsa. Velimir. Better that I bear the responsibility."

Velimir shook his head and chuckled. "You fool. You have gathered far more power for Dimitri than anyone else by systematically murdering his offspring. And they say *I* suffered from delusions of grandeur!"

The sanctimoniously regretful look in Tamasin's eyes got under Peri's skin. She pushed past Velimir, pale, the familiar murder shining in her eyes.

"Do not dare to speak Velimir's name as if he was some kind of filth beneath you. He is a far better person than you could ever hope to be! He would give his own hard-won life back for Ewynne and would never be as presumptuous as you are."

"You are proving your nature, Peri, and thus my point," Tamasin said with a sad, disappointed look in her eyes. "I fear you have me at a disadvantage, but Zalbov will assist me. I will not allow you to ascend!"

"Fine!" Peri slashed at Tamasin. But despite being wounded, Tamasin evaded the slash easily, leaving Peri wide-eyed. Zalbov lunged at her with remarkable speed and force, but Velimir had been ready. The orcish monk's head flew into the wall with a *thud*, spraying blood all over Tamasin on its way.

"Very well," Tamasin said, holding up a hand. Peri and Velimir tried to advance, but Tamasin had raised an invisible shield against them. They tried to push through, but the shield didn't budge. Tamasin's breath was short, and her lips were starting to pale, the red dot spreading in her abdomen. "My shield won't last forever, so I will have to enlist...Ewynne's help."

Ewynne scoffed. "Are you out of your mind? I will never help you with anything!"

"Sadly, you have no choice. You see, being one of Dimitri's weak offspring, there is a spark of the Edge even in you. With someone of Peri's caliber, I could not hope to command it. With you, however, it is like squeezing intestines in my hand. I regret it has come to this, but now you must welcome the wrath in your blood, little Ewynne." She tensed her trembling fingers and whispered some words in Vysokian.

Ewynne jerked and spasmed. Then she erupted in a long, wailing scream. The others watched in horror as she flailed in anguish, gasping and weeping. She started to contort, her body transforming into a skinned corpse that grinned and stared with yellow demonic eyes. There was nothing but murder and madness in its eyes, and it gleefully lunged at Peri.

The fucking *sanctimonious bitch. Thinking herself an altruist, a hero, saving Valkama.* Peri shook with fury, tears of uncontrollable rage streaming on her cheeks. She charged, the frosty blade slicing a wide arch through the air. "No-one hurt it! No-one hurt Wyn. Or I'll rip your head off!" she heard herself screaming through a dark red haze—the rage suffocating her, barely realizing her environment. A sound in the distance. Someone shouting.

"Peri! Peri! Don't give in! Don't! There is no use in attacking her. She is shielded!"

Velimir tried to establish contact with his sister, to make her listen. She was hacking at Tamasin quite uselessly, the blade bouncing from the slightly diminished shield. The Edge was struggling to get in control of her.

"Peri! Get a grip! We won't hurt Ewynne, I promise!"

He wasn't getting through. Out of the corner of his eye, he kept looking at the creature Ewynne had become that followed him and tried to shred him into pieces. He dodged the creature and shielded the others from it, remembering all the time that his little sister was suffering inside the abomination. It was supernaturally fast and raked at him with venomous claws. Without Jussuf's healing and since fighting defensively, he kept taking damage. Being indoors, Kauno could not call her nature allies to help. Razeem tried his counter-magic tricks, but none seemed to have any effect on either the demonic apparition or Tamasin's shield.

"Kill...just kill..." Peri growled, nothing human in her eyes. She grew. She screamed. Her head split open and sprayed blood and black ooze. Her flesh melted away, and she was now a glittering skeleton, golden orbs spinning in its eye sockets, keening. Her sword clattered away, and the creature clawed furiously at Tamasin's shield. Tamasin herself had retreated towards the wall she leaned her elbow against, sweating profusely.

Velimir whacked the demon that was Ewynne with the flat of his sword to ward it off. It wailed. "My brother! I thought you loved me..." Its face was Ewynne's again, and Velimir hesitated. Just long enough for the creature to growl and swipe low, tearing a large wound into his abdomen. He toppled on his knees and his ears buzzed. He heard a faint cheer, but it faded away, and he realized it was a mortal wound. All right then...

Mother, I did well, didn't I? They might live. I didn't get to live very long, but I helped my sisters. Please, please may they live. I will not complain about my own demise. Then, darkness.

47
SHUNYATA SKIES

KIRIL TURNED HIS ATTENTION BACK TO HIS PHYSICAL body, having dwelt for a while in the spacious internal peace he had found while hanging in the wind-swept tree. He opened his eyes and frowned. He was no longer in the dank cell of the House of Apathia. He was no longer tethered to the body of the gaunt little mage. There was still this vaguely humanoid shape occupying space around him, the one in which he had flown over the war-torn lands while his body was writhing at the end of the rope.

He looked at his hand and saw nothing, yet it felt as if he had a hand. He imagined having a hand, and instantly a translucent, iridescent hand materialized in front of his eyes. He looked around and found himself floating above a mass of soft, white clouds, surrounded by lucid and peaceful infinity. Every fiber of his incorporeal being was charged with magic, and the environment brimmed with it.

Suddenly, a crystal pond in the shelter of three syca-mores softly whispering in the wind appeared in front of him. A man was sitting on a rock under the trees. He was rather nondescript with plain, friendly features and sand brown hair, perhaps in his forties. He wore the simple brown garb of a monk and had a dove sitting on his shoulder. The man smiled up at Kiril. "You can assume your familiar form if you like, Kiril Belaja. Or any other that you can think of. Welcome to Shunyata Skies."

The bird on his shoulder looked familiar, though last time Kiril had seen it, it had looked like a gray pigeon. Now it was a luminous white dove. It was as if the bird and the man were made of frozen light, just like everything else here. Kiril floated next to the man and imagined having a body. It promptly materialized, luminous and transparent, resem-bling the one he had as a younger man. He sat down.

The plain-looking, luminous monk smiled. "You are get-ting the hang of it. At Shunyata Skies, there is no need for gross matter. You can dwell in its peace without a corporeal form. Or will any pleasures or scenes of beauty you desire into existence."

"Really?" Kiril imagined a cozy but enormous library, with shelves covering its walls all the way to the ceiling, the smell of books, leather, dust, and ink. Sure enough, as soon as the image formed in his mind, he now sat in such a li-brary with the dove and the plain-looking monk, in cozy armchairs facing a fireplace.

"Are you...are you Lord Milostra? Am I hallucinating?" Kiril was familiar with the descriptions of the god's avatar when it suited Milostra to take a human form—if the dove was not a clue enough.

"I am he, and you are not hallucinating. You made an extraordinary choice—a choice that transcends the ego and its desires. You put aside your own happiness for that of another, even if it meant spending your eternity in a cell without magic, without freedom. That set you free and attracted you to my presence."

"I...just couldn't. Not after I hung in Yggdrasil. It showed me...the truth. I suppose there is no other word for it. That there is just one pain, and all living things share it. I couldn't condemn her for the sake of my own freedom. Especially as she was trying to do the right thing. The tree showed me that the separation between my pain and someone else's is, ultimately, an illusion."

The luminous white dove cocked its head. "Such drastic measures you took, and therefore you were able to learn so much in such a short time. For most souls, it takes eons."

The mass of silvery clouds parted for a moment, and down at the bottom of the shaft of light, Kiril could see the cell he had just departed. A small, gaunt man sat there, cross-legged, hands on his knees, eyes closed. "He is...*I am*...still there?" It felt less strange than one would have thought.

Milostra nodded and the luminous dove hopped on Kiril's knee. "It is an emanation of you, made of gross matter. No different from what you ever were, really, but you have gained the freedom from imagining that whatever body and mindstream you currently inhabit is all that there is. If you don't want to return to it—and I don't see why you would—it will stay there infinitely."

"But...who am I now? *What* am I?"

"You are a soul that has started to awaken. You are in the fields of infinite potential, where there are no blemishes or evil or pain."

"Will I stay here? Are there any other beings here?"

"Plenty! You just aren't used to perceiving them yet. And yes, you could stay here. You could have eternal peace, manifest anything you want into existence. But should you choose, you can also inhabit a body again. Be warned, though...a human body is a source of intense attraction and aversion. Passion. Everything that disturbs the peace of mind. There are no guarantees that you would not fall back on your path."

"What about Jelena? Is she—?" Kiril started to ask. Another shaft of light was formed as the clouds parted. Down below, he could see a stony balcony overlooking a lush valley. A crystal stream tumbled down the slopes, overgrown with ferns and other foliage. Bell-shaped white little spring flowers grew everywhere, and Kiril felt as if he could smell their sweet scent. Jelena sat on a bench hewn in stone. She was clutching the dove amulet, and her eyes were closed. She was pale and trembling.

"The boon triggered as soon as you revealed your deception to the jailors. She is at her home, at the Valley of the Lilies of the Elysian Fields. She is naturally upset, as she thinks your plans have failed and worries about your fate."

"Then..." Kiril hesitated just for a moment. He knew perfect peace now, and he knew secrets the runes at the bottom of the Well of Urd had shown him when he fell from the tree. He could contemplate the secrets of the universe for all eternity. He could observe whatever he could think about, create from luminous subtle matter any scene that pleased his imagination. Inhabiting a body again would carry the risk of being enthralled with poisonous thoughts, along with all the hardships that were part of embodied life. But without a body, he could not directly interact with others who had not found their way to Shunyata Skies. Not with the woman he loved. Not with the son he had failed. Nor anyone else he might be able to help now that he…knew more. "I want to be corporeal again. To go to her. I will accept the limitations that come with a body and hope I will be wiser this time."

"Then your wish shall be granted. I know that you and Jelena were planning to seek out your son Velimir. Well, the Dimitrian turmoil is about to come to fruition, and he is involved. We, the Three, have a keen interest in the outcome. Come, let us create a new body for you and enter the Elysian Fields."

Kiril became firm flesh again. He felt more dense and coarse, more limited. More sharp and impatient. The body and the mind were familiar but more spacious and light than they had been before. He and the nondescript monk with the luminous dove landed softly on the stony balcony. He reached out to touch Jelena's arm.

48
THEATER OF TIME

VELIMIR BLINKED AND OPENED HIS EYES. STILL CORPO-real, but somewhere else. He looked around and found himself at the stage of the Theater of Time. Dozens of dead hornets and birds covered the stage. There was a white painted bench under a maple tree bright in autumn colors. A withered corpse sat on the bench, a book still open in its arms.

"Greetings, Velimir," spoke a serene voice as Irina stepped from the shadows.

"So, this is how I die the second time," Velimir said.

"Die? Perhaps, momentarily. But no, you are not dead. You can't be. You are one of the Deathless now. The ritual of your resurrection saw to that."

"The Deathless?" Velimir frowned. He'd not heard the term before.

"They walk the face of Valkama, in the spotlight and in

the shadows. Those who never perish. Not all of them see that as a blessing."

Tamasin, translucent now, screeched and raised her fist. "It is not right that he should get to be Deathless! Not him! He is evil!"

Irina glanced at her. "The Deathless are good, evil, and anything in between, just like mortals," she said then turned her gaze back to Velimir.

"Miss I-orchestrated-a-mass-murder-and-leveled-a-city has thoughts about evil now," said a familiar voice.

Velimir turned and gasped. *Peri!* And the rest of her companions. Ewynne was pale and shivering, but back to her original form, no sign of the beast she'd been.

Irina smiled briefly at Peri and smoothly raised her hand in greeting. "The prophecy is at its final stage now. The fate of an enormous reservoir of transcendental energy is at hand. My role is that of an observer. I pray that you will choose wisely, Peri of Eilean de Taigh-Sholais."

Tamasin glared at Peri and whipped her translucent arm out in a chopping motion. Nothing happened. She tried twice more, her eyes widening in shock, her teeth baring.

"That is futile," Irina said to her. "You linger, but you are dead. Your involvement in this matter is finished."

Tamasin balled her fists. "I can't have failed! I can't!" she insisted. "I am the weapon of the One True God, the God of The Void that will cleanse the evil that allows gods such as Veit or Sjenka to exist! God spoke to me, chose me to execute his plan!"

"Indeed?" A new voice spoke up. A luminous being—a radiantly handsome young man with golden eyes, chiseled features, smooth skin, a lean body, and luminous wings—strolled onto the stage. "Tamasin, dear child."

Tamasin took a few steps back and raised her hand as if to conjure a shield. "Dimitri! Stand back! Your evil shall *not* prevail! I was raised to serve your plan, but in the loneliness of the mountains, I found the true god!"

Dimitri threw his head back and laughed. "Did you, now? All those cold winter mornings. Sleepless nights spent in prayer in the cold of your cell. Fasting so that you were half dead from thirst and hunger. Enduring unimaginable hardships, fervently praying for guidance. Pray tell, little Tamasin—who do you think you were talking to? Who do you think planted the seeds of your plan?" the celestial chuckled.

Tamasin gasped a few times, as if choking. "It...it isn't true..." she said in a small and hesitant voice.

Dimitri's flawless face split into a venomous, patronizing smile. "Of course it is true. You really left yourself wide open, my dear."

"No...It isn't true..." Tamasin slowly collapsed on her knees, whispering. "It isn't..."

Irina turned to face her, wearing a tiny frown of impatience. "Enough. My brother is correct. It is quite true. Your zeal and self-righteousness blinded you, and now you will pay the price. Go," she said sharply.

Tamasin gasped and swallowed. A tear formed in her eye as she stared at the dead hornets in stunned silence. Then, in a blink of golden dust, she vanished.

Dimitri turned to face Irina, and a spark of anger surfaced in his golden eyes, so similar to Velimir's. "Sister," he said.

"Greetings, my lost brother. You have destroyed much to get your way, yet in the end, the wildcards of fate prevailed,"

Irina said. She spoke in that serene, unperturbed tone that Velimir had once found so annoying. Except now it was being turned on the celestial behind all the chaos.

"Tsk. Gloating doesn't become you, Irina," Dimitri said and smoothed a few golden locks behind his ear. "True, this is a setback. Tamasin in her self-righteous hubris would indeed have made a perfect vessel for me. It was amusing to observe her delusions, too. But it is not over just yet."

"No, it is not," Irina said. She clasped her hands and turned to face Peri. "Now it is time to decide what to do with the sum of the Dimitrian essence. And the choice falls upon you, Peri of Eilean de Taigh-Sholais."

Peri's eyes were hard as flintstones, gleaming like steel. She looked wild and very angry. "What are my options?" At her words, Velimir felt an uneasy chill.

"The essence has now reached a singularity of enormous potential," Irina explained. She took a few steps closer, regarding Peri's tense and angry face from her height. "Only one mortal remains that could harness it, namely you. The first option is to allow it to dissipate, to release it to float in the infinity of the ether. It would merge with all other wild matter of the multiverse, having lost what bound it together as a deathly potential. You would be free to go on with your life."

"And the other option?" Peri's mouth was a tight line.

"The other option is to assume all the essence to yourself," Irina said. "That would make you a god for all intents and purposes. You would succeed in what many have sought and failed. It would transform you irrevocably—but in what exact manner is not for me to say."

Peri was quiet for a moment, scowling, eyes hard and

dark, mouth grim, pacing. Velimir tried to catch her eye, to establish that warm connection that was always between them, but Peri wouldn't meet his eye. Then she spoke.

"Perhaps I should take it after all! Damn it, I could kill… the likes of Silas and Radek Rosinin…all the assholes of the world…see them all dead! All those who always ruin everything…" She rubbed her hands together as she paced. "I could use my power to make sure no-one ever hurts my family again!"

"Peri! No! You have said it yourself. It cannot be controlled," Ewynne said, shocked.

"I don't care!" Peri yelled. "I don't care about anything but that you and Velimir won't suffer again! In fact…I control the essence now, don't I?" She glanced at Irina, whose face remained without emotion.

"At my approval, yes," answered Irina. Dimitri smirked and crossed his arms.

"Fine! I summon here one Radek Rosinin!" Peri snarled, glowing momentarily, the features of the glittering skeleton shining through her flesh. Dimitri chuckled.

The fearful, cowering thing shivering on the stage was nothing like the Radek of Velimir's memories. This Radek's body was strangely deformed, full of whiplashes and blisters. His eyes were sunk into his head, fear and submission marking his face like it never had in life. Yet Velimir recognized his stepfather. The features were forever imprinted in his darkest memories. This pitiful thing was essentially what the man had tried to reduce Velimir to when he was growing up under his yoke. *But you never succeeded.*

"Take it out on him, Velimir!" Peri cried. "Torture him! I will…create some hot pokers or vats of acid or thorn mats or something! Velimir, kill him, gut him, whatever. Then I will resurrect him and then you can kill him again!" Peri's flashing eyes and anger were frightening to behold.

"Please, Velimir..." Radek whispered. "They have tortured me so much already..."

Velimir drew breath as he pondered the situation in front of him. He had, for seemingly endless years, dreamed of this very scenario. He well remembered the fear and humiliation and rage and pain. Nobody would blame him for releasing it on Radek. The man had brought this all upon himself. Velimir thought about a garrote slicing through his mother's neck. Perhaps squeezing the life out of this thing and sending it to the next hell awaiting it would kill the memories, banish their dark, slithering forms from the deep fjord of his mind—the fjord that hid the things he didn't want to think about but that haunted him.

Peri cackled in a voice that was raw and shrill. "Oh, they have tortured you, have they? Well boo fucking hoo. You... you miserable, rotten motherfucker. You tortured Velimir all his life! You tortured his mother!"

Very true. But somehow the idea of brutalizing what was left of Radek failed to exhilarate Velimir. He could fan the flames of his bloodlust if he so chose...but it didn't bring him the kind of pleasure it once did. For a moment he remembered Connor's eyes in the memory of a world that never was. What he was truly seeking—peace, lightness of being, the lion heart of the boy in the rainbow world—was in the opposite direction of whatever petty, short-lived pleasure Velimir might derive from indulging his old hate.

He tried to establish eye contact with his sister. "Peri..."

But Peri paid no attention to Velimir's lack of enthusiasm.

She glared at Radek, who was cowering, anticipating a blow, inefficiently covering his head with his arms. He was pathetic.

"Sorry not sorry if I don't pity you, you cowardly child- and wife-beating bastard!" Peri screamed. "You always thought nobody could stop you—you and others like you!"

"Peri!" Velimir spoke loud enough to interrupt her. "I have done too much torturing and killing in my time. It never healed the pain. It only fed it. As for you," he spoke to Radek, "it is difficult, but not impossible, to find a better afterlife."

Radek frowned and worked his mouth, uncomprehending.

Irina nodded. "Once upon a time," she said, looking serenely in the distance, "there was a child, just an infant. He had no notion of passage of time, of gender, of labels or concepts. He smiled when he saw a butterfly flap its iridescent wings in the sunlight. He reached his little chubby arm towards it with simple delight. That child had no idea that he would be named Radek."

Radek didn't look up. "I...don't remember." His voice cracked.

To Velimir, the hate felt like old, stale water leaking from a cracked bucket. The all-powerful presence of Radek that had molded Velimir's life, that sometimes still came to his dreams, was no longer tangible. It was a memory, no more real than any translucent scene playing at the stage of the Theater of Time. A wave in the ocean of his mind. A reflection in the unbreakable mirror of his mind. All that was left of it was this pitiful thing, a plaything of demons who recognized a mediocre bully with delusions of grandeur when they saw one. "If you want the torment to stop, my stepfather, you must redeem yourself. Try to remember the infant you were—the infant desperate for kindness and love you later grew to despise. There lies your hope."

He turned his back on Radek.

"Velimir..." the man tried. But it was Irina who answered. "Go back whence you came, little man, and cling to the words of the one you tormented." With a smooth motion of her hand, Radek faded away.

Peri had stopped her pacing and stood there wild-eyed, hair frizzy. She took a few steps back and sank against the wall, the wind of rage in her sails somewhat gone.

"Peri, sister," Velimir came to her, taking her in his arms so that he could face her. The others kept a respectful distance. Velimir spoke in a low voice so that only Peri could hear. "Remember when I talked about becoming a god, and you yourself told me how a power like that corrupts? How you told us that being a god, as you put it, 'sucks'? How you pushed me to think about Tomoe and how I destroyed what we had because I wanted a power greater than that of mortals?"

Peri shivered in Velimir's arms, balling her hands into fists, shaking her head vigorously.

Velimir held her steady. "I loved Tomoe, too. I wanted nothing but to keep her from harm and give her all she desired. Do not do this for love. We would just lose you—me and Ewynne."

A tear rolled down Peri's cheek, her face softening.

"Do not become the Lady of Wrath, sister..." Velimir ventured on, the two of them in the magic world of their own no-one else could ever share. "You know that we share a link...that we are two pieces of the same soul. You know how I was when I was committed to becoming wrath. You will be like that, as well. There is too much passion and anger in you for it to end otherwise."

Peri closed her eyes and took a shuddering breath, shaking her head.

Velimir stroked her arm. "I plead with you. I want you here, with us."

Peri uttered a long sigh. "You speak the truth..." Her voice was quiet, her eyes downcast. "I don't know what came over me. I just wanted to kill...them all."

Velimir took her hand in his own. "Well, Peri, you've been through a lot. You turned into the Edge and went on a rampage, experienced my painful memories, saw Ewynne tortured...I guess you are allowed a bit of instability under the circumstances," he said.

Peri lowered her voice to a whisper. "It...feels...So. Fucking. Awesome. *You* know."

"I do. But it is poison. It is borne of Dimitri's rage. You taught me the truth of it."

Peri squeezed his hand, then lifted her head and faced Irina.

"No," she said. "I don't want to absorb the essence. It would probably be best if it was dissipated. But I will not give it up just like that."

Dimitri's smug smirk vanished as he bared his perfect teeth and jabbed a finger at Peri. "You would consider becoming a pathetic mortal?" the celestial snapped.

Peri remembered Janis Pulaski, the legless beggar she had shared a bottle of expensive port with. "If nothing else, age will diminish you. Happens to us all," Janis had said.

Not if I have anything to say about it, Peri thought.

Dimitri's lips curved to a gleeful smile as he witnessed Peri's hesitation. "I have felt how you savour it. You *love* it! Don't lie to yourself! Don't diminish yourself! Own your birthright!"

"Here's the thing," Peri said, pointedly ignoring Dimitri and addressing Irina. "That pathetic mortal part. I would give up Dimitri's power if you'll make me immortal, so that I never age. Do that for me, and I'll just fuck off and get on with my life."

"I see," Irina answered, her face enigmatic as usual. "And why do you want that?"

Peri shrugged. "I like adventure. I like the vigor of youth. I want to see all of Valkama. I don't want to grow old and weak. *Ever.*"

Irina stroked her chin and pondered for a moment. "Your motives may be less than altruistic, but very well, your wish shall be granted. The Three have their reasons. The ritual you performed in Dimitri's old sanctuary already has made your brother Deathless. Evil forces are aligning against him, so it is well that he would not have to face them alone. It will be as you wish. If you give up the Dimitrian essence, you shall never wither and get old."

"Fuck yeah!" Peri shouted. "Then take the motherfucking essence and hurl it into the ether. I don't want to become whatever monster it would make me, no matter how awesome it might feel."

Dimitri's mouth opened wide as he started to fade, his face distorting in horror. He spotted Casimir, perched on Ewynne's shoulder. "No! No! Casimir! Tell her!

The imp shook his head and waved sadly.

As the moments passed, Dimitri's face turned softer and younger, the face of an adolescent boy. "Father…" he whispered, then disappeared in a blink of golden dust.

"So it is done," Irina said. "I am glad of your choice, Peri of Eilean de Taigh-Sholais. I trust it was the right one."

Velimir gasped, and conflicting emotions alternated on his angular face.

"Velimir? What is it?" Peri asked.

"It is mother and Kiril…" he motioned across the stage to where three people had appeared.

The third person, a nondescript, middle-aged monk, greeted Irina, who saluted. The other two people—the lean, feline, black-clad mage and the blonde, round-shouldered woman—looked overwhelmed and held each other's hands. Peri and Velimir approached the group.

"Peri of Eilean de Taigh-Sholais—a newly minted Deathless by choice," said the monk. "Is it correct that you plan to travel to Zmaj-Vostok with your brother, to bury his true love, the warrior Tomoe?"

Peri tilted her head and crossed her arms at waist. "It is," she said warily.

"It all adds up! I have talked with Lord Milostra here," Irina smiled as Peri and Velimir widened their eyes in surprise, "and it seems that in the Far East, there is a prophecy we believe to be centered around Velimir. It speaks of a warrior of divine blood returned from the land of the dead, who will ride from the West and have a crucial role when a great evil which threatens not only Zmaj-Vostok, but the whole of Valkama as we know it. It also mentions burying a…*ronin* lady love of his, returning her to her ancestors' soil. And that the warrior once as evil as a demon is now a force of good."

"Could be pure coincidence," Peri said dryly. She glanced at Velimir, but her brother's eyes were fixed on his mother and Kiril, as if unsure whether they were real or not. The two stared back but opted to wait until Milostra was done talking.

Peri sighed. "It seems that I'm destined to save the world yet again. Oh well, if I get to ride to Zmaj-Vostok with Velimir, I guess it doesn't matter too much."

"You will not have to travel alone," said Milostra. "If you accept, I will send my favoured devotee to act as your cleric and healer, and she is accompanied by a very loyal and accomplished magician. It is not usual for souls to be sent back to Valkama from beyond the veil, but these are volatile times. The fate of Dimitri's essence was only a prelude. True evil is brewing." The god of compassion and forbearance glanced at Jelena and nodded.

Jelena stepped forward, and Velimir ran to his mother, almost crushing her with his fierce embrace, hot tears running down his cheeks.

"Mother...you heard me, didn't you?"

She stroked his broad back and pressed her cheek against the cold metal of the breastplate. "I did. I heard you praying to me in the land of despair. I sent you strength and hope with every fiber of my being. I never stopped loving you, no matter what. I love you today as I loved you the first time I laid my eyes upon you in our kitchen all those years ago. I always will, my golden-eyed boy."

Velimir savoured her presence. His mother wore the sand brown robes and the dove amulet of Milostra's clergy, and the god had referred to her as his favoured devotee. He'd ask her all about it very soon, but right now he just wanted to hold her and marvel at being reunited. Gods help it, they'd never be separated again.

Velimir lifted his head and let his mother go. He turned to Kiril, and both of them looked afraid, scared to face each other's gaze for fear of the truths that lay behind it. Velimir only had hazy memories of the weeks before he had stabbed Kiril and left him to die. He had a vague recollection of fear and doubt in his oldest friend's tormented eyes—and of threatening and menacing Kiril like he had threatened and menaced everyone else. *But the boy with the lion heart in the rainbow world would be brave enough to seek amends with those he wronged.* Velimir took a deep breath and took the first tentative steps, then Kiril, back and forth until the men were face to face. And in that moment, their faces crumbled, and they wept like children. They threw their arms around each other, holding on as if to never let go.

"Forgive me..." they both whispered at almost the same time, then looked each other in the eye, laughing and crying.

"You will have plenty of time to talk when you travel together," Irina said to the reuniting family. Velimir drew back from Kiril to face the celestial. "But there is someone else who wants to meet you before I send you all where you wish to go."

Connor then appeared there on the stage. The girls rushed to him, but before they could reach him, the sage came to Velimir and hugged him like he had hugged the girls when he had met them the last time. Velimir hesitantly returned the gesture—it still didn't quite feel like he had the right. The girls joined the embrace, and Connor acknowledged them by squeezing them, but his attention was still on Velimir.

"Little boy left to die, born anew..." Connor said. "You did what I asked you to do. You saved Peri—and Valkama—from a grim future. I know of your guilt over my death. Let go of it. Consider it fully paid by the act you committed here today."

"I do not know if I can," Velimir said. How could it ever be made up? How could he make amends for taking such a life, the life of the man who had loved the easily angered boy in the rainbow world and nurtured his lion heart? Yet Peri and Ewynne had freed him of the guilt.

Connor nodded and patted his arm. "I wish that you would."

For a few moments the four savoured the moment. Connor felt like flesh and blood, but he was translucent and radiant. The moment was transient—Connor belonged to the Blessed Isles, while Velimir, Peri and Ewynne would soon return to Valkama. Therefore, the embrace was tinged with a certain melancholy.

"Now you are free, children," Connor said. "You did very well. I have yet some news. Eoghain the Wanderer heard your heartfelt prayer for this Genjiro you had grown to care about. The creaking of ropes in the wind and the soaring of the waves you invoked carried your words to the Otherworld."

Peri swallowed and bit her lip. "I...have come to realize that Eoghain and faith means more to me than I ever thought at the island. What about Genjiro?" Connor's gentle smile was reassuring, yet she still felt a moment of dread. Had she been too impious? Indifferent to faith all her life yet expecting Eoghain to help her when she was desperate?

"Genjiro was found worthy of release from the geas. His

soul drifted to the Otherworld, from where he was free to move on."

Peri uttered a sigh of relief. "That's fucking awesome. Um, sorry. That came out the wrong way. I mean, I'm extremely grateful, praise be to the Voyager, Beloved of the Zephyr, all that stuff." Peri grinned, but her eyes glistened. "Can I talk to Genji, somehow?"

"I am afraid not—at least not here. His soul has passed to the sphere of reflection—Yomi, as it is called in Morishima. It is a place where unfulfilled souls wait to be reborn. Perhaps, if you reach the Hanamori lands, you can talk to him in a shrine."

Peri glanced at Velimir. "I will try. We're going to travel to Morishima and seek his family, see all of Zmaj-Vostok on the way. Wyn is coming, too."

Connor held something out to her, pulled from the pocket of his robes. "Peri, I want you to take this amulet. Evoke it if you have a need of me, and I will find you if it is possible for me to do so. Don't do it just for social calls, though—planar traveling is not easy." Velimir chuckled at his words, and the girls smiled.

"But we'll be traveling to the other side of the world," Ewynne said. "Zmaj-Vostok. Will you hear us from there?"

"I'll hear you, Ewynne. It may be a bit more complicated to find you, but I'll do everything in my power to do so. And so, until then, farewell, children."

And Connor was gone.

"Now is the time for goodbyes," Irina said, "All of you will be teleported to Valkama—to a location you have ties to. Razeem al-Farouq, faithful servant of Juris the Ever-Vigilant, where do you wish to go?"

Razeem saluted the celestial by placing his palm over his heart. "Of that I have no doubt," he said in his deep and firm voice. "I wish to go to my family, to spend time with them after this long campaign. The Order or the Eye also needs rebuilding after having abandoned its ideals out of fear. That will be my next mission."

Irina returned the salute and nodded. "Say your good-byes then, and your wish will be granted."

Razeem turned to Peri and saluted her, too. "Peri, I am glad that you made the right choice. You are impious and irreverent, and you were tempted by evil. But in the end, you chose good. And you prevailed. Don't ever let the honor of your spirit die."

Peri tilted her head and grinned. "Oh well, I guess you helped me with that. Razeem, thanks for being the annoying, nagging dad figure," she answered and high-fived the old paladin, who returned the gesture somewhat clumsily and smiled.

Next, the old paladin's expression turned somber and sincere as he turned to Velimir. "And Velimir, being a part of your redemption is one of my greatest reasons for pride. You are a noble and good man and can do much with your skills. It has been the ultimate honor. Fare well, and godspeed as you traverse the desert. May Juris watch over you. I will pray for you all."

Velimir shook the paladin's hand, clasping it with his other hand. "Farewell, Razeem. I wish you well. I will welcome your god's blessing and your prayers."

And then Razeem was gone.

Irina turned next to Kauno and extended a finger to lightly touch Varpu's beak. The bird rubbed his head against the finger. "Kauno, the friend of animals, one among the spirits. Where do you wish to go?"

Kauno consulted Varpu, cupped in his hands. Then he lifted his head. "Kauno goes back to Yalifa, to seek a band of troubadours that are Sjenka's apostles. That is what the spirits whisper to Kauno."

Irina gestured to Peri and the others with a hand. "Very well. Say your goodbyes, and you will be teleported to the Cathedral of the Three in Wallila Gate."

Kauno extended his arm towards Peri, Velimir, and Ewynne, and Varpu uttered a small chirp. "Kauno is sad to part ways with old friends...but Kauno will go where the spirits beckon. You will meet spirits of the East now, and Kauno hopes we will exchange tales one day again."

"I very much hope for the same," Peri said. "Thank you for everything, Kauno." Ewynne hugged Kauno and petted Varpu's head.

Kauno fixed his eyes on Velimir. His gaze was usually carefree even in the most dire of circumstances, but now there were traces of worry and sadness in it. "Now resolute and courageous spirits are drawn to you, Velimir," Kauno said. "But there are also spirits of pain, spirits that cast long shadows. Don't give them power over you."

Velimir had learned to pay heed to Kauno's warnings, even when they concerned forces he was not able to perceive. This was to be taken seriously. "I will keep that in mind. Thank you for your support and compassion through everything, Kauno."

Then Kauno, too, was gone.

Irina focused on the rest. "Now the question of your destination remains," the celestial said.

The group looked at each other, unsure who should speak first.

Ewynne grinned. "Let's go to the Crossroads Inn a few miles from Lughani Vos," she suggested. "It's on the way to the Dimitrian temple. We need to go there to get Tomoe's urn, but I think there is a bit of catching up to do before that."

"That, I find, is something of an understatement," Kiril said. "But yes, a solid plan."

The others agreed.

"So let it be done then," Irina said. "Farewell."

"Bye. I hope this wasn't too shitty of a gig for you," Peri said. "I know I was a bit of a pain at times…"

"I am an immortal spirit, child," Irina smiled. "Such things pass quickly for me."

There was no booming and cracking. No earth-shattering thunder. No lights in the skyline. Just a sudden silent moment, and they stood before the familiar weathered door of the tavern, on a road winding through the fresh-scenting pine wood like they never had been away from Lughani Vos.

"I guess that means it's over now," Ewynne said, not quite able to believe it.

"So it would appear," Peri nodded.

"How does it feel not to have the Dimitrian blood anymore?" Velimir asked his sister.

Peri looked down at herself, like she was considering the question for the first time. "Better. Not like being in a murky pond where a sea snake is lurking just under the surface. But somehow…emptier as well. Hey, let's go get drunk and catch up!"

"I'll pass the drunk part, but I will be happy to catch up,"

Kiril said.

"I really want to hear how you ended up here, mage," Peri said, glancing at him with a small frown. "That speech you made when we last met didn't exactly sound like Milostra's credo."

Kiril laughed then took Jelena's hand. "Well. You probably won't find it hard to believe that a lot has happened since—my being beheaded by you notwithstanding."

And without another word, they headed for the tavern.

ACKNOWLEDGEMENTS

My friend Wietske Beeksma continues to be generous with her time and brilliant suggestions. My husband and my dogs continue to be my rocks.

A new member of the team, I want to thank my editor P.J. Hoover for being willing to do things in a different way and being a delight to work with.

ABOUT THE AUTHOR

CHARLIE FREELANDER IS AN ADVENTURER, GAMER, AND author of *The Legacy of Wrath* series. She spends her time volunteering at ships around the world, daydreaming about being an action hero, and boldly sharing the magic of her own inner-world through fiction. Charlie's passion for fantasy video games started at a young age and inspired her deep love of worldbuilding and her insights about the struggle between good and evil. When she's not working on her next books, you can find her curled up with her dogs, reading about the gritty yet poetic anti-heroes who inspire her.

Sign up for exclusive character art and regular tidings at Charlie's website: www.charliefreelander.com

Milton Keynes UK
Ingram Content Group UK Ltd.
UKHW030147051224
452010UK00001B/75